THE EVENTER'S TRILOGY

Eventer's Dream
A Hoof in the Door
Ticket to Ride

Caroline Akrill

The Eventer's Trilogy

This 3-in-1 edition published 1994 by Diamond Books
77–85 Fulham Palace Road
Hammersmith, London W6 8JB

Eventer's Dream
© Caroline Akrill 1983
First published in 1981 by Arlington Books

A Hoof in the Door
© Caroline Akrill 1982
First published in 1982 by Arlington Books

Ticket to Ride
© Caroline Akrill 1983
First published in 1983 by Arlington Books

All titles republished by Dragon Books in 1984,
and first published by Armada in 1990

The Author asserts the moral right to be identified
as the author of this work

Set in Times

Printed and bound in Great Britain

ISBN 0 261 66423-9

For Lizzie
in memory of some very similar vases

1

Uncertain Advantages

"The thing is," Nigella said, giving the teapot a vigorous shake, "that if you *did* decide to come and help us out, we couldn't pay you much."

"Hardly anything at all, really," Henrietta said. "Just pocket money wages. But on the other hand, there would be certain advantages."

I sat beside the stone-cold Aga in the antiquated kitchen and I thought of the pot-holes in the drive. I remembered the straggling laurel bushes that bordered it, smelling of damp and leaf-mould and fox. The broken park railings. The dead elms. The grim old house with its blind and shuttered windows and the heavy atmosphere of age and neglect and decay.

"Certain advantages for whom?" I enquired. I couldn't imagine that they could possibly be for me.

"For us, naturally," Henrietta said. "Because we would have someone to organize the stables. And for you Elaine, because you would have a job, and somewhere to live, and a stable and keep for your horse."

"I haven't got a horse," I said.

"Oh, but you will have," Henrietta said confidently. "I mean, if you want to go eventing, you will need a horse to do it on. Unless," she added in an uncertain tone, "you were thinking of using one of ours?"

"Oh, no," I said. "That wouldn't do at all."

In actual fact, it was exactly what I had in mind. The truth of the matter was that I couldn't possibly afford to buy a horse of my own and I planned to find myself a sponsor in the shape of a sympathetic employer, who would provide me with a mount and a chance to compete. So far though, I had drawn a blank. This was my fifteenth interview and already I was planning my escape.

Henrietta looked relieved. "I'm glad," she said. "Eventing can be a bit risky and horses are so expensive these days. One just can't afford to keep breaking legs and things."

"Quite," I said.

I wondered why I had accepted the invitation to tea in such unpromising circumstances, when the situation was so clearly hopeless. Any sensible person, confronted with a pair of prospective employers like Nigella and Henrietta in their skin-tight jeans, their out-at-the-elbow anoraks and their cut down wellingtons, all liberally coated with horse hairs and mud, would have fled the place on sight.

Nigella squinted down the spout of the teapot. Her long dark plait was speckled with hay seeds and tied at the end with bailer twine. When she had tried to pour the tea, nothing had come out. She poked a ball point pen energetically up and down the spout. "I don't suppose eventing is any more risky than any other equestrian activity," she commented, "provided that horse and rider are properly prepared." After a bit of fishing about inside the pot, she managed to flip a sodden brown lump on to the table. She splashed tea into three chipped red beakers. We helped ourselves to milk from a bottle and

8

damp sugar straight out of a packet. "Sorry it's a bit informal," Nigella said.

Henrietta looked round the kitchen in a vague sort of way. "There *were* some biscuits," she said. I wondered how long ago there had been biscuits. Last week perhaps, or last month. There certainly didn't seem to be any today.

"Can you cook?" Nigella said suddenly. "I mean, nothing too special, not cordon bleu or anything like that. Just cakes and puddings and pies and things."

"And biscuits," Henrietta added. "We like biscuits."

I swallowed a mouthful of musty tasting tea. I was prepared for this. After all, I was an experienced interviewee by now and I had discovered that people who advertised for help with horses often wanted anything from a gardener to a children's nanny and merely offered the horses as bait.

"The advertisement didn't mention cooking," I said firmly. "It just said, 'Help wanted in small, friendly, private stable'."

"Ah," Henrietta said, looking guilty. "So we did say private. We thought we might have."

"You mean it isn't?" I said, surprised.

"Not exactly," Henrietta said. She stared at the tea bag. Her wild mane of auburn hair flowed over her shoulders and on to the table. It was full of knots and it looked as if it hadn't been combed for months.

"We do take the odd livery," Nigella admitted. "Well, perhaps rather more than the odd one."

"And we do let out horses for hunting now and then," Henrietta said. "Well, perhaps more often than not."

"In that case you are not a private stable at all," I

9

said. "You are a commercial enterprise. You are running a business."

"Only in a manner of speaking," Nigella said. "And not out of choice. We are not motivated by profit. We only do it to live."

"We wouldn't dream of doing it if we didn't have to," Henrietta said in a defensive tone. She picked up the ball point pen and poked at the tea bag. "Having to earn a living is the most frightful bore."

"But in your advertisement you distinctly said it was a private stable," I reminded them. "It just isn't true." I pulled the page torn from *Horse and Hound* out of my pocket and spread it on the table. The advertisement was ringed with red crayon. "Small, friendly, private stable . . ."

"I wish you wouldn't keep *on* about it," Henrietta said. "It isn't as if it really matters." She rolled the tea bag over and leaned closer to it, narrowing her eyes.

"We *are* friendly," Nigella said.

"You are not private," I said.

"We *are* small," Nigella argued. "That's two out of three."

"It's still misleading," I said, "and also illegal. You can't say things that aren't true in an advertisement. You could be prosecuted under the Trades Descriptions Act. It's misrepresentation."

"Heavens," Nigella said. "How awful. I had no idea."

"This tea bag," Henrietta commented, "isn't a tea bag at all."

"What else did we say in the advertisement?" Nigella scanned the page, interested.

"It's a mouse."

10

We transferred our attention to the tea bag. It was definitely a mouse; very small, very saturated, and very dead. Nigella clapped her hand over her mouth and let out a low moan.

"If it's any consolation," Henrietta said, "I should think it was practically sterilized by the boiling water." She lifted the mouse up with the ball point pen and plopped it down on the advertisement. Nigella watched, appalled, as she wrapped it into a neat parcel.

"It was a natural mistake," I said. "It was exactly the same shape and size as a tea bag. It was even the same colour."

"A blatant case of misrepresentation, I'd say." Henrietta slipped the parcel into her anorak pocket. "Would you like to see the horses?" she enquired.

I could hardly refuse. Once we were outside I hoped that I would be able to make my escape. As it was I allowed myself to be conducted to the stables.

The stable block had once been grand. It was built in the traditional square with a clock arch. The stables were lovely, large, airy loose boxes with blue brick floors and green three-quarter tiled walls. There were cobblestones and a lead water trough, a dovecote and a proper mounting block. It was the sort of stable yard I had dreamed of working in, except that the same air of shabby neglect I had seen everywhere else was here as well, only more so. The paint on the woodwork had long flaked away, broken windows were stuffed with rags or patched with cardboard, doors hung at drunken angles, tiles were missing from the roofs and grass grew unchecked between the cobbles.

11

Henrietta led the way into a tack room where a jumble of saddlery was heaped up anyhow on a table. She untangled a brittle-looking headcollar and presented the damp little parcel to a large black and white cat who was curled up on a moth-eaten day rug. The cat sniffed it suspiciously and backed off. He jumped down from the table and stalked off with his tail in the air, looking offended. "Ungrateful beast," Henrietta said.

The first horse was a gaunt, ewe-necked thorough-bred mare who rolled her eyes and seemed disinclined to leave her stable. Henrietta flipped her in the ribs with the headcollar rope and she flew out of the door like a champagne cork and skidded on the cobbles.

"This is the old bay mare," Nigella said.

I stroked the old mare's faded brown face. The deep hollows above her eyes were full of dust.

"What's her name?" I asked.

Nigella looked blank. "She hasn't actually got a name," she said. "She's just the old bay mare."

The old bay mare scuttled back into her stable. There was a bit of a set-to with the black horse who lived next door. He dived round the box and refused to have anything to do with Henrietta who was finally obliged to grab him by the tail, whereupon he gave in and dropped his nose into the headcollar. Out in the yard he assumed an anxious expression and began to prance on the spot, lifting each of his legs in turn, as if he was performing a *piaffe*.

"He has a lot of nervous energy," Nigella explained. "He simply *never* stands still. It's very wearing and inconvenient at times, but he's perfectly

12

all right when hounds are running, he goes like a bomb."

The black horse's stable had blocked drains and the bedding squelched. The soles of his prancing feet showed the soggy, smelly indications of thrush. I noticed these things and my heart sank into my boots.

Henrietta led the next horse out for inspection with the headcollar yanked up so tightly that I imagined that he must surely be throttled. But the grey horse didn't appear to notice. He was preoccupied with Higher Things. He put on a noble expression and stared into the distance above our heads as if we were beneath his notice.

"This is The Comet," Nigella said. "He's a bolter."

Bolter or not, The Comet presented a fine picture standing four square on the cobbles. Somehow it didn't seem to matter that his coat was streaked with yellow and the top of his tail resembled a scrubbing brush. "We've tried everything to improve his braking system," Nigella said. "Martingales, gag snaffles, twisted bits and check reins, but nothing makes the slightest difference. He just sets his neck and away he goes."

"Luckily he always heads for home," Henrietta said. "Which could be regarded as an advantage. Although it must be said that he has lost us some very good clients."

"I don't suppose he would be suitable for eventing?" Nigella suggested. "He is a very fast horse and he is as brave as a lion."

But even without looking at his mouth, I could see that The Comet was past it. "He is the right size," I said. "About sixteen-three, and he is the right type, threequarter-bred; but he is too old and besides, a horse with a good mouth and a controllable nature is a prime requirement for eventing. After all, it isn't a race. Think of the show-jumping. Think of the dressage." So as not to damn the horse completely, I said, "I suppose you have tried schooling?"

Henrietta looked astonished. "School The Comet?" she said incredulously. "What a joke." She dragged the grey horse back into the stable and removed the headcollar.

"We shall have to sell him, I suppose," Nigella said. "It seems a shame to part with such an impressive animal, but what else can we do?"

"We'll send him to auction," Henrietta decided. "Without a warranty. It's the only way to get rid of him. People who know him wouldn't have him as a gift."

I looked at a bad-tempered chestnut gelding who swished his tail, flattened his ears and made snapping noises with his teeth and I thought of the grey horse. I imagined him standing under the hammer, wearing his noble expression as the bids flew. Then I imagined him later, when his reputation had spread and he was known in every sale ring in the country as the grey horse who was a confirmed bolter. I could visualize his final destination only too well, and the fact that he would meet his fate with that same lofty indifference only made it harder to bear.

Henrietta now produced a moth-eaten roan with tall boxy feet like a donkey's. "This is Nelson," she said.

Nelson regarded us solemnly out of his one eye.

The eyelids of the other had been stitched together over the empty socket after some fearsome accident which didn't bear thinking about. I looked in despair at his scurfy coat and his hollow flanks, and the way in which, once back in his stable, he took a few wisps of dry hay in his soft little mouth and chewed them with every appearance of discomfort.

I knew I had to harden my heart to all this. I told myself firmly that sentiment didn't pay. I couldn't possibly come here, I couldn't take the job, it was out of the question. If I came to work in this awful place it would be the end, the absolute finish of my eventing ambitions. I would never find a sponsor to provide me with a decent horse. I would never get the chance I so desperately wanted. I would be sunk before I had even begun. The only thing to do was to leave at once. I would plead a pressing engagement. I would make my excuses now, straight away.

I turned to Nigella. "What exactly do you mean by pocket money wages?" I asked.

Nigella led the way past a row of stables which housed two hunter liveries. They were considered not worth looking at. She seemed embarrassed by this mention of hard cash, as if it was something one never mentioned in polite company.

"You would have to ask Mummy," she told me. "She isn't actually here at the moment. It's her Meals-on-Wheels day."

Henrietta brought out the last horse in the yard. It was a stunningly beautiful bay mare.

"Isn't she lovely," Nigella breathed. "I should be used to her by now, I know. But she still takes me by surprise every time I see her."

The bay mare stretched out her long elegant neck

and nuzzled Henrietta's pocket. Her coat was fine and smooth and her legs and her tail were silky black. Her eyes were dark and gentle and on her face there was a perfectly shaped star.

"She's terribly well bred," Nigella said. She recited an impressive pedigree.

"She was unbeaten in the show ring as a four-year-old," Henrietta said. "Champion at the Royal and practically every other County Show you can think of."

I said I could quite believe it.

"Of course," Nigella admitted. "That was before it happened."

"Before what happened?" I said faintly.

"Before she started to slip her stifle," Henrietta said.

I wasn't surprised; after all the other defective horses I had seen, if the bay mare had been fitted with an artificial limb, I would hardly have batted an eyelid.

"When that happened," Henrietta continued, "she was sold as a brood mare."

"She was still a very valuable animal," Nigella said. "Because of her breeding. She sold for well over four figures."

"Then what happened?" I said.

"Then they discovered that she was barren," Nigella said sadly.

"So we bought her," Henrietta said, slapping the mare heartily on her neck. "Because she was the most fantastic bargain, and she was the most beautiful horse we had ever seen."

"But that means you just keep her as a pet," I said, astonished. "If you can't breed with her and

16

you can't ride her either!" I was amazed that people in such obviously straitened circumstances had given a home to a totally useless animal. By this act of mercy, Henrietta and Nigella soared in my estimation. I could almost overlook their shortcomings in stable management. They were redeemed.

"Can't ride her?" Henrietta said, frowning. "Of course we can ride her."

"If we couldn't breed with her and we couldn't ride her either, there would really be no point in keeping her," Nigella explained carefully. "Horses are very costly animals to keep. The price of corn alone is astronomical."

"Not to mention hay and shoeing," Henrietta added. "And you can't even get free straw in return for stable manure any longer, not like the old days."

"But what about the slipped stifle," I wondered. "Is it cured?"

"Oh no," Nigella said. "It still happens. When it does, we just turn her away for a month or however long it takes to come right again."

"But you don't hire her out for hunting," I said. "Not when you know it could happen at any moment."

"It doesn't happen every day," Henrietta pointed out. "To be fair, she sometimes lasts half a season. And nobody has ever complained." She grinned.

"They are always too worried about the mare," Nigella said, suppressing a giggle. "They think they have broken her leg. They are terrified almost out of their wits."

"They think they are going to be sued," Henrietta spluttered. "They think we will make them pay for the horse!"

17

I had to laugh. It was grotesque. It was just too awful for words. We all leaned on the bay mare and the tears poured down our cheeks. I forgot all about my sponsor and my future prospects and when Nigella suggested that I should start work next week, I was too shattered to argue.

2

Mutual Disagreements

When I rang Lady Jennifer to get some hard facts about the job she was enthusiastic but evasive. "But my *dear*," she cried in ringing tones when I enquired about hours of work and days off. "You will be such an *enormous* help to us all, a marvellous asset! We shall be most *understanding* about your days off. It will be such *fun* to have another young person about the place, we have no other help whatsoever – you can't *imagine* the turmoil we live in!"

Actually, I could imagine it only too well. As soon as I could get a word in edgeways, I enquired about the pocket money wages.

"But of course you shall have pocket money," Lady Jennifer trilled. "We wouldn't *dream* of expecting you to help out without remuneration! We shall come to a mutual agreement the very *second* you arrive. You are intending to arrive?" she added with a trace of anxiety. "You haven't changed your mind?"

I said I hadn't. It hardly seemed the moment to mention that I was only accepting the job on a temporary basis, until something more promising turned up.

"And what about your parents?" Lady Jennifer wanted to know. "Do you think I should have a *teeny* little word? Just to reassure them that their daughter will be in excellent hands? To say how absolutely *thrilled* we are? After all, you are only seventeen . . ."

"I don't think so," I said hastily. "I really don't see the necessity."

My father heartily disapproved of my desire to work with horses and the fifteen interviews had left him feeling distinctly edgy, especially in view of the fact that many of my school friends were already propping up the dole queue. He had seen my six month apprenticeship at a top training establishment as a complete waste of time and energy, despite the fact that I had been accepted on a Working Pupil basis and had paid for my instruction myself with hours of hard labour every day. I had gained a qualification at the end of it, but still he wasted no opportunity to remind me that in his opinion, the horse world had nothing to offer but low pay, bleak prospects, and broken promises.

It went against the grain to admit to myself that he might be right. Certainly there seemed to be no jobs vacant in eventing yards at all, and the two jobs I had been offered as a result of the fourteen interviews had both been in dubious little riding schools offering squalid accommodation in caravans and a few pounds in return for a 70 hour week. With the Fanes at least I would be able to hunt, and as the hunting field was supposed to be the best training ground for event horses and riders, I wouldn't be completely wasting my time. Also, it was a relief to be able to tell my father that I had landed a job at last, but as I knew he would take a dim view of the pocket money wages, I decided that the less he knew about the job the better.

It was agreed that I should arrive by train the

following Monday. Lady Jennifer met me at the station and I could hear her voice even before I got off the train. She was a tall, thin person in a crumpled raincoat and a headscarf the size of a small tablecloth. Like the black horse, she seemed to have a lot of nervous energy and she threw the tiny station into confusion by blocking the passenger exit with her delapidated shooting brake.

"I won't keep you waiting a *minute* longer than necessary," she shrilled at the trapped passengers. "It's so *frightfully* thoughtless of me, I can't think *why* I did it. I must have been *insane* to park here." She emptied her handbag on to the bonnet in a fruitless effort to find the car keys and finally located them in the ignition.

Whilst all this was going on I was loading my case into the back. I had wondered why all the windows were steamed up and when I opened the rear doors I could see why; the shooting brake was full of hounds. They were sitting on all the seats and I couldn't imagine where I was going to sit. I considered the passenger seat. The two lemon and white hounds who occupied it regarded me in an encouraging manner. The nearest one had a long dribble of saliva suspended from its dewlap. I decided on the back seat. The four hounds already seated shuffled up obligingly to make room and arranged their heads four deep in order to inspect my person.

Lady Jennifer got into the driving seat and slammed the door. This acted like a starter's pistol to the hounds, who dived into position for the journey. The two on the passenger seat put their front paws on the dashboard and pressed their noses to the windscreen. My neighbours put their paws on the back of the front seats and craned forward avidly as the shooting brake bucketed away. The smell of dog was overpowering.

"You won't mind if we drop the young entry off first?" Lady Jennifer enquired, swerving to avoid a cyclist and causing a hound to slip off the dashboard and hit its chin on the glove compartment. "We walked them this summer and they *will* keep coming back. I can't *tell* you how inconvenient it is. The Hunt Staff get *furious*."

I hoped the young entry didn't live very far away. If they did I thought I should possibly suffocate before we got there. I wound down the window in an effort to get some fresh air. As soon as they got wind of this, all four hounds launched themselves across me and jammed their heads out as far as their shoulders, pinning me back in the seat. I managed to extract myself from the jungle of hind legs and waving sterns and gained the comparative comfort of the empty end of the seat. I didn't dare open the window.

Lady Jennifer applied the brakes smartly outside a collection of whitewashed buildings. A sign announced that we had arrived at the Midvale and Westbury Hunt Kennels. This was a relief, but as soon as the shooting brake juddered to a stop our hounds dived under the seats as one man. They refused to budge. Lady Jennifer and I were obliged to drag them out by the scruff of their necks whilst they pretended to be dead. Once out of the brake they crept across the yard with their sterns dragging on the concrete. They looked anything but happy to be home.

Lady Jennifer unbolted the iron grille door of the

exercise yard with furtive care and we stuffed our hounds inside. In a trice they had cheered up and were indistinguishable from the rest of the pack. We might have got away undetected but they put their paws up on the bars with the rest and set up a terrific racket. The noise brought a young man in a white kennel coat to the door of one of the buildings. He looked rather cross.

Lady Jennifer decided that attack was the best form of defence. "William," she shrilled indignantly. "Your hounds have been trespassing *again*. They have upset all my refuse bins. I simply will *not* tolerate it. If it happens again I shall have them shot."

William looked taken aback by this. He went rather red. He opened his mouth to say something, but Lady Jennifer was already on a different tack.

"Elaine," she said briskly. "This is William, the Second Whipper-in. William, this is Elaine, our new groom." She made for the shooting brake. It was all very awkward.

"Hello," I said. "I'm sorry about the hounds. I'm sure she wouldn't really have them shot."

William didn't reply. He just stared. He ran his hand through his ginger hair and left it standing in peaks, stiff with bran. "New *groom*," he said in disbelief. "New *groom?*"

"That's right," I said. "New groom."

William still didn't know what to make of it. He turned and shouted to someone inside the building. "Hey, Forster! Come out here a minute! The Galloping Fanes have gone and got themselves a groom!"

I wasn't sure that I liked the sound of this. I

looked round for the shooting brake but Lady Jennifer was having trouble of her own with the gears. Terrible crashing and grinding noises accompanied the shunting backwards and forwards.

Forster had the kind of looks that belong to dangerous young men in novels. He had a dark handsome face and black hair that curled almost to the collar of his coat. I could tell he thought himself rather special by the way he leaned indolently against the door frame and looked me up and down in an amused sort of way.

"You must be barmy," he drawled, "to go and work with that collection of old screws."

For one terrible moment I thought he meant Lady Jennifer and her daughters. Then I realized that he was referring to the horses.

"You have seen the place?" William wanted to know. "You do know what it's like? You have *seen* the horses?"

"Horses!" Forster gave a contemptuous laugh. "There isn't a sound animal in the yard, or a properly fed one either. The Fanes don't need a groom, they need a knacker."

"As long as they don't call us," William said, grinning. "We don't want them. All the hirelings boiled up together wouldn't feed hounds for more than a week."

I didn't want to listen to any more of this.

"Excuse me," I said. "I have to go."

"Wait a minute," William said. "I asked you if you had seen the place. You wouldn't be going there sight unseen would you? You haven't taken the job *blind*?"

There was genuine concern in his voice but I was so offended by their attitude that I hardly noticed.

"Yes, I've seen the place," I said crossly. "And I've seen the horses, so I know what it's like. But it might interest you to know that things are going to be rather different in future. We are going to reorganize the yard and the business. There are going to be a lot of improvements." I looked round anxiously for the shooting brake and saw that it was moving in my direction.

"And who is going to pay for these improvements?" Forster enquired in a sceptical tone.

"More to the point," William added, "who's going to pay you?"

"That's my affair," I snapped. As the shooting brake came alongside with the passenger door flapping, I jumped in and slammed the door as hard as I could. The crash caused Lady Jennifer's foot to slip off the clutch. As we bounced away Forster was laughing his silly head off. The last impression I got of him was that his teeth were sickeningly white.

If Lady Jennifer was alarmed by this show of temper in her new employee, she didn't show it. She hummed a little tune as she drove in her erratic manner along the Suffolk lanes heaped with golden leaves. I was too preoccupied to notice the glory of it. I sat in silence and I wondered, not for the first time, what I had let myself in for. I realized that the callous comments which had made me so angry, were probably no more than the truth. But if I had been a fool to accept responsibility for a bunch of old crocks, if I had been a worse fool to accept a job with no prospects and quite possibly no money either, I didn't want to be told so, not yet, and certainly not by Forster or William. I had to give it a try first. I had to give it a chance.

As the shooting brake flew along the lanes, leaving eddies of leaves in its wake, I grew more optimistic. It would give me great satisfaction, I decided, to show the Midvale and Westbury Hunt a thing or two. In my imagination I saw the Fanes' tumble-down yard restored to its former grandeur. It could be the finest livery stable in the county. We could have the most luxurious loose boxes, the most magnificent stable yard, the cleanest tack and the fittest, best turned-out horses that ever graced the hunting field. Not only that, but we could have the best hirelings available anywhere. My imagination soared. By my own skill I saw myself turning my collection of lame ducks into beautiful equine swans, so expertly produced, so superbly schooled, that people would queue up to ride them.

Untrimmed branches pinging against the sides of the shooting brake brought me back to earth. We turned in at the lodge gates where one vulpine creature leered down from the top of its post and the other lay nose down in the grass, choked with ivy.

"Welcome to Havers Hall," Lady Jennifer said. She leaned over unexpectedly and squeezed my hand with her long, bony fingers as the shooting brake bucked and leapt over the pot-holes.

Nigella and Henrietta were waiting, a reception committee of two on the front steps. If anything, they looked even scruffier than I remembered them. They grabbed my cases and bore me up into the hall as Lady Jennifer swerved off round the back of the house in a shower of gravel.

"Welcome to our humble home," Nigella said brightly. "Family seat of the Fanes for eight generations."

"Clobbered by death duties, turned down by the National Trust," Henrietta added. "And shortly to be condemned by the local council."

I wasn't sure if this was supposed to be a joke or not. I smiled politely. The hall was vast and icy cold. There were no carpets and precious little in the way of furniture either. The ornate plaster ceiling was patched with damp and mould. The two huge stone fireplaces which dominated either end were heaped with dead ash.

"It isn't very cosy, is it?" Henrietta said. "I expect it's a bit stark for your taste?"

"It's certainly very large," I said. "And very grand."

"*Was* very grand, you mean," Henrietta said peevishly. "You may as well say what you think."

"Take no notice of Henrietta," Nigella said. "She gets a bit prickly at times. She can't help it. She finds it hard to accept that she is one of the *nouveaux pauvres*."

"I'm not poor," Henrietta objected. "Can anyone be described as poor," she asked me, "who owns a Vile secretaire?" She led the way up the dusty wide staircase. Her wellingtons squeaked on the bare oak treads.

I wasn't sure what a secretaire was. "I wonder you keep it," I said. "If it's so awful."

Henrietta paused to look at me in astonishment. "It isn't awful," she said. "It's magnificent."

"Vile is the name of the maker," Nigella

explained. "William Vile. Henrietta's very proud of her secretaire, it's her dowry."

We walked along a gallery landing lined with darkened oil paintings. Now and again there was a gap and a rectangular patch of lighter coloured wall.

"Do people have dowries these days?" I asked.

"I don't think so," Nigella said. "It's a pretty feudal idea. Still, Henrietta has hers."

Henrietta opened one of the doors along the landing and I followed them into a large, dark room filled with an unwholesome smell of damp. There was a chill air in the room which brought out goose-flesh at the back of my neck. In the half light I could make out a vast, carved wardrobe, a bed of unusual height and solidity, and another huge, empty stone fireplace. The only other furniture was a dark oak chest, shaped like a coffin. Henrietta began to heave mightily at some wooden shutters which stretched from floor to ceiling.

"Well?" Nigella said in an uncertain tone. "What do you think?" She dumped my case on the single piece of threadbare carpet. "Do you like it?"

I didn't like it. I didn't like the dark, or the cold, or the smell. As my eyes got used to the gloom I saw other things that I didn't like. There was a dead jackdaw in the hearth. There was an angry Eliza-bethan lady on the wall. She clutched an orb to her chest and she glared at me balefully, as if the whole of her misfortune must surely be my fault. It was terrible. It was frightening. I had never been in such an alarming room in all of my life. I tried to work out how I was going to tell Nigella that I couldn't sleep here. Not possibly. I wouldn't dare to close my eyes even for a minute. I tried to find the right words to explain how I felt without causing offence. And all the time Henrietta yanked at the shutters and Nigella waited expectantly for me to speak.

I took a deep breath and suddenly Henrietta and the shutters flew aside with a resounding crash. October sunshine flooded over us and the room was filled with the warm, earthy smell of grass and dying leaves and plough. Across the park I saw old turf like worn velvet, and oak trees, red and golden. The river lay like a blue and silver ribbon and all along the banks the willows leaned. Beyond, the Suffolk landscape stretched, brown and green and gilded and somewhere, even beyond that, was the sea.

"Oh," I said. "It's perfect. It's absolutely beautiful."

"I'm so glad," Nigella said with relief. "It wouldn't be everyone's idea of a comfortable room."

After a conducted tour of the mahogany panelled bathroom and a recital of its deficiencies, Nigella left me to unpack. Henrietta didn't follow straight away. She stood thoughtfully in the doorway and watched me stow my belongings in the giant wardrobe. She had picked up the dead jackdaw and she swung it by the legs in an absent-minded manner, as if it was a handbag.

"You must have been pretty desperate for a job to come here," she said unexpectedly. "I don't expect you will stay."

"Not stay?" I said. "Why shouldn't I stay?"

"Because you want to event. Because you only took the job until you can find something more suitable. Because this is an awful place," Henrietta said. "And you know it."

"It isn't true," I said. "It's a very nice place. Of course I shall stay."

I couldn't look at her. I kept my eyes on my new breeches, my eventing breeches, strapped with soft creamy suede, and still in their tissue wraps. Unworn. When I looked up, Henrietta had gone.

I covered up the Elizabethan lady with my tweed jacket. She didn't seem quite so angry any more, but I couldn't stand the accusation in her eyes.

3

A Nice Long List

Supper was served at the kitchen table. Nigella grabbed roaring hot plates out of the Aga which, she explained, was having one of its over-enthusiastic days. The plates warmed our faces and stuck to the table. They were crusted with dried up mince decorated with solidified potato and peas like lead shot. It was probably left over from the Meals-on-Wheels.

Lady Jennifer was not present at this repast, having departed for some committee meeting or other clad in a suit which dated from the New Look and a Hermes scarf with a small darn in it. When Nigella had distributed some frighteningly strong, bitter coffee and woody apples, I suggested that she might like to outline the daily stable routine for my benefit.

"Stable routine?" Nigella said, and her eyebrows rose up and vanished into her thatch of a fringe.

"We don't actually have a routine," Henrietta said absently. She dangled her apple peel which she had carefully cut into a long curly spiral from her little finger. "Do I throw it over my left shoulder or my right?" she wondered.

"You must have some sort of routine," I said. "You must do certain jobs at certain times."

"Isn't she thinking of salt?" Nigella wanted to know. "Isn't it salt you throw over your shoulder?"

I said I thought it was. "What time do you start in the mornings?" I asked her. "What do you do first?"

"We feed first," Nigella said. "Doesn't everyone feed first?"

"I think apple peel probably only works on Halloween night," Henrietta said glumly. She threw the spiral over her shoulder anyway. It landed in the sink.

"Then what do you do?" I said.

"Then we muck out," Nigella said.

Henrietta went over to the sink and peered into the clutter of dirty dishes. "It's a W," she decided.

"W for William," Nigella said.

"William," Henrietta said in disgust. "Who on earth would want *William*." She came back to the table and began to hack savagely at her naked apple.

"When do you do the watering?" I persisted. "When do you give the horses their hay?"

"Look," Henrietta said in an irritated tone. "You're not at the training centre now. You can forget all about routines and things. We don't have them."

I could see that I was going to have to make a firm stand if anything at all was to be achieved. "If we are going to reorganize the yard," I said, "we shall have to work to a routine. It's the only way to be efficient."

"And if there is one thing we need to be," Nigella said in a heartfelt voice, "it's efficient."

"I thought I might spend my first day mucking out," I suggested. I knew that the loose boxes hadn't been cleaned out properly for months, possibly years, and that the corners were packed solid.

32

"It won't take you all day," Henrietta said. "Even if you do the lot."

"It might," I said, "if I do each one properly. If I turn out all the bedding and disinfect the floors and flush out the drains. If I wash down the tiles and scrub out the mangers and the water buckets."

"That *will* be lovely," Nigella said.

I knew it wouldn't be.

"If I look after the stable work," I said, "you will both be free to cope with the exercising."

There was a silence.

"We don't exercise the horses every day," Nigella said cautiously. "We couldn't possibly. We only take them out on alternate days, if that. On the days they are not ridden, we turn them out for a few hours in the park."

"But hunters need to be taken out every day," I said. "They should have been having steady road work every day for months already to strengthen their limbs and to build muscle, to condition their hearts and their lungs. If they are not exercised properly, how do you expect them to get fit?" I had been on a tour of inspection before supper and I knew that none of the horses was even half fit. It occurred to me that perhaps they didn't need to be. That half a day's hunting on one of the Fanes' hirelings would be enough for anybody.

"I don't know how you expect us to exercise nine horses every day *and* do all the stable work," Henrietta said crossly, "when we haven't any staff. When you know perfectly well that we've been without any help whatsoever."

"We've done our best," Nigella added. "But no two people could cope with nine stabled horses. It

33

just isn't possible." She stared down at her apple pips and assumed an air of total exhaustion.

All this was hardly encouraging, but on my tour of inspection I had discovered several deficiencies that I felt bound to mention. I decided to get it over with.

"The tack room will have to be sorted out," I said. "It's a disgrace. Some of the tack will have to be replaced. We need pegs and saddle brackets. We need Neat's Foot oil and metal polish. We need thread for repairs and needles and soap. And that's not all. There are other things."

"Oh?" Henrietta said in an uneasy voice. "What other things?"

"There only seems to be one set of grooming tools," I said. "We need more. The horses need to be clipped. We need clippers and blankets, rugs and rollers and bandages."

Nigella was looking alarmed.

"Is that all?" Henrietta enquired. "I wonder you can't think of anything else. Perhaps we can find you a pencil and some paper. Then you can make a nice long list."

"What a very good idea," I said.

There was another silence whilst I waited for the pencil and paper. Nobody moved.

"We never make lists," Nigella said awkwardly.

"I shall need the vet," I continued. "To rasp Nelson's back teeth. He has some nasty sharp edges very high up and he can't chew his food properly. I shall need the blacksmith as well. There is hardly a horse in the yard whose feet don't need attention and anyway, I need him to pare away some of the

34

black horse's foot, so that I can treat the thrushy bits."

"Hrmm," Henrietta said.

"What exactly do you mean by 'hrmm'?" I said impatiently.

"Heavens," Nigella said hastily. "Did you say thrush?"

"Also," I said, warming to my theme. "There isn't much in the feed room."

"There almost never is," Nigella admitted.

"There's hardly any bran left. The corn bin is only a quarter full."

"I don't know why you are telling us all this," Henrietta grumbled. "It isn't as if we don't already know."

"The horses need to put in condition," I said. "They are far too poor to start the season. As they are, they won't last a month. We need high protein food. We need fatteners. Some of the horses need boiled food, especially the old." I stopped myself just in time from adding "the lame and the sick".

"You are absolutely right," Nigella said. "We do." She stared unhappily into her coffee. It had gone cold and it was covered with a fragile metallic skin.

"We need barley and linseed. We need chaff for mixing, and sugar beet pulp. We need high energy foods, oats and barley and cubes. There isn't any rock salt."

"All these things we suddenly need," Henrietta said in an acid tone. "We never needed them before."

"You need them now," I said.

"Only because you say so," Henrietta snapped.

I tried not to lose my temper, but it was hard to

understand their attitude. They seemed totally unwilling to grasp the realities of the situation.

"Look," I said. "Either you want to run a decent yard, or you don't."

"Oh, we do," Nigella assured me. "We really do."

"What you don't seem to realize," Henrietta said, "is how incredibly difficult it is to manage. How impossibly expensive things are. Look at hay, for instance."

"I did," I said. "There's only half a ton in the barn."

"Is that all?" Nigella said. "I didn't realize we were as low as that. It won't last any time at all."

"It certainly won't," I said. "Especially if we feed by the book and allow the horses all the hay they can eat."

"As you seem to do everything by the book," Henrietta said waspishly. "Maybe you should consult it on our behalf. It might tell us how we are going to pay for all these things you expect us to provide at the drop of a hat. Or perhaps you intend to pay for them out of your own pocket?"

"I can't pay for them," I said. "I'm absolutely broke. I've been out of work for four months and I'm down to my last pound."

"Then you know how *we* feel," Henrietta said, "because we haven't a bean either."

"Not to put too fine a point on it," Nigella said despondently, "we're at a very low ebb. Financially, I mean."

They both looked depressed.

There was a lengthy silence whilst we all thought about it. Henrietta filled in the time by picking little bits of crinkly wood from the sleeve of her jumper. Then she piled the bits into a pyramid on her plate.

"Of course," I said eventually. "Increased efficiency doesn't necessarily have to cost money."

"A few minutes ago," Henrietta pointed out, "it sounded very expensive."

"After all," I said, trying to be optimistic, "the hunting season is only a couple of weeks away."

"Is it really?" Nigella said. "As soon as that?"

"And that means," I went on, "that there will be money coming in from the hirelings."

"Which, according to you," Henrietta reminded me, "won't last a month."

"And then there are the liveries," I continued.

"When they pay," Nigella said. "Which doesn't seem to be too often."

"I shall make sure that they pay," I said firmly, "and as we improve the yard, we shall get more."

"Get more liveries?" Nigella said, interested. "How will we get more?"

"By recommendation," I said. "We could even advertise."

"We're not very good at advertisements," Henrietta commented.

"There are plenty of spare boxes," I said. "There's no shortage of room. We are in the ideal position, the Hunt is almost on the doorstep. Even one really high class livery would add tone to the yard."

"Tone," Nigella said warmly, "is just what we need."

"The boxes are beautifully built," I said. "The yard is rather splendid." I pushed away the memory of the missing tiles, the broken windows and the peeling paint. Even the empty corn bins receded.

"The hacking must be marvellous, especially now, when there are miles and miles of stubble fields; and where else could livery clients ride in such a beautiful park?"

"It's true," Nigella agreed. "Our facilities are ideal. We are in the perfect situation. I can't imagine *why* we get so depressed."

"We'll give it a try," Henrietta decided. "You can have a free hand. We will do it your way, even though it entails lists and graphs and charts. Whenever it is possible, we will do it by the book."

"And in the morning, Henrietta and I will exercise every horse," Nigella promised. "We will make a fresh start. We simply can't *help* but be successful."

It seemed to me that we couldn't afford not to be.

4

If Something Isn't Done . . .

True to their word, the next morning Nigella and Henrietta prepared to give their attention to the exercising.

"How many hours of exercise does each horse have to be given on this daily routine of yours?" Henrietta enquired, peering over the half door into the black horse's stable.

"Two," I said. I was scrubbing out the black horse's feet with soap and water and he wasn't enjoying it one little bit. Finding his legs immobilized, he was obliged to content himself with rolling his eyes, snaking his neck, and rotating his tail like a windmill.

Nigella's head appeared beside Henrietta's. "Two hours?" she exclaimed. "You do realize that means eighteen hours of exercising *every* day? Nine hours solid riding for each of us. You can't be *serious*."

"Of course I'm serious," I said. "You can double up. You can take two horses each." I let go of the black horse's foot and he pumped his leg up and down a few times in an anxious sort of way, to reassure himself that it still worked. I had scrubbed out the evil-smelling gunge in the cleft of his frogs and trimmed the ragged bits. He didn't seem to be lame and I thought that if I could treat the rotten bits with Stockholm tar and keep him on a dry bed, he probably wouldn't need professional treatment.

He did need the blacksmith though, his shoes were paper thin.

"I don't see why we shouldn't," Nigella said. "One of the liveries has lost a shoe, so he can't do any road work; that leaves eight horses to exercise, so if we take four out at a time . . ."

"Four at a time," Henrietta said in alarm. "Four!"

"Not each," Nigella said patiently. "Two each. Four altogether. One lot in the mornings and one in the afternoons."

"Better still," I said, "one lot before breakfast, and one lot after. Then we shall have more time."

"More time for what?" Henrietta said.

"More time for strapping, tack cleaning, renovating, painting and weeding," I said. I stepped out of the way of the black horse who was having an experimental trot round the box, lifting his scrubbed feet like a hackney.

"Sometimes," Henrietta said in her clear voice as they departed in the direction of the tack room, "it's better not to ask."

For the first period of exercise, Nigella decided to ride the old bay mare and lead the black horse, and Henrietta elected to ride the bad-tempered chestnut and lead The Comet. There was a bit of a fracas when the old bay mare decided she didn't like the idea of communal exercise and refused to leave the yard. She suddenly dug in her toes and jibbed so strongly that Nigella was forced to let go of the black horse. He decided that his stable was the safest place and dived off past the bad-tempered chestnut who, not being one to let a golden opportunity pass by, lunged forward with bared teeth and almost displaced Henrietta, who was fiddling with her stirrup

40

leathers. The Comet, unimpressed by all these goings-on, stood rocklike on the cobbles, even though his withered leading rein had snapped and dangled uselessly under his chin. Eventually, the black horse was captured, an even more withered rein was clipped on to The Comet, and they clattered off leaving me to do battle with the black horse's drains.

It took me ages to clear all the sour, soggy straw out of the stable and to scrape out the sides and the corners. I trundled six wheel-barrow loads to the steaming, sprawling muck heap behind the barn. Then I swept out the stable and prised off the drain cover. I poked about hopefully for a while with the end of the pitchfork, but it was packed solid. In the end there seemed nothing for it but to unblock it by hand. I steeled myself to the task and laid a sack down on the bricks. I was lying on my stomach with my arm down the drain up to my armpit, groping in the unspeakable depths, when I heard footsteps. Footsteps and voices.

"I've just about had a beakful of this place," an angry female voice proclaimed. "I can't stand the lousy dump a minute longer. What's more," the voice went on, getting angrier by the second, "I'm going to find the Misses Fane and tell them so, just you see if I . . ."

The voice tailed off as the footsteps came to an abrupt halt outside the stable. A large person wearing pink dungarees stretched to the very limits of their endurance appeared in the doorway. She had cropped hair dyed a stark white blonde, and her red, rather puffy face was decorated with a cupid bow of

chalky pink lipstick, hooped eyebrows, and a matching pothook at the corner of each eye drawn with
thick orange pencil.

"Who the devil are you?" she demanded in a
belligerent tone.

A dead white face framed by a floppy pageboy
haircut peered round the dungarees. When the face
spotted me lying on the sack it gave a little yelp.

"I'm Elaine," I managed to say. "I work here." I
couldn't get up at once because I had finally managed to get my fingers round the last solid plug of
filth. It came away suddenly, with a loud sucking
plop and a shower of evil-smelling black droplets.
The Pink Dungarees didn't flinch, but the white face
ducked.

"*Work* here?" the Pink Dungarees exclaimed in
tones of disbelief. "Since *when*?"

The owner of the white face came out from behind
the dungarees in order to gape at me in stupefaction.
She was a small, thin girl of about fourteen. I
scrambled to my feet. I was splattered all over with
liquid manure and I knew that I reeked.

"Since this morning," I said. "I've only just
started, so I haven't had time to get anything organized yet." I wiped the worst of the black stuff off on
to the sack in case anyone offered to shake hands.
They didn't.

"And who the hell are you to organize anything?"
Pink Dungarees said scornfully, planting her hands
on her hips.

"I'm qualified," I said. "I've got my Horsemasters
Certificate."

"You and a thousand others," Pink Dungarees

scoffed. "Who do you think you're going to impress with that?"

"I trained with Hans Gelderhol," I said.

A glimmer of interest appeared between the pothooks. "Gelderhol the Eventer?"

"Is there another Gelderhol?" I enquired.

"*Gelderhol*," the white-faced girl said in a breathless voice. "You trained with Gelderhol?"

"Shut it, Doreen," Pink Dungarees snapped. She was determined not to be impressed.

"All the same," Doreen breathed. "*Gelderhol*."

"Gelderhol or not," Pink Dungarees said. "It'll take more than you to lick this hole into shape. It'll take an army."

"I may get one," I said. "I may take working pupils." I had only just thought of it. It seemed a splendid idea.

"Trainees," Pink Dungarees said in disgust. "They're *all* we need. Anyhow, who'd want to train in a dump like this?"

"It won't be a dump when I've finished with it," I said in an annoyed tone. I wasn't prepared to spend the morning sparring with Pink Dungarees. I had far too much to do.

"You're not being very fair, Brenda," the white-faced girl said, suddenly showing a bit of spirit. "You're not really giving her much of a chance."

"She hasn't got much of a chance," Pink Dungarees retorted. "Not working for the Fanes; where the devil are they anyway?" She glared round the yard as if she expected to catch them hiding somewhere.

"The Fanes are out exercising," I said crossly. "They won't be back for at least an hour. So I

43

suggest that you either tell me what you want, or go and wait somewhere for them to come back." I turned back into the stable, picked up the metal grid and jammed it back over the drain. I had wasted enough time. I picked up the stiff brush and began to sweep the drain clots towards the door.

"Now look here, Miss Busy Bee," Brenda said angrily. "I'll tell you what I want! What I want is a bit of service! A bit of value for money, that's what I want!"

I stopped sweeping. "Value for what money?" I said.

"You're not explaining yourself very well, Bren," the white-faced girl said anxiously. "She doesn't know who we are."

"*We*," Brenda pronounced, pursing her rosebud lips, "are livery clients. And what is more, *we* are not satisfied, and *if something is not done* about it, *we* are leaving."

"Oh, I wouldn't do that," I said hastily. I put the brush down. It hadn't occurred to me that I might be dealing with livery clients. The livery clients I had encountered at the training centre hadn't looked anything like Doreen and Brenda. They had been sober, middle-class sort of people who came into the yard dressed in tweed jackets and breeches and sometimes slipped the students fifty pence for saddling their horses. I cursed myself for being so offhand. After promising the Fanes more livery clients, the last thing I wanted on my first morning was to have to tell them they had two less. "I'm sorry," I said. "I didn't realize. If you tell me what's wrong, I'll do my best to put it right."

"You can get the bloody blacksmith to my horse,

44

for a start," Brenda said. "The creature's had a shoe off for a week and he's footsore. How can I get the beast fit without a decent set of shoes?"

"I'll organize it," I said. "Leave it to me. If I can, I'll get him here tomorrow."

"And where's the mineral supplement?" she said. "Ordered and paid for three weeks ago and still not arrived."

"I don't know," I admitted. "But I'll find out."

"My pony is supposed to have damped hay," Doreen said in her timid voice. "He's got a cough. He's supposed to have paste spread on his tongue twice a day. I don't think they remember."

"I'll remember," I promised. "I'll give him the paste. I'll dunk his hay."

"We'll give it one more week, Busy Bee," Doreen said threateningly. "If things don't look up, we're off."

"I quite understand," I said.

There was a lot of snorting and muttering and slamming of stable doors after this, but eventually the Pink Dungarees left, with Doreen scuttling along behind.

The next interruption wasn't long coming. I had just poured a bucket of water down the drain and was listening to the satisfying gurgle as it cleared, when there was a scraping noise at the door and two delighted faces appeared in the crack. The two faces were swiftly joined by four more. It was the young entry.

I was not at all pleased to see them. Apart from already having suffered one set-back in the form of Big Brenda, I knew that there was no way I could get the hounds back to the kennels as Lady Jennifer had taken off earlier in the shooting brake, it being her day of duty at the Oxfam Shop. I rattled the bucket at them, hoping to frighten them away.

"Home," I commanded them sternly. "GO HOME."

But the young entry were overjoyed to hear my voice. They tried to fight their way in through the partly opened door and succeeded in trapping their shoulders and their necks to the accompaniment of howls, yelpings and choking noises. When I kicked at the door to free them, they burst into the stable and leapt at me in an ecstasy of lickings and slobberings. Their coats were wet and black and sticky where they had been rolling in the fields of burned stubble.

I was trying to stay on my feet, fending them off with the bucket, when I heard galloping hooves on the drive. I dropped the bucket and rushed outside with the young entry bounding at my heels, expecting to see an escapee. The Comet perhaps, or the old bay mare. It was Forster.

He was in his scarlet, mounted on a rangy liver chestnut whose coat was running with sweat. His boots were splattered with mud and his white breeches were streaked with black. He was in a blazing temper.

"Damn you, Ladybird, you useless cur," he raged as soon as he set eyes on the young entry. "And you, Landlord! Hike back there you bloody little fiends, or I'll break your miserable necks for you!"

He kicked his horse towards them, cracking his whip. The young entry cringed away and dived behind me for protection. I backed away from the plunging hooves, treading on paws and sterns as I went, setting up a succession of agonized yelpings.

"Don't you dare hit them," I shouted. "If you touch them with that whip, I'll report you to the RSPCA for cruelty!"

Forster gave a bark of laughter. I stood my ground, feeling foolish because of the young entry peering anxiously round and through my legs. "If they were well treated at the kennels," I said defensively, "they wouldn't keep coming back here."

Forster yanked the liver chestnut to a standstill. "They keep coming back," he said angrily, "because they were ruined by your crazy employers. They slept on the beds and gobbled scraps in the kitchen like lap dogs. These are supposed to be working hounds, not *curs*!" He threw a booted leg over the horse's neck and jumped down on to the cobbles. The liver chestnut dropped its head thankfully and let out a long, gusting sigh from its distended nostrils. "How would you feel," Forster said, "if you had been up since four, had a hard morning's cubbing, and then had to do a six mile detour because half the pack decided to go visiting?"

"I suppose I might feel a bit peeved," I said, keeping my eyes on the plaited leather thong with its muddy red lash flickering on the end like a serpent's tongue.

"Peeved," Forster said in disgust, "is not the word I would use to describe it." He coiled up his whip, and as if by magic the young entry crept out from behind my legs and prostrated themselves at his feet, grovelling and fawning in the most sycophantic manner possible. One of them actually started to lick his boots.

I was exasperated by this fickle behaviour and I

was also uncomfortably aware that I was still splattered with dried sludge from the black horse's stable. Normally, it wouldn't have mattered, but for some reason it mattered now.

"I suggest you take your toadying curs off back to the kennels," I said crossly. "You're not the only one with a job to do." I started to walk off, but Forster got hold of my elbow.

"Hold on a minute," he said. "I'm sorry if I frightened you. I was angry."

"Obviously," I said.

"They don't hate me, you know," he said, gesturing at the young entry, sprawling contentedly at his feet. "They have to learn discipline. If they don't, they can't hunt, and if they can't hunt, they have to be destroyed. It's as simple as that."

"It isn't simple," I said. "It's heartless."

"They're not pets," he said. "You couldn't keep a foxhound as a pet. They're hunters and scavengers by nature. They're not a domestic strain." One of the young entry laid its head on his knee and gazed up at him with adoration in its eyes. "So how's the job?" he asked.

"The job's OK," I said. "If you're really interested."

"If I wasn't interested," he said, "I wouldn't have asked."

"So now you've asked," I said, "and I've told you. So perhaps you'll let go of my arm."

"I'll consider it," he said.

We stood and stared at each other. I told myself that he was arrogant and conceited and heartless, and that I hated him. But he was in his scarlet, with his hounds at his feet. He was muddy and tired, and there was blood on his face where a bramble had jagged him. And the mocking, sneering façade was gone. So my eyes dropped first, and I felt the colour rush to my cheeks. I knew how very, very easy it would be to fall for Forster.

"Elaine," he said, letting go of my arm. "Why are you so determined to make a fool of yourself?"

"I don't know what you mean," I said faintly.

"The Fanes are the laughing stock of the county," he said. "Surely you realize that."

"I needed a job," I said.

"You don't need this job," he said. "I can get you a better one."

"Another job?" I looked up in surprise.

"Felix Hissey needs a groom. His girl's leaving. She's got," he hesitated, " . . . personal problems."

"Felix Hissey?" I said. "You mean Felix Hissey, the Pickle King?" I had heard of Felix Hissey. His company sponsored the two largest Three Day Events in the country. Not only that, but they awarded two annual scholarships so that promising young event riders and their horses could train with the National Coach. A job with someone like Felix Hissey was the golden opportunity I had been waiting for. I couldn't quite believe my ears. I wondered if it was Forster's idea of a joke. But he looked perfectly serious.

"He's a good employer," he said, mistaking my silence for lack of enthusiasm. "It's a well paid job. There's also a very nice flat."

"How soon does he need someone?" I tried hard to sound casual.

"By the end of the month. He hasn't advertised yet. Good jobs are hard to come by in the horse

49

world and when he does there'll be hundreds after it. If you want to get in first, you'll have to be quick."

"But the end of the month is only two weeks away!" I said.

"Two weeks too long, I'd have thought." Forster thrust his foot into the liver chestnut's stirrup and swung himself into the saddle. At once the young entry were on their feet, sterns waving, ready to be off. Things were beginning to move rather too fast for me.

"But I've only just taken this job," I said in dismay. "I only started this morning!"

Forster shrugged. "So what? Hissey was out with us this morning and he'll be out again on Thursday. Do you want me to put a word in for you?"

"I don't know," I said, agonized. "I need time to think about it."

The liver chestnut sidled towards the clock arch, wanting to leave. Forster kicked it in the ribs. It obliged him by standing still and chucking its head up and down. "Listen Elaine," he said impatiently. "You've no prospects here. You haven't a hope in hell of earning a decent wage. If you pass up this opportunity, you're a fool."

"I know," I said. "It isn't that I don't want to take it. I do. But it's so sudden. I can't just walk out, not just like that. I should feel a cheat."

"The Fanes are not averse to a bit of cheating themselves," Forster said. He cuffed the liver chestnut's neck with his coiled whip. It stopped chucking its head and arched its neck, opened its mouth, and rattled the bit against its teeth.

"It isn't the Fanes I'm thinking about," I said miserably. "It's the horses."

I couldn't expect Forster to understand this. I only had to think of Nelson with his one eye and his hollow flanks, and the old bay mare with her gallant air and her dusty, threadbare coat, to feel a pull at my heart. And who would treat the black horse's thrush and school The Comet, if I didn't? And across the yard, Doreen's pony coughed and coughed and Brenda's cob with its pink nose and white eyelashes rested a footsore hind leg.

"You'll have to give me a little time to decide," I said. "I have to think things out."

"I'll ring you," Forster said. "On Wednesday night." He raised his whip in a salute and loosed his reins. The liver chestnut plunged across the yard. "By the way," he added, "you're very pretty." He disappeared under the clock arch and the young entry gambolled obediently after him without so much as a backward glance.

I went into the tackroom and I looked in the little spotted mirror on the wall. I couldn't see anything pretty. I saw my mother's pale blonde hair, but whereas hers had always been lightly permed and set into a distinctive style, mine hung straight to just below my ears and because I had cut it myself, it was a bit lopsided. My too pale skin was decorated with black splodges from the drains and my father's eyes stared back at me, grey and wide and rather vacant. Compared to the robust and colourful Fanes, I looked washed out and faded; I looked like a ghost. No, I saw nothing pretty in the tackroom mirror.

Hooves sounded and the Fanes clattered in from exercise, pink-cheeked and breathless, with cascades of wind-blown hair. "We've just passed the young entry on the lane," Nigella gasped. "It was jolly bad luck that you were here by yourself. I bet Nick Forster was *hopping*."

"I hope you didn't let him get away with it, anyway," Henrietta said, sliding down the bad-tempered chestnut's shoulder. "I hope you gave as good as you got. It isn't as if it's *our* fault."

I took The Comet by his withered rein. "He wasn't all that angry," I said. "In fact, he was rather nice about it."

"Oh," Henrietta exclaimed in a knowing manner. "*Was* he!"

"I think we ought to warn you," Nigella said anxiously, "that he's not all that nice to know. He's got a terrible reputation."

"He's had an affair with half the county," Henrietta said, "including Mrs Lydia Lane, whose husband threatened to shoot him."

"And they do say," Nigella continued, "that he drinks rather more than he should."

"The Hissey groom was keen on him for ages," Henrietta said. "You wouldn't believe how badly he treated her. In the end, he was so insufferably awful to her at the Hunt Ball that she packed her cases and walked out."

"I see," I said. That explained why Forster had appeared so concerned about getting me a better job; it hadn't been done out of kindness, but because Felix Hissey had been left in the lurch, and Forster was responsible for it. I took the old bay mare by her bridle.

"I hope you don't think we are being prissy,"

Nigella said. "We're only telling you for your own good."

"After all," Henrietta added. "It's better to know these things. It's as well to have them pointed out."

"Thanks," I said. "I appreciate it."

I led The Comet and the old bay mare back to their stables. I had been up long before anyone else, and their beds were laid thick and clean and sweet, with banked up sides, scrubbed pails of clean water, and piles of newly shaken hay. The horses showed no surprise or gratification at their increased comfort, accepting it as their due. The satisfaction should have been mine. But somehow it wasn't. And it was all Forster's fault.

After that, the day went from bad to worse. Whilst the Fanes were out with the second lot of horses, I decided to ring the blacksmith. There was a dingy little room next to the kitchen which served as an office; if a wobbly table heaped with yellowing newspapers and copies of *Horse and Hound* dating back to the year dot, could be termed an office.

The office housed the telephone, and in my efforts to locate the local telephone directory, I pulled open the drawer in the table. It was stuffed with invoices. I might have closed it again if I hadn't noticed that one of them was from the blacksmith, and had his telephone number on the top. When I pulled it out, I noticed that it also had a little green sticker on the bottom saying YOUR CHEQUE WOULD OBLIGE. The next one I pulled out was of a more recent date and it had a different sort of sticker on it, a round one proclaiming THIS ACCOUNT IS OVERDUE in angry red letters. The next one was bigger altogether. It occupied a larger space and was edged in black. It threatened legal action if the account was not settled within ten days. The invoice was dated two weeks ago.

I sank down into a chair and looked through the invoices. There were dozens and dozens of them, not only from the blacksmith, but from the saddler, from the vet, from local farmers who had supplied hay and straw, and from the corn merchant. Some of them were almost a year old and none of them was receipted. They were all unpaid.

I knew now why the blacksmith hadn't been called, why the corn bins were empty and why the mineral supplement hadn't arrived. How could you call a blacksmith who was taking legal action to recover payment for past services? How could you place an order with a corn merchant who regretted that he must refuse any further credit and cease all future deliveries until the outstanding invoices were cleared?

I don't know how long I sat in that dismal little room, telling myself what a complete and utter fool, what a blind and crass idiot I had been. Asking myself how I had imagined, even for a minute, that by my own inept and inexperienced hand, I could salvage such an appallingly hopeless business.

My father had always numbered over-confidence and misplaced optimism amongst my prime failings. These defects, being completely alien to his own nature, he considered to be a character weakness inherited from my mother, a born optimist, who had left home for a man fifteen years her junior when I was ten. In view of this, it was hardly surprising that he should feel that pessimism and modesty were more solid attributes. Nevertheless, it didn't help to speculate how much he was going to enjoy being proved right again. How he would relish the opportunity of being able to say "*I told you so*. Haven't I always told you that there is *no future in horses*."

Even Hans would have to smile to see me now. Just as he had smiled when I had outlined to him the plans I had made for my career, so tidily and confidently expounded, so forlornly and improvidently arranged. He had listened to me carefully, with his blond head slightly on one side, and one long, beautifully polished boot ledged in the bottom rail of the paddock fence. And when I had finished, he had sighed.

"So you think you go to an event yard, eh?" he had said. "You think you find a place to take you, with no trouble? And you think, even if it happens, that you are allowed to ride these event horses? You, with no experience at all? And you imagine that these kind people you find, because you work hard and they are pleased, that they let you compete on these horses, these good horses worth so many thousand of pounds? You think it will happen this easy?"

I had nodded. Standing there in all the euphoria of my newly awarded qualification, I had been sure that it would be.

But now I knew differently. And as I walked slowly up the dusty oak treads to my bedroom and started to repack my cases I was glad that Hans Gelderhol, The European Champion, The Golden Boy of Eventing, couldn't see me now.

5

Liquid Assets

I waited until the Fanes came into the kitchen for their tea. Then I told them I was leaving.

"*Leaving*?" Nigella said in tones of the very greatest astonishment. "But you have only just arrived!"

"I know," I said. "And I'm sorry. But I thought I could be useful. I really thought I would be able to cope."

"I knew she wouldn't stay," Henrietta exclaimed. She turned to Nigella in exasperation. "Didn't I tell you she wouldn't? Didn't I warn you that she was just using us as a stopgap? Only taking our job until she found something better?"

"I'm not leaving because I've found something better," I said. "I haven't found another job. I haven't anything else in mind at all." This was true. I had considered applying for the job with Felix Hissey and I had decided against it. For one thing I didn't want to get involved with Nick Forster and his sordid affairs, and for another I hadn't the face to take a job where I would be bumping into the Fanes every five minutes. Then there were the horses. I had to steel myself not to think about them. I had made up my mind that the only thing to do was to make a clean break. I had to leave the area; to creep back home with my tail between my legs; to start again, scanning the *Situations Vacant*. The prospect was depressing, to say the least.

"But if you haven't found another job; if you haven't anywhere else to go," Nigella said, mystified, "why are you leaving?"

"I'm leaving because things are worse than I ever imagined," I said. "I'm leaving because of *these*." I threw the sheaf of unpaid invoices on to the kitchen table.

The Fanes stared at them in silence.

"Oh," Henrietta said eventually in a flat voice. "Those."

"You can't run a yard without money," I said. "No one can. You have to pay the bills. You didn't tell me you were bankrupt."

"We are not exactly bankrupt," Nigella said in her careful way. "At least," she added, "not yet."

"Where did you find them, anyway?" Henrietta demanded indignantly. "We didn't employ you to pry into our private affairs. Or to search through our drawers."

"I was looking for a telephone directory," I said wearily. "I wanted to ring the blacksmith."

"I'm rather glad you didn't," Nigella said with a hollow little laugh. "He would have been awfully cross."

"I'm the one who's entitled to be cross," I pointed out. "You should never have employed me. You can't afford to employ anyone. I wonder you even had the nerve to place the advertisement. No wonder you wouldn't discuss my wages."

"You're not entitled to any wages yet," Henrietta flared. "You've hardly done anything!"

Nigella picked up the invoices. She flipped through them in a desultory manner. "They do seem to have built up a bit," she admitted. "But I expect we will manage to pay them off. After all, the hunting season is almost here, and there will be money coming in from the hirelings and the liveries. You said so yourself."

"Hirelings have to be fed," I reminded her. "They also need to be shod. And your liveries are leaving."

"What do you mean our liveries are leaving?" Henrietta cried. "That's a lie!"

"It isn't a lie," I said. "I saw Doreen and Brenda this morning. They told me." After the traumatic visit of the young entry I had completely forgotten to mention it.

"They don't *mean* it," Nigella said. "They keep on saying it. They just use it as a threat. But they would never actually *leave*. I'm sure of it."

"They do mean it," I said. "They've given you a week to get the blacksmith and the mineral supplement. Otherwise," I added, remembering Brenda's words, "they're off."

"That's blackmail," Henrietta muttered. "They've no right."

"They've every right," I said.

Nigella put the invoices back on to the table. "Things are pretty bad," she said. "We may as well admit it."

I wondered if she realized quite how bad things were. "In a week," I said, "the oats will be gone altogether. In a week there won't be a horse left in the yard with a full set of shoes on."

"It won't worry you," Henrietta snapped, "since you won't be here."

"In a week," I said, "you won't have any hay left at all."

There was a silence in which Nigella stared at the

invoices in a distressed manner, and Henrietta picked angrily at her sleeve which was unravelled almost as far as the elbow. I told myself that I shouldn't feel emotional about it. There was nothing I could do. It wasn't my problem. I blinked hard and studied a sepia photograph on the kitchen wall. Under the fly blown glass, Lady Jennifer, willow-slim and elegant, posed her hunter for posterity. Something about the horse was familiar. I looked closer and I saw that it was the old bay mare, fit and sleek and in her prime. The photograph was pasted to a piece of cardboard scattered with thunder flies, and in one of the lower corners there was some writing in faded ink. "Little Legend" it said, "1947". The old bay mare was nearly forty years old.

I stared at the photograph and I wondered when she had stopped being Little Legend and become just the old bay mare. It didn't take much imagination to picture the steady decline of the stables, to know that every year there would have been less to spend and less people to care. Like a gallant old pensioner, the old bay mare had weathered the hard times. She had lost her comfort, her youth and her looks, but she still had her spirit. She deserved a better end.

"Nigella," I said. "If there was some way; if things were not quite so hopeless, I wouldn't leave."

"I know," she said, "and there is a way."

Henrietta looked up from her elbow. "Which way is that?" she enquired in a suspicious tone.

"We shall have to sell something," Nigella said. "Although to be honest, there is not a lot left."

"Well, don't look at me," Henrietta said. "I only have my secretaire; and I'm not selling."

"Then it will have to be my vases," Nigella decided.

Selling the vases meant that I had to drive the shooting brake to London. I had passed my driving test before I left the training centre, but since then I had not driven at all. My father flatly refused to allow me behind the wheel of his beloved Morris Minor. It was his most cherished possession and he was very proud of the fact that it was still in the same gleamingly pristine condition as when he had driven it out of the showroom twenty years ago. So I was a bit alarmed at the thought of having to face the London traffic with a valuable cargo of vases.

The next morning, after a herculean effort in the stables and a shortened form of communal exercise, we peeled off our anoraks and wellingtons and rushed upstairs to change into town clothes. It only took me a few seconds to flip through the hangers in the wormy, carved wardrobe and realize that I hadn't anything resembling town clothes with me at all. I couldn't even find a clean shirt. I flew along the passage to tell Nigella and bumped into Henrietta, who was already changed. She had added fluorescent purple socks and scuffed pink spikey-heeled shoes to her awful drainpipe jeans and topped it all with a horrific moth-eaten fur coat with padded shoulders. She didn't look as if she had even combed her hair.

After that I settled for jeans and a roll-necked jersey under my hacking jacket which made a nice rustic contrast to Nigella, who appeared in something that looked suspiciously like a pink openwork bedjacket which tied at the neck with a grubby piece of satin ribbon, the inevitable drainpipes and red tap-dancing shoes.

I set off gingerly down the drive, steering the shooting brake in and out of the pot-holes, trying to avoid the bumps. The Fanes sat nursing the vases on the back seat.

"Heavens," Henrietta grumbled. "I hope you're not going to drive like this all the way to town. Can't you drive in a straight line?"

"You're jolly lucky I can drive at all," I pointed out. "It wasn't a requirement of the job. It wasn't mentioned in the advert."

"Quite a lot of things weren't mentioned in the advert," Nigella remarked, cranking down her window to dispose of some withered dahlias which had been sitting in the neck of her vase. "It's a bit of a sore point."

None of my previous driving experience, not even suffering brake failure after stalling the land rover whilst ferrying Hans round the cross-country course, had prepared me for the terrors of negotiating the London traffic. It was fearful.

The Fanes were no help. Whilst I was being honked and hustled and trapped in the wrong lanes, narrowly avoiding being rammed by taxi cabs or mown down by buses, they yelped and clutched their vases and bounced up and down in their seats, shouting out conflicting directions as to the quickest way to get to Knightsbridge.

Finally, after whirling round and round a one-way system in a state of near hysteria, we arrived at an underground carpark. There was a portable sign blocking the entrance saying FULL. In a trice, Nigella was out of the shooting brake and had heaved the sign aside.

"Drive on in," Henrietta commanded. "We shall have to bribe someone to find us a space."

I drove into the gloom and almost knocked over the attendant who was hot-foot after the person who had removed his sign. He leapt aside and banged angrily on the roof with his fist. I stamped on the brake, released the clutch and stalled the shooting brake. Henrietta, who was holding both vases, shot forward in her seat and screamed, and Nigella, who was coming along behind, walked into the rear doors.

The attendant took advantage of the confusion and grabbed Nigella by her bedjacket, demanding to know what she thought she was up to, moving his sign. Full was full, he said. And that meant everybody. It took Nigella quite a while to calm him down, but eventually she tripped round the front of the shooting brake and stuck her head in at my window.

"Has anyone got any money?" she enquired.

There was a silence.

"He says he'll do it for a pound," she said urgently. "If we leave the car unlocked and the keys in the ignition, he'll move it into the first vacant space."

The attendant leered at us. Regretfully I handed over my last pound coin. I was not too sure when or if I would ever see another.

We took it in turns to carry the vases through the streets. They were very large. They were also very heavy. They had fat bulbous bodies and little thin necks with nasty little handles shaped like ears attached to them. Not only that but they were decorated all over with ladies and butterflies and trelliswork in vivid shapes of gold and burnt umber. They were the most hideous vases I had seen in the whole of my life. I couldn't imagine that anyone could possibly want to buy them.

We turned into the main entrance to Harrods and stepped on to the escalator.

"Nigella," I said as we sailed majestically upwards. "What if they don't *want* them?"

Nigella was standing in front of me with her hands clasped round the belly of her vase and its neck lodged under her chin. "It'll be all right," she said in a muffled voice. "Honestly."

"Of course they'll *want* them," Henrietta interposed from behind in an acid voice. "We've been dealing with Harrods for years. We should know what they want by now."

When it seemed that we could go up no further, we stepped off the escalator and began to weave our way through an endless maze of tapestry armchairs. At the end of it all there was a glittering chandelier, an empty suit of armour, and the entrance to the Fine Arts Department.

Almost as soon as we had stepped inside, the Fine Arts Gentleman came hurrying over. He eyed the vases with obvious pleasure and ushered us into an inner sanctum. He seemed to be an old friend.

"What is it this time?" he said, relieving us of the vases and placing them reverently on a baize-topped table. "Central heating perhaps? Or a winter holiday in the Canaries?"

"No such luck," Nigella said. "We need to refurbish the stables. The cost is horrendous."

"I can imagine." The Fine Arts Gentleman pulled out an immaculately folded handkerchief on which to polish his eyeglass. "Provenance?" he enquired.

Henrietta rummaged in the pockets of her verminous fur coat and handed him a screwed up piece of paper. He smoothed it out carefully on the table and studied it.

"They've been in the family for two hundred years at least," Nigella said. "They're Cantonese. They are supposed to be rather valuable."

"They are indeed," the Fine Arts Gentleman agreed. "They are an extremely fine pair of Cantonese porcelain baluster vases. Circa 1780, unless I am very much mistaken." He screwed in his eyeglass and turned one of the vases upside down in order to examine the base. A thick brown soup rolled slowly out of the neck, down his trouser leg, over his beautiful suede shoes, and spread in a glutinous pool on the carpet. The inner sanctum was suddenly filled with the most disgusting smell.

"Oh!" Nigella gasped in dismay. "Mummy's dahlia water!"

The Fine Arts Gentleman recoiled, catching his breath.

"We're most terribly, awfully sorry," Nigella cried. She tried to mop up some of the soup with a paper handkerchief. It was thick and slimy. I thought that if I didn't go outside, I should probably be sick. Henrietta had already backed away as far as the door and had her hand clamped across her mouth.

When the Fine Arts Gentleman had recovered himself sufficiently, he paid us £2,000 for the vases. It wasn't quite enough to pay all the bills, but it was enough to get us out of trouble. On the way home, Henrietta composed a little song to mark the occasion. It was the first time I had heard her sing. She was surprisingly good.

6

Thunder and Lightning

A few days later we were in the thick of preparations for hunting, when Nigella came back from the post-box at the end of the drive, gleefully waving a letter.

"It's in reply to our advertisement," she shouted. "Come and see!"

The Fanes had placed another advertisement in *Horse and Hound*, but this time I had been allowed to compose it.

Small High Class Livery Yard in the Midvale and Westbury Hunt Country (I had put) *has a few vacancies for the coming season. Apply: Havers Hall, Westbury, Suffolk.*

There had been little point in adding a telephone number since our line had been disconnected. There hadn't been enough money left to buy clippers *and* pay the telephone account, and the clippers had seemed more important. We were desperate to attract more liveries because we needed a regular source of income; the vases had bought us time, but already the bills were building up again.

At the time of the letter, Henrietta and I were engaged in clipping the black horse. It was no easy task. Backed into a corner and held firmly by the nose and a foreleg, we managed to make him stand fast, but he soon discovered that if he put his mind to it, he could send ripples along his skin like wind through winter wheat. It slowed up the clipping considerably, and the motor had begun to overheat. We were glad of a break.

Henrietta released the black horse who immediately shook himself like a dog and began to sag at the knees as a preliminary to getting down in the box for a good roll. We thwarted him by tying him to the hayrack. I threw a blanket over his naked hindquarters and we left him to have a good fidget whilst we went up to the house to investigate the letter.

Nigella was in the kitchen making coffee. The letter was lying on the table. I picked it up. It was typed on thick, cream paper and there was a business heading at the top. "THUNDER AND LIGHƷNING LIMITED" it said, and underneath there was an address in Clapham.

"It's obviously a double glazing firm," Nigella said in a jubilant tone. "One of the very best. You only have to look at the paper: it's embossed." She chipped enthusiastically at a lump of solidified sugar and dropped the bits into our mugs. There weren't any biscuits; we had no time for cookery.

"Read it out, read it out," Henrietta said impatiently jiggling my elbow. "Don't keep it all to yourself."

Dear Sirs (I read),

Having noticed your recent advertisement in *Horse and Hound* I am writing to enquire if it would be possible for you to take three hunters at full livery for the coming season? Owing to the nature and timing of our engagements, we are not able to hunt more than two or three times a month, but my colleagues and I have found it unsatisfactory to hire horses in the past.

Should you have a vacancy, I would be grateful if you would quote your terms, in order that we may come to a decision as soon as possible.

Yours faithfully,

J P Jones

pp. Thunder and Lighȝning Limited.

"Glory," Henrietta gasped. She sat down on a kitchen chair with a thump. "Three liveries! *Three*."

"And business types," Nigella said gloatingly. "Exactly the sort you wanted, Elaine. High class liveries, to add tone to the yard."

"We had better write back," Henrietta said, becoming agitated. "*Immediately*. They may have written to other places. We must get in first." She ran into the office and began to search frantically for notepaper and a pen.

"Sit down Elaine," Nigella said. "You must write our reply. And I will post it when I go out with the second lot of horses." She sat beside me and looked expectant. Henrietta managed to unearth a clean sheet of notepaper with the family crest in one corner, and a ball point pen which turned out to be red. This necessitated another search. Finally I was able to begin.

Dear Mr Jones (I wrote),

Thank you for your enquiry. I am pleased to confirm that we have sufficient vacancies to accommodate your three hunter liveries for the coming season . . .

"That's good," Nigella said appreciatively. "That's really good."

68

I also have pleasure in quoting our terms, which are as follows:

I looked up at the Fanes. "What are our terms?" I said.

Henrietta shrugged her shoulders in a vague sort of way.

"We don't actually have any set terms," Nigella said. "So you can put what you like."

"You must have some idea of what you charge," I said. "What about Doreen? What about Brenda?"

"Ah," Nigella said uneasily. "They have been here a long time."

"They pay for their own foodstuffs," Henrietta pointed out. "They pay the blacksmith, and they do all their own exercising."

"All the same," I said, "I would like to know what they pay."

"Actually," Nigella admitted. "It's five pounds."

I was astounded by this piece of information. The rent of the stable alone was worth five pounds a week, and the Fanes had been supplying hay and straw, not to mention the labour involved in mucking out and feeding.

"You're crazy," I told them. "You're absolutely mad. You deserve to be bankrupt."

"If we had charged more, they might have found somewhere cheaper," Nigella protested. "Then we wouldn't have had anybody."

"And ten pounds a week in cash," Henrietta added, "is very handy."

"Ten pounds a week for two liveries," I said crossly, "is *pathetic*."

"All right," Henrietta said, nettled. "If you think you are so jolly clever, *you* fix the livery rates."

"You are quite right, of course," Nigella said hastily. "We haven't been charging enough. You had better adjust the prices, Elaine. We are completely in your hands; make it ten, if you like."

I turned my attention back to the letter. There was no point in starting an argument. When it came to costing, the Fanes were hopeless. They hadn't a clue.

Full Livery (I wrote) £25 per week
Shoeing and Veterinary Fees extra.

"Twenty-five pounds," Nigella gasped. "For a week!"

"They won't pay it," Henrietta said in a scandalized voice. "Twenty-five pounds for a livery is far too expensive. Honestly Elaine, sometimes I wonder whose side you are on. This may be our one chance to make a success of the yard, and you are going to price us out of business!"

"Twenty-five pounds a week is reasonable," I said firmly. "At the training centre, the hunter liveries paid thirty-five."

"But we are not the training centre," Nigella said. "We haven't the staff for one thing, or the facilities."

"And we're fed up with hearing about the training centre," Henrietta said. "We find it very boring."

"And I find you very boring," I snapped. "I thought you wanted to run a high class yard? I thought you wanted to attract quality liveries?"

"We do," Henrietta said in a grumpy voice. "You know we do."

"We are only being cautious," Nigella pointed out. "We are not trying to be difficult."

70

"If we agree to charge twenty-five pounds," Henrietta said, "what about Brenda? What about Doreen?"

"Their rates will have to go up as well," I said. "And if they don't like it, they will have to move out."

"I realize that we have to be economic," Nigella sighed, "but it does seem a bit hard. After all, they are old clients; and Brenda is sure to take it badly. She can be very difficult."

"You can leave Brenda and Doreen to me," I said. "If they want to stay, they can have their livery at a slightly reduced rate. Brenda is no fool, she must know how much it would cost to keep her horse elsewhere. We are not going to be a cut price establishment."

"Better a full cut price establishment," Henrietta grumbled, "than an empty high class one."

"It didn't take you long to foul things up, Busy Bee," Brenda commented when I told her that her livery had gone up to twenty pounds, but as a concession to her long residence she would no longer have to pay for her own foodstuffs. "I thought something like this was in the wind. Well, I can't say things haven't improved, so I expect I shall have to cough up; but Doreen won't. She's only a kid. She won't be able to afford it."

"I've thought about Doreen," I said. "Her livery is only a pony, so it won't cost so much. It doesn't need the corn for one thing. I thought we would charge her fourteen pounds a week, and as she likes to hang around the yard perhaps she could help out sometimes, in the evenings perhaps, or at weekends.

If we paid her a pound an hour, we could deduct it from her livery bill. We could do with an extra hand, and it isn't as if she would have to do it all the year round; her pony goes out to grass in the spring."

"I've got to hand it to you, Busy Bee," Brenda said grudgingly. "You've got all the answers."

The Fanes, who were secretly terrified of Brenda, were much impressed with these negotiations, but they were alarmed at the thought of having to pay Doreen a pound an hour. They were slightly mollified when I explained that they would not actually be required to hand over hard cash, which was something they were incredibly mean about and would go to inordinate lengths to avoid. As soon as there was some regular income coming into the yard I meant to pin them down on the subject of my pocket money wages. There was no point in mentioning it until then, because the Fanes were as broke as I was.

We didn't get any more replies from the advertisement, so we were more than a bit anxious about the response to our letter to Thunder and Lightning Limited. Every day Nigella ran down to the postbox at the end of the drive and every day she returned with another bill we couldn't pay. But there was no reply to our letter.

"I told you twenty-five pounds was too much," Henrietta said bitterly. "I told you they wouldn't pay it."

"If they can't afford twenty-five pounds a week," I retorted, "we don't want them anyway." But even I began to wonder if I had pitched our prices too high to start with; that maybe we would have been better to start low and fill the yard as Henrietta had maintained.

One morning when Nigella came back from the postbox there was a letter for me. It was from my father. Now that I had landed a job which had lasted all of a fortnight, and rather more especially, I suspected, because the Fanes had a title and a grand-sounding address, he had softened in his attitude. He was prepared to come to visit me.

This change of heart was something of a mixed blessing. Whilst I was pleased to think that at last my father might be beginning to accept my choice of career, I was vastly alarmed at the prospect of having to introduce him to the Fanes. I knew that Havers Hall and its occupants would not be quite what he expected. Also, that seeing me in such down-at-heel circumstances, he would immediately smell exploitation and demand to know how much I was being paid in wages, if I was covered by Employers' Liability Insurance, if my National Insurance Contributions were being paid, and a dozen other niggling little details he considered important. To further complicate matters, the date he had suggested for his intended visit was the day we had planned to take some of the horses cubbing, as a pipe-opener for the opening meet. It was all very inconvenient.

I mentioned the last problem to Nigella who, with her customary tact, said that I should on no account try to put him off, for fear of causing offence.

"He doesn't want to come until mid-morning anyway," she pointed out. "And as the meet is at eight-thirty, you could leave early and be back by then. When they meet in the village, they always end up by drawing the edge of the park, so it isn't as if you will be far away. And Mummy will be home, it isn't her Meals-on-Wheels day and she would be delighted to meet your father."

Mummy was delighted. Lady Jennifer immediately identified my father as a Good Cause.

"But *Elaine*," she shrilled. "How simply *marvellous*! Of course your father must pay us a visit. I shall be absolutely *thrilled* to entertain him."

The day before the entertainment was due to take place she bucketed down to the village store in the shooting brake and returned with a box of livid iced fancies and a packet of custard creams which, in the Fane household, represented the height of extravagance.

I hadn't the heart to tell her that my father refused to eat commercially produced confections of any kind because he was convinced that the white sugar they contained poisoned the system.

7

A Friend of a Friend

The cubbing morning was dry and bright, with just the right amount of autumnal nip in the air. The meet was at the Westbury crossroads, which meant that we could hack there.

Our party consisted of Nigella on the mare-who-sometimes-slipped-a-stifle, Henrietta on the black-horse-who-never-stood-still, myself on the bad-tempered chestnut, and Doreen, who because her pony had not completely recovered from its cough had been allowed to take the old bay mare. There was also a solitary client, a Mr McLoughlin, described by Lady Jennifer as a friend of a friend, who after much deliberation had been allocated The Comet, the only horse in the stable who was up to weight.

To our consternation, when he arrived, Mr McLoughlin turned out to be small and spindly and not very experienced. However, there was no time to do anything about it and he professed himself overwhelmed to be presented with The Comet who, clipped and newly shod, with a neatly pulled mane and tail, looked a picture.

Now that there were three of us and Doreen working in the yard, the horses were beginning to look reasonably presentable. They were still rather too lean, especially the old bay mare, whose age was against her, and Nelson. Nelson had found having his jaw put in a metal clamp and a file rasped along his back teeth up to his eye sockets an alarming experience. He had spent the rest of the day rattling his mouth in the water bucket, which by evening stables was topped with froth and lined with tooth chippings. The next morning, though, he had cheered up and when I went into his stable I found him standing on bare brick; during the night he had not only eaten his corn feed and his hay net, but also his bedding. I had high hopes of Nelson.

The black horse still looked like a racehorse after the Derby. His nervous energy would never allow him to maintain any condition, but his thrush was drying up, his coat was glossy, and he had a certain dashing attraction that captured the eye. The Comet, the bad-tempered chestnut, and the mare-who-sometimes-slipped-a-stifle all looked smart and well-covered. They were not one hundred per cent fit by any means, and they lacked muscle, especially behind the saddle, but I couldn't help feeling pleased as we set out in the watery sunshine with our breath hanging in the air like smoke, the horses bright-eyed and well shod, and the saddlery, even if it was not new or even very modern, soaped and, thanks to Nigella's hideous vases, mended and safe.

The only dubious note was struck by the Fanes themselves who didn't appear to possess any riding garments other than the drainpipe jeans. Even so, with the addition of old-fashioned leather riding boots with laces up the front, baggy tweed costume jackets which probably originated from the Oxfam Shop, and their hair in long plaits beneath their bowler hats, they achieved a certain period charm; all the same, I hoped that they would manage something rather better for the opening meet.

Hounds were already waiting at the crossroads when we arrived; the black horse went into a *Piaffe* at the sight of them. The Master, a round, red-faced man with a waxed moustache, wished us a cheery good morning as we clattered up, and the Huntsman, who looked lean, hungry and irritated, favoured us with a curt nod. The rest of the field consisted of two middle-aged women on big raw-boned thorough-breds, a boy on a piebald cob, and a tall, thin, nervous-looking man on a threequarter-bred bay gelding.

Nigella, Doreen, Mr McLoughlin and I stood our horses quietly in the lane a little way apart from the others. The black horse fussed and fidgeted about and arched his neck and swished his tail. His neck and shoulders were already patched with sweat. Mr McLoughlin, with his stirrups too short and his toes pointing firmly towards the ground, seemed to be perfectly happy and confident on The Comet, leaning forward every now and again to clap him affectionately on the neck. I had ridden The Comet out to exercise several times and I had found him an obedient and intelligent horse, if at times rather world-weary in his attitude. At some time in his life someone had schooled him with great care and I found it hard to reconcile this with the Fanes' assertions that he was a confirmed bolter. If this was so, he had yet to show his true colours.

"I wonder if the pups are out," Nigella said. She stood up in her stirrups, scanning the pack for familiar faces. "The trouble is that when they are all together, it's nearly impossible to tell them apart."

William and Forster were holding up hounds on

the little grass triangle in the middle of the cross-roads. When William saw us, his jaw dropped and he stared at the horses in open astonishment. After that, when he wasn't paying attention to hounds, he stared at Henrietta instead. Henrietta ignored him. Forster on the other hand, immaculately mounted on a grey, hardly gave us a glance. But when one of the young entry recognized Nigella's voice and came gambolling across the lane to greet us, he kicked his horse after it and sent it scuttling back.

He lifted his hat to the Fanes. I hoped with all my heart that he wouldn't say anything about the job. I felt myself grow hot and I lifted my saddle flap and fumbled with the straps, pretending to tighten my girth.

"I tried to ring you on Wednesday," Forster said. "There seemed to be something wrong with the telephone."

"We've got a faulty line," Henrietta said smartly. "It's a cable fault."

"Is that so?" Forster gave her a cool look. "The operator seemed to think you had been disconnected."

Henrietta shot him a glance of pure hatred before being carried out of earshot by the black horse, who was executing a *passage*.

"I take it that you've decided against the job," Forster said, "otherwise you would have let me know."

"Yes," I said. "I would . . . I mean, I have . . . and if you wouldn't mind, I would rather not discuss it." I felt hatefully embarrassed. Forster had kept his voice low so that the others wouldn't hear, but all conversation had stopped and I knew everyone was staring. My face had turned scarlet.

Forster seemed to find it very amusing, it was obviously the kind of situation he enjoyed. "I shall have to come and visit you at the Hall," he said, and this time he didn't trouble to keep his voice down. "I'm sure Lady Jennifer won't object."

Nigella gave me a startled look. I opened my mouth to protest but I was saved from having to reply by the bad-tempered chestnut who, realizing that my hands had turned to jelly on the reins, took advantage of the situation to dive forward with flattened ears in order to sink his yellow teeth into the neck of Forster's grey.

The grey horse shot backwards in dismay and bumped one of the thoroughbreds, who began to spin round like a top, lashing out at everything in sight. The tall, thin, nervous man's horse leapt in the air and catapulted him out of the saddle on to the lane. In the resulting confusion, Nigella and I sought the refuge of the grass verge where the rest of our party had collected.

"Serve him right," Henrietta commented in a valedictory tone. "Ought to have been *his* neck."

Soon afterwards, the Master decided it was time to move off. We followed hounds along the lane and across a track towards the first covert. The tall, thin, nervous man rode in front of us, holding his horse tightly and shouting at it. The horse was upset and refused to walk; it pranced along unhappily and kept shaking its head, making the man more nervous than ever.

"I do wish people wouldn't overmount themselves," Nigella said in a low voice. "He'll ruin that lovely animal; not only that, but he'll frighten himself to death at the same time."

"I'll keep an eye on him," Henrietta promised. "If the horse has him off again, I shall offer him fifty pounds for it. He'll probably be only too pleased to accept."

At the first few coverts of the day there was not a lot of action; as it was so close to the new season, the hunt didn't want to cull the cubs, just scatter them. We were told to ring the coverts with orders not to send the cubs back, but to let them get away. The coverts seemed to be full of foxes. They ran out everywhere, streaking away across stubble and plough, whilst hounds blundered about in the undergrowth. At one point, a young fox ran straight between the black horse's front legs, causing him to go totally rigid for at least a minute. It was, Henrietta declared, the longest she had ever known him to stand still on his own account.

As a reward for scattering the cubs, the Master informed us that we could expect a run at the next draw if hounds were diligent enough to put out an old dog fox who had given good sport for three seasons without losing a hair of his brush. The draw was a long straggling copse and we were positioned at set intervals on the ride that surrounded it, each person out of sight and sound of the others. The draw was planned like a military operation and everyone was given a part to play, something that is never possible after the opening meet, with fields of hundreds for the Master to control.

I was sent to watch a triangle of scrub at the end of the copse, which finished in a vast field of plough, stretching off into the sky, speckled with gulls and pewits. The bad-tempered chestnut and I stood on the ride, listening. The silence was total.

Nothing happened for ages and just as I had decided that nothing ever would, and even the bad-tempered chestnut had lost interest and was chewing a twig, I heard the Huntsman's voice. There were some rustlings and cracklings and a, "Leu in there, try over," followed by a yelp. Then a hound spoke inside the copse and almost immediately another joined in. The bad-tempered chestnut stiffened to attention, his ears pointed forward like a terrier.

A few seconds later there was a holloa, a shrill, spine-tingling scream along the ride, and almost simultaneously Forster steamed past, galloping hard, with a couple of hounds at his horse's heels. After a moment's hesitation I followed. Flying round the edge of the copse, the bad-tempered chestnut and I suddenly came across Henrietta standing in the middle of the ride, holding her hat in the air.

"Don't come any further," she shouted. "Don't cross the line!"

The bad-tempered chestnut applied his brakes and skidded to a halt. The black horse, knowing there was to be a run, was in an agony of impatience, plunging and dancing all over the ride and frothing at the mouth. It was all Henrietta could do to hold him with one hand. Suddenly there was a staccato burst on the horn and the entire pack flashed across the ride between us. The Huntsman crashed after them, cheering them on. The black horse leapt in the air and carried Henrietta after them even before she had time to cram her hat back on to her head.

The bad-tempered chestnut and I followed at a more cautious pace. I wanted to be sure that hounds were all out of the copse and that the Hunt Staff had got away first. I didn't want to find myself galloping in the middle of the pack and in front of the Master on my first day out.

By the time we had negotiated the headland of the plough, the rest of our party had joined us and hounds were strung out two fields ahead. It was marvellous to be riding across country again. The bad-tempered chestnut didn't have much scope because he was a small, compact horse with a naturally short stride; but he was very game. He tackled everything that came his way. He slithered down and scrambled up the sides of ditches the bigger horses took in one massive flying leap; he shrugged his way through brambles and undergrowth the thin-skinned blood horses baulked at; and he laboured manfully over the plough. Whenever we hit grass or stubble, he showed a surprising turn of speed. Galloping along with the wind stinging my face, the chestnut neck stretched in front of me, and the regular thud of hooves beneath me, I felt alive again for the first time since I had left the training centre.

Another dozen or more riders joined the field as the morning wore on. Hounds had begun to slow down and were swinging in a wide circle when I looked at my watch and realized that it was time to leave. Punctuality was one of my father's strong points and I knew he wouldn't be even a minute late. I pushed the bad-tempered chestnut on slightly to catch up with Nigella, who was riding slightly in front. Doreen and the old bay mare were well behind but I could see the black horse and The Comet almost two fields ahead, practically level with the

Master. Mr McLoughlin was by no means being run away with; his reins were lying loose upon The Comet's neck, his seat was waving in the air, and he was having the ride of his life; worth every penny of the twenty pounds I intended to charge him.

"Can't you stay a little longer?" Nigella gasped, when we were stirrup to stirrup and I had shouted that I was about to leave. She added something about turning for home anyway and having to watch The Comet, but I lost most of it in the rattle of hooves as we dropped off a bank into a narrow lane. The lane seemed a good place to make the break, so I pulled up and set off for home. The bad-tempered chestnut was as reluctant as I was to leave when hounds were running. He clamped his tail to his rump, fixed his ears back and sulked.

Along the lane we came upon the tall, thin man struggling to load the bay horse into his trailer. The horse was rearing and rolling its eyes and the man was shouting and hitting it with the end of the headcollar rope. I dismounted and stood behind the horse, slapping its hindquarters and making encouraging noises and the bad-tempered chestnut did what he could by snaking out his head and snapping his teeth, and eventually the bay horse went up the ramp. As I fastened the breeching, the tall, thin man told me that the bay horse was only on trial, and that, by jove, it was off back the first thing in the morning; he couldn't wait to see the last of it. I was relieved to hear it because the bay horse was far too high couraged for him, it deserved better than the tall, thin man; and I knew that he would be a different person on a more suitable horse. He wasn't cruel, only frightened; but fright can make even a timid man into a tyrant where horses are concerned.

By the time I had mounted up again and reached the Hall, it was a quarter past eleven and my father was due to arrive at half past. I rubbed down the bad-tempered chestnut, rugged him up and left him warm and dry with his mash and his hay and dashed up to the house. There was just time to jump in and out of a luke-warm bath, which was the best the hot water system could achieve, to drag on some clean clothes and to clatter downstairs where I found Lady Jennifer laying out the iced fancies and the custard creams in her own little sitting room.

The sitting room was the only furnished reception room in the house and it was enhanced by Henrietta's Vile secretaire. Lady Jennifer was all prepared for tea with an electric kettle sitting on the hearth, together with a teapot with the silver plate rubbed off, and some china cups and plates of assorted design. A single bar electric fire only just failed to banish the chill from the air. It was not quite gracious living, but I was touched and grateful. I only hoped my father would be.

At exactly half past eleven we were hovering by the front door and we heard the sound of a car on the drive. I felt incredibly nervous. I was almost glad that my father had chosen a hunting day to visit. At least, with the Fane sisters out of the way, the setting was serene. And Lady Jennifer, as she swept down the stone steps in her ancient tweeds with her hair pinned into an untidy bun, looked the picture of impoverished gentry.

The immaculate Morris Minor came to a careful halt and my father got out and gave me a perfunctory kiss on the cheek. I was just beginning to introduce him to Lady Jennifer when there was a wild shriek from somewhere in the park.

As we turned towards it, we heard thundering hooves and a riderless horse came into view with reins and stirrups flying. The horse was The Comet and he was heading for the stables at full speed. Lady Jennifer barely had time to grip my arm with her bony fingers, when three couple of hounds, sopping wet from the river, burst through the remains of the yew hedge and hurled themselves upon us with yelps of joy. My father, with admirable presence of mind, opened the door of the Morris Minor to take refuge, but before he could set foot inside, one of the young entry beat him to it and seated itself proudly upon the driver's seat, awaiting the inevitable transport back to the kennels.

All this happened in an instant and it was followed up by the arrival of the old bay mare with Doreen aboard, hatless, her hair flopping over her eyes and her cheeks pink with exertion. They cleared the yew hedge in fine style and almost landed on top of us.

"We tried to turn them," Doreen shrieked. "But Mr McLoughlin hit a tree!" She hauled furiously at the old bay mare to prevent herself being conveyed back to the yard and kicked her wildly in the ribs. "He's lying in the park! Felled like an ox and as dead as a doorknob!"

Lady Jennifer, who throughout this recital had been crying, "Oh! Oh!" in dismay, now turned deathly pale and set off at a run for the park gate, dragging my father with her. I jumped up behind Doreen, but the old bay mare refused to jump back over the hedge with an extra passenger and after a few nerve-racking tries, we abandoned the idea and made for the gate as well.

In the event, Mr McLoughlin was not dead. He had risen from the spot where he had been felled by an overhanging bough whilst grappling with The Comet's iron will, and he was tottering towards us. His bowler hat was broken, there was blood flowing from his brow, and his breeches were streaked with grass stains. As Lady Jennifer loosed hold of my father and rushed to support him, the hunt swept past us like the Charge of the Light Brigade on the trail of the old dog fox who was heading for the certain safety of the plantation. With the ground vibrating under our feet, we made for the park railings where, just as we were engaged in heaving Mr McLoughlin over the top, more galloping hooves, whip crackings, and some colourful old English language heralded the arrival of William, red hot with temper over the desertion of his hounds.

All of this was like a nightmare. When we got back to the Morris Minor it was packed with hounds. The upholstery was soaked and steam was coming out of the open door. Noses were pressed expectantly against the windows. The Comet, who had returned to his stable only to find the lower door closed against him, paced up and down the drive looking anxious. He had broken his reins.

Somehow I managed to push the young entry out of the car. They took one sideways look at William's whip, tucked their sterns between their legs and fled across the park towards the plantation.

My father and I faced each other across the ruined upholstery. His tie was askew and his good suit was patched with damp. Mr McLoughlin's blood was on his cheek and his hair was standing up in a crest. To one side of us, Lady Jennifer was supporting the injured party, who appeared to be deliberating as to whether he should remount The Comet. Doreen and the old bay mare were engaged in a private battle, churning up the gravel.

My father, who prided himself on being articulate and erudite, could find no words to suit the occasion. When he did speak it was in a voice stupefied by the passage of events.

"Elaine," he said faintly. "My *dear* child."

8

Eventer's Dream

Mr McLoughlin was persuaded not to remount, which was a great relief to everyone. He seemed to feel that he might lose his nerve if he didn't get back into the saddle right away, but Lady Jennifer assured him that this was nothing but an old wives' tale, and Doreen was allowed to lead The Comet and the old bay mare back to the stables.

When the friend of a friend had been conveyed to a bathroom to be cleaned off, and a sticking plaster had been applied to his head, he got out his wallet.

"No, no," Lady Jennifer cried, aghast. "Put it away! We wouldn't *dream* of charging you for such a *ghastly* experience. We couldn't *bear* to take any fee whatsoever!"

This foiled my plan somewhat, because I had been quite prepared to charge him twenty pounds, having decided that falls and minor injuries were an integral part of the chase. But Mr McLoughlin was not to be put off, insisting that I took not two, but three ten pound notes, and maintaining that until he had left the field to assist Doreen to turn the wayward hounds, he had been more than satisfied with The Comet. In fact, the horse had given him the best ride he had ever had.

We were all deeply impressed by this show of open-handed sportsmanship. Lady Jennifer, in particular, was quite overcome and fussed over

Mr McLoughlin, offering him tea and brushing his jacket, and setting him on his way with promises of even better sport on the day of the opening meet. "And not a *mention* of payment," she warned him. "We shall be *delighted* to mount you, *absolutely* free of charge." Even I nodded agreement to this, secure in the knowledge that Mr McLoughlin's sense of fair play would never allow it.

After Mr McLoughlin had departed, and to my utter amazement, not only did my father stay for tea and sit on the sofa nibbling an iced fancy of a particular poisonous shade of green, but he and Lady Jennifer got on like a house on fire. The expected interrogations regarding wages and other matters related to gainful employment failed to occur and in no time at all they were both sitting on the sofa, sipping gin of dubious origin and giggling in a remarkably silly manner, whilst my father's jacket steamed in front of the electric fire. My father was still in a good humour when he drove away an hour or so later, seated on a split *Equivite* bag for the better protection of his person. He had invited Lady Jennifer to lunch the following week.

In due course Nigella and Henrietta returned, still boiling with excitement over the fabulous sport they had seen and totally unaware that anything untoward had happened to their client. When I related all that had taken place, Henrietta was vastly amused, but Nigella got into rather a state, maintaining that it was her fault for failing to watch The Comet who invariably took off when his head was turned for home. She was appalled to hear of Mr McLoughlin's injury and of the desecration of the Morris Minor and even the sight of the three ten pound notes failed to banish her remorse.

By the time we had finished in the stables, Nigella had worked herself up into a fever of anguish which Henrietta said was quite a regular occurrence due to over excitement after hunting, being a question of genetics and an inherited trait which had occasioned some of the Fane ancestors to have completely lost their marbles. This was hardly a comfort to Nigella who, far from being her calm and careful self, went around the yard as if demented, spilling the corn and dressing the horses in the wrong rugs, with her eyes unnaturally bright and two red spots burning on her cheeks.

When we finally repaired to the kitchen there was a letter waiting for us on the table. It was from Thunder and Lightning Limited, and it informed us that we could expect the three hunters to arrive two days prior to the opening meet. They had noted our terms with pleasure and found them to be extremely reasonable.

All this was too much for Nigella who, when Henrietta had read the letter aloud, placed her head on the kitchen table and sobbed and sobbed.

I felt a bit weak at the knees myself.

Two days later, we were out exercising when we passed some horses in a dealer's field. There was nothing unusual in this as we passed the field practically every time we rode out. It was usually peopled with a few nondescript animals and a flock of geese who sometimes opened their wings and hissed at us, making the horses shy. Today the geese were on the far side of the field amongst some rank clumps of grass, and they didn't bother us, but amongst the plain and pottery dealer's stock, there was a magnificent bay horse.

"Heavens," Nigella exclaimed. "Just look at that in Harry Sabin's field!" And we stopped to have a look.

The horse was a threequarter-bred gelding of about sixteen-two and he was absolutely beautiful. He was a rich, dark, whole colour with black points, and when he trotted across the field to investigate our horses, he moved like a dream.

"He certainly is some horse," Henrietta said admiringly. "You don't see too many with his sort of quality."

"You don't see too many with his sort of quality in Harry Sabin's field," Nigella said. "I wonder how he came by it?" She leaned forward over the old bay mare's bony shoulder and tickled the bay gelding under its chin. "He's very friendly."

The bay gelding stretched out its neck enquiringly towards the old bay mare. He wasn't clipped, and his thick coat had a soft, satiny gloss. The old bay mare squealed and tossed her mane like a four-year-old.

"There has to be something wrong with it," Henrietta decided. "There has to be a snag somewhere; otherwise Harry Sabin wouldn't have it. He doesn't deal in high class animals like this." She stood up in her stirrups and peered over the hedge at the horse's lower limbs, as if she expected to discover some appalling deformity.

I stood in the lane with Nelson and the bad-tempered chestnut and I thought that the bay horse looked familiar. I had seen him somewhere before.

"It might not be something you can see," Nigella pointed out. "It could be gone in the wind or have an irregular heartbeat. It could be a crib-biter."

"It's the tall, thin man's horse," I told them. "The one Henrietta was going to offer him fifty pounds for."

We all stared at the bay horse.

"So it is," Nigella said, astonished.

"Let's go and ask Harry Sabin how much he wants for it," Henrietta said. "It might be cheap."

We rode down a track which led into a dirt yard. There were a few ramshackle buildings and a scruffy cottage with its thatch patched with corrugated iron. There were some chickens scratching in the dirt and a blue-eyed, cream pony was wandering loose, like a dog. A wiry, weathered little man in a brown warehouse coat was tinkering about under the bonnet of a cattle waggon.

"Harry!" Nigella called. "How much is the bay gelding?"

Harry Sabin looked up from his tinkering in a leisurely sort of manner. "Now, Miss Fane, which bay gelding would you be talking about?" he enquired.

"You know which one we mean, Harry," Henrietta said. "The one in the top field."

"Ah," Harry Sabin said in an enlightened tone. "*That* bay gelding."

"How much is it?" Nigella said.

Harry Sabin straightened up slowly and put down his spanner. "That bay gelding," he said ruminatively, "come very expensive."

"Come off it, Harry," Henrietta said impatiently. "How expensive?" The black horse, who was being

92

led beside The Comet, began to dig a hole in the dirt with one of his front hooves. Henrietta jerked his headcollar rope and he stopped for a few seconds and then began again with the other foot.

"Why would you be interested in the bay gelding, Miss Fane?" Harry Sabin asked, narrowing his foxy eyes and squinting up at Henrietta. "Is it that you haven't enough mouths to feed already?"

"All right," Henrietta said, annoyed. "If that's how you feel. I wasn't going to buy it anyway." She turned The Comet towards the lane.

"Harry," Nigella pleaded. "Just give us a price; a rough idea of what he's worth."

The blue-eyed, cream pony ambled round the back of the bad-tempered chestnut, who shuffled his quarters round, hoping to get a shot at it. I felt a bit impatient with the Fanes. They couldn't afford to buy the bay gelding. They were just wasting Harry Sabin's time, and he knew it. He softened though, as people often did, for Nigella.

"Well now," he said thoughtfully. "What he's worth, and what I'm asking for him, that's two entirely different things."

"Cut the cackle, Harry," Henrietta snapped. "How much?"

"Two thousand," Harry Sabin said.

"Heavens!" Nigella gasped. "*How* much?"

Harry Sabin shrugged his shoulders indifferently. "That's a class horse, that is."

"It jolly well needs to be for that sort of money," Henrietta snorted. "It's ridiculous. You'll never get it."

"Not from the likes of you, maybe," Harry Sabin said disparagingly. "He's entered for Warners

Wednesday week. They know a good horse when they see it in Leicestershire. They pay a good price there for a horse with class."

"It looks as if he could be the genuine article then," Henrietta said with regret as we rode back down the track. "It's a pity. Just imagine, he could have been ours if he'd been a wind-sucker or something."

The bay gelding trotted alongside us, displaying natural carriage and a long, low lingering stride behind two drooping strands of barbed wire. Without the tall, thin man on the top, he looked even more impressive. I took in his substance and his clean hard joints, his fine sloping shoulder and his beautifully balanced neck, his youth and his presence, and I wished with all my heart that I had two thousand pounds. If I had scoured the world for my ideal event horse, I might never have found him, and yet here he was in Harry Sabin's field. So close, and yet so impossibly out of reach.

9

A Tricky Customer

I just couldn't stop thinking about Harry Sabin's bay gelding. The same afternoon, perched on a wobbly saddle-horse, slapping whitewash on the ceiling of a stable allocated to the Thunder and Lightning liveries, I decided that I would have to go back and have another look at him. I knew that if I could find one thing wrong with him, one defect which would make him unsuitable for eventing, I would be able to forget all about him and that would be the end of it.

I could hardly tell the Fanes where I was going because they would have thought I was mad, so I said that the smell of the paint was making me feel peculiar, and I put a saddle on Doreen's pony on the pretext of testing its wind to see if it would be fit for the opening meet. I trotted out of the yard feeling rather silly on the pony: it was only thirteen-two, and very narrow; my feet were almost level with its knees.

The bay gelding was no longer in the top field. The geese were there, running up to the hedge and making a brave show, and the dealer's stock were there, hardly troubling to raise their heads from the scrubby grass, but the bay gelding was not. There was nothing for it but to ride down the track into the dirt yard where Harry Sabin was still tinkering about under the bonnet of the waggon.

"Harry," I said. "Can I have a ride on the bay gelding?"

Harry Sabin straightened up and looked at me with his foxy eyes. "Now then, young lady," he said, "which bay gelding is that?"

I pointed to the bay gelding who was standing in one of the ramshackle buildings behind a slip rail.

"Well now," Harry Sabin said doubtfully. "That's a very expensive horse, that is."

"I'm looking for a good quality animal," I said. "I need a high class horse. I want to event." I was quite surprised to hear myself say it.

"Eventing is it?" Harry Sabin looked at Doreen's pony and scratched his head with the spanner. "That do seem a bit small for the job, I can see that."

"The pony isn't mine," I said hastily. "It's at livery with the Fanes. I came with them this morning. I work for them."

Mentioning the Fanes was obviously the wrong thing to do. Harry Sabin went back to his tinkering under the bonnet of the cattle waggon. "That isn't a horse for the Fanes," he said. "They don't pay that sort of price. I've sold a few horses to the Fanes in my time; they don't pay at all if they can help. I know the Fanes."

"It isn't for the Fanes I'm looking," I said. "It's for myself."

But Harry Sabin had lost interest in me as a potential customer. He didn't bother to reply. I got off the pony and tied him up with a piece of baler twine I found lying in the dirt. I leaned over the bonnet and faced Harry Sabin eyeball to eyeball. "Harry," I said. "The horse is the right type and he's the right height. He's also the right age, if he's the

five-year-old I take him to be. But I have to be sure
he has the scope and the temperament and the
courage for the job. If you won't let me ride him,
how will I know?"

Harry Sabin grinned at me. His teeth were the
colour of old piano keys. "I daresay you won't," he
said. "And I daresay you won't have two thousand
pounds, neither."

"If the horse isn't suitable," I pointed out, "I
shan't need to have."

"That you won't," Harry Sabin rubbed his chin in
a thoughtful manner. "And you say it's not for the
Fanes?"

"They don't even know I'm here," I said. "I made
an excuse to get away. I can't stay long, otherwise
they'll come after me."

This worked like a charm. "Best put the pony
round the back then," Harry Sabin decided. "If they
see that from the lane, that might just give you
away." He seemed pleased to be part of a conspiracy
against the Fanes. He waved his spanner in the
direction of one of the tumbledown buildings. "Saddle's in there. Bridle's there as well, but that might
need taking up a strap or two to fit." He went back
to his tinkering looking vaguely triumphant.

I led the pony round the back of the buildings and
I went to get the tack. The saddle was an awful old
thing with a bumpy serge lining, and the bridle had
a driving bit. I carried them over to where the bay
gelding was standing. My heart was jumping with
excitement as I ducked under the rail, took a few
paces aside, and stared at my dream horse.

Close to, he was every bit as good as he had

97

looked in the field. He had the class and the conformation of a show horse. His coat was rich and glossy, his eyes were large and clear and intelligent, he had a good top line, strong, short cannon bones with tendons like iron bands, big flat knees, short sloping pasterns and healthy open feet. He also had a perfectly formed five-year-old's mouth. Try as I might, I couldn't fault him, and as Nigella had noticed, he was very friendly, and didn't once offer to put his ears back when I picked up his back feet and lifted his tail.

When I tacked him up, he opened his mouth obligingly for the driving bit, and stood like a rock whilst I girthed up the lumpy saddle. It was all too good to be true. I led him out into the yard. Harry Sabin shuffled across in order to leg me into the saddle and lead me to a rusted metal gate which opened into a field. The bay gelding had a long, swinging walk.

"He even walks like a show horse," I said.

"That's just what he was," Harry Sabin said. "A show horse."

"Why *was*?" I asked.

Harry Sabin shrugged and dragged open the rusty gate. "Temperament," he said.

"What do you mean?" I said. I had seen the horse out cubbing and hadn't felt that he had looked anything more than upset by bad horsemanship, but suddenly, especially after Doreen's pony, I felt a long way from the ground. "What's wrong with his temperament?" I asked.

But Harry Sabin refused to be drawn. "Just you sit tight, young lady," he warned. "That's a very expensive horse, that is, and don't you loose him. He's entered for Warners Wednesday week."

I rode through the gate feeling less than confident. Harry Sabin dragged the gate shut and went back to his tinkering. The dealer's stock in the top field trotted up to a gap in the hedge which had been filled in with a rusty bedstead and regarded the bay gelding with interest.

I walked and trotted him in a few cautious circles, noting his natural balance and steady head carriage and the fluent regularity of his stride which augured well for dressage. He didn't feel like a rogue horse. He was responsive and well-mannered and cantered a perfect figure eight with a simple change, and galloped for a short burst displaying a long, low stride, and a willingness to pull up when asked. My confidence almost fully restored, I looked round for something to jump.

There was nothing in the field except a broken down chicken coop, so it had to be that. I cantered him slowly towards it and left him to his own devices to see how, and if, he would tackle it. It was essential to find a horse who really enjoyed jumping because I needed a willing partner. The bay gelding pricked his ears forward and looked neither to the left nor the right, lengthened his stride into the coop and took off heavenwards in the most enormous leap I had ever experienced.

He jumped so high that I flew upwards out of the hateful little saddle and crashed down again right on to the pommel. It was agonizing. The bay gelding, feeling me loosened in the saddle, cantered on for a few strides with his head tucked into his chest, then he put in one almighty buck that sent me hurtling over his shoulder. I hit the ground with a thump that knocked all the breath out of my body and the bay gelding cantered off, cleared the bedstead with a yard to spare, and joined the dealer's stock who, overcome by the excitement of it all, thundered round and round the field like a cavalry charge.

I sat on the ground for at least five minutes, too sore and winded and shaken to move. I had always hated falling off and I had never got used to it. Eventually I staggered to my feet and made for the bedstead. My eyes were watering and I could hardly walk but I wanted to catch the bay gelding before Harry Sabin discovered that I had loosened his expensive animal, entered for Warners Wednesday week. I was halfway between the coop and the bedstead when another terrible thing happened. There was a hammering along the lane and the Fanes came into view mounted on Brenda's cob and Nelson.

Almost without thinking, I ducked down and made for the cover of the hedge, hoping against hope that the Fanes wouldn't notice the bay gelding in amongst all the others. But the sound of skidding hooves on tarmac told me that they had seen him and Henrietta's voice carried clearly across the field.

"Look," she said. "He's got a saddle on. And a bridle. He must have thrown his rider or something. We'd better catch him."

Horrified, I peered through the hedge and watched them ride along the lane until they came to the track which led to Harry Sabin's yard. Then I saw Henrietta dismount. She ducked under the wire, walked up to the bay gelding and took him by the rein. She led him towards the yard and Nigella followed with the horses.

Totally defeated, I limped to the gate, wondering how on earth I was going to explain my behaviour to the Fanes. Henrietta had never trusted me from the start and I could imagine how triumphant she would be to discover my deception. I had reached the gate to the yard and was still out of their line of vision when I heard Harry Sabin's voice.

"That's very good of you, Miss Fane," he said in a deeply respectful voice. "That's very good of you indeed. I was just expecting my lad to come and give him a spot of exercise and he just managed to slip the rail and get out of the shed. I'm much obliged to you and that's a fact."

"If you're that obliged, perhaps you'll consider dropping the price you're asking for him then," Henrietta said as she remounted Nelson. "Say four hundred?"

"That just isn't possible, Miss Fane," Harry Sabin said regretfully. "That wouldn't be economical at all. That's a very high class animal and I wouldn't take a penny less than two thousand for it, and that's the truth."

"Oh well," Henrietta said ungraciously. "Please yourself."

"I don't suppose you've seen our groom, Harry?" Nigella enquired. "The one who came with us this morning? She took out one of our liveries, a chestnut pony."

"Well now," Harry Sabin said, considering it. "I might have seen her along the lane not more than half an hour ago."

101

"Might have?" Henrietta said. "What do you mean, might have?"

"I can't say that it was definitely her," Harry Sabin said. "I've been busy on the waggon and there get to be a lot of horses along the lane."

As Henrietta and Nigella trotted back down the track, I eased my way carefully through the gate. Harry Sabin was standing by the cattle waggon holding the bay gelding, cackling with delight at having scored against the Fanes.

"Thanks for not giving me away, Harry," I said. "I thought I was done for then. I hope the horse is all right."

"That's lucky for you he is," Harry Sabin chuckled. "I told you not to loose him."

"But you didn't tell me what a wicked buck he had in him," I protested. "I might have stayed on if you had warned me."

But Harry Sabin was unrepentant. "But then he might not have bucked you," he said. "And I should have been sorry I'd mentioned it." He led the bay gelding back to his ruined stable. "A good sharp clout or two'll soon teach him some manners, young lady. It don't do to let them get the upper hand. He'll find his master in Leicestershire, and no mistake."

I followed them into the stable and watched Harry Sabin drag off the lumpy saddle. "He's a beautiful ride," I said. "I don't think I have ever ridden a better horse; and he certainly can jump."

"But can you stay on him when he do?" Harry Sabin wondered. "That's not much good if you can't." He pulled the bridle over the horse's ears. The bay gelding dropped the driving bit, stuck out his head and lifted his upper lip in a gesture of disgust.

"Two thousand pounds is a lot of money," I said. "For a horse with a buck like that." It wasn't. Even with my limited experience, I knew that he would make twice the price at Leicester Sales. I ran my fingers through the bay gelding's silky coat and he turned his head and nudged hopefully at my pockets. I found him an old boiled sweet, gone soft and furry. "I'll give you fifteen hundred for him," I said.

Harry Sabin shouldered the saddle and regarded me in a sceptical manner.

"Subject to vet," I added.

"Subject to you getting the money," he said.

"Subject to you accepting my offer, for a start," I said.

I followed Harry Sabin across the dirt yard to the shed where he kept his awful saddlery; then I followed him back to the cattle waggon where he picked up his spanner and started tinkering. I had reluctantly decided that the conversation had come to an end when he straightened up and poked the spanner into my chest.

"You send your vet," he said. "And you bring me fifteen hundred in cash; I don't take no cheques since I've had a bad one off the Fanes. I'll keep the horse no more than a week. If you're not here with the cash by Monday week, he's off to Warners Wednesday, and that's the finish of it."

10

Can't Make It Tonight

Halfway back to the hall I had to dismount and walk beside the pony because I was so sore. I was within sight of the gates when a van slowed down alongside me. It was the flesh waggon from the kennels with Forster at the wheel.

"What happened to you?" he enquired, leaning over the passenger seat. "Did the brute throw you?"

"No," I said, embarrassed. "I'm walking because I'm too heavy for him. I'm giving him a rest."

"You're a liar," Forster said, grinning.

"I'm not," I said, but without conviction, because even if I wasn't yet, I supposed that I soon would be.

"I suppose you've fallen off Harry Sabin's bay gelding," Forster said.

I stopped walking and stared at him. Doreen's pony immediately dropped its head and started to graze.

Forster shrugged. "It was just a guess. Almost everyone has." He stopped the van and pulled up the handbrake.

"Including you?"

"Including William. The Master sent him to try it. He thought it might make a good hunt horse if he could get it at the right price."

"I'm glad he didn't," I said with relief. "It's far too good for a hunt horse."

"Thanks a lot," Forster said in a sarcastic tone. "I suppose you think we ill treat our horses, as well as our hounds."

"Not ill treat exactly," I said. "You're just too rough."

"We're paid to catch foxes," Forster said. "Not to practise the finer points of dressage." He leaned over further and pushed the passenger door open. "Sit down for a minute. You look as if you need to."

It crossed my mind that it might not be wise to sit in a van with Forster in a deserted lane, but I lowered myself carefully into the seat. There was a winch in the back of the van and a dead cow behind it. The cow was slimy and it stank. I averted my eyes hastily.

"Sorry," Forster said. "I've been to collect a casualty. I had to pull it out of the river."

"Nick," I said. "I'd be glad if you didn't say anything to anyone about me going to try the bay gelding. You're not supposed to know. No one is. It's supposed to be a secret."

"What on earth for?" he said curiously. "Don't tell me the Fanes are thinking of buying it."

"No," I said. "I am."

Now it was Forster's turn to stare. "You are?"

"I want it for an event horse," I said. "It's perfect. It's just the kind of horse I need."

"It's expensive though," Forster said. "At least," he corrected himself, "it's expensive for Harry Sabin."

"It's expensive for me as well," I admitted ruefully. "I'm broke. And I've got to find fifteen hundred pounds in cash by Monday week, otherwise it's going to Warners."

"How the devil are you going to do that?" Forster said, astonished.

"I haven't a clue," I said.

Forster laughed. Then, seeing that I wasn't laughing as well, he leaned his elbows on the driving wheel and rubbed his chin. "How about your parents?" he suggested.

"My father doesn't have any money to speak of," I said. "And what he has is invested in a building society. He wouldn't touch that, and anyway, he doesn't like horses."

We sat in silence for a few seconds.

"The only thing you can do," Forster said eventually, "is to find yourself a sponsor."

"I had thought of that," I said. "But who?"

"Well," Forster said, considering it. "It isn't as if you're a well known event rider with a string of past successes to your credit. You're an unknown quantity, so you can't expect the big companies to be interested. They wouldn't be prepared to back a struggling amateur because they are only in it for advertising purposes, and they wouldn't get enough publicity out of you to make it worth their while."

"I know," I said. "So it's hopeless really; and I can't go to my employers. The Fanes haven't a bean."

"The only person I can think of," Forster said, "is Felix Hissey."

"No thank you," I said flatly. "I don't think that would do at all."

"Why on earth not?" Forster wanted to know. "Felix Hissey is very into eventing and he might just be interested. His company sponsors two of the biggest events in the country."

"He also has an unexpected vacancy for a groom," I said. "Which you may well have a guilty conscience about."

"I see," Forster said resentfully. "So you've been tipped off by the scandalmongering Fanes."

"They aren't really scandalmongering," I protested. "They were only telling me for my own protection."

"I'd like to hear what else they told you," Forster said vengefully. "The next time I see those two, I'll crack their stupid heads together."

"You must admit though," I said, "that when you offered me the Hissey job, you did have an ulterior motive."

"So what if I had?" he said angrily. "It would have done you a good turn at the same time. Nobody in their right mind would want to work for the Fanes."

"Thanks for the compliment," I said. "Thanks a *lot*." Now it was my turn to feel nettled. I was fed up with Forster and the stench of the cow was beginning to turn my stomach. "I have to go now," I said. "I'm late already and the Fanes will be frantic."

"Oh no, Elaine," Forster said. "You're not going anywhere yet." He put out a hand and pinned me back in my seat.

I wasn't sure that I liked the way things were going. I had let go of the reins and Doreen's pony had moved further along the verge, still pulling at the grass. "I do have to go," I said anxiously. "The Fanes . . ."

"The Fanes can go to hell," Forster said. He put his arm round my shoulders.

I could see that I would have to make a firm stand if I was to keep the situation under control. I removed his arm. "I'm sorry, Nick," I said. "I really can't stay any longer. I am supposed to be working, after all, and there's a lot to be done in the yard; we've three new liveries coming in tomorrow."

Forster looked as if he might object, then he shrugged. "All right," he said. "If you're so determined to be conscientious, I'll see you on your day off. When is it?"

"Er . . . I haven't actually got one organized yet," I admitted. "We've been so busy, it didn't seem fair to ask."

"I don't suppose you've organized yourself any wages yet, either," he said in an exasperated tone.

"Well, no," I said. "How could I? There hasn't been any money coming into the yard. The Fanes are on their uppers. There didn't seem any point in going on about it."

"Honestly, Elaine," he exploded. "I said you were barmy the first time I saw you and I was right. You're the biggest idiot I've ever met! *Nobody* works without being paid for it; you must be round the twist!"

This was the last straw. I gave him a shove and dived for the door handle. "I'm not staying here to be shouted at," I told him. "I've had enough."

"Suit yourself," he said coldly. "Girls like you deserve all they get." He turned the key in the ignition. The engine roared.

"I *beg* your pardon?" I exclaimed. I felt my face flush with anger. "I think you might be mistaken there; *you're* the one with the lousy reputation!"

"I'm not talking about reputations," he said. "I'm talking about working for peanuts. I like my job; I like the hounds and the horses and the hunting, I even like the foxes; but I wouldn't work for nothing, and my employers respect me enough to pay me a decent wage. You girl grooms moan about being underpaid and overworked, but it's your own fault, you let yourselves be exploited all the way along the line. You're fools." He kept his eyes on the road. "And you're one of the biggest fools of all, Elaine, if only you would realize it."

"I want to work with horses," I said indignantly. "I want a chance to event. I didn't realize that eventing yards were so few and far between, or that it was going to be so hard to find a job with a decent wage. People don't seem to be able to pay very much. There doesn't seem to be much money about in the horse world, when you get close enough to find out."

"Rubbish," Forster said, but his voice was suddenly less angry. "There is money in the horse world, but people have got used to having horse-mad girls on tap for cheap labour. It's going to take them a long time to learn that if they want a decent groom they have to pay a decent wage, even if it means they have to keep fewer horses."

I was touched by this, and even a little ashamed. "I'll talk to the Fanes," I decided. "Now that we've got these new liveries, I'll tackle them about my wages, and about my days off. Perhaps I am a fool, but you must admit that the Fanes are an extreme case; I can't help feeling sorry for them. They were once a very fine family, but they have fallen on such hard times; they are a dying breed."

"The Fanes," Forster said, "are a pain in the arse." He grinned. His humour was almost fully restored. "Elaine, if you really want to tackle Felix

Hissey about Harry Sabin's bay gelding, he'll be at the opening meet. He always parks his box in this lane; you can't miss it, it's a navy blue Lambourne. He leaves at two o'clock sharp every hunting day, and he comes back to his box for a quiet sandwich and a drink before he drives home. It might be a good opportunity to catch him. I can't promise that he'll be interested, but it's worth a try."

I was so delighted with this piece of information that I forgot about my injury, and the slimy cow, and Doreen's pony, who was almost at the Hall gates, having eaten himself home. I leaned over and gave Forster a peck on his cheek. This was a tactical error, because I somehow got caught up in his broody dark-fringed eyes and almost before I knew it, he had taken hold of the back of my neck and stretched out his other hand to turn off the ignition. He was just closing in when I saw two faces, framed in the window beyond his shoulder. It was the Fanes.

I let out an involuntary yelp. Forster drew back, startled, and turned round in his seat. When he saw the Fanes he wrenched open the door.

"What the hell are you up to?" he shouted in a furious voice. "Creeping about and spying on people!"

"We weren't actually creeping about," Nigella objected. "You didn't hear us coming. You had your engine running."

"How dare you play fast and loose with our groom anyway," Henrietta cried, her cheeks flushed with anger and excitement. "We guessed she was up to something! She said she was only going out to test the pony's wind and she's been gone for hours, she was going to meet you all the time!"

110

Forster jumped out of the van. "And what if she was?" he demanded angrily. "Since when have you been her nursemaid?"

I staggered out of the flesh waggon in order to cope with all this. My back had stiffened up and I was none too steady on my feet. I knew that I looked hot and dishevelled, and in the circumstances, I could hardly blame the Fanes for jumping to conclusions.

"Oh, Elaine," Nigella said reproachfully. "How *could* you?"

"And with *him*, of *all* people," Henrietta shouted. "After we warned you about his reputation!"

Forster took a threatening step towards Henrietta.

"Don't you dare lay a finger on me!" she shrilled. "I know your type!"

"Not, perhaps, quite as well as you would like," Forster said in an icy voice.

Henrietta backed away, her face crimson. "How dare you," she choked.

"We honestly didn't mean to spy on you, Elaine," Nigella said in a harassed tone. "But you had been gone for ages, and you had said you felt peculiar. We were getting anxious and then we saw the pony loose on the grass verge; we *are* supposed to be responsible for you, whilst you are living under our roof."

"Or to be strictly accurate," Forster snarled, "half of one." He jumped into the flesh waggon, slammed the door, and roared off down the lane.

I walked painfully up the drive behind the Fanes, leading the pony, whose mouth dripped green froth. My head was spinning. Suddenly there were so many things to consider that I didn't know where to start.

Certainly I couldn't deny that I had spent the afternoon with Forster without revealing the truth or telling lies, so I decided that the best thing to do was to leave things as they were and let the Fanes think what they liked. But for the rest of the afternoon, you could have cut the atmosphere in the stable yard with a knife.

I got through evening stables early and went back to the Hall to telephone the vet. He agreed to examine the bay gelding the following day and I arranged to ring him at his surgery in the evening for his report. After that I boiled some kettles of water to augment my bath and soaked my aches and pains and washed my hair. Then I went down to the kitchen prepared to do some cooking because by this time I was feeling pretty remorseful about upsetting the Fanes.

I found the kitchen table heaped with offerings for a Help The Aged jumble sale, currently being organized by Lady Jennifer, who obligingly cleared a corner for me whilst I stirred the Aga into action. Amongst the pressed sugar bowls and the fairground Alsatians, there was a portable television set.

"It can't *possibly* be a working model," Lady Jennifer decided. "It would be just *too* generous for words."

"It won't be much use to anyone if it doesn't work," I pointed out. "You will have to test it."

"Could you be an absolute *angel* and test it for me, Elaine?" she wondered, considering a wobbly plastic cakestand before applying a fifteen pence sticker to it. "I simply haven't a *clue* about electricity."

I promised to try it later. When Lady Jennifer had

112

priced all the junk, she swept it into cardboard boxes and transported it to the front hall where jumble stretched from floor to ceiling, emanating a smell of B.O. and mothballs. A few minutes later she raced through the kitchen in her crumpled raincoat, bound for a spell of night duty with the Samaritans.

"Oh," Henrietta said when she came into the kitchen. "Biscuits."

"And a pie," I said. "And a cake and a pudding. It's a sort of apology for this afternoon."

"As a matter of fact," Nigella said. "We've been talking about that."

"And we've decided," Henrietta added with her mouth full of biscuit. "That we were probably a little hasty. After all, it's your life, and you're over the age of consent, so you can do what you like."

"Oh," I said, taken aback. "Thank you very much."

"Although we must point out," Nigella said, "that we are a little concerned about your choice of friends." She leaned over the table and sniffed the cake appreciatively.

"And as we have our reputation to consider," Henrietta went on, adopting a serious tone. "We must ask you to protect yourself against any possible consequences."

"I see," I said. I wondered what possible consequences could arise from a peck on the cheek.

"I hope you don't mind us being so forthright," Nigella said. "But Nick Forster does have a very sticky reputation, although one has to admit that he is rather devastating to look at."

"If you happen to like the dark, dangerous type,"

Henrietta said, licking her unwashed fingers. "Personally, I don't. I think he's a nasty piece of work. By the way," she added, "where did the television come from?"

"It's a jumble offering," I said. "I promised that we would test it."

Henrietta kicked off her wellingtons and transferred her attention from the biscuits to the television set. There was no aerial, so she spent some time poking bits of wire into the back and fiddling with the controls, achieving a lot of zizzing noise and a row of shivering dots on the screen. Finally she had the brilliant idea of wiring the set up to the lightning conductor. This was a wild success and resulted in an excellent picture.

As the Fanes had never previously owned a television, the jumble set was an event worthy of celebration. Nigella disappeared into the depths of the cellar and returned decorated with cobwebs, clutching a dirt encrusted bottle of cloudy red wine out of which she strained terrifying lumps through a tea cloth. Then we sat round the kitchen table eating pie and taking cautious sips of the wine, with our eyes glued to the television set, and it was all very jolly.

By the time we had started our second glass of wine, we were even jollier still. The Fanes were anticipating their high class liveries due to arrive the next morning, and I was imagining myself collecting fifteen hundred pounds from Felix Hissey and riding into the yard in triumph on Harry Sabin's bay gelding. We were watching a top twenty record show.

"Look at him," Henrietta said, waving her fork at the screen. "He's got striped hair."

The singer with striped hair was replaced by the compère who had two lots of earrings and a furry chest.

"We've got a real treat for you now, folks," he crowed. "Live in the studio; currently number eight in the charts and climbing fast – *Can't Make it Tonight*, by Thunder and Ligh⅂ning Limited!"

Nigella laid down her fork on the table. "What did he say?" she said.

As the first beats of *Can't Make it Tonight* thundered out, the group appeared on the screen. There were three of them. They wore black leotards and leg-warmers which revealed unexpected areas of puny, unattractive flesh. They wore necklaces, bangles and earrings, vivid lipstick and heavy eye makeup. They didn't have striped hair. They didn't have any hair at all. They were completely bald.

There was no mistake, because as the camera followed their gyrations across the stage, it caught the name of the group emblazoned across the front of the drums. Thunder and Ligh⅂ning Limited it said, with the familiar jag of lightning replacing the t.

11

High Class Liveries

The next morning we set about morning stables in an agony of apprehension, listening with half an ear for the sound of the horsebox which would deliver our three liveries. We didn't know what to expect. We didn't dare to imagine. But as the day passed and no horsebox arrived, our expectations began to fade.

By five o'clock it was already dark, and as we lit the barn lanterns which hung outside every other stable door, creating our own Dickensian world of flickering golden light and stamping hooves, an atmosphere of ostlers and old inns and stagecoaches, we began to realize that our liveries were not going to materialize. The general feeling was of anti-climax, coupled with a mixture of relief and dismay.

Henrietta slammed the doors of the prepared stables in a gesture of disgust. "They were never coming in the first place," she said. "It was probably a trick. It was just a stupid joke." She gave me a suspicious look, as if I might be responsible for it.

"Perhaps it's just as well," Nigella decided. "They weren't exactly the type of clients we were hoping for. They might have worn lipstick at the opening meet. They might have worn mascara and eye shadow and spangles on their cheeks."

"And just think of those three bald heads," I said. "Even with a velvet cap on top, they would still have

116

looked a sight." Now that it wasn't going to happen, we could voice our unspoken, unspeakable fears.

"They probably have a drink problem," Nigella said. "And they might have had groupies. There might have been unmentionable goings-on in the back of the horsebox."

"Not only that," I said. "But I expect they are on drugs. They probably smoke pot or worse. They might have arrived at the opening meet stoned out of their minds. They would have got us thrown out of the Hunt."

"All the same," Henrietta grumbled. "We could have used their seventy-five pounds a week."

Nigella and I fell silent, depressed by the thought of the money aspect; and in the silence we heard the unmistakable hum of an engine on the drive.

The custom-built horsebox turned into the yard under the clock arch. The stable lanterns were mirrored in its gleaming black coachwork. They caught at the Rolls Royce insignia on the bonnet. When the driver jumped out, the door with its narrow red trim closed behind him with a discreet clunk. Muffled scraping noises issued from the rear of the box.

"Are you the Misses Fane?" the driver asked. He wasn't wearing lipstick. He wasn't bald. He was a thin, blond-haired, anxious looking man in a tweed jacket and Newmarket boots.

The Fanes stared at the horsebox with their mouths open. I said that we were. I asked, although I already knew, if he had brought the horses for Thunder and Lightning Limited.

The driver introduced himself as Chick Hayes. He handed me a set of keys. Special delivery, he said, of three horses and a horsebox. "The Lads" had suggested that he should leave us to it. They had a gig tonight in Norwich and he was supposed to be in charge of the lighting. So we would have to excuse him if he nipped off because he was already late. And "The Lads" didn't like him to be late; they didn't like it at all.

I asked Chick Hayes if we could expect "The Lads" to be attending the opening meet. To my relief he said no. They had a concert on Saturday and they wouldn't be hunting until Thursday, when we should arrange to have the horses plaited and loaded for ten fifteen sharp. As the horses were all new, he said, it might be a good idea if we gave them an hour or two with the hunt on Tuesday, so that we could give "The Lads" an idea of what they were like to handle. Then, if any of them turned out to be tricky, we could ring him up to enable him to swop it for a better one. He couldn't chance anything happening to one of "The Lads", they were a valuable commodity. And the Insurance Company didn't like the idea of "The Lads" going hunting; they didn't like it at all.

Even the Fanes were taken aback by the revelation that "The Lads" hadn't felt it was necessary to select their own hunters; and that any bad ones would be exchanged as if they were no more than a pound of apples. I felt that such a cavalier attitude could spell trouble in store, and I was rendered even more uneasy when I remembered that "The Lads" had not felt it necessary to send anyone to inspect our yard before they had accepted our livery terms. I was heartily glad that we were to be spared the presence of Thunder and Lighℑning Limited at the opening meet.

When Chick Hayes had sped off towards the Norwich gig in a Bedford van which had come along behind, the beautiful horsebox was left in solitary splendour in the centre of the yard. The lanterns reflected in the paintwork like orange globes and the Fanes and I stood and stared at it, mesmerized, like children round a Christmas tree.

"Well," I said eventually. "I suppose we had better get the horses out."

I began to unbolt the ramp. The Fanes, after a moment's hesitation, came to help. The ramp swung down smoothly to reveal three horses, a bay, a chestnut and a blue roan, staring at us over partitions padded with real hide. I had seen luxury horseboxes before, but even the box which Hans Gelderhol used to transport his event horses had been nothing like this. The paintwork was sparkling, unblemished white, the padding was soft black leather, the floors were fitted with anti-slip matting, and the inside of the box was lit like a film set.

Nigella unbolted the breast bar and untied the bay, who stepped down the ramp in an unhurried, mannerly way, pausing at the foot to look round at his new surroundings. He was a quality blood horse with a sensible, kind expression. He wore a black mohair rug piped in red with a jag of lightning in the corner instead of initials. He had matching kneecaps and tailguard, red bandages and a nut brown anticast roller and headcollar with solid brass fittings.

"Wow," Henrietta breathed, taking it all in. "Wow."

"Now this really *is* my idea of a high class livery,"

Nigella said, delighted. "If we can attract clients with horses like these, we are made. Our problems are over."

"From what I have seen and heard of 'The Lads'," I reminded them, "our problems might only just be beginning."

We stabled the horses and changed their mohair rugs for lined and piped jute night rugs with pure new wool under-blankets. Then we fed them and began to unload the saddlery from the groom's compartment in the horsebox. It was all top quality German workmanship with stainless steel bits, stirrup irons and buckles. In the homely light of a lantern suspended from the centre beam, we stowed the fine saddlery in our shabby tackroom and folded the beautiful rugs carefully on the centre table. When it was all finished we stood back and drank it all in; the silvery gleam of the metalwork, the soft glow of fine supple leather, the luxury of the rugs with their scarlet piping, the glitter of the brass fitted headcollars.

"One day," Henrietta said, "all our saddlery will be like this." And her eyes were hungry in the lantern light.

Nigella said nothing, and I knew that she was thinking what I was thinking. That if it didn't work out; if it turned out to be wrong and all this richness was taken away again, how terribly hard it would be to bear. That after all our struggles, after all the moth-eaten rugs, the patched and threadbare blankets, the old and withered leather, the rusted and pitted metalwork, to be able to feast our eyes on such fabulously extravagant things was food for the soul. So we stood looking but not saying, for a long time, whilst the stable cat purred around our ankles.

After all that, I almost forgot to ring the vet. I left the Fanes investigating the baby cooker and the fridge and the buttoned hide seating in the living compartment of the horsebox, and fled up to the Hall to get the report on Harry Sabin's bay gelding.

I was only just in time because the vet had finished his surgery and was in the act of going out of the door in his hat and coat when the telephone rang. He was pleased to inform me that the bay gelding had a completely clean bill of health which would cost me fifteen pounds. Yes, he was sound in every way and as far as he could tell, eminently suitable for a tough competitive sport such as eventing. There was just one thing that he felt bound to mention. That when he had been galloped to test his wind, and to assess how quickly his heartbeat and respiration returned to normal after exertion, he had put in a buck, the violence of which had almost launched Harry Sabin's lad into outer space.

12

Flight of The Comet

On the morning of the opening meet the Fanes appeared in beautifully cut, navy blue habits with scarlet waistcoats. Their wild hair was wild no longer, it was coiled and netted below silk hats. They wore veils over their faces. They looked absolutely beautiful. I stared at them in amazement, quite unable to speak.

"We thought you would like it," Nigella said. "We did it as a surprise. We don't actually have any proper hunt coats and breeches and things. The habits belong to Mummy. They are almost antique."

"We have to live up to our high class image, after all," Henrietta said. "Although if we break our necks, it will probably be your fault. We haven't ridden sideways for ages."

They tripped off across the cobbles to heave down the side-saddles which reposed under canvas covers on the topmost brackets of the tack room, leaving me to organize the rest of our party.

There were seven horses going from the yard. Mr McLoughlin, not surprisingly, had expressed a desire not to be reunited with The Comet. Nigella determined to ride him herself, which allowed him the use of the mare-who-sometimes-slipped-a-stifle. Henrietta was taking the black horse, Brenda was taking her pink-nosed cob, Doreen was taking her pony, and a friend of hers was hiring the bad-tempered chestnut. This had left me with the scintillating choice between the old bay mare and Nelson.

I was a bit worried about the old bay mare because when I had ridden her out to exercise a few days previously, I had thought she was off-colour. The Fanes had dismissed this as a figment of my imagination, especially in view of the fact that I had taken her temperature which had been completely normal, 100.5 after two minutes. But since then I had noticed that she hadn't been finishing up her feeds, and although I couldn't find anything specific to put my finger on, I was uneasy about taking her hunting. So it had to be Nelson.

Taking Nelson actually suited my plans perfectly. The fact that he wasn't hunting fit and was only up to half a day provided me with an excuse to leave early. I planned to take him slowly, keeping to the rear of the field, so that I could slip away undetected at one o'clock and be waiting for Felix Hissey when he returned to his box at two.

We set off down the drive in a little cavalcade led by Brenda's cob, slapping down his soup-plate feet in a purposeful manner, his persil-white tail swinging above his thickset hocks.

"We're going to be late, Busy Bee," Brenda grumbled. "It'll take half an hour to get there and all the free booze will have gone."

But the Fanes were unconcerned about being late and we progressed at a leisurely pace. The lanes were jammed with horseboxes and trailers and I felt my heart speed up under my hunting shirt as we passed the navy blue Lambourne not far from the

Hall gates. We were overtaken by throngs of late-comers hammering along towards the meet. Children cantered past us along the grass verges with their ponies already in a lather, and now and again we drew aside for a solitary scarlet-coated subscriber, loping along at a ground-covering trot, striking sparks from the lane.

The opening meet, traditionally held on the first day of November, is an important social event in the hunt calendar and I was anxious that we should create a good impression. I was satisfied that the horses looked as good as was possible in the short time that had been available. We had all worked hard on them and the Fanes, after a characteristic objection to plaiting up ("We never plait manes," Nigella said. "We find it a waste of time,") relented after they had watched me plait Doreen's pony. Henrietta, who had never hitherto plaited anything other than her own tangle of hair, proved a dab hand, moving from stable to stable with her damp sponge and comb, needles and thread, plaiting up the horses with incredible speed and neatness, singing in her clear, high voice, a plaiting song composed on the spot.

> "Silver needles and golden manes,
> Cold in the stable, ice on the lanes,
> Silver needles and golden manes,
> Seven hunt plaits for the Galloping Fanes."

When we got to the village green where the meet was taking place, it was murder. Brenda and Doreen battled their way through the crowds towards the pub carpark where the tail end of the punch was being distributed.

The rest of us waited well away from the scrum, in the centre of which I caught the occasional glimpse of Forster in his blue velvet cap, his dark hair curling over the collar of his scarlet coat; he looked out of temper; and William, hot and flustered with the effort of keeping hounds together, had a face the colour of a radish.

I looked around at the scarlet-coated subscribers, wondering which of them was Felix Hissey. I hadn't the remotest idea what he looked like. There must have been five or six hundred mounted followers at the meet, not to mention all the foot people. I couldn't imagine how we were going to get any hunting at all, but Nigella said that the Huntsman would draw all the worst coverts first, in the hope that those members of the field who had only come out to be seen and photographed would become discouraged and go home.

The Galloping Fanes in their stunning outfits attracted a lot of attention at the meet. They smiled obligingly for the photographers who seemed to be under the impression that they were visitors from the Quorn. They certainly looked very grand, but I was a little worried about how Nigella would fare on The Comet without a leg on each side.

Nigella's prediction came true in that we had drawn three coverts before we got a run, by which time the field had thinned to about two hundred. This was still bad enough because there was a melée in every gateway and a queue of adamant refusers at every jumpable place. To get any sort of ride at all I

125

had to take my own line. This seemed a good idea until I got my first taste of Nelson's jumping system.

Nelson's missing eye made no difference to him on the flat whatsoever but his method of tackling an obstacle was unconventional to say the least. He galloped towards it with great enthusiasm, holding his head low and cocked slightly to one side, giving the impression of rushing through space with nothing in front. But as he neared the obstacle he gradually began to slow up, until by the time he had reached it he was almost at a standstill. Then suddenly, just as I had decided that he had refused, he sprang over it like a cat and took off at the speed of light towards the next ditch.

This, together with the fact that I was still sore from my collision with the bay gelding and unable to concentrate on hunting due to my forthcoming meeting with Felix Hissey, didn't add up to a very enjoyable morning, and it was with a feeling of relief that I looked at my watch and saw that it was after one o'clock, time to leave.

Hounds were in the vicinity of home as Nelson and I traversed the lanes. Groups of people were already engaged in loading up their horses, or leaning against their cars and horseboxes, smoking or gossiping or eating sandwiches. With Nelson's stitched up eye socket and his bobbing ears in front of me, and the hollow clop of his boxy feet below me, I practised what I would say when I met Felix Hissey, and the more I practised, the more nervous I felt. I knew I had to convince him that the bay gelding and I had a great future, that we were a solid investment, but when it came to finding the right words it was not so easy. Whichever way I put it, I was still asking him to part with fifteen hundred pounds, probably more, which was pretty bare-faced cheek. I could hardly blame him if he saw me off with a flea in my ear, but I should have to risk that. I wanted the bay gelding more than I had ever wanted anything, and Felix Hissey was my only hope. I had to try to talk him into it.

Nelson bounced over a heap of rust red bricks which was all that remained of the demesne wall and trotted over the spongy old turf. As I was on the far side of the park, I decided to ride along the river bank until I came to the bridge where the lane crossed the river and where, not more than five hundred yards away, I had seen the navy blue Lambourne horsebox parked earlier in the day. I was just consoling myself with the thought that at least my plans had not been jinxed by the Fanes, when I became aware of thundering hooves somewhere in the distance behind me.

I turned round in my saddle, half expecting to see the young entry with William or Forster at their heels. I saw The Comet instead. There was a steady relentlessness about his coming and as he came nearer, I saw that Nigella was shouting and hauling uselessly at the reins. She had completely lost control.

I pulled up Nelson, cursing the Fanes for their gift of turning up when they weren't wanted, thinking that now I had the additional worry of shaking off Nigella before I got to see Felix Hissey. I was sure that The Comet would stop when he got to us but The Comet did no such thing. He swept past without faltering in his stride with Nigella clinging on, her face taut with horror. It took me a few seconds to realize why. It was because the only thing that separated The Comet from his stable was the river.

I clapped my heels into Nelson's astonished sides and he leapt into a gallop. His neck stretched out and the clods flew but it was useless to try to catch The Comet. I could see the river looming closer by the second, but the sight of it did nothing to daunt the runaway. He galloped furiously and unwaveringly towards the bank and he launched himself into the air. I heard Nigella's terrified scream as they appeared to hang in space and the next moment there was a tremendous splash as they hit the water. They vanished from sight and their backwash flooded the banks.

As Nelson skidded on to the bank, I threw myself out of the saddle and stared helplessly into the river. I had no idea of what I should do. After a few seconds I saw The Comet's head emerge a little way down stream, but Nigella didn't come up at all. I stripped off my jacket and struggled to free myself from my boots. Nelson, quite oblivious to the emergency, dropped his head and began to graze.

I was just about to jump into the water when I heard a faint noise from the opposite bank and first Nigella's arm and then her head appeared under a willow. At the same instant I saw Henrietta galloping towards us on the opposite bank, followed by Mr McLoughlin on the mare-who-sometimes-slipped-a-stifle. Screaming to them that Nigella was in the river, I jumped on to Nelson in my stockinged feet and made for the bridge.

When I arrived on the opposite bank, Nigella was being hauled to the water's edge on the thong of Mr McLoughlin's hunting whip. We leaned over and dragged her out of the river, and we sat her, heaving and choking and blue with cold, upon a stump. Water streamed from her beautiful habit and her hair was plastered to her shoulders.

"The Comet," she gasped as soon as she was able to speak. "He's drowned!"

"Never," cried Mr McLoughlin valiantly. He pointed to The Comet's bobbing head. The horse was swimming strongly away from us, straight up the middle of the river.

"Oh," Nigella cried. "The horrible brute." She burst into agonized sobs.

Henrietta and I set off after The Comet along the bank, hoping to tempt him out with the promise of equine company. But The Comet was having none of it. We followed him across the park, over the lane, and for almost a mile until the river had widened into mud flats fringed with reed. There, amongst rotting barges and watched by two majestic swans, The Comet hit the shallows and waded out, only slightly obstructed by the side-saddle, which had settled itself beneath his belly.

Henrietta led him home with his sides heaving like a bellows. His saddlery was stuck with reeds, and steam rose from his every part. Henrietta herself was not the elegant sight she had once been.

I followed on Nelson, trying to ignore the curious looks we collected from the occupants of land rovers and horseboxes returning from the hunt. I was grieved to know that I looked just as odd, hatless and bootless and jacketless, with a hole in the elbow of my yellow hunting shirt and the ends of my stock flying in the breeze.

"We shall have to sell The Comet after this,"

Henrietta said grimly. "He'll have to go. We can't possibly keep him any longer. He will kill someone in the end." And as a navy blue Lambourne horse-box inched past us in the lane and I hid my face to preclude any future recognition, she added, as one who is struck with an extremely sensible idea, "Perhaps we can send him to Warners with Harry Sabin's bay gelding."

13

A Raison d'Etre

All I could think about now was getting to see Felix
Hissey. I knew that it was no earthly use waiting
until the next hunting day because we had to take
the Thunder and Ligh⁷ning liveries out and I would
never find an excuse to shake off the Fanes. So I
watched and waited for my chance, and on Monday
afternoon it came. A lorry trundled down the drive
to collect the jumble.

After we had loaded the junk and tied a tarpaulin
over it, the Fanes and Lady Jennifer squashed into
the cab beside the driver to organize the unpacking
at the village hall. Within five minutes of their
departure, I was speeding along in the shooting
brake, on my way to the pickle factory in Bury St
Edmunds.

The pickle factory was in the old part of the town
behind a Georgian terrace. Above the gates there
was a wrought iron arch in the centre of which there
was a sign in the shape of a round-faced, red-
cheeked man with a jolly smile and a crown studded
with silverskin onions and chilli peppers. I drove
into the yard and was directed towards the office by
a white-coated man unloading cauliflowers from a
lorry.

The office was up a lot of narrow flights of stairs
above the factory where lines of women in overalls,
with their hair tied up in scarves, shouted to each
other over the clank of the machinery and the clink

131

of glass and the roar of piped music. There was a powerful smell of vinegar.

Behind a door at the top of the last flight of stairs I came upon the round-faced, red-cheeked man of the sign, bending over a desk, sniffing at little piles of orange powder.

"Take a sniff," he invited. "I'm trying to decide which has the best bouquet."

I was breathless from the climb, and in my anxiety to do the right thing, I leaned over and inhaled the nearest pile. The fine dust rose up into my nostrils. I sneezed, dispersing orange powder in a cloud all over the desk.

"No, no," the Pickle King said in reproof. "Not like that, like this. *Gently.*" He leaned over another pile and gave a short, delicate sniff, closing his eyes and flaring his nostrils. "You test the aroma. You don't take it like snuff."

I tried again. "I can't smell anything at all," I confessed.

"That's because you haven't a nose," the Pickle King said with regret. "There are not many about these days. People don't realize what a disastrous effect our polluted environment has on the olfactory senses; a good nose today is a very rare find." He settled himself down behind the desk and waved me into a chair. "As you haven't a nose," he said cheerfully, "perhaps you should begin by telling me what other redeeming qualities you have." He beamed at me expectantly.

"I beg your pardon?" I said.

"Your qualifications," he said. "Your experience. Have you ever worked in a pickle factory before?"

"Mr Hissey," I said nervously. "I don't want a job in the factory."

A look of enlightenment spread over the Pickle King's cherubic face. "Then you must be the girl groom young Forster was telling me about," he said. "I should have guessed. I can see you are the outdoor type."

"I haven't actually come about the groom's job either," I said.

The Pickle King's face fell. He frowned.

"I've come about Harry Sabin's bay gelding," I said, and I blurted out the whole story; about my eventing ambitions and the misery of not being able to find a job which paid a living wage, and of having to accept work with the Fanes, and how we had come across the bay gelding in Harry Sabin's field and how, if I didn't do something about it, it was going to Warners on Wednesday week. I was just mentioning the importance of having the fifteen hundred in cash, when the Pickle King held up a restraining hand.

"Wait a minute," he said in a disbelieving voice. "Am I hearing you correctly? Are you asking *me* to buy *you* a horse?"

"Not exactly," I said, but then, "well, yes. I suppose I am."

"But I hardly know you," he exclaimed, and his eyes were round with astonishment. "We only met a few minutes ago!"

"I don't actually want you to buy the horse for *me*," I tried to explain. "I just want you to put up the money. It would actually belong to you. You would own it."

133

"Oh," the Pickle King said. "How extremely generous."

"I don't seem to have put this very well," I said anxiously. "But the truth of the matter is that I want to event and I've found the perfect horse, but I haven't any money. I need a sponsor."

"I don't sponsor people," the Pickle King said firmly.

"Not people," I said. "Only one person. Only me."

"Especially people I don't know," he added. "So I'll say good morning." He scrambled up from behind his desk and made for the door.

I grabbed him by his jacket. "Mr Hissey," I said desperately. "I only need a chance. I have a promising future; ask Hans Gelderhol."

The Pickle King paused with his hand on the door knob. "Hans Gelderhol?" he said. "*That* Hans Gelderhol?" He nodded towards a framed photograph on the wall.

"Oh yes," I said. "That's the one I mean."

"And Hans Gelderhol thinks you're good?"

"Ask him," I said. "Ring him up. Ring him now."

The Pickle King made his way back to the desk and stretched out a hand towards the telephone. He hesitated. "If Hans Gelderhol thinks you're so good," he enquired, "why doesn't he take you on himself?"

"He did ask me," I said. "I refused."

The Pickle King flopped back into his chair. "You refused a job with Hans Gelderhol?" he said incredulously. "You *refused*?"

I nodded.

"Why?"

"Personal reasons," I said.

The Pickle King looked at me suspiciously. "What personal reasons?" he asked.

"They're personal," I said indignantly.

The Pickle King waved me back into my chair. "I only asked," he said placatingly, "because most girls would give an arm and a leg to work for Hans Gelderhol."

"I know," I said. "Hans Gelderhol can have any girl he wants, and now and again they do get a ride. But they don't get paid good wages, and they don't get the good horses. He keeps those for himself."

"Well, naturally," the Pickle King said. "He *is* the star." He stared at me thoughtfully. "So you wouldn't join the bandwagon," he said. "You didn't fancy it, eh?"

"Didn't fancy what?" I said faintly.

The Pickle King chuckled. "Don't think I don't know the Golden Boy," he said. "I know Hans. I know him very well indeed."

"There was nothing improper," I said. "I was just a student. But the inference is that if you haven't a wealthy family behind you, you haven't a chance. I want to prove that it isn't necessarily so. I want to do it on my own."

"Correction," the Pickle King said. "You want to do it on my money."

I couldn't deny it.

The Pickle King frowned at me over the desk, and his forehead was furrowed with genuine perplexity. "Assume for one moment, Miss Would-Be-Event-Rider," he said, "that I rang Hans Gelderhol and he gave me a glowing report on your potential; then further assume that I purchased this bay gelding on

135

your behalf. What would I stand to gain from it? Can you give me one valid reason why I should back a completely untried novice horse and rider? Why I should spend fifteen hundred pounds on a total stranger?"

It was the question I had been dreading. There was nothing for it but to tell the truth. "You were the only person I could think of," I said. "Everyone knows you are interested in eventing, you must be, or you wouldn't be a patron. I know you sponsor events and give prize money and expensive trophies to those who have made it to the top; I thought there might be a chance that you would consider helping someone right at the bottom for a change." It sounded unlikely, even to my own ears.

"I might," the Pickle King said.

I could hardly believe it. I almost jumped out of my chair.

The Pickle King held up a restraining hand. "I only said that I might, not that I would." But his eyes had begun to sparkle. "I'm not Father Christmas; I work hard for my money, and when I spend it I want to be sure I get good value in return. How do I know that you would be good value, Miss Would-Be-Event-Rider?"

"Oh, Mr Hissey, I *would* be," I assured him. "I work hard and I would train hard. I *wouldn't* let you down; you could ask Hans to give me a reference."

"I could," the Pickle King agreed. "And I most certainly would."

"And the horse is good value," I said eagerly. "It's actually very cheap. It's the right type and the right age, and it's sound in every way because I've had it vetted. It's exactly the horse for the job, you could go and see it for yourself."

"Oh, I would," he said. "Make no mistake about it."

"It would be a good investment," I urged him. "Even if it didn't make the grade, you would still come out with a profit at the end of the exercise. You couldn't possibly lose money."

"Unless it broke its neck," he said.

"There is such a thing as insurance," I pointed out.

"An insurance premium on an event horse is very costly," he said solemnly.

"You wouldn't have to pay the running costs," I told him. "I can keep a horse in the yard where I work; it's a condition of the job."

"You must be earning a very good wage," the Pickle King said, "to be confident that you can afford the upkeep of an event horse; the training, the transportation, the entry fees, not to mention the best quality food, the supplements, the shoeing, the saddlery, the veterinary charges."

There was nothing I could say to this. The Pickle King leaned back in his chair and stuck his thumbs into the pockets of his jolly yellow waistcoat. He regarded me in amusement. He knew perfectly well that I wasn't earning a bean. Everyone who hunted in the Midvale and Westbury country knew the Fanes.

"Now, in my yard," he observed in an innocent tone, "I do pay extremely good wages. I pay more than the NAG rate for the job; and as a concession, there happens to be a vacant stable, with keep, for a horse that might, just might, you understand, be an eventer."

"Mr Hissey," I said, appalled. "That's bribery!"

"No, no," the Pickle King said comfortably. "It's known as setting a sprat to catch a mackerel."

"But I already have a job," I said. "I'm not sure that I want to leave. At least," I added, "not yet."

"The trouble with horse-mad little girls," the Pickle King said sternly, "is that they don't realize, don't *want* to realize, that they are being exploited. If I worked my pickling ladies the hours that you are expected to work, and paid them the rate you are getting, I would have the union down on me like a ton of bricks."

"Mr Hissey," I said. "Are you saying that if I take your job, you will buy the bay gelding?"

"The problem is," he continued, "that in the horse world, apart from in the racing sector, there is no nationally supervised training scheme, just a rather fragmented examination system . . ."

"Mr Hissey," I interrupted. "Am I right? Is that what you are saying?"

". . . Which is, in any case, undersubsidized, oversubscribed, and leans rather too heavily towards the art of instruction; therefore a really good well-trained groom, like a good nose, is a rare find." He rocked back in his chair towards the desk and gave me an angelic smile. "Are you a really good, well-trained groom, Miss Would-Be-Event-Rider?"

"Yes," I said, wanting to be truthful. "I believe I am."

"Then what I am saying," the Pickle King said, "is that in all propositions laid before a man of business, there must be a raison d'être, an inducement, a benefit."

"Mr Hissey," I said. "I think you are a snake in the grass."

Unabashed, he beamed at me over the piles of orange powder. "I dislike conducting interviews," he continued. "It would give me great pleasure to tear up the advertisement I was about to insert in *Horse and Hound*, to be spared the agony of sorting through an avalanche of unsuitable applicants. Consequently, if you will consider my job, in return, I will consider the bay gelding. Now, Miss Would-Be-Event-Rider, do we have a bargain?"

"Yes, Mr Hissey," I said. "We do."

14

A Very Old Mare

The old bay mare was flat out in her stable and I couldn't get her up. I was dressed for hunting, but I couldn't leave her because I knew in my bones that she was going to die. It was Doreen's half-term, and she stood in the doorway, wide-eyed. Her white face was almost transparent with dismay.

"Go and find Nigella," I said. "Tell her the old bay mare is worse; that I am going to stay behind, and that you are to take the blue roan instead of me."

"Oh, I *can't*," Doreen moaned. "The Fanes won't like it."

The old bay mare's eyes had sunk and her breathing was fast and shallow. I had heaped rugs on top of her but her ears, when I felt them, were like wet leather gloves left out in a frost.

"The Fanes will have to lump it," I said. "I can't go off and leave her like this."

"What did you say?" Henrietta exclaimed, appearing at the door with her plaiting box under her arm. "Can't go? Of course you can go. It isn't as if you can do anything for her, after all. She's pretty far gone already; she won't notice if you are here or not."

"I'm going to stay," I said. "I've called the vet."

"I thought we had decided not to call the vet," Henrietta said peevishly. "You know he won't be

140

able to do anything, and he'll charge us the earth just for the visit."

"I've called him anyway," I said. "There might be a chance. Doreen will take the blue roan."

"Oh, I don't *know*," Doreen wailed. "I've never ridden it before."

"You see," Henrietta said. "She won't. She's hopeless."

"Ow," Doreen squeaked, offended. "I'm *not*."

"Then go and get your hunting clothes," I said crossly. "This minute."

Doreen went off, looking uncertain. The old bay mare managed a tremulous sigh, although she was really past caring.

"If she falls off . . ." Henrietta warned. "If she damages the horse . . ."

"She won't fall off, and she won't damage the horse," I said, "because you will be there to see that she doesn't."

"Hrmm," Henrietta said, and she went off to change with a disgruntled air.

The Fanes were not able to use their side-saddles on the Thunder and Lightning liveries for fear of causing sore backs and confusion over the aids, so they were forced to ride astride. I had offered them the loan of the stretch jodhpurs I wore for exercising, but they had refused. When they appeared in the yard, ready to mount, I could see why. Amongst the jumble offerings they had discovered several pairs of ex-cavalry elephant-ear breeches in a vibrant shade of ginger, and appropriated them for their own use. No self-respecting rider would have dreamed of wearing them, but the Fanes thought them delightful.

141

"Wait until you see my other pair," Henrietta said gleefully. "In black and white houndstooth check."

Doreen, legged up into the blue roan's beautiful *Stübben* saddle, whispered that she couldn't wait.

"There are some smaller sizes," Nigella said benevolently. "We should sort out a pair for Doreen."

Doreen followed them out of the yard, looking troubled.

When the vet came I asked him if there was any hope. He examined the old bay mare and he took her temperature and he listened to her failing heartbeat.

"No," he said. "I'm afraid there's no hope at all. She's a very old mare and there would be no point in trying to prolong her life. It wouldn't be fair; in fact, it would be unkind to try. It's far better to just let her slip quietly away; she isn't in any pain."

He helped me to heap the blankets back on to her. "You mustn't be too sad," he said. "After all, it's quite a privilege these days, for a horse to be allowed to die of old age."

Outside in the yard, he asked if I had bought the bay gelding. I told him about my financial position and about Felix Hissey's offer, and that I had six days in which to make up my mind.

"You'll go to Hissey's place, of course," he assumed. "It's exactly what you want; a well-paid job and a chance to event. There's no decision to make, as far as I can see."

"It seems that there isn't," I said. "In fact I've already told Felix Hissey that I'm willing to take his job. He's going to see the bay gelding tomorrow. It all rather hinges on whether he likes it or not."

The vet patted my shoulder. "He can't help but

like it," he said. "It's a grand horse." He left me with two bills, fifteen pounds for vetting the bay gelding, and an eight pound call-out fee for the old bay mare. I knew Henrietta would be furious when she saw it.

I was prepared for a solitary vigil with the old bay mare, but not long after the sound of the vet's car had died away Lady Jennifer appeared with two mugs of coffee on a tin tray. They were accompanied by the last of the biscuits and a new packet of raw cane sugar. I didn't need to be told where the latter had come from. Lady Jennifer had been to lunch with my father the previous day; already he was making his influence felt.

Lady Jennifer settled herself down on the straw and gently lifted the old bay mare's head into her faded tweed lap. And whilst we waited, she told me about her youth and the many hunters she had owned, and how, although never beautiful, Little Legend had once been the envy of the country because of her speed and her courage. And as she related all this, her eyes grew damp, and she wiped tears off the old bay mare's nose with a crumpled paper tissue.

"I mustn't be sentimental," she sniffed. "It's so *terribly* silly of me, and it doesn't help at all."

When the old bay mare finally stopped breathing with a single long, shuddering rasp, Lady Jennifer closed her eyelids over her sunken eyes as gently and carefully as if she had been a human and lifted the lifeless head from her lap; then she went out of the stable to summon the flesh waggon.

I saddled up the bad-tempered chestnut and went out for a ride so that I shouldn't have to witness the indignity of the old bay mare's departure. I knew that it really made no difference at all what happened to her once she was dead, but I was haunted by something William had said when Lady Jennifer and I had returned the young entry to the kennels on the day of my arrival; that all the hirelings together wouldn't feed hounds for more than a week. Well, the old bay mare had been fatter when she died than she had been for a long time; she wouldn't disgrace us now. The sheer awfulness of it brought on a few more tears before I managed to pull myself together, and turned the bad-tempered chestnut for home.

Henrietta and Nigella received the news with regret unclouded by any hint of sentimentality or remorse and soon fell to relating in tones of high excitement the happenings of the day; describing in glowing terms the impeccable behaviour and the general excellence of the Thunder and Lightning liveries. They had been particularly impressed by the blue roan, who, "even with a fool like Doreen in the saddle", had been in the first flight to the end.

They were just contemplating the alarming possibility of letting the liveries out as hirelings when their owners were otherwise engaged, when there was a determined thumping at the front door. I went to answer it.

It was William. He stood in the portico, shuffling his feet and looking as if he would vastly prefer to be somewhere else. He was sorry to have made such a row, he said, but he had knocked a couple of times before and nobody had heard. I said it was perfectly all right and would he like to come in.

"No," he said awkwardly. "I won't come in, if

that's all right with you. It's very kind of you to ask, but I'd prefer not."

I wondered if he had come to see Henrietta, and had lost his nerve, or if he was the bearer of a message from Forster who had not spoken to me since the incident in the lane, or if it was the lingering odour of B.O. and mothballs that had caused him to turn red to the gills with embarrassment.

But it was none of these things.

"We were sorry about the old mare," he said. "She's been a good horse in her time. We thought you might like to have these." He pushed a brown paper bag into my hands and made off down the steps before I could even say thank you.

Inside the bag, scrubbed and burnished, were the old bay mare's shoes.

15

A Good Day's Hunting

"Whatever 'The Lads' happen to be like," Henrietta said, "we must make sure that they enjoy themselves. Our livelihood depends upon it."

We all agreed that we would do our best, but on Thursday morning it was bitterly cold and raining hard.

"They won't come," Nigella decided. "They are sure to be fair weather riders. I wouldn't send my worst enemy hunting on a day like this." But we plaited up just in case, and at ten fifteen a white Mercedes drew into the yard.

"The Lads" were a lot smaller, younger and punier than they had looked on the television, but they were friendly and optimistic and they were looking forward to their day with the Hunt, rain or no rain.

"Heavens," Nigella exclaimed when she was introduced to them. "I thought you were bald!"

Johnny Jones leaned towards her and unpeeled one of his sideburns. "We are," he said. "This is a wig."

"Oh, please," Nigella said, dismayed. "Don't take it off."

"It's only 'is 'ead," Sammy Pike said reassuringly. "It ain't indecent exposure."

When "The Lads" were introduced to their horses, they all wanted the blue roan. Things got so heated that Nigella was forced to take charge and allocate the horses size by size. So Johnny Jones got the blue roan because he was the smallest and puniest, Solly Chell got the chestnut, and Sammy Pike, because he was the tallest, got the smallest horse, which was the bay.

Whilst "The Lads" changed into their hunting clothes we tacked up their horses and loaded them into the horsebox and as soon as we had pointed them in the direction of the meet, we began to fly round getting ourselves and our own horses ready. We knew it was essential that we turned out; we had to keep an eye on our livelihood. It was still pouring with rain.

It was not a day on which to feel responsible for someone else's enjoyment. The Fanes and I missed the meet because we had to hack there, but it didn't matter, the first two coverts were blank anyway. The weather had worsened by the time we arrived at the third draw, a wind-lashed thicket perched on the top of a hill and exposed to the full force of the elements. There was a vicious east wind coming off the sea which gave an icy edge to the squalling rain. Henrietta said we were standing on the highest part of Suffolk and that there was nothing on the same level between us and Russia. I didn't know if this was true or not, but it certainly felt like it, and I decided that this day would be the end, the absolute finish, of the Thunder and Lightning liveries.

"The Lads" stood in a miserable huddle with their coat collars up and their backs to the battering wind. Their faces were blue, their expensive hunting clothes were soaked, and water dribbled off their hats and their horses' chins. Nigella and I placed ourselves a little way off and shivered. I could feel water beginning to seep down my neck and my thighs were numb. The mare-who-sometimes-slipped-a-stifle and the bad-tempered chestnut stood with wretchedly bowed heads, whilst Henrietta and the black horse squelched ceaselessly up and down. It was utterly dreadful. Then, like a miracle, we heard the Gone Away.

In the flurry of the first few minutes, struggling to regain our circulation, we could see that "The Lads" were no horsemen. They sat with loose reins and flapping legs and they had no idea how to control their horses at all. It was clear that this would lead to disaster because the country was treacherous. The stubble fields of the autumn were almost all gone, replaced by wide acres of deep, sticky plough criss-crossed by greasy tracks studded with loose flints. The yawning banked ditches which divided the land were not improved by the rain, their sides were slimy with exposed clay, and their dug out gullies gushed with yellow water.

As the Field dived after the Master, the Fanes and I held back, ready to pick up the pieces of our livelihood. We were certain that they would come to grief; it wasn't a day, or a country, for riders without experience.

"They'll be killed," Henrietta gasped in a despairing voice. She sat down hard and fought the black horse gamely with slippery reins, her sodden apron flapping against his ribs. "Think of their insurance company! Think of our seventy-five pounds a week!"

But it was the horses I was thinking about, forseeing sprains and strains and broken limbs, and at the third ditch we came upon the blue roan, upside down and stuck fast, kicking like a turtle.

"Oh, glory," Nigella moaned. "Where's Johnny Jones?"

We scanned the grey and buffeted headland, expecting to see him lying injured, but Johnny Jones was not in sight. Then, from the depths of the ditch, we heard an inarticulate noise.

"He's here!" Henrietta shouted. "He's under the horse!" Panic-stricken, she leapt off the black horse, slid down the side of the ditch, and began to tug helplessly at the blue roan's reins. The tail end of the Field, near blinded by the rain, flew past, splattering her with mud.

"No! No!" Nigella cried. "You'll never move her like that! We shall have to use stirrup leathers!"

I dragged the leathers off the mare-who-sometimes-slipped-a-stifle's saddle and yanked off the irons. As I threw the leathers to Nigella, the black horse, unable to bear the sight of the departing hunt without protest stood on his hind legs, dragging the bunch of slippery reins from my grasp. I dived for his head and in an instant the mare-who-sometimes-slipped-a-stifle and the bad-tempered chestnut realized that they were free and trotted off smartly in the wake of the tail-enders.

"Let them go!" Henrietta yelled, as I lifted my foot to the black horse's stirrup to be after them. "Don't leave us! Johnny Jones may be injured; you may have to ride for help!"

Somehow the Fanes managed to get the leathers under the blue roan's withers whilst I held on to the black horse who plunged about like something demented.

"Now," Henrietta commanded, her face shining

149

with rain and red with exertion, and her habit trailing in the mud. "PULL!"

They pulled. The blue roan pressed her head forward and flailed her legs mightily. She rolled over on to her side. Then, with a heave and a grunt, she was up the bank and standing safely on the headland. Johnny Jones lay flattened into the mud at the bottom of the ditch, saved by the hollow of the gully. He sat up and poured water out of his boots. "If this is hunting in Suffolk," he said, "you can keep it."

"Nonsense," Henrietta said briskly. "You're having a lovely time." She helped him up the bank and legged him back on to the blue roan.

A woman in a bowler hat rode up to us, leading a chestnut horse. "Excuse me," she said. "Is this one of yours?"

"No," Nigella said firmly, wringing ditch water out of the bottom of her apron. "It isn't," and then, "Wait a moment," she said. "I believe it is." It wasn't the bad-tempered chestnut, it was the chestnut livery.

"All this isn't really happening," said Henrietta grimly, as she took hold of the black horse's rein as a preliminary to the search for Solly Chell. "It's just a nightmare. I shall wake up in a minute."

I threaded the irons on to the leathers, put them over my shoulders, and mounted the chestnut livery. Johnny Jones was a speck in the distance.

"What about me," Nigella enquired. "I haven't got a horse." Henrietta legged her up behind me on the chestnut livery and we set off along the headland. The black horse progressed across the plough in a series of giant leaps and the chestnut livery cantered at a sedate pace with his double burden. The wind whipped our clothes and slashed our faces with icy rain. "I think this day might turn out to be the worst of my life," said Nigella.

Two fields on we came upon Sammy Pike and the bay horse wandering up and down a banked ditch in a dazed manner, looking for a way to cross. Across his cheekbone there was a bloody gash and a rapidly gathering bruise. He told us that he had been galloping behind someone when their horse had thrown up a flint.

"Well, if you must gallop on someone's tail," Henrietta said. "Remember to keep your head down."

Nigella wondered if the cut should have a stitch but Sammy Pike said no fear.

"But you'll have a scar," Nigella said anxiously.

"Yeah," Sammy Pike said, pleased. "I've always wanted a scar on me face."

"Heavens," Nigella said in a low voice. "There's no way of understanding some people."

Henrietta was demonstrating to Sammy Pike the correct way to approach the banked ditch. "When it's dry you have a choice between scrambling down it, or flying it. But when it's wet there's no choice, you simply have to fly it. You must approach it at a controlled gallop because you need plenty of impulsion to get up the bank and to take you over the top. If you approach it too slowly, your horse will never make it, and if his back legs slip back into the ditch, throw yourself clear so that he doesn't roll on top of you. Come on, I'll give you a lead."

She trotted the black horse away from the ditch and turned him towards it. "And don't ride on my tail," she shouted to Sammy Pike, "because if I don't make it, you will land on top of me!"

The black horse galloped at the ditch like the old hand he was, leapt up the bank and flew over the top with his tail and Henrietta's hair, which had escaped from its coil, streaming out behind them. Sammy Pike, his eyes lit with excitement, urged the bay after them. He had no idea of how to control a horse at a gallop with his slack seat and flapping arms, but the bay bounded up the bank and flung itself heroically across the gap, landing with several yards to spare.

"I hope you realize what a super horse that is," Henrietta said severely, as she dispatched him in the approximate direction of the hunt.

Nigella and I and the chestnut livery made our way along the top of the bank until we came to a tractor crossing. We traversed the headland of a vast plough field and breasted a long rise of stubble without any sign of Solly Chell or the bad-tempered chestnut, but when we reached the top of the rise, we saw a small crowd gathered round a horse in the lane below.

A woman with a child on a leading rein trotted up the rise towards us. "I wouldn't go any nearer unless you must," she called. "It's broken a leg. They've sent for the humane killer." She pointed to a small white van bucketing across the lower stubble towards the lane.

"Henrietta," Nigella said in a horrified voice. "The horse in the lane looks like our bay mare!"

Henrietta's face stiffened. She lifted her whip hand. The black horse shot forward and flew helter-skelter down the rise. He stretched out his neck and

152

raced the white van towards the knot of people in the lane.

The chestnut livery, sensing the urgency of the situation, leapt after him. He galloped down the rise as fast as his legs would carry him and Nigella and I clung on grimly, slipping further and further sideways. "Don't shoot the mare! Don't shoot her!" Nigella screamed. "She hasn't broken a leg, she's just slipped a stifle!"

With a determined effort of willpower, we managed to stay on the chestnut livery until we saw that Henrietta had arrived in the lane, seconds before the Terrier Man climbed out of the van with the killer in his hands.

"Don't you dare shoot this mare," she cried dramatically. "She's ours!"

Nigella and I hit the stubble together, still clutching each other like Siamese twins. The onlookers gasped, unused to such goings-on, but the Terrier Man was unimpressed.

"She ain't no good to you now, Miss," he said dismally to Henrietta. "Her leg's broke."

Nigella and I picked ourselves up from the stubble. The bay mare's hind leg hung uselessly from her hip. When she moved, she hopped on three legs. I had never seen a slipped stifle, but it looked broken to me.

"You can see for y'self," the Terrier Man said gloomily. "It's definitely broke."

"Nonsense," Henrietta said. "Put that gun away. You know you're not supposed to shoot any animal without a veterinary opinion."

"I don't need a vet to tell me its leg's broke," the Terrier Man said stubbornly.

Nigella untangled herself from the stirrup leathers and picked up the mud-caked end of her apron. She walked into the lane and without a word, took the bay mare by the reins and began to lead her away. The mare hopped obligingly after her. By the time they had covered a hundred yards, she was already putting the injured leg to the ground, although she was still hopelessly lame.

"There you are," Henrietta said in a satisfied voice. "I told you it wasn't broken." She turned the black horse and rode off down the lane after Nigella.

The Terrier Man shrugged his shoulders and plodded morosely back to his van where his charges could be heard yapping and scrabbling in their cages. The crowd of foot-followers began to break up, and I mounted the chestnut livery and followed the Fanes, thinking that I would probably never experience anything like this if I went to work for Felix Hissey, and wondering if I should be glad or sorry.

When we arrived at the Thunder and Lightning horsebox, we found Johnny Jones and Sammy Pike ensconced cheerfully in the cab with a half empty bottle of Scotch between them. Far from having had a disastrous day, they had thoroughly enjoyed it and couldn't wait to come out again. We all accepted a drink, being in need of something to revive us, and got a bit giggly, especially when we opened the back of the box to hospitalize the bay mare, and saw the liveries' legs had been bandaged so loosely that they had concertina'd round their ankles like schoolboys' socks. By the time we had rebandaged the horses, Nigella had gone into one of her flat spins and was being eaten up with anxiety over drink and driving and the safety of the horses, whereupon Johnny

Jones assured her that it was perfectly all right because Solly Chell did all the driving and he never touched a drop. This only made matters worse because Nigella reminded us that for all we knew, Solly Chell might be lying unconscious, half-drowned in a ditch somewhere, not only that, but we were a horse short, and what did we intend to do about it. Didn't we realize that it was getting dark, and shouldn't somebody call the police . . .

The situation was finally saved by the sound of hoof beats on the lane which heralded the arrival of Solly Chell mounted on the bad-tempered chestnut, still bursting with the exhilaration of the chase. He had fallen from his horse when it had veered away from a refuser at a ditch, and he had captured the bad-tempered chestnut as it had trotted by. He had no idea that he had started out on one horse and ended the day on another.

16

King in a Pickle

Nelson and I toiled up the immaculate pea-gravelled drive lined with reproduction street lamps, towards Winter Place. I had tried to telephone Felix Hissey at the factory but I had been unable to speak to him; he was at home, they had said, indisposed.

I needed to see him because he hadn't been out hunting the previous day, and I wouldn't see him at the Saturday meet because I wasn't going; there wasn't a horse for me to ride. In a week we had lost the old bay mare, the mare-who-sometimes-slipped-a-stifle was out of action, probably for the rest of the season, and The Comet had been declared unsafe. This left us with only three hunters, and we had Mr McLoughlin to mount. The season had only just begun and already we were short of horses.

Winter Place was a large, four square neo-Georgian house built of red Suffolk brick with a lot of long white-painted windows. It was very smart and very silent. Nelson and I crunched our way round the back and into the stable yard. There were four garages and three loose boxes. I wondered how much I would enjoy working in this tiny, spotless yard, and if I would be lonely. Felix Hissey's two cobby hunters regarded us with astonishment; they didn't seem accustomed to visitors at Winter Place.

I put Nelson in the empty stable and stroked the noses of the cobs. All through my school years, at the training centre, and even at the Fanes', I had worked with people of my own age. I didn't know solitude and I was bothered by it. I was even more bothered when I met the cross, grey-haired housekeeper, who set her mouth in a grim line and said she would ask if Mr Hissey was prepared to see me.

I told myself firmly that the bay gelding would make up for all this and I followed the grim housekeeper through the hall lined with hunting prints, into a small room lined with books. Felix Hissey was lying in an armchair with his foot propped up in front of him. It was encased in plaster of Paris from the knee downwards.

The Pickle King glowered.

"Oh no," I said weakly. "You *didn't* . . ."

"You don't think, Miss Would-Be-Event-Rider," he snapped, "that I would contemplate the purchase of a horse I hadn't ridden?"

"I don't know," I said helplessly. "It didn't occur to me."

"It didn't occur to you to warn me that it had a buck like a jerboa either," the Pickle King expostulated.

I wasn't sure what a jerboa was, but I felt the bay gelding slip irretrievably from my grasp. "Mr Hissey," I said. "I'm terribly sorry."

"I might have expected it from that lugubrious fool, Harry Sabin," he said in disgust. "But not from you, Miss Would-Be-Event-Rider, I expected better things from you."

"Mr Hissey," I said, ashamed, "what can I say?"

"You can start by saying when you intend to begin work in the yard," he said. "I can't do a thing with this damned leg – which, I might add, Miss Would-Be-Event-Rider, could have been avoided if you had seen fit to give me prior warning."

I couldn't argue. It was true that I had been negligent, and because of it I had lost the bay gelding; and even without the bay gelding I would have to come to Winter Place. It was my penance. "I expect I could leave the Fanes on a fortnight's notice," I said.

"And how am I expected to look after my horses during this fortnight?" the Pickle King enquired peevishly. "With this leg, and without a groom?"

"I'll come twice a day," I said humbly. "I'll cut out their corn and turn them out in the daytime in their New Zealand rugs. I'll give them two small soft feeds morning and night and plenty of hay. I shall have to let them down, there's no point in trying to keep them fit. You won't be riding again for at least six weeks."

"Six weeks," the Pickle King said resentfully. "The season will be over!"

"It won't," I assured him. "You will be hunting again before Christmas."

"Christmas," he said in an explosive tone. "Pah!" He lapsed into a miserable silence.

"Mr Hissey," I said. "Would you like me to see to the horses before I go?" It seemed the least that I could do.

"Yes," he said grudgingly. "Thank you . . . and get Mrs Short to show you the flat . . . you'll get forty pounds a week all found and the use of the pick-up . . . one day a week off in half days during the hunting season and two full months off with pay in the summer . . ."

158

"Thank you," I said. "You're very generous." I had never felt more unhappy in the whole of my life.

"Oh," he added. "And there's the money." He pointed to a fat manilla envelope on the desk.

"Money?" I said stupidly. "What money?"

"The money for Harry Sabin's bay gelding," he said. "I've never ridden a better horse in my life."

"Nigella," I said. "I'm leaving in a fortnight."

Nigella looked up from the *Horse and Rider* she was reading. "Oh *Elaine*," she sighed. "Not again!"

"I mean it this time," I said. "I've written out my notice. I've got another job." I told her about Felix Hissey and the bay gelding.

"I can't believe it," she said. "How could you do this to us? We thought you were happy here."

"I have been," I said. "I honestly have been. I feel terrible about it; but I have my future to think of, and this is the only way."

"Why didn't you talk to us about it?" she wondered. "You didn't mention the bay gelding; why didn't you tell us? Why did it have to be a secret?"

"If I had told you," I said. "If we had discussed it, you couldn't have done anything, and Henrietta . . . well, Henrietta would have interfered."

"Yes," Nigella agreed. "She would." We fell silent, thinking about Henrietta. "I shall have to tell her," she decided. "She won't like it, and I expect she will make your last two weeks as difficult as possible, but I can't not tell her, can I?"

"No," I said. "You can't."

"I had hoped," Nigella said, getting up from the table, "that you would stay with us for years and years." She went out of the door rather quickly, but not before I had seen that her eyes were bright with tears.

"Elaine," Lady Jennifer said. "As you are not hunting tomorrow, could you *possibly* help me with the jumble sale?"

"Oh dear," I said. "Must I?" I had planned to collect the bay gelding and take him to Winter Place; but Lady Jennifer was not to be put off.

"I'm so *frightfully* short of helpers," she sighed. "I just don't know *how* I shall manage; and it isn't as if I would need you all day, it doesn't begin until two o'clock."

I sighed inwardly. I knew it would take me all morning to finish my work in the stables, and added to that I had to get to Winter Place to look after the cobs as well. If I helped Lady Jennifer with her awful jumble sale, I would have to put off collecting the bay gelding until Sunday. It was a nuisance, but I was fond of Lady Jennifer and I didn't want to refuse.

"Of course I'll help," I said. "I'll be delighted."

Mucking out alone in the deserted yard when everyone had left for the Saturday meet I told myself that I should be feeling elated, that surely I must be one of the luckiest people alive. At last I had landed a good job with a fair living wage and regular time off; I had never received a penny from the Fanes, and they still owed me the pound I had loaned them in the underground car park. I hadn't had a day off either, in the month I had worked for them. Was it only a month? It seemed longer than that.

I told myself that not only had I landed a good

job, but that I also had the bay gelding, I had the potential event horse I had dreamed of; and yet I still couldn't shake off a feeling of blankness; there was a sort of hollow void where the elation should have been. I wondered if perhaps now that it had actually come to it, I was getting cold feet about the task ahead, if it was nerves that were anaesthetizing the bit of me that should have been bursting with joy. Perhaps I should have stayed with Hans Gelderhol when he had offered to take me on in his yard. He would have given me a few pounds a week and I could have become one of his acolytes. The acolytes had a few doubtful privileges, but sponsored event horses were not among them. Hans Gelderhol had said that I was "promising", but what did that mean? It meant that I had a lot to learn, and professional training was expensive; everything to do with eventing was expensive; eventing was a rich person's sport, whichever way you looked at it. Well, thank heavens for Felix Hissey. Felix Hissey was a rich man. I thought of Felix Hissey sitting with his foot up, whilst everyone else was at the Saturday meet, and I was ashamed.

Preoccupied with all this, I led The Comet out in his New Zealand rug and loosed him into the park. There was a Harrods van in the drive. I wondered if Lady Jennifer knew it was there and I decided that she did, because the front door was standing open.

I lit the boiler in the feed room and put in the barley and the linseed and the water to cook very gently so that it would be ready to make into a mash when the horses came in from hunting. I filled hay nets and water buckets, I tidied the tack room and I swept the yard and I wondered why I felt flattened.

161

Did everyone who suddenly found themselves in possession of everything they had ever wanted feel flattened? I didn't know. I went to get changed for the jumble sale.

On our way to the village hall, we met Henrietta, riding home on the black horse. It was only half past one, so I knew that something must be wrong.

"He's a bit lame," she explained. "So I thought I had better bring him back."

My heart sank. The horses were going down like ninepins. Now there were only two hirelings left out of six, and one of those had only one eye. I couldn't imagine how the Fanes were going to get through the season. I jumped out of the shooting brake to look at the black horse's legs. I knew it couldn't be thrush causing the lameness because his feet were now completely clean and sound.

Henrietta had said nothing at all about my notice and I had found this hard to understand because I had expected a scene. "There's really no need to fuss," she said in an irritated tone, as I ran my hands down his legs and felt his hooves for heat. "He's probably just stepped on a flint or something. I'll look at him properly when I get him home."

"I can't find anything wrong with him," I said, puzzled. "If you could trot him up the lane for a little way, I might be able to see where the trouble is."

"Elaine!" Lady Jennifer shrilled anxiously. "We must not delay a *moment* longer, or we shall be *terribly* late!"

"You'd better go," Henrietta said hastily.

I jumped back into the shooting brake, still watching the black horse for any clue to his unsoundness. Henrietta rode him towards the Hall. He broke into an anxious trot, impatient for his stable and his supper. He trotted remarkably well for a lame horse.

Outside the village hall, a queue of determined looking women had formed. When the doors were opened they raced for the stalls and everything seemed to fly into the air at once. I had no idea that a jumble sale was such hard work. We worked flat out all afternoon and our tins of silver overflowed.

"You won't be expected to lift a *finger* in the stables this evening," Lady Jennifer promised. "The girls will do everything. You look absolutely *exhausted*. I can't begin to tell you what a *marvellous* help you have been."

At the end of the sale, when Lady Jennifer had collected all the tins and was seated at a trestle table counting the piles of silver, surrounded by a bevy of jubilant ladies, I wandered outside to get some fresh air. It was beginning to get dark as I walked slowly down to the village green, nursing my inexplicable emptiness. I stood on the grass remembering the morning of the opening meet, and like an echo, I heard the sound of the hunt returning to the kennels.

I moved into the shadow of a tree and I watched them pass by in the fading light. The horses clopped past the shadowy cottages on lengthened reins and hounds ambled beside them with lowered sterns. The young entry must have been there, although I wouldn't have known which they were, Forster was there, and William, and the Huntsman, with the horn tucked between the buttons of his coat. And following them home came Brenda on her pink-nosed cob, and Doreen on her pony, and further behind still came Nigella on Nelson and Mr McLoughlin on the bad-tempered chestnut. They all looked very contented and companionable, and the lights pricked out from the cottages around the green, and nobody saw me, under the tree.

17

Another Legend

"Harry!" I called. "Harry Sabin! Are you there?" The dirt yard was deserted. There was nobody tinkering with the cattle waggon. I wondered if I was too early, if Harry Sabin was still in bed. I had set off at six thirty; before anyone at the Hall had been up, in order to feed and muck out the cobs, and make the spare box ready for the bay gelding at Winter Place. Then, with the manilla envelope in my pocket, I had driven the shooting brake to Harry Sabin's yard, hoping to ride the bay gelding to his new home, and still be back at the Hall in time to help with morning stables. I shouted again.

This time the door of the scruffy patch-roofed cottage opened and Harry Sabin shuffled out in his carpet slippers.

"Harry," I said. "I'm sorry to be so early, but I've brought you the money."

"Now, young lady," he said cautiously, rubbing his unshaven chin. "Which money is that?"

"You know perfectly well," I said. "It's the money for the bay gelding. You wanted it in cash. Before Monday."

"Ah," he said in an uncomfortable tone. "The bay gelding."

"Harry," I said. "The bay gelding is *here*?" Some part of my insides tied themselves into a nasty little knot. The bay gelding wasn't in the stable with the slip rail because it was now occupied by a big grey horse. Neither had he been visible in the top field with the dealer's stock. I pulled the manilla envelope out of my pocket and my heart began to beat heavily under my jersey. "We made a bargain, Harry," I said. "Fifteen hundred pounds in cash. You said you would give me until Monday. You *promised*."

"Well now," Harry Sabin said, embarrassed. "That's a little bit difficult, that is."

"What's difficult about it, Harry," I asked. "Where is the bay gelding?"

Harry Sabin looked down at his greasy carpet slippers. He stuck his hands into the pockets of his warehouse coat. He shrugged his wiry shoulders and he looked at me with his foxy brown eyes. "That's a little hard to say, Miss," he admitted.

"Oh, Harry," I said, agonized. "You've sold him, haven't you? After we had made a bargain; after you had given me time to find the money!" I couldn't believe he could have done such a thing. "Oh, *Harry*," I groaned. "And it isn't even *Monday* yet!"

"I never thought you'd get the money," he muttered. "And that's the truth of it."

"But Felix Hissey put up the money," I said in despair. "Felix Hissey came to try him. He was going to be my sponsor, surely you *knew*!"

"Felix Hissey never said nothing to me," Harry Sabin said. "Neither did you for that matter, and Felix Hissey got his leg broke. That didn't look as if he'd be interested after that. That didn't look promising."

"Where did you sell him to?" I demanded. "Who bought him?" I had wild ideas of going after them, trying to buy him back.

166

"I didn't ask no questions," Harry Sabin said. "The waggon had London plates on it."

I could see it was no use. "How much did they give you?" I asked him bitterly. "As a matter of interest, how much did they pay?"

"Sixteen hundred," he said, adding in a disparaging tone, "That was a better offer than yours, anyhow."

It seemed incredibly, unbelievably unjust that I should have lost the bay gelding for a hundred pounds; when a hundred pounds, or two or even three, would have been nothing, absolutely nothing, to Felix Hissey.

"Did they pay you in cash?" I said, catching at a straw. If they hadn't, I wondered if I might be able to trace them through their bank.

"I told you," Harry Sabin said sullenly. "I don't take no cheques."

It was hopeless. I walked slowly back across the yard to the shooting brake. I was completely stunned. Numb. I might have driven away without another word, but as I passed the ramshackle building, the grey horse nickered to me and I recognized The Comet's familiar greeting. The Comet!

"Harry!" I yelled. "What the devil is The Comet doing in your stable?"

"He's going to Warners," he said defensively. "Instead of the bay gelding."

"Oh no," I shouted. "He is NOT!" Suddenly, I could hardly see straight. I turned round on Harry Sabin and pushed him aside. I grabbed the bridle out of the shooting brake and flung away the slip rail. I yanked the bridle on to The Comet, who was so astonished that he had his mouth open even

167

before I got the browband past his nose. I was livid. My anger exploded into flashes of bright, bloody red. I was boiling with anger, and my fury was directed against Harry Sabin; the people who had deprived me of the bay gelding; the Fanes. Everybody. I dragged The Comet out of the stable and vaulted on to his back.

"Harry Sabin," I hissed. "You are a bent, slippery, double-tongued rogue!" I clapped my heels into The Comet's sides and he flew out of the yard in a cloud of dirt. Down the track and out on to the lane The Comet flew, round the corner and across the verge and along the tarmac. Faster and faster went The Comet, but I didn't care. I couldn't have stopped him and I didn't even try. Up the Hall drive The Comet thundered, swerving under the clock arch and skidding to a halt on the cobbles.

Henrietta was crossing the yard with a hay net. "Goodness," she said in a calm voice. "You've brought The Comet back. Whatever for?"

"Whatever for!" I shouted. "*Whatever for*? Because he was going to Warners, that's what *for*!"

"I thought you knew," Henrietta said. "I was sure I had mentioned it." She frowned.

"You can't send a horse like The Comet to a *sale*," I cried. "He's dangerous! He's a bolter! If you declare it, he'll go for meat! If you don't, they'll find out and they'll sue you; then they'll shoot him anyway!"

Henrietta shrugged. "He's no use to us," she said. "What else can we do with him?"

"You can sell him to me," I said furiously. "*I'll* buy him."

Nigella appeared. "Buy The Comet?" she said,

astonished. "Why should you want to buy The Comet?"

"And anyway," Henrietta enquired. "How will you pay?"

This was the last straw. "I'll pay with the wages I should have had from you!" I cried. "With what I should have been paid for sorting out your messy yard! For caring for your crocked up horses! I'll pay for The Comet with the money you owe me!" I howled.

"Will it be enough?" Nigella said cautiously. "You have only been here a month."

"If it isn't enough," I told her furiously. "I shall make it up somehow."

"Since you are buying The Comet," Henrietta said coolly, "he had better stay. Perhaps you should put him in his old stable."

I slid off The Comet. My legs almost gave way as I hit the cobbles; they seemed to be made of jelly. The Comet clopped beside me across the yard. I was trembling all over. I told myself that this was the end. I had had enough of the Fanes. I couldn't stand them for a minute longer; they were driving me insane. I would take The Comet to Winter Place. I would pack my case and I would ride there; The Comet and I would go together. I wouldn't even stay to work my notice; we would go today. This morning. Now.

I opened the door of The Comet's stable. It was already occupied. By Harry Sabin's bay gelding.

My whole world went round and round. I thought I must be going mad. I clutched The Comet for support.

"We knew you would be pleased," Nigella said. "At least, we hoped you would be."

"Although you rather spoiled things," Henrietta said severely. "We didn't expect you to leave so early. There was to have been a proper presentation; with Mummy and Doreen and Brenda; and even Mr McLoughlin was going to come."

I went into the stable. I felt the bay gelding's satiny neck and I touched his mane. It was true. He was real. He was standing in The Comet's stable.

"How . . ." I stuttered. "How . . . did you find the money?"

"Henrietta sold her secretaire," Nigella said. "It was the only way. It was the only thing we had left."

"It was nothing," Henrietta said diffidently. "People don't really have dowries any more. It's a pretty old-fashioned idea."

"But Henrietta," I said weakly. "You *loved* your secretaire."

She shrugged. "It was only a piece of furniture, after all."

Suddenly, it all began to fall into place; the Harrods van, the black horse's invisible lameness, Lady Jennifer insisting that I should help at the jumble sale, the Thunder and Lightning horsebox with its London plates; even Harry Sabin must have known.

"You were all in the plot!" I exclaimed. "You all schemed against me!"

"Not against you," Nigella corrected. "*For* you."

"And you schemed as well," Henrietta pointed out. "When it came to getting what you wanted, you schemed more than anybody."

I couldn't argue; but the Fanes, through their interference, had put me in a very difficult position.

"I don't want you to think I don't appreciate what you have done," I said, agonized. "But the situation isn't as simple as it looks. I *have* to take Felix Hissey's job, because he has broken a leg and he can't look after his horses. I *promised*!"

"You must do as you wish, of course," Nigella said. "But when Mummy went to see Mr Hissey yesterday morning, he was very understanding. He said that he wouldn't hold you to your side of the bargain if, in return, we agreed to livery his horses free until Christmas."

"And to be perfectly honest," Henrietta said. "It suits us very well, because we are extremely short of horses."

"You don't look all that pleased," Nigella said anxiously. "I hope you don't think we have gone too far. We only did it because we didn't want you to leave. We thought you didn't really want to leave either, that all you really wanted was the bay gelding."

"And now that you've got the bay gelding," Henrietta added with a touch of her customary malice, "perhaps you would be good enough to take The Comet back to Harry Sabin."

"The Comet isn't going back to Harry Sabin," I said heatedly. "He isn't going to Warners!"

"Oh no," Henrietta said. "I forgot. You are going to buy him with the money we owe you."

I stared at her in exasperation. I couldn't tell by her expression whether she was joking or not. I felt upset and disorientated. The Fanes had turned my life upside down and inside out, and I didn't know if they had done it to please me, or to suit their own convenience. I just couldn't work it out. I was dumbfounded.

"Do have a ride," Nigella said. "I'll go and get some tack." She returned with a Thunder and Lightning saddle and bridle and she put them on the bay gelding. "Please notice," she said, as she led him into the yard, "that we've had him shod." His shoes were buffed and polished, curiously bright.

"By a stroke of luck," Henrietta said. "His feet were the same size as the old bay mare's."

I was beginning to feel rather ill. The morning had assumed an unreal quality. Nigella legged me into the saddle and we progressed out of the yard, towards the park.

"We've even given him a name," Henrietta informed me. "We were going to call him Little Legend, after the old bay mare; but as he isn't so little, we decided to call him Another instead."

"Another?" I said. Even in my dazed state of mind, it seemed an odd name for a horse.

"Another Legend," Nigella explained. "It seemed a good name for an eventer. You must admit, it does have a nice ring to it."

I had to admit that it did. The Fanes dragged open the park gate. Then they perched on some sagging rails and looked expectant.

"We can't wait to see you in action," Nigella said admiringly. "He really is magnificent. He's every bit as beautiful as the bay mare. We never thought," she added wonderingly, "that we would ever own an eventer."

"He'll be a marvellous advertisement for the yard," Henrietta said. "We might get more event

172

horses as liveries. He could open up a whole new world for us."

"But he isn't an event horse yet," I pointed out. "He might not even make it. Preparation takes years and it is very expensive. I don't think you realize quite how much it is going to cost. We shall need saddlery and show jumps, we shall need to build a cross country course and mark out a dressage arena. There will be professional training to pay for, and entry fees and transport. An event horse costs a *fortune* to produce." The prospect of being sponsored by the Fanes in their precarious financial position was terrifying. "How shall we possibly afford it?" I asked them. "Without Felix Hissey to pay the bills?"

"Oh, don't worry," Nigella said comfortingly. "I expect we shall manage somehow; we always have."

"But how?" I wanted to know. "*How*?"

"I don't know," she admitted. "But we've got the horse, and that's a start."

"And we've got a business," Henrietta reminded me. "More or less. Such as it is."

"So do ride him for us," Nigella pleaded. "We're just *dying* to see how he goes."

I turned the bay gelding away from the fence and trotted him across the park. I was too stupefied to appreciate how he bent his glossy neck, how the light wind lifted his silky mane, and how he threw out his toes for the sheer joy of being alive. I was too shaken by the traumas of the morning to realize that I didn't have to go to Winter Place, that I had my eventing prospect, and that life with the Fanes would never be dull, never be lonely.

I was too preoccupied with the difficulties that lay

ahead. Hans Gelderhol had prophesied disappointment and frustration, he had warned that I would be bruised and struggling; but he had not promised me failure and I knew that I must cling to that.

Like learning about riding, he had told me, life will be bumpy at first. All these dreams, these fine ideals, they will be damaged; it is in the way of things. If you are ever to succeed, you must be steadfast. You must hold very, very tight to your dream.

Well, it had been bumpy all right, and there would be more and bigger bumps to come. But as I rode across the old turf on Another Legend, owned and sponsored by the Honorable Nigella and Henrietta Fane of Havers Hall, High Suffolk, I was holding very tight to my dream.

A Hoof in the Door

Caroline Akrill

For Elaine
in memory of a very similar accident

1

A Driving Ambition

"You don't think, Elaine," Nigella Fane said in an enquiring tone, "that The Comet is beginning to step out a bit?"

Almost before the words were out of her mouth, the dog cart hit a stone on the lane and bounced in the air. Nigella grabbed the side of the cart, and I snatched up the reins which had hitherto been lying unattended across The Comet's dappled rump. Lulled by the rhythmic clopping of hooves, the rumbling of wheels, the creaking of leatherwork, and the blissful warmth of the spring sunshine, I hadn't been paying any attention to the horse at all. I had been admiring the scenery, yet I had quite failed to notice that the scenery was slipping past at an accelerated rate.

I stood up in the cart and yanked the slack of the reins through the terrets. "Steady boy," I said warningly, "slow down now." But The Comet wasn't listening. His ears were set ominously for the way ahead and they didn't even twitch in my direction.

"I told you we should have fixed him with a bearing rein," Henrietta Fane said in an irritated voice from the back seat. "If he really gets going there'll be no holding him. You know what he's like."

I knew only too well, since The Comet was my

horse. I had foolishly accepted him in lieu of unpaid wages after an argument with the Fanes.

"People haven't used bearing reins since the days of Black Beauty," I told Henrietta crossly. I hauled uselessly at The Comet's cast-iron mouth. "They're probably illegal."

"A pity," Henrietta commented acidly, as the cart began to sway from side to side in a discomforting manner, "because The Comet obviously needs one."

I made no reply to this, being almost rocked off my balance. I lurched back into my seat and wedged my feet firmly against the front of the cart in order to get a better grip on the reins. As I sawed furiously at the grey horse's Liverpool bit, I wondered if anyone else in the history of horsemanship had ever been run away with at the trot; because between the wide-banked ditches thick with cowslips, under the vast and luminous East Anglian sky, The Comet was certainly running away now. His neck was set solid, his head was down, his rump was swinging in a determined manner, and his front legs were shooting out like pistons, achieving elevation and suspension worthy of a dressage horse.

"Perhaps you should try the brake," Nigella suggested. Her voice was calm, but the knuckles of one hand showed white on the outside rail. With the other hand she clutched her hat. It was a small, red, satin pill-box with a polka-dot veil. Nigella considered it just the thing for driving.

I looked round for anything which resembled a brake. I had found the ramshackle cart in the gloom of the disued coach-house behind the stables at Havers Hall, where it had been mouldering away for decades. If it had ever had a brake, it certainly didn't have one now.

"There isn't a brake," I said helplessly. "There's nothing to control the speed with at all, apart from the reins."

"Then kindly tell that to The Comet," Henrietta yelped, "because he doesn't appear to know, and I'm not enjoying this very much!" I wouldn't have changed even my own unenviable position for Henrietta's. She was riding with her back to us on a fragile little dickey seat suspended above the lane, with her feet jammed against a wobbly foot-rest.

By means of a herculean effort, I managed to get back on my feet in order to set the whole of my weight and strength against The Comet, leaning backwards on the reins like a Roman Charioteer. Eight stones and three pounds of dead weight did nothing to impede the grey horse's progress whatsoever, particularly as one of the reins snapped almost immediately. I hurtled backwards, almost knocking Henrietta off the dickey seat. Henrietta was still screeching when a car came round the bend.

The car braked furiously and skidded. It swerved out of our path and mounted the bank in a desperate and noble attempt to avoid taking off our outside wheel. As we bounced against the opposite bank I caught a momentary glimpse of the driver's ashen face, before The Comet's ironshod hooves carried us relentlessly on.

"I don't want to add to your troubles," Nigella gasped, "but the wheel on my side is behaving in a very peculiar fashion.'

I had time for one last despairing heave at The Comet's plank-like jaw, before being completely

9

thrown off my feet by an appalling jolt and a rib-cracking rebound, followed by a prolonged splintering crash. The Comet, the lane, the banks and the sky seemed to spin round like a kaleidoscope, and when I opened my eyes again I was lying amongst the cowslips and the rogue wheel was bowling along the lane quite on its own and almost out of sight.

The Comet stood serenely on the tarmac attached to two broken shafts. Nigella, her pill-box slightly askew, stood at his head, surveying the remains of the dog cart which were scattered across the lane like kindling. "Well," she commented, as much to the horse as to anyone. "That seems to be the end of that. I can't say I'm sorry."

Henrietta scrambled up from the ditch, rubbing her elbow and looking murderous. Her anorak was split from top to bottom and her wild, waist-length hair was stuck with twigs and bleached grasses. I lay where I had landed, wondering if I would ever walk again, much less achieve my ambition to become a leading light in the world of the Three Day Event. When I had recovered sufficient nerve to move my head, I found myself facing a poster nailed to the trunk of a stagheaded oak.

The Midvale and Westbury Hunt
POINT-TO-POINT
April 25th
First Race at 2 P.M.
Hon Sec O. T. V. Bloomfield
Shrubbery Farm, Kettleton

I sat up, discovering with a flood of relief that I seemed to have retained the use of my limbs. "Nigella," I said urgently, "I've just had an idea!"

10

Henrietta gave me a vicious look. She was examining a cut in her leg through a torn flap in her jeans, "Well, if you wouldn't mind," she said in a sour tone, "we would prefer not to listen to it. Breaking The Comet to harness so that we could give driving lessons was your idea, if you care to remember and it hasn't exactly been a roaring success; we might all have been killed."

"Yes, quite honestly, Elaine," Nigella said in a resigned tone, turning her attention from the shattered dog cart to the lacerated sides of her favourite stain-laced, tap-dancing shoes, "it might be advisable to wait until we have recovered from the effects of this idea, before you suggest anything else."

"But look at the poster," I implored them. "We could enter The Comet for the Point-to-Point!"

There was a silence whilst the Fanes looked from me to the poster, to The Comet; then, "How much money do you get if you win first prize at a Point-to-Point?" Henrietta asked.

"I don't know," I admitted, "but quite a lot I should imagine. Hundreds probably."

"If we could win just enough to buy Legend a dressage saddle," Nigella said thoughtfully, "and some jump stands with proper cups and pins . . ."

"The Comet *must* have qualified," I said. He's sure to be eligible. He's hunted for most of the season, and he goes like a bomb. Nothing, *nobody*, can catch The Comet once he gets into top gear."

We all looked speculatively at the grey horse, weighing up his chances. The Comet was embarrassed to find that he had suddenly become the centre of our attention. He raised his head in the unbecoming Liverpool bit and the blinkers, and he

11

stared intently into the far landscape, as if he had unexpectedly caught a glimpst of someone he knew.

"But who will ride hm?" Henrietta said. "Which one of us will race?"

"Oh, I must," I said firmly. "After all, it's my event horse we are financing."

This was not strictly true, because Legend was actually owned by the Fanes. They had bought him when they had realized that if I didn't find a sponsor to provide me with a potential event horse, I would leave them at a crucial time, when only our combined efforts had saved their floundering livery yard from bankruptcy.

"It can't be you, Elaine," Nigella pointed out in her careful way, "that wouldn't do at all. Imagine the conequences if you had an accident. If you broke an arm or a leg our event horse wouldn't have a rider and that would be the end of our sponsorship. No," she decided, "it will have to be me. I will ride The Comet."

I didn't like the sound of this. It was true that Nigella had ridden The Comet more often than any of us, but while hunting last season, he had bolted with her and galloped straight into the river, practically drowning them both. I still saw Nigella's face in my nightmares, blanched and frozen, as the grey horse thundered unwaveringly towards the river bank.

"I think we'll forget about the Point-to-Point," I said. Already I was sorry I had mentioned it.

But the Fanes had taken to the idea and they were not to be put off.

"We certainly *won't* forget about it," Henrietta declared. She set about removing the broken shafts from the tugs on The Comet's driving pad. "It's a stupendous idea! All Nigella has to do is sit tight and steer and let The Comet run himself out. Then she can pull up and collect the money."

Even Nigella raised her eyebrows at this over-simplification of Point-to-Point racing. "But at least I shall be racing over a properly laid-out course," she said, "and it will be properly organized and stewarded. It won't be at all like the rough-and-tumble of the hunting field." She straightened her pill-box and slapped The Comet confidently on his neck. I knew from experience that there was no point in further argument.

We returned to the hall in ignominy, bowling the wheels of the cart like hoops, and leading The Comet up the pot-holey drive with his traces tied in knots at his sides like a farm horse returning from the fields. Against its backdrop of long-dead elms, Havers Hall looked grey and shabby in the sunshine. Its stucco was cracked, its brickwork was pitted, and its rows of windows were firmly shuttered against the rains of winter which had continued to seep in through the rotten woodwork.

The horses behind the sagging iron railings of the park raised their heads at the sound of the Comet's hooves. Ahead of them stretched a long idle summer of relaxation. There were three high-class horses belonging to our most valued clients, a pop group called Thunder and Lightning Limited. There was a thickset, pink-nosed, grey cob owned by Brenda, the Fanes' first-ever livery client, and there was a chest-nut pony which belonged to our half-witted, part-time stable help, Doreen. Apart from the liveries, there were also the Fanes' own collection of cut-price, equine misfits, the hirelings, who were rented out during the season to unsuspecting clients who fancied a day with the Midvale and Westbury Hunt. They were all there, made fat and contented by verdant spring grass; the mare-who-sometimes-slipped-a-stifle, the bad-tempered chestnut, Nelson, with his stitched-up eye socket, and the black-horse-who-never-stood-still. Amongst them I could see the dark bay gelding that was Legend, his summer coat already gleaming through on his shoulders and his flanks. I stopped and called to him and after a moment of hesitation, he left the others and ambled lazily towards the fence.

I rummaged in my pockets and came up with a few damp and unworthy horse nuts. Legend ate them without enthusiasm, then screwed up the end of his nose in disgust, displaying a row of short, yellow teeth.

In the precious few months that I had known him, the good-looking bay horse had proved himself to be everything I had hoped for. I had no way of knowing if I would ever manage to break into the distant, expensive and exclusive world of the Three Day Event, but I did know that I had found the perfect horse with which to try. Legend was the embodiment of all my hopes and all my ambitions. Ambitions, I reflected with a twinge of misgiving, that Nigella and The Comet were about to risk their necks for.

2

A Few Pounds Short

"These fences," Nigella commented, "look a bit big from the ground."

They did. Four feet of solid, black birch, as wide as they were high, in one instance flanked with a nine foot open ditch. Stouter hearts than Nigella's would have failed at the sight of them.

"If you're having second thoughts, there's still time to change your mind," I told her. "It isn't too late. We can easily scratch."

We stood on the Point-to-Point course with our hands stuffed into the pockets of our anoraks and the ever-present East Anglian wind numbing our cheeks. All around us the Point-to-Point Committee and the Hunt Supporters' Club were busily engaged in raking up birch clippings and strapping hurdles together to act as wings. The Clerk of the Course, clad in ancient sheepskins and threadbare cords, was hammering in signs proclaiming WINNERS' ENCLO-SURE, and FIRST, SECOND and THIRD; and in a convenient hollow below us which theoretically should have been out of the wind but somehow managed not to be, men in duffle-jackets fought the catering marquee, the canvas slapping and billowing like the sails on a galleon.

"There's no question of jibbing now," Henrietta said sharply. "The horse is qualified, fit and entered. We're not pulling out for anything."

"As the owner of the horse, I think I'm entitled to make the decisions," I pointed out, irritated by the way Henrietta had assumed control of the situation. "It isn't actually your affair."

"As the owner of the eventer we are supposed to be financing," Henrietta snapped, "it's more my affair than anybody's."

"And as the rider of the horse, and the person who is more involved than either of you," Nigella put in, "I think you should both shut up."

She set off resolutely to walk the course which consisted of sixteen fences over three and three-quarter miles of undulating flint-studded clay, her beautiful, brown hair streaming out from beneath a knitted purple helmet, pulled down firmly over her ears. Nigella was taking the race very seriously and had been out running before breakfast every day for a week. Henrietta and I trailed along behind, feeling unfit.

At the open ditch we came upon William and Nick Forster, the two young whippers-in to the Midvale and Westbury Hunt. They were armed with rammers, spades and a wheel-barrow, and they were working their way round the course, filling in holes.

"You're not serious about racing the old grey?" William pushed his cap to the back of his ginger thatch and stared at Nigella as if she was mad.

"I certainly am," Nigella said. "And what is more, I shall probably win." She was dwarfed by the fences but her confidence was unshaken.

William was impressed but doubtful. "Well, the old horse does have a fair turn of speed when he likes," he allowed. "He definitely can travel."

"And he definitely can jump," Henrietta added,

16

launching herself down into the clay-walled ditch. "He *never* stops. He's as brave as a lion."

I looked at the dark, forbidding fence with the gaping yellow ditch behind it, and I thought that The Comet needed to be.

Forster didn't speak to us. He just continued to thump at a displaced sod of turf and he kept his face turned away. He had avoided me for several months after an embarrassing scene which had involved the Fanes. He made no secret of the fact that he thought I was crazy to work for them. He had wanted me to give in my notice, and he had even helped me find another job with a good wage and the prospect of an event horse thrown in. But the Fanes had foiled him by buying Legend, and I had lost the incentive to leave. I wanted to tell Forster that I had been grateful for his help and say that perhaps we could carry on where we had left off; but I didn't have the nerve, and anyway, the Fanes would have overheard. They disapproved of Forster because of his racy reputation, and considered him to be an unsuitable and unsettling influence.

So I stood, awkward and silent, whilst William kept a covert eye on Henrietta, who was his secret passion, and the Fanes in their knitted helmets energetically paced out the ditch in a snowstorm of kapok emerging from the split in Henrietta's anorak. The Fanes shopped for their clothes at *Oxfam* and *Help the Aged*. I wouldn't actually have liked to wear Nigella's white quilted ski-pants which didn't fit and bagged at the seat, and had a lot of zippers in unexpected places, nor could I have worn Henrietta's electric-blue, satin disco trousers with black leg-warmers on top, but in my conventional groom's winter uniform of lovat-green Husky, cords and Hunter wellingtons, with my pale, straight, uninteresting hair stuffed under a tweed cap, I suddenly felt unutterably boring and drab. No wonder Forster wasn't interested in me. I turned to go, thinking that I would make my way back to the Fanes' delapidated shooting brake, when: "How's the event horse, Elaine?" Forster asked.

"The event horse is OK," I said, flustered, "the event horse is fine."

"Except that it's a little short of funds, and the Fanes have got to do damned fool-hardy things like racing the old grey to finance it." Forster's voice was friendly enough, but the final thump he gave the turf was a vicious one.

"There isn't any cash," I admitted. "After the hunting season the income from the yard has dropped off to practically nothing." There was no point in pretending. I tried not to look at Forster. I knew all about his rather insolent mouth, the way his black hair curled over the back of his collar, and the thick curve of lashes over his blue eyes.

"And did you really expect that there ever would be any cash?" Forster enquired. "Knowing the Fanes as you do, did you honestly expect it?" He threw the rammer at the wheel-barrow where it landed with an almighty crash. "Honestly, Elaine," he said in an exasperated voice, "I said you were a fool to go and work for them in the first place, but I never imagined you would let them trap you into working for them for nothing for ever."

Henrietta had noticed our conversation and immediately decided that it was time to leave.

"Elaine!" she shouted, "we're going back to the car! Are you coming?"

"Anyhow," Forster went on, as the spade clattered into the wheel-barrow beside the rammer, "I hope you're going to try for the Hissey Scholarship this year."

I waved at Henrietta to let her know that I would follow. "Try for the what?" I said.

"Felix Hissey's training scholarship for event riders," Forster said. "He's always given a couple every year, but this year he's giving more, and it's being properly organized through the BHS. You have to be eighteen and have a promising young event horse to participate." He paused and raised his shoulders. "Well, you're eighteen, and you've got a promising young event horse . . ."

"I've also got the Fanes," I pointed out, "and Legend is their property, I can't just do as I like." As if to reinforce this, there was a further shriek from Henrietta.

"*Elaine!*" she yelled. Do come *on!*"

"Anyway," I said, remembering, "Felix Hissey probably wouldn't even let me try for it; after all, I did turn down his job."

"Turning down his job won't enter into it," Forster said. "Felix Hissey doesn't do the choosing any more, it's all done by the BHS, he just puts up the money."

I had never seriously considered trying for a training scholarship before. Now it seemed to be the perfect solution. So perfect, in fact, that there just had to be a fly in the ointment somewhere, and I rather suspected that the fly would turn out to be the Fanes.

"I'll get you the details, anyway," Forster said. "I might be able to give them to you at the Point-to-Point."

"But please don't say anything to the Fanes about it," I begged him. "I shall have to ask them first, and they might not like the idea." I ran off up the course towards the Fanes, pleased on two counts. Forster was speaking to me again and there was a chance, if remote, of a training scholarship. Things were looking up.

On the way home we made a detour in order to visit *Help the Aged*, because Nigella needed a suitable jersey to race in.

"It's Mummy's duty day," Henrietta said. "She's sure to find us something."

Lady Jennifer Fane was equally confident. "But I *know* I shall be able to put my hand on the *very* thing!" she trilled. "You can't imagine how many jerseys people bring to the shop, we turn away simply *hundreds*!"

She flung open several drawers, but all she could find was a pale green angora trimmed with a little pocket and a button.

"No, no," Henrietta said. "That won't do at all. We need a big, thick jersey with a stripe across the front or hoops on the sleeves."

Lady Jennifer looked at us in genuine despair. She was tall and thin and highly strung, and she had Given Her Life to Charity. "I'm *frightfully* sorry," she said. "I can't offer you *anything* with stripes or hoops." We might have been customers in Harrods.

"We really need a man's jersey," Nigella said. She flicked along a rail of dubious looking garments and discovered a pair of ginger velvet knickerbockers. She pulled them out and surveyed them with admiration tinged with regret. "Size eight! Could anyone possibly be that size?"

Lady Jennifer disappeared through a bead curtain and returned bearing a red jersey of immense proportions. It was clumsily knitted and mis-shapen, but she laid it out on the glass-topped counter as if it was the finest cashmere. "I really don't know if this would be of the *slightest* use to you at all," she said. "But it is the most *marvellously* warm colour, and I do have another in the most *heavenly* shade of blue."

"What we really need is a two-tone jersey," I explained. "It's for the Point-to-Point. Nigella ought to have racing colours in red and blue to match the silks on my cross-country hat."

Lady Jennifer had done her best, but now she looked defeated. A lot of wispy, grey hair had escaped from her unwieldy french pleat. "I haven't got a red *and* blue jersey, Elaine," she sighed, "only a red jersey and a blue jersey."

"I know what to do," Henrietta declared. "We can pull the sleeves off the red one, and fix them on to the blue one." She leaned over the red jersey and picked experimentally at the sleeve joint, to ascertain that all this was possible.

"Oh," Lady Jennifer shrilled in alarm, "I *really* don't think . . ."

"We'll buy them both," Nigella interposed hastily, "naturally."

"And *naturally*," I said in a low voice to Nigella, "you have some money to pay for them, because I haven't."

"It's all right," Nigella said reassuringly, "we can probably open an account."

"We don't have accounts at *Help the Aged*," Lady Jennifer said sharply.

"Perhaps we could do a swop then," Nigella suggested. "Your jerseys for ours."

Lady Jennifer frowned. She wanted to help us, but her loyalty to The Cause was being severely stretched. "Not Henrietta's," she said firmly. "Henrietta is so *frightfully* hard on jerseys. She picks at the wrists *constantly*; she always did, even as an *infant*."

This proved to be true, because when Henrieta took off her anorak, her jersey was unpicked practically to mid-arm.

"Mine's all right anyway," Nigella said. She pulled off her slightly discoloured Arran and replaced it with the red jumper. Apologetically, she added, "We shall have to have yours as well, Elaine."

I hadn't expected this. I was fond of my good navy guernsey. It had been a Christmas present from my father and I was loath to part with it.

"Come on, Elaine," Henrietta said impatiently. "Hand it over."

Unhappily, I peeled off my Husky.

The Comet stood at the start of our improvised Point-to-Point course as if hewn from stone. With his noble bearing and his distinguished good looks, he could have been a top-flight steeplechaser. But Nigella, in the quilted ski-pants, to which, as a concession to horsemanship, she had added jodhpur boots frilled at the ankles with withered elastic, and

22

a hard hat with a ventilator button missing, looked anything but a jockey.

Henrietta raised the flag, fashioned by means of a twig and a small, white, housemaid's apron, discovered during the ritual laying of rat-poison in the attics, and a legacy of the Fanes' former gentility.

"Once round," she commanded, "at half speed." But it was clear, once the flag had dropped and the first furlong had been covered, the horse had other ideas.

The Comet galloped like an express train with an unrelenting thunder of hooves and his yellowing tail streaming like a banner behind him. He flew unerringly over the wild, unrimmed hedge, bore onwards in a wide half-circle across the park, and took, without the least falter in his stride, the log pile which was part of Legend's painfully built cross-country course. After this he made an unscheduled turn to the left, and despite Nigella's determined efforts to screw his head round to the right, he continued at a powerful speed towards the stable yard and the comfortable privacy of his own loose box.

"Henrietta," I said, "what happens if he does that tomorrow?" I thought of the network of lanes with their slippery tarmac, the jaunting gin-and-tonic traffic, and the fast running river which had flooded its banks, all of which lay between The Comet and his stable; the stable where he stood like a statue for hours and hours and dreamed his mysterious dreams. Despite the fact that the grey horse was lofty and self-absorbed, and feigned indifference to man or beast, or perhaps even because of it, I felt something catch hold of my heart and give it a little twist.

"How can it possibly happen tomorrow?" Henrietta said scornfully. "He's hardly likely to make a bolt for home, because he won't know which direction to take; he won't know where he is! After all," she added, as she tossed away the twig and tied the apron round her waist with a flourish, "he isn't a homing pigeon."

We slung The Comet's saddle from the spring balance we used for weighing hay nets in the barn. It weighed twenty-five pounds. Nigella had weighed herself on the scales outside the village chemist, and even with five extra jumpers and her long riding boots, she couldn't make more than nine stone two pounds. The starting weight, which included the saddle, irons, leathers, girth and breastplate, was eleven and a half stones.

"Weights," I told them. "We shall be expected to provide weights."

"What sort of weights?" Henrietta wanted to know.

"The sort of weights you carry when you're eventing," I said. "In a weight cloth with pouches on each side, and straps to attach it to the saddle."

"What are they made of, these weights?" Nigella wondered.

"Lead," I informed them. "Lead pipe normally, you cut it up into pound and half-pound pieces, and then you hammer them flat."

"We haven't any lead pipe," Nigella said, dismayed. "I'm sure of it.

"Can't we use something else?" Henrietta suggested. "Sugar or something?"

We lapsed into giggles, thinking of The Comet struggling round the Point-to-Point course with panniers full of sugar packets.

"There must be *something* else we can use," Henrietta said.

"No," I assured her, "it has to be lead."

Nigella subsided on to a convenient hay bale. She looked weary and oddly rounded in all the jerseys, topped off by the awful blue one with the red sleeves. "Where on earth are we going to get lead from, at this time of night?" she sighed.

We all fell silent, thinking about it, then: "I think I know," said Henrietta, and she vanished into the darkness with a torch.

"I expect she's seen a piece of pipe lying around somewhere," Nigella said, but when Henrietta returned, it wasn't with a piece of pipe.

Where she had found the wide strip of lead flashing with the prettily scalloped edges, neither Nigella or I thought fit to enquire. But the next time it rained, I noticed that the little portico with the doric columns and the pointed roof which sheltered the main entrance to the hall leaked like a sieve.

3

A Maiden's Race

There was a flurry of race-cards as I led The Comet into the paddock.

"Hold on a minute, miss!" A steward ran after me in order to tie a number on my arm. He looked at The Comet in admiration. "Nice horse, miss," he said, "got a powerful hindquarter on him."

The powerful hindquarter was the result of dragging half a tree round the park as part of being broken to harness, but there was no time to go into this with the steward. "You mind you don't get him kicked, miss," he warned. "Some of these beggars are over the top." Other horses were piling up behind. One of them ran backwards and stood on end, pulling the leading-rein out of its attendants grasp. There was a short interval of chaos until it was recaptured.

I led The Comet along the inside of the rails. Some of the other runners in the Ladies' Race were already parading, sidling along with their tails up, rolling their eyes and snatching at their bits, upset by the atmosphere of excitement, the proximity of the jostling crowd, and the hoarse shouts of the bookmakers. The Comet was unmoved by it all. He stalked along, looking regal. People looked him up hastily as he passed them by.

"Good-looking grey, what's its number?"

"Grand sort of animal that."

"Number twenty-two. The Comet."

"My God," somebody else exclaimed, aghast. "It's the Fanes' old grey! It's unstoppable!"

In the middle of the paddock, Nigella waited in her red and blue. Henrietta stood beside her with the saddlery. She looked unfamiliar and even vaguely fashionable in one of Lady Jennifer's ancient tweed suits which dated from the New Look. When the steward had finally managd to get all the runners forward, he waved us in to saddle up. There were nine runners, all bays and chestnuts. The Comet was the only grey.

Nigella looked pale but composed. She pulled off the paddock sheet and Henrietta put on the weight cloth, followed by the number cloth and the saddle. The Comet stood like a statue whilst I reached under his belly for the girths.

"Some of the others look a bit hot," Nigella remarked, taking in all the plunging and snorting going on around us.

"With a bit of luck they'll wear themselves out before they get to the start," Henrietta said. "I reckon Mrs Lydia Lane's horse is the one to watch."

Mrs Lydia Lane's horse was a massive foam-flecked bay, who pinned his ears back and lashed out as a groom pulled up the surcingle. Mrs Lydia Lane wore beautiful calf boots with silky trousers tucked into them like a Cossack, and a dark and glossy fur coat. She looked very glamorous.

"No wonder Nick Forster found her so attractive," Henrietta commented.

I didn't rise to this, being engaged in replacing the paddock sheet.

"It was the talk of the county, at the time,"

Henrietta went on. "There was quite a scandal. I do believe that her husband threatened to shoot him."

"I don't know why you are telling me all this," I said, flipping The Comet's tail over the fillet string. "It isn't as if I'm actually interested."

"Oh," Henrietta said innocently. "I thought you were."

It was not the moment to fall out with Henrietta. I led The Comet back into the walk-round. He may have been a bolter, but he was mine, and I was proud of him. He had taken everything in his implacable stride; the early preparation, the journey, the arrival and the unfamiliar surroundings, the noise and the bustle of the course; and now he sailed round the paddock with the demeanour of one who paraded in public every day of his life. He looked a wise, experienced, sensible and powerful horse, in fact just the kind the punters tend to fancy for the Ladies' Race. He had no breeding entered on the race-card, no impressive thoroughbred blood-lines, and no previous form whatsoever. He was just *The Comet. Grey Gelding. Breeding unknown. Aged.* But already the odds were shortening on the Tote from rank outsider to 8–1 against.

Buoyed up by the general excitement and the sense of occasion, I had lost most of my former uneasiness about the Point-to-Point, but now, through a gap in th crowd, I saw the winner of the last race being led down to the horse-boxes with distended nostrils, pumping sides and lowered head. His neck was black with sweat and there was blood on one of his hind legs. I was suddenly terribly afraid for The Comet.

"Turn your horses in please!" the steward

shouted. Everyone stopped on the perimeter of the ring and turned their horses' heads to the centre. Up on the number frame, Nigella's name and The Comet's number had appeared. Henrietta removed the paddock sheet for the last time and tightened the girths. She legged Nigella into the saddle. Nigella's hands were trembling as she took up the reins, but she still managed to give me a reassuring smile. "It'll be all right," she said. "Really."

Outside the paddock I unclipped the leading-rein and pulled it through The Comet's snaffle rings. "Nigella," I pleaded, "do take care. Please don't take any chances."

Mrs Lydia Lane's horse flew past us with an enormous bound which nearly unseated his jockey. Next to The Comet, the rider of a raw-boned chestnut took out her teeth and handed them to her attendant for safe-keeping. The huntsman, dressed in his scarlet with brass buttons flashing in the sunlight, rode forward to lead the parade of runners on to the course.

"Good luck!" Henrietta shouted after Nigella. "Make sure you're the first back!" She was bright-eyed and flushed with excitement. In contrast, Nigella looked cool and determined.

Mrs Lydia Lane's horse was the first to canter away towards the start, shaking its head, scattering froth like snow. The Comet cantered steadily; it was easy to distinguish the grey with the red and the blue.

"We'll find a good place to watch from," Henrietta said in an agitated voice. "Over there, up on the rise! We should be able to see the whole course from there!" She set off towards the rise at a run, dodging through knots of people.

"Here," Forster's voice said. "You might need these." He gave me some papers which I stuffed into my pocket, and he put a pair of binoculars into my hands. I tried to thank him, but he was gone, jumping into the Hunt Land Rover which bucketed after the runners to take up its position on the course.

I ran after Henrietta. My heart felt like a stone in my chest. I knew that horses were irretrievably injured at Point-to-Points, that in the back of the Hunt Land Rover there were green canvas screens put up to spare the feelings of the crowd; and that afterwards the owners went home with empty lorries and broken hearts. At that moment I loved The Comet more desperately than I had ever loved anything in the world, and I couldn't bear the thought of losing him.

"Henrietta," I cried wretchedly. "What if something awful happens?"

But Henrietta was beyond-hearing. "They're calling the roll," she exclaimed, "they're all lined up. The Comet's in the middle. They've already called Nigella, I saw her turn her head!"

The loudspeaker above our heads crackled into life. "They're under starter's orders," the commentator said.

Below us, beside the uneven line of fidgeting horses with the black fences stretching in front of them I saw the white flag rise. My heart started to pump violently, the flag dropped, and suddenly all the horses were galloping towards the first fence. The Comet was in the middle of a tight bunch. I didn't know much about Point-to-Pointing, but I knew that this was the worst possible place to be. I could imagine the thunder of hooves to the front, to the sides and behind. I could see the huge, black fence looming nearer with no room for error, yet with no possible way to see a stride into it. I closed my eyes and in the next few seconds my heart stopped beating altogether and I probably stopped breathing as well.

"They're all over the first," the commentator said.

Henrietta grabbed the binoculars. "He's lying third . . . It's a good place to be! Keep him steady, Nigella . . . Hold him back . . . They're spreading out a bit, good . . ."

I couldn't bear to watch, but then on the other hand, I couldn't bear not to. I saw the bunch of horses swing round to the next fence; they were not so close together now. The leaders jumped, one, two, and then the grey horse sailed over and made a perfect landing. The next horse fell. Uniforms appeared out of the crowd and carried off the jockey without the teeth. The raw-boned chestnut galloped gamely after the field, reins and stirrups flying.

"He's dropped to fourth," Henrietta said with disappointment in her voice, "the others are overtaking him."

The line of horses, strung out like a necklace, took the open ditch without mishap and completed the first circuit. At the next fence another horse fell. It scrambled to its feet and shook itself like a dog before setting off towards the horse-box park with several spectators in hot pursuit. The jockey limped back down the course, shaking her head at the St John's Ambulance Brigade. Mrs Lydia Lane's bay was going strongly in the lead, it looked a sure winner, and half way round the second and last circuit The Comet had fallen back to sixth.

"At least he's all right," I breathed, "even if he isn't going to get a place, he looks as if he's going to finish the course safely."

"Don't underestimate his chances," Henrietta said, "he's coming up!"

And The Comet was coming up! Now he was fifth, and suddenly he was fourth! Even from so far away it was plain to see that The Comet had taken the race into his own hands. Nigella was a mere passenger. She could no more hold him back than she could have held back a ten-ton truck with the brakes off. As we watched, the grey horse's stride settled into the familiar relentless gallop, the powerful hindquarters went to work, the iron neck stretched out; The Comet was away!

"He's third!" Henrietta yelled. "He's second!"

"But he'll never catch the bay!" I screeched. "He'll never do it!"

The crowd had begun to shout as Henrietta and I raced pell-mell down the side to the finish. We were there in time to hear the thunder of approaching hooves as the bay come round the bend, stretched out at a flying gallop, and coming up behind him was The Comet. On and on came The Comet with his raking stride, on and level with the bay, and as the crowd roared their approval, on and on came the grey and the blue and the red, into the lead and past the finishing post. But as Henrietta clutched my arm and screamed, "He's won!" The Comet galloped on and over the black birch fence, and was galloping

32

away over the next, with Nigella glued helplessly to the saddle like a wet rag.

"And it's the grey, it's number twenty-two, The Comet, with number eighteen in second place, and number twenty-five third . . ." the commentary tailed off in an uncertain manner. "I have got it right, haven't I?" the commentator was heard to say. "This was the second circuit?"

The crowd was flabbergasted. The cheers died on their lips. "Oh, *no*!" Henrietta shrieked in despair. "Stop him, Nigella! Stop him! You've got to weigh out! We'll be *disqualified*!"

The rest of the runners had pulled up and were staring in consternation after The Comet. Some looked uncertain as to whether or not they should follow.

"She's gone on," Mrs Lydia Lane's jockey said, "I'm going to lodge an objection." She turned the dripping bay and rode away towards the steward's tent.

Henrietta and I stood as if frozen to the ground, and all around us the arguments raged.

"If the horse has won, it's won, and that's that!"

"No, it has to weigh out immediately afterwards. If the jockey doesn't weigh out, the horse is disqualified. You can't argue with the rules!"

"The rules say the winner's the first horse past the post, there's no rule that says it can't go on to jump a few more fences if it wants to!"

"I tell you the prize will go to the bay, the grey will be disqualified, although if you ask me, it's a damned shame . . ."

Suddenly though, unbelievably, there was an outburst of delighted clapping and The Comet appeared, cantering back up the course, with Nigella still in the saddle. "Sorry," she panted apologetically. "Couldn't stop. Had to run him into a thicket."

I grabbed The Comet by his bridle and ran with him towards the steward's tent. The crowd surged along beside us determined to see fair play. Outside the tent Mrs Lydia Lane's jockey was haranguing the chief steward who had refused to accept her objection on the grounds that a "reasonable period of time" had not yet elapsed. The Comet had not been disqualified. He was cheered and applauded all the way to the winner's enclosure.

Nigella slid down from the saddle and fell against the hurdles. She was wet with sweat and her face was as red as her jumper. She staggered through the well-wishers towards the weighing-out. Somebody threw a rug over The Comet. The grey horse was steaming like a turkish bath. His nostrils were lined with vermilion and every vein stood out in high relief. His breath came in huge, sobbing gulps. I was never so proud of anything or anybody in the whole of my life.

The weighed-out signal was given, and Nigella appeared beside us with the saddlery. We walked The Comet slowly back to the horse-box. Henrietta pressed her face against his sodden neck. "I never imagined," she said, "that any horse of ours would ever win a Point-to-Point."

"Any horse of mine," I corrected her.

"What did you say?" Henrieta said, releasing The Comet.

"Any horse of mine," I repeated, "The Comet belongs to me."

"Well," Henrietta said dismissively, "in a manner of speaking."

"More than in a manner of speaking," I said. "I took The Comet instead of wages. You didn't want him. You were going to send him to Leicester Sales without a warranty. He would have ended up being knackered."

"Never mind about all that," Nigella said hastily. She remove The Comet's bridle and put on his headcollar. "Where did you get the binoculars?"

"Oh," I said, remembering, "they belong to the Hunt." I also remembered the papers in my pocket. I knew what they must be. Sooner or later I would have to tackle the Fanes about the scholarship, but not now, not today.

We sponged The Comet with warm water and disinfectant, and dried him with old towels. He let out a long, shuddering sigh and rubbed his face against Henrietta's tweeds. "Whoever would have thought," she commented, with a sly, sideways glance at me. "that any horse of Elaine's would have won a Point-to-Point?"

4

Training the Event Horse

"Two hundred and seventy pounds is an awful lot of money for a dressage saddle," Henrietta said. "It's a *fortune*."

We sat at the table in the flagged kitchen, nursing mugs of coffee. It was the evening of the day after the Point-to-Point, the time of reckoning. It was already dark outside the curtainless, stone-mullioned windows, and in the dusty iron chandelier above our heads three lights burned out of twelve.

"But if we are going to buy one," Nigella reasoned, "it may as well be the best." She flipped through the pages of *Training the Event Horse* which she had ordered from the local library and adopted as her Bible. "*A badly-made dressage saddle can not only place the rider in the incorrect position, but also unbalance and affect the movement of the horse . . .*" she quoted. "We don't want that to happen, do we?"

"No-o," Henrietta allowed reluctantly. "But all the same, two hundred and seventy pounds!"

"I agree that we need to buy a good one," I said, "but I don't see why it can't be second-hand. As long as it fits Legend properly, I think one that has been used a bit would be just as good as a new one, if not better."

"Why didn't I think of that?" Henrietta leaned in front of us and grabbed the current issue of *Horse and Hound.* She turned to the classified advertisements, and as she perused them, she chewed a piece of her hideously tangled hair. "Of course, just because we happen to want one, there won't be a second-hand saddle to be had." She was right. There wasn't.

"Then we'll advertise for one," Nigella decided. "If we can get one for a hundred and fifty pounds, we will still have enough for the jump stands and the cups and pins." She went off in search of pen, paper and envelope.

The Event Horse Training Fund had done well out of the Point-to-Point. The first prize for the Ladies' Race had been a hundred pounds, and as we had each speculated five pounds on The Comet for an outright win, our winnings on the Tote had amounted to another one hundred and thirty-five pounds.

Nigella returned with a piece of damp, cockled crested notepaper and a pen. Together we drafted a brief advertisement TOP QUALITY ENGLISH OR GERMAN DRESSAGE SADDLE WANTED, GOOD CONDITION. URGENT. This was followed by our address. Short as it was, it still set the Training Fund back almost ten pounds.

All day I had been waiting for a suitable moment to broach the tricky subject of the Hissey Scholarship. Now I took the details out of my pocket and put them on the table.

"That's a very official-looking document," Henrietta said at once, eyeing the application form in a suspicious manner. "I hope it isn't anything to do with our sponsorship. We did agree that it was to be a personal arrangement. We're not going to sign anything."

"It's nothing like that," I assured her. "It's just something I want to discuss with you both. It's the details of the Hissey Training Scholarship."

"Hissey?" Nigella said, looking up from writing the envelope. "You mean Felix Hissey?"

"Yes," I said, "he awards a scholarship every year to six of the most promising young event riders and their horses. I rather thought we might try for it."

"We?" Nigella said guardedly. "Of course, what you actually mean to say is 'you'."

"No wait a minute," Henrietta said heatedly. "That's just another form of sponsonship; you don't need another sponsor, you've got us."

I had known it was going to be difficult; that the Fanes would want to do things in their own way. "But Legend and I are going to need professional help if we are to make any progress at all," I told them, "and the scholarship provides for a whole month's training with one of the very top international instructors. It's the chance of a lifetime."

"And who's going to do your work whilst you are away on this whole month's training with a top international instructor?" Henrietta demanded to know. "We can't possibly spare you for a month; we wouldn't be able to manage. It's out of the question."

"The course is held in the spring," I pointed out. "After the hunting season; it's never a busy time."

"Oh," Henrietta said grumpily, not in the least mollified. "*Is* it."

"The thing is," Nigella said in a reasonable tone, "that surely we can pay for professional tuition as and when we need it? After all, that's what our fund raising scheme is for."

38

"I don't think you realize," I said patiently, "quite how much professional tuition costs."

"I don't think we want to be bothered with Felix Hissey and his scholarship," Henrietta said firmly. "We can make it on our own."

"Profession tuition," I went on, "costs about twenty pounds an hour."

Henrietta choked on her coffee. "*How* much!"

"I did warn you how much it would cost to produce an event horse," I reminded her. "You knew it wouldn't be cheap."

"I didn't expect it to be cheap," Henrietta spluttered, "but twenty pounds!" She turned an incredulous face to Nigella. "We seem to have chosen the wrong business; we shouldn't be hiring out hunters at twenty pounds a day, we should be training eventers at twenty pounds an hour!"

"We could be," I said, "if we are sucessful at training this one. But you have to prove that you have the ability first, you have to have some form behind you."

"You're right about that, anyway," Nigella said. She opened *Training the Event Horse* at a page of photographs. They showed Trisha Phillpots during her early eventing successes with Fly On Brightly, then later, instructing potential, young event riders and horses.

"How many hours of professional tuition are you going to need?" Henrietta wanted to know.

"How can anyone possibly tell?" I said airily. "Two, three, five or six hours a week."

"Oh, goodness," Nigella gasped, "surely not." She turned over the pages of her Bible to ascertain if this could be so.

"She's kidding us," Henrietta said. "What does the book say?"

"Of course, if you still think we can manage to pay for it," I continued, "there's no point in even considering the scholarship."

"Now, let's not be too hasty," Henrietta said. "We may as well keep our options open."

"*Professional training and advice are essential to the potential event horse and rider*," Nigella read. "*Expert training can take a less than brilliant combination to the top, the lack of it will prevent even the most gifted horse and rider from achieving their potential.* You can't argue with that," she concluded.

"Perhaps we should just consider the *possibility* of a scholarship," Henrietta suggested. "I mean, as Elaine already had the details, we may as well see what Felix Hissey has to offer."

I spread the sheets out on the table. "What he has to offer is a month's course with a top international instructor, all expenses paid . . ."

"When you say all expenses," Nigella enquired, "do you mean everything; tuition, food and lodging for the rider, and keep for the horse?"

"Yes," I said, "everything."

"So it's worth quite a lot," she said pensively, "if you work it out at twenty pounds a hour."

"About a thousand pounds," I said.

"A thousand pounds!" Henrietta exclaimed. "Glory!"

"Of course," I said, "if you still think it isn't worth trying for, if you're still not interested . . ."

"Read on," Henrietta commanded. "We're interested."

"First of all you have to make a provisional entry

40

on the form supplied, giving full details of yourself, your previous experience, and your horse. Then, if your entry is accepted, you are invited to go to a combined training competition, where the selection committee make a short list of prospective candidates."

Nigella turned to the index of *Training the Event Horse* in order to look up combined training.

"It means dressage and show-jumping," I informed her, "at a fairly basic level."

"That wouldn't be a problem," Henrietta said, "would it?"

"Well," I said doubtfully, "if we get the dressage saddle and jump stands . . ."

"No," Henrietta decided, "it wouldn't be a problem."

"After that, the short-listed candidates take part in a mini-event held over two days. The selection committee watch the candidates schooling and competing, and then they make their final decision. They announce the names of their six chosen scholarship candidates at the end of the competition."

"Do you have to pay anything for the two-day event?" Nigella said cautiously.

"No," I said, "it's completely free for the short-listed candidates."

"And do you have to pay an entry fee to apply in the first instance?" she asked.

"No," I said, "that's free as well."

"Then it seems to me that we can't afford not to try for it," said Nigella.

Now that they had made a decision in favour of the scholarship, the Fanes began to panic in case something should prevent our participation. Nigella handed me the pen. "Fill in the application form, Elaine," she urged. "When is the closing date of entry?"

"When's the combined training competition?" Henrietta said, anxiously craning over my shoulder. "Do we have enough time to prepare?"

"And what do we need to be able to go," Nigella said in an agonized voice, "apart from the dressage saddle and the jump stands?"

"The combined training is next month," I told them, and added that we would need another saddle, suitable for cross-country and show-jumping. I could make do with the rugs, rollers and bandages we already had, but Legend would also need a double bridle; there wasn't a double bridle in the yard, and even the snaffle bridle I was using for schooling was pulled up to the top holes, and the bit was almost an inch too wide.

"So even if we get the dressage saddle and the jump stands with the money we already have," Nigella mused, "we still need another saddle and bridle, which will cost us almost as much again."

"I could use one of the old hunting saddles," I said. "Even the one I'm using now would do at a pinch, but it's very straight in the seat, and not at all forward cut. It isn't really built for the job." I didn't add that the stirrup leathers had a distressing tendency to fly off backwards when Legend took one of his unexpected, exaggerated leaps, and that the girth straps were cracked and withered.

"You can't go without the proper equipment," Nigella said, "it would look unprofessional, and I'm sure it would affect your performance." She thumbed through *Training the Event Horse* until she came to the chapter on saddlery. "*A general purpose saddle with a reasonably deep seat and knee and thigh rolls, is essential for the comfort and safety of both rider and horse*," she read.

"So we shall have to do a bit more fund raising," Henrietta declared. She jumped up and vanished into the squalid little scullery which served as our office and returned with a folded schedule which she placed triumphantly upon the table. "And Rendlesham Horse Show might be just the place to do it!"

"Rendlesham Horse Show?" Nigella said, interested. "Might it really?"

I looked at the schedule, not at all sure that Rendlesham Horse Show was a good idea. Henrietta leaned over my shoulder and flipped back her hair, giving the programme of events her very closest attention.

"We can enter the mare-who-sometimes-slips-a-stifle in the ladies' hunter class," she decided. "That's fifty pounds, and another fifty if she wins the championship . . ."

"She couldn't win the championship," Nigella objected, "not possibly. The bigger horses always win."

"And the bad-tempered chestnut in the riding horse class," Henrietta went on. "He may not always go very sweetly, but no one could deny that he's exactly the right stamp . . ."

"But the bad-tempered chestnut's coat isn't through," I said. "We were saying only this morning how terrible he looks."

"And look at this!" Henrietta's finger stabbed at the schedule. "A working hunter class! It's just the thing for Legend; and look at the prize money –

43

seventy five pounds, *and* a trophy. We could sell it, it might be worth hundreds!"

"You can't sell a perpetual challenge trophy!" Nigella cried in horror. "It has to be given back after a year!"

"But you must enter the working hunter class, Elaine," Henrietta insisted. "After all, it could be regarded as part of your training."

This was true. It would be good experience for Legend to jump in the ring, and the fences would be soundly constructed, solid and natural. I resigned myself to some fairly blatant pot-hunting. Nigella was already filling in the entry form. "Pity we haven't got a horse who can really jump," she said, thoughtfully, "the prize money is so much better."

"But then we would have to join and register with the BSJA," I pointed out, "otherwise you can't compete."

"That's true," Nigella agreed, "it's best to stick to the show classes."

Henrietta picked up the schedule and sat down in her chair, still persuing it. "Did you notice that there's a private driving class?" she said. "I don't suppose . . ."

"No," Nigella said flatly. "Certainly not."

"We've done with driving," I said. "We haven't a vehicle any more, and anyway, The Comet's done his bit for the Training Fund."

"Ah, well," Henrietta said regretfully, "as you wish."

5

Show Business

"Will exhibitors in class five, ladies' hunter, mare or gelding, please make their way to collecting ring?"

As the announcement was relayed across the showground, I secured Nigella's coiled-up hair with a couple of long pins, helped her to fit the veil over the brim of the silk hat, and pinned on to her lapel the smallest of creamy yellow roses to match her primrose waistcoat. The result was absolutely stunning. The navy side-saddle habit, cut narrower in the sleeve, tighter in the waist, and longer in the apron than was now quite fashionable, had belonged to Lady Jennifer when, in her youth, she had ridden with the cream of Leicestershire.

Henrietta looked up from the mane of the mare-who-sometimes-slipped-a-stifle with a plaiting needle in her mouth. "Where's that fool, Doreen, with the numbers?" she managed to say. "She's going to make us late." She stuck the needle in her jersey and stood on tip-toe in order to nip the dangling piece of thread from the very last plait with her teeth.

Doreen appeared at my side as she spoke, trailing numbers and white tape and looking gormless. She was a thin, pale schoolgirl with a floppy page-boy haircut, who helped out in the stables whenever she could in return for the part-livery of her chestnut pony. "*Every*body's here," she informed us, "even the hunt. That Mister Forster, Elaine, he wanted to know if you was here. I told him you was."

"You were supposed to have been running an errand for us, not gossiping with the hunt," Henrietta said irritably, turning over the numbers and squinting at the secretary's crabbed writing to discover which was to be attached to Nigella.

I heaved the suede-seated side-saddle on to the mare-who-sometimes-slipped-a-stifle and wondered if I would have an opportunity to talk to Forster. He would be pleased, I knew, to hear that I had posted off my application form for the Hissey scholarship.

We put Nigella up on to the saddle, straightened her apron, and snapped the elastic over her boot. She pulled up the mare's girths as we set off through the horse-boxes towards the flags and marquees which surrounded the main ring.

Rendlesham Horse Show was held in a clearing hewn out of the forest, and the air was filled with the scent of resin and the sharpness of the sea. Years of falling pine needles had left the ground dry and naturally resilient, carpeted with short, soft grass, and the result was a perfect all-weather riding surface.

The bay mare arched her glossy neck with its border of tight, black plaits, and lengthened her stride, appreciating the going. As we had expected, there was not another horse in the collecting ring that could hold a candle to her.

"She's sure to win," Henrietta muttered, "providing the leg holds out."

Inside the ring the two hunter judges signalled that they were ready to begin. Nigella, displaying a smart piece of showmanship, managed to be first inside the rails.

It was years since I had been to a horse show. I stood at the ringside with Doreen and Henrietta, drinking in the half-remembered sights and the smells and the sounds of it; the elegant hunters walking out in front of the sparkling white rails, the banks of spring flowers around the grandstand, the huge marquees, and the row of little trade-stands with their pennants fluttering angrily in the breeze. The ground vibrated with the thud of hooves, and from an adjacent ring came the regular crash of show-jumping poles accompanied by sympathetic moans from the crowd who stood six deep at the ropes. From the members' tent came the muted sound of laughter and the chink of glasses, and the occasional whiff of beer mingled with the scent of pine and bruised turf and the heady tang of the sea.

Just as the ladies' hunters were about to be waved on into a trot, everyone was asked to hold back in order to accommodate a late arrival.

"Oh, no," Henrietta exclaimed in disgust, "it's the landlord's daughter."

The landlord's daughter was Janie Richardson, who hunted with the Midvale and Westbury, and was greatly admired both for her looks and the quality of her horses. Her father was a rich publican, and her most striking feature was a mass of coal-black hair permed into a vast and solid frizz. It was a miracle that the frizz managed to fit under a silk hat, but she had flattened it down somehow and imprisoned it into a bun at the back of her neck, although as she trotted past us, I saw that fetching little spirals had drifted onto her blush-tinted cheeks.

47

The landlord's daughter was very pretty in a stagey sort of way, but she was not beautiful like Nigella, nor as elegant, but Henrietta groaned. "If there's any horse that could match up to the bay mare," she said, "it's Janie Richardson's Summer Nights."

When Janie Richardson had found a space, the hunters were allowed to trot on, and the judges gave their attention to Summer Nights. He was a nicely-made blue roan which turned to black on his face and his legs, and he had a white mane and tail which gave him a fairy-tale quality, enhanced by his pretty rider with her coal-black locks. The judges then turned back to Nigella and the bay mare, and it was clear that they were comparing the two. Henrietta fumed, furious that Janie Richardson had turned up.

The steward waved the class on into canter. The mare-who-slipped-a-stifle cantered off smoothly, with professional ease. She was no stranger to the show ring, having been many times a champion before she had suddenly and inexplicably begun to slip her stifle out of joint. When her owners had discovered that her disability was as incurable as it was unusual, they had sold her as a brood mare, only to have her returned as barren. Thus the Fanes had bought her for a song to join their stable of cut-price, slightly imperfect hirelings.

The canter sorted the class out in no uncertain manner. Some of the bolder horses began to yaw and pull, sweating up in anticipation of the gallop they knew was to come. One of them managed to get its head down in order to give three huge consecutive bucks right in front of the judge. Its rider, with any hopes of a prize dashed, asked

48

permission to retire, and rode out through the collecting ring, her shoulders bowed with disappointment.

The mare-who-sometimes-slipped-a-stifle galloped like a dream, long and low, with strides that ate up the ground. She steadied and balanced herself beautifully on the corners, and she fairly flew down the straight, with Nigella sitting on top looking charming and aristocratic, and as cool as a cucumber. The glory of this was entirely missed by Henrietta, who kept her eyes glued to the mare's inside hindleg, as if she expected it to drop off at any moment.

To our chagrin, Summer Nights galloped just as well, and we were in an agony of apprehension as the class came back to a walk, and the judges conferred on their preliminary placings. They looked at Nigella and the-mare-who-sometimes-slipped-a-stifle for a long time, but they pulled Summer Nights in first.

Doreen let out a squawk of dismay. "It's not fair," she complained. "Our horse is much nicer than that one; it looks as if it should have rockers on it."

I could see her point. "But the class isn't over yet," I told her. "The judge has to ride them and see them run up in hand."

"If Nigella just gets the second prize," Henrietta grumbled, "we shall only get twenty pounds instead of fifty." It sounded anything but sportsmanlike.

When the line had assembled, the judges asked Janie Richardson to ride out in order to give them an individual display. Summer Nights performed impeccably, trotting out with a long and level stride, striking off into canter on the right leg, and stretching out into a sweeping gallop. But when the riding

49

judge was put up into the saddle, he became a different horse. Whether it was the extra weight he objected to, or her heavy-handed way of riding, was not altogether clear; but he completely lost all his fluent, forward-flowing movement. He trotted with an over-collected chopped stride, he cantered sideways like a crab, and when he was asked to gallop, all he could achieve was an agitated tail-swirling scuttle. Janie Richardson covered her eyes in shame and we knew that it was all over for Summer Nights.

Even though all this was to our advantage, Doreen and I felt sorry for Janie Richardson, but Henrietta was openly delighted. "Serves her right," she chortled, "for coming in late."

The bay mare, who was used to strangers clambering into her saddle, gave the riding judge a superb ride; you could tell that she was enjoying every minute, and that the uncomfortable ride she had had on the first horse only heightened her appreciation of the second. Even the in-hand display went without a hitch. It was no surprise at all when Nigella was handed the red rosette. Doreen gave a little shriek of joy, and Henrietta rubbed her hands in satisfaction. "That's our first fifty pounds in the bag," she said. I knew it was for the Training Fund, but it sound terribly mercenary.

The bay mare led the winners in their lap of honour, with her polished hooves flying over the turf and the satin rosette fluttering on her bridle. When we caught up with Nigella in the collecting ring, a gentleman in a camel-hair coat was asking if she would care to name a price for the mare.

Nigella, knowing full well that the horse had never been sound for longer than a month at a time, smiled down upon him with regret. "I'm sorry," she said graciously, "but I'm afraid that we could never bear to part with her."

The gentleman, who was very taken with Nigella's beautiful face, and her hand-span waist in the old-fashioned habit shrugged his camel-hair shoulders in good-natured resignation and patted her boot in an affectionate manner. He was glad, he was heard to remark as he walked away, that there were still people left in the world to whom money wasn't everything.

Henrietta, dressed for her class in my best two-way stretch breeches, my Weatherall tweed with the velvet collar, and my deep-pile high-crown hat, with her hair in two long plaits tied with velvet ribbons, looked extremely smart. The bad-tempered chestnut, who had looked like an advanced case of moult, had been newly clipped for the occasion; with his neatly pulled tail and his plaited mane, he resembled the ideal riding horse, but in temperament he was nothing like one.

The trouble was that the bad-tempered chestnut loathed and detested other horses. He loathed and detested them all, quite without exception, and every morning, given half a chance, he would launch himself at his stable companions with a hatred undimmed by familiarity. When we led him out of the horse-box at the show there were so many horses for him to hate all at once, that he didn't know which way to turn. He contented himself with flattening his ears, arching his neck, and grinding his teeth.

"If only he didn't have that nasty spiteful look in

his eye," Doreen moaned, "he'd be such a pretty horse."

The bad-tempered chestnut replied to this by letting fly with a back leg, catching Doreen on the shin.

"Ooooow!" she wailed. "He's kicked me, the horrible thing!"

"Then you shouldn't walk behind him when I'm saddling up," Nigella told her in a reasonable voice. "You know what he's like."

When we reported to the collecting ring, the show programme was running fifteen minutes late. The steward, who was looking harassed, informed us that the riding horse class would begin just as soon as the hunt had given their display.

"Oh," said Henrietta, crossly, "how annoying. I rather wanted to get this over with." The bad-tempered chestnut was being an absolute beast, hopping from foot to foot, with his chin pressed against his chest, hoping that one of the other horses would come within striking distance of his back legs so that he could get a shot at it.

"I'm beginning to wonder if this was such a bright idea after all," said Nigella, in a voice of foreboding.

Above the crowd I caught a glimpse of scarlet. William and Forster and the huntsman were advancing across the showground with a path opening in front of them and the bitch pack at their horses' heels. When the bad-tempered chestnut saw them, he completely exploded, whether from anger or excitement one couldn't really tell. He flew backwards into the ring and began to plunge up and down in a succession of rapid *Croupade* and *Courbetes*, to the vast amusement of the ringside, some of whom applauded as Henrietta stuck gamely to the saddle with her plaits flying, rating him with some rather unladylike language.

The bitch pack flowed into the ring in a wave of lemon and white as the commentator began his introduction to their parade. "The Midvale and Westbury hounds, one of our oldest Suffolk packs of fox-hounds, with their huntsman, Tony Welby, and their whippers-in, have kindly consented to be with us today . . ."

Henrietta, finding herself to be a reluctant participant in the parade, and looking distraught, finally raised her stick and gave the bad-tempered chestnut a mightly thwack on his ribcage. As she expected, he stopped leaping up and down and shot forward, but even Henrietta could not have foreseen what happened next.

As Forster rode past, flicking his whip to bring up a loiterer, the bad-tempered chestnut recognized a well-known adversary, whipped round before Henrietta could spot him, and planted two hind shoes firmly in the chest of Forster's grey. The grey, shocked and horrified by such unexpectedly anti-social behaviour, leapt backwards into the pack, scattering hounds left and right to a chorus of yelps and howls of anguish. He cannoned tail-on into William's cob, who rocketed forward with such velocity that William was left sitting on the grass, only yards from Forster who, precipitated over the shoulder of his grey, had landed spreadeagled like a starfish.

All this had happened within the space of half a minute and the commentator, struck all of a heap by the turn of events, could only struggle with a few disjointed sentences. ". . . Hunting the country from the coast to . . . seems to have been a mishap . . . catch the loose horses before they . . . hounds . . . seems to be the end of the . . ." The rest was mercifully drowned by the band who manfully struck up into *If You were The Only Girl in the World*. It seemed singularly inappropriate as Henrietta crept out of the ring leading the bad-tempered chestnut, and the huntsman galloped after William's cob, who had high-tailed it into the collecting ring, and was causing havoc amongst the assembled riding horses.

The crowd, who had relished every second of this unplanned and hair-raising pantomime, now gave its entirely sympathetic attention to Forster who, tight-lipped, and rubbing his hip, limped after his grey who in the infuriating manner of horses who suspect that they have the momentary advantage, snatched mouthfuls of grass with a cautious eye in his direction and strolled to a new patch as he approached, always managing to be fractionally out of reach.

Hounds by this time had melted away into the ring-side, and were being fed sweets and crisps and ice-cream and other forbidden things. One of them was blissfully rolling in some droppings, another sat down in the centre of the ring and scratched itself. It was not the impressive display that either the hunt or the show committee had anticipated.

Henrietta, Nigella, Doreen and myself hid ourselves away behind the members' tent until we heard the riding horses being called. We knew that not even the rousing cheer that went up as the hunt, remounted and reassembled, re-entered the ring to begin their parade afresh, would appease the fury of William and Forster and the huntsman, who knew full well that half of their subscribers had been standing at the rails to witness their embarrassment.

The bad-tempered chestnut, with all passion spent, went quite well in the riding horse class. The judges gave him some long and favourable looks, and he even managed to put his ears forward at times, such as on the approach to the two small jumps he was asked to negotiate, and during his gallop. The result of this was that Henrietta came cantering out of the ring with a yellow rosette. It may not have been the one she had wanted, but in the circumstances it was very creditable.

It was lunchtime by now, and the working hunter class was not until half past two. We despatched Doreen to fetch some sandwiches, and Henrietta and Nigella went off with their rosettes to collect the prize-money from the secretary. I was left to lead the bad-tempered chestnut back to the horse-box.

Half way across the ground I was dismayed to see that Forster was walking towards me. He was not alone and there was no way I could decently avoid him. I knew he would still be simply livid about the fracas with Henrietta and the bad-tempered chestnut, and I had really hoped that I wouldn't have to face him until things had cooled down a bit. Yet I knew I would have to apologize for the Fanes sooner or later, and I steeled myself to get it over with. I needn't have bothered.

The other person with Forster was Janie Richardson. Forster had his arm around her. I thought he might have removed it, when he saw me, but he didn't. He just gave me an icy look and said, "I'd have that bloody horse destroyed, if I were you."

Then Janie Richardson giggled and slipped an arm around his waist, and they walked on, looking into each other's eyes.

I felt curiously numb as I led the bad-tempered chestnut up the ramp of the horse-box, unofficially borrowed from Thunder and Lightning Limited, who had ill-advisedly left it parked in the coach-house. I rugged and bandaged the chestnut and gave him a hay net. Then I turned my attentions to Legend and my thoughts towards our appearance in the working hunter class. Or at least, I tried to; but the image of Forster with Janie Richardson kept getting in the way.

6

A Working Hunter

The pinewoods were inviting; they were dark and cool and silent, and very, very private. I would have given a lot to be able to ride away into them; to lose myself in their deepness, to ride through and beyond them, out into the brown and green and gold of bracken and gorse and tree-lupin, where the soil grew light and sandy, and dipped its pebbly fingers into the grey, unwelcoming turbulence of the North Sea.

But as I worked Legend steadily on the edge of the showground and his head gradually came down on to the bit, and he settled into his regular, fluent stride, I was cross with myself for becoming so easily depressed about Forster, when there should be other, more important things on my mind.

I told myself that there had never been anything at all serious between Forster and me, and there probably never would be. After all, he thought me a fool, he had told me as much often enough; and I worked for the Fanes whom he detested. There was also his reputation to consider. I had been warned about him times without number, so there was no earthly reason why I should get so overwrought about seeing him with Janie Richardson. Nevertheless, every time I thought about it, I felt as if I had been kicked in the stomach.

I decided not to think about it. I forced myself to

put it out of my mind completely. I thought about the Training Fund and the scholarship instead, and I concentrated exclusively on schooling for the working hunter class which was due to begin in less than half an hour. Legend and I trotted faithfully in circles and serpentines, and cantered figure eights with simple changes of leg, and threw in some transitions and half-halts for good measure.

Things were going very smoothly by the time I heard the first call for the working hunters. I rode Legend back to the horse-box, pleased by his swinging stride, his row of immaculate plaits, the eager curve of his black-tipped ears, and the silky gloss of his bay coat.

"Legend don't half look lovely," Doreen said in a wistful voice. She held him whilst Nigella put an extra gleam to his coat and his black legs with a rubber, oiled his neat hooves, and applied vaseline highlights to his nose and round his dark, thoughtful eyes. Henrietta pulled off his tail bandage and brushed out the bottom of his straight, sleek tail, exhorting me to hurry and put on my jacket. Then, with my hat brushed and my boots shining after the ministrations of Nigella's rubber, I set out for the main ring on my sponsored potential event horse, glad of the new, nut-brown double bridle we had purchased out of the Training Fund, but hoping that the stirrups wouldn't fly off the saddle.

We left Doreen walking Legend round the collecting ring whilst we walked the course. There were five fences to be jumped and they were well spread out, with lots of grass between them because, unlike a show-jumping course which has to be jumped with precision and accuracy involving much placing and collection, they were to be jumped at a good, hunting pace, not a gallop, but a fairly brisk canter.

The first jump was a plain, brush fence about three feet high, constructed of birch. "Like the Point-to-Point fences, only smaller," Nigella commented. The second was a log pile made of old railway sleepers stacked one on top of another to a height of about three feet six. The third was a gate with the top bar painted white.

"That needs to be jumped fairly accurately," Henrietta said, pushing it with her foot and setting it swinging on its pins. "It isn't fixed."

The fourth fence was a combination which consisted of a hay rack with a rail in front of it, and an upright rustic post and rail. Nigella paced the distance and we decided that it would be three good strides between the two. I could see that I would have to be cantering fairly fast to get it right, and I could also see that the post and rail was narrow and had no wings; it would be all too easy for a horse to dodge out to the side of it and Legend, although he hardly ever refused a fence, was not averse to dodging out of a difficult one, if he thought that he could get away with it. The combination fence was going to be my bogey.

The last fence was a bank made with a double row of straw bales covered with artificial grass and topped with a hog's back of silver birch poles. It was over four feet high, with a spread of about five feet six, and it was set at a crafty angle, so that after flying the combination, you had to steady up immediately in order to negotiate a hair-pin bend, then muster enough impulsion to manage the spread. It was a cleverly designed course which demanded absolute control, brain-power, and a bold horse with plenty of scope, yet to the crowd at the rails, accustomed to the thrills of the *Puissance* and the colourful fences of the show-jumping arena, it must have looked incredibly boring; five drab fences to be galloped over in the shortest possible time.

When we got back to the collecting ring, the steward was chalking up the numbers in the order of jumping which had been decided by means of a draw. He recognized Henrietta by the length of her plaits. "The hunt is parading again at four," he said, giving her a jovial poke in the ribs with his chalk. "I hope you won't let us down. We're expecting it to be just as good as the last one." Henrietta flushed at this reference to her earlier catastrophe; she was not yet ready to regard it as a joke.

I was fifth to jump which was just where I would have chosen to be. I would hate to be drawn first, because I needed to see how the other riders tackled the course, and I wouldn't want to be further down the list because of the suspense of waiting a long time to jump. As it was, Henrietta, Nigella and I stood at the rails to watch the first few. The judges were standing in the centre of the ring with their clipboards, the jump stewards took up their positions, and the first of the working hunters, a flea-bitten grey with a roman rose and pink-rimmed eyes, cantered round the ring, waiting for the bell. Doreen was still walking Legend round the collecting ring.

When she heard the bell, the aged woman-rider of the grey cantered one more circle before turning into the first jump. The grey pricked his ears at the brush fence as if it was the one obstacle in the world he had been longing to jump. He cantered at it with

60

evident enthusiasm, then suddenly changed his mind and dug in his heels at the very last moment, stopping on a violent skid, gouging two deep channels out of the turf, and landing with his pink nose on the clipped birch.

The aged woman-rider, who had shot up his neck and lost her hat, struggled back into the saddle, applied her stick to his ribs and set him back at the fence. The grey sailed over. This performance was repeated at every fence, but the pair were totally defeated by the combination, and the judges were forced to ping their bell for elimination. On the way out the grey cleared the first two fences in reverse order and without hesitation, which must have been simply infuriating for the aged woman-rider.

The next horse to jump was a little black cob with three white stockings and a blaze. He looked the sort of horse you see on chocolate boxes and calenders, but he was not the sort of horse you expected to see in a working hunter class.

"He'll be in trouble over this course," Henrietta commented. "He's very short-coupled and short-striding, he just doesn't have the scope."

The little black cob sailed over the brush and the sleeper-pile in fine style, but he tipped the gate, which swung wildly and fell as he approached the combination. He cleared the hay rack, took an incredible five and a half short strides, and screwed himself up and over the rustic post and rail, dislodging the top rail with his hind legs and almost losing his rider in the process. The hair-pin bend, though, presented no problem at all, and by whipping up a certain amount of speed, his rider bustled him over the spread. The crowd gave him a round of applause for a game effort.

The third horse was a handsome chestnut gelding ridden by a determined-looking young man in a bowler hat and brown butcher boots. They cantered round the ring looking as if they meant business, and they did. They achieved a perfect round and a burst of spontaneous applause as they finished. I missed the last half of it because I was looking for Legend. When I had been ready to mount, neither he nor Doreen were anywhere to be seen in the collecting ring. They were finally found half-way across the showground, Doreen having decided to join the queue for a milkshake, and taken the horse with her. Henrietta delivered them back, Doreen by the scruff of her neck, still gripping a blue and white straw between her teeth. Nigella, displaying sound economic reasoning in the midst of high tension, said she should be allowed to go back and finish it, milk-shakes being the price they were.

"One day," Henrietta promised, as she bolted back across the showground, "I'll wring her skinny little neck."

After a few cantered circles in the collecting ring, I put Legend at the practice jump. It was a thin, rustic pole balanced on two jump stands, not at all like the solid fences we had constructed in the park, and he clipped it carelessly with his heels. The second time he jumped it with inches to spare, so I left it at that and walked him over to the main ring entrance to wait our turn. The last horse to jump before us was very hot. It raced at its fences and went into the combination so fast that it couldn't even take off in time for the second part and crashed through it, taking the rails on its chest.

There was a short delay after this, whilst the judges decided whether it counted as a knock-down or a refusal, but as the horse had not actually left the ground, it was counted as a refusal, and the rider was told to jump the combination again. This time the horse managed to scrape over with one and a bit strides in between the fences, but it completely failed to negotiate the hair-pin bend and flew straight past the bank instead of jumping it. After another circuit of the ring, the rider managed to steer it into the bank and the horse cleared it like a steeplechaser, and galloped past us into the collecting ring.

"Goodness," Nigella gasped, "it's almost as bad as The Comet."

"It's worse," said Henrietta. "The Comet jumps a lot better than that; at least he doesn't flatten over his fences."

It was my turn. Legend and I trotted into the ring to a breathles shriek of, "Good luck, Elaine!" from Doreen, who had torn herself away from the milk-shake stand and arrived in the nick of time to see Legend perform.

I had been very nervous just before the class, but now I was actually in the ring, and although I was very much aware of the crowd pressed against the rails, my nerves were steady. With the soft thud of Legend's rhythmically cantering hooves in my ears, and the supple reins of the double bridle between my fingers, I was ready and waiting for the bell, and as soon as it went I turned Legend into the first fence.

I was half-expecting him to put in one of his silly,

exaggerated leaps over the birch brush, but he didn't; his ears pricked forward, his stride lengthened into it, and he jumped it perfectly. On we thudded, over the sleeper-pile, across the springy turf and into the swinging gate. We cleared it with no trouble at all. Now for the combination.

I knew I had to keep up a fairly brisk pace to get the stride right, and I also knew that the tendency is for both horse and rider to slow up instinctively when two fences loom ahead instead of one. In my anxiety to do the right thing, I pushed on too hard and I rushed Legend out of his stride. It was entirely my fault that he met the hay rack slight wrong and took off too late and too close to the fence. He went up like a lift, both stirrups flew off the Fanes' hateful old saddle, and I crash-landed back on to it only just in time to stay with him as he put in two racing strides and soared up over the post and rails. He could so easily have run out instead, because I wouldn't have been able to do a thing about it, but he carried on and took me over without so much as a look to left or to the right.

I was back in balance with him in time to make the hair-pin bend, and we cantered on towards the bank, lengthened into it, met it exactly right and flew over, stirrupless but triumphant, landing to the sound of applause and the shouts of the jump steward who came running with the stirrups and leathers.

The Fanes were delighted although their delight turned to agitation as six out of the fourteen horses left to jump went clear, which meant that eight of us went into the next phase of the class with similar marks.

But I didn't doubt for a moment that Legend would win the class. In the showing phase he performed as impeccably as I had known he would. He trotted and cantered and galloped and stripped better than any of the others; even the handsome chestnut gelding ridden by the young man in the brown butcher boots was well and truly outclassed. When everything goes so well, it all begins to have a dreamlike quality, and I was in a daze by the time the judges had hooked the triple-tier red rosette on to Legend's new double bridle. I almost forgot the lap of honour and followed the other prize-winners into the collecting ring. I had to be shooed back by the steward.

We cantered in front of the grandstand whilst the band played *If You Knew Susie* in quickstep tempo and the crowd did a hand-clap which turned to cheers as we gave them a spirited gallop along the rails. Legend would dearly have liked to do it again, knowing that it was really his triumph, but I brought him back to a trot as we neared the collecting ring, and rubbed his neck gratefully with my knuckles. I knew he had won the class in spite of my riding, not because of it.

There was a splash of scarlet at the ringside. It was worn by someone who stood alone at the rails beside the blackboard which still had the numbers chalked upon it. Forster didn't smile or acknowledge me at all; but our eyes locked for a brief moment before he turned and walked away.

7

The Message of the Dressage

"Working trot down centre line, at L circle to the left twenty metres diameter, X to M leg-yielding . . ." The pages of *Training the Event Horse* fairly flew, as Nigella went in pursuit of the explanation to this new mystery.

I knew all about leg-yielding, having spent hours watching Hans Gelderhol, the golden boy of eventing and three times European Champion, instructing dressage riders at the training centre where I had studied for my Horsemaster's Certificate. "It's just a matter of the horse giving to the lateral aids and moving on four tracks," I explained, "it's a perfectly simple exercise." I didn't add that I had never actually tried it.

"It doesn't sound simple to me," Henrietta said grimly, "it sounds jolly difficult. How on earth can any horse move along on four tracks all at once?" Henrietta hated dressage.

"There seems to be a separate track for each leg," Nigella said, having finally come to rest at the appropriate page of her Bible. "*The horse moves along at a slight angle to the side of the arena, with his head slightly bent away from the movement, and the rider uses the lateral aids, the leg and the hand on the same side. When the horse is on four tracks,*" she read, "*one hind leg moves to a position between the*

66

forelegs, and the other moves outside the forelegs.
Here, you can see how it works in this photograph."

Henrietta took the book with a sigh of resignation.
"I shall never understand it," she groaned. "I don't
even see why I have to try."

"You have to try because I need all the help I can
get if I'm to stand any chance at all of winning a
scholarship," I said severely. "I must have someone
standing in front to check if Legend is actually
moving on four tracks; I won't be able to tell myself.
Somebody has to know what we're aiming for!"

We were out in the park, trying to master the
sequence and the rules of the dressage test for the
combined training competition. A week after Rendlesham Horse Show I had been accepted as a
suitable candidate for the Hissey Training Scholarship for potential event riders, and had been sent an
invitation to compete in the combined training competition to be held in three weeks' time. Three weeks
should have given me ample time to prepare, but
the way things were going it seemed as if I needed
three years.

"This horse," Henrietta said, squinting at the
photograph, "is amazingly like The Comet; younger
of course, and smarter, and a bit more dappled, but
very like The Comet all the same."

"That's Genesis," said Nigella, who by this time
knew all the intimate details of the horses and riders
pictured in *Training the Event Horse* by heart. "He
belonged to Lala Thornapple and he was one of the
team when Great Britain won the Olympics. He was
only six years old at the time and that's incredibly
young for an Olympic horse. He was an equine
infant prodigy."

"You're not supposed to be looking at the horse anyway," I told Henrietta impatiently, "only noting the position of its legs to see if you can tell me when Legend is moving on four tracks."

Henrietta gave her attention to the horse's legs and decided that she probably could.

"Then, let's start again," I said, "and you can stand at the end of the arena and judge the leg-yielding."

Henrietta pulled a face but she jumped down from the rusted iron rail where she had been perched beside Nigella and went to take up her position. Our dressage arena was marked out with oil drums begged from the local garage and painted white with black letters on them. We had marked the centre X with an armful of straw and Legend had wasted the first quarter of an hour by refusing to walk across it, snorting, and running sideways and rolling his eyes. For all the fuss he made I might have been asking him to walk over an elephant trap.

"Right," Nigella decided, "we shall begin again." She settled her Bible and the printed dressage sheet on her lap in order to bang a small saucepan lid with a tablespoon. This was intended to represent the bell, and it made Legend jump. I had to trot him round a few times before he could forget about it. Finlly, we entered the arena.

"I'm sorry, Elaine, but you're already eliminated," Nigella informed me. "*Any horse failing to enter the arena within sixty seconds of the bell being sounded shall be eliminated.*"

I stared at her in indignation. She was still wearing the zippered ski-pants although they were no longer the unsullied white they had been. She also wore the red pill-box with the veil pulled up lest it should impede her view of *Training the Event Horse*. Her hair was tied back with baler twine and her feet were shod with the red tap-dancing shoes. She was nobody's idea of a dressage coach.

"You might have warned me," I complained. "I had no idea!"

"You may begin again," she said patiently, "but do remember on future occasions. Now, enter at working trot, at X halt and salute . . ."

Legend and I rode wearily out of the arena and re-entered at a sitting trot, managing to achieve a level halt at X.

"Don't let him swish his tail!" Nigella cried in alarm. "*Grinding the teeth and swishing the tail are signs of nervousness or resistance on the part of the horse and will be penalized in the movement concerned and also in the collective mark at the end of the test.*"

"He isn't grinding his teeth, and he was only swishing his tail at a fly," I said crossly. "How can I possibly be expected to control that?"

"Also," Nigella continued, "*the use of the voice is prohibited and will be penalized by the loss of two marks.*"

It was maddening. We would never make any progress at all at this rate. "They only mean you can't say things like 'canter on' to the horse!" I cried in exasperation. "We're only practising, after all!"

"I'm only telling you what it says in the book," Nigella said in a defensive tone, "I'm only reading out the rules."

"And I'm beginning to see why you need professional tuition," Henrietta said morosely from the end of the arena.

Later in the day we went on a spending spree. We went into our local saddlers and explained that we wanted to buy a really good general purpose saddle suitable for cross-country and jumping. The sales lady, who was small and grey-haired, with close-cropped hair and a leather jerkin, regarded us with interest tinged with apprehension. In the days when I had first gone to work for the Fanes, they had run up huge bills for everything connected with their livery yard, and the saddlers had been one of the creditors who had been obliged to threaten to sue. We had managed to pay them before they did, but it was hardly surprising that they should hesitate to supply us now.

"It's perfectly all right," Nigella assured the sales lady. "We've got the money, honestly." She opened her bead-encrusted dorothy bag and displayed the Training Fund in the form of a wad of notes. The sales lady, reassured by this glimpse of hard cash, sped into action.

By the time I had clambered in and out of two dozen saddles, all varying in their length, shape, design and fitting, I was no longer sure what I wanted and I couldn't tell if any of them were going to fit Legend either.

"Fetch the horse," Henrietta commanded, "we shall have to try them on."

Even the sales lady thought this to be an excellent idea, and in no time at all Legend was standing in the back yard amongst the jumping poles and stands, whilst the sales lady placed saddle after saddle on his

70

back and we squinted at them from all angles. Eventually, after much agonizing and several try-out runs up and down the road involving the addition of girth and leathers and irons, we found one that suited us exactly. By the time we had paid for the saddle and some jump stands with cups and pins, we had spent almost two hundred and fifty pounds. This meant that taking into consideration the double bridle, which had cost seventy pounds, we only had fifty pounds left, and with that we had to buy a dressage saddle.

"Where on earth are we going to find a dressage saddle for fifty pounds?" I asked Nigella, as I drove the shooting brake down the road with its back bristling with jump stands, and Henrietta followed sedately behind on Legend. "I'm sure it's going to be impossible, and there's no question of doing any more fund-raising between now and the combined training competition, there isn't time."

"I know," Nigella admitted. "But I expect something will turn up. It usually does."

And it did.

On the Monday morning after the advertisement for a saddle had appeared, we received one letter. It was written in the most hideous scrawl and signed with a totally illegible signature, but the gist of it was that the writer was the possessor of a dressage saddle which she was unable to use any more and might be willing to sell. There was no further information than this, no size or make or price, but it was the only reply we had, and we were desperate. Armed with the dorothy bag containing our last fifty pounds, we set out.

71

Luckily, the letter had been written on headed notepaper, so we didn't have any trouble in deciphering the address. It took us two hours to reach the small Oxfordshire village, and the house was easy to find, having two stone gateposts surmounted with rearing horses. They were a lot nicer than the Fanes' ivy-clad vulpines, one of which had toppled off its perch long ago and never been replaced.

We drove up an immaculately maintained drive, passing a small stone-built stable yard, and parked in front of a mellow stone house with a sundial cut in above the door.

"We won't get a dressage saddle for fifty pounds from here," Henrietta said in a depressed voice. "People who live in houses like this always buy the very best things, they never have anything cheap."

My heart began to lower itself down into my boots. I felt sure that she was right. We got out of the shooting brake. Through the long leaded windows of the house I could see good oak furniture, gilt framed pictures and the glint of silver on every available surface. I felt thoroughly despondent. It hardly seemed worthwhile lifting the solid brass knocker on the front door.

The door was opened by a nurse. She didn't look too welcoming. She was wearing a dark blue dress with a starched apron and black shoes and stockings. She didn't have a frilled cap. "Yes?" she said, raising her eyebrows at us in a questioning manner. "What do you want?"

Nigella immediately launched into a long explanation about the advertisement and the dressage sadle and the letter we had received. The nurse frowned a bit and looked disapproving, but she let

us in and left us standing in a small, panelled hall.
We hoped she had gone to hunt out the letter-writer.

The hall was lined with framed photographs of
horses. When we looked closer we saw that they
were event horses.

"Look," Henrietta said, stabbing at one of them
in astonishment. "It's the horse in the book! It's
Genesis!"

There were a lot of photographs of Genesis,
performing dressage in a boarded arena, sailing over
show-jumps in front of a crowd of spectators, galloping over cross-country fences.

"It can't be Lala Thornapple's house," Nigella
whispered incredulously, "it just can't be!" But it
was.

Lala Thornapple came trotting into the hall hot-
foot after the nurse. She was wearing a baggy, red,
track-suit with white flashes and I saw at once why
her writing was so awful, her hands were crippled
with arthritis. They were set in impossibly knotted
positions and it made shaking hands very difficult.
Lala Thornapple was old, I suppose, but her lined
face was pink, and her eyes were as bright and
sparkling as a child's. She seemed delighted to see
us, and gave us a guided tour of the pictures,
sometimes forgetting which horse was which and
what they were doing at the time, which made it all
rather confusing.

"What about Genesis?" Nigella asked. "Is he still
alive?"

"Alive?" Lala Thornapple threw up her gnarled
hands, astonished to think that anyone could ever
doubt it. "Of course he's alive! He's out there in the
stables," she gestured through the window at the

stone-built stable yard. "They're all out there, all of these horses are in the stables; would you like to see them?"

It occurred to me that some of them must be very old by now but, "Oh *yes*," Nigella breathed, "we *would*."

"Not without a coat, Miss Thornapple," the nurse said hastily, and whilst she was helping her charge to get her arms into an anorak, she looked at us over her shoulder and frowned and shook her head. We all looked at her blankly, not knowing what she meant.

The nurse came with us down to the stable yard looking on in resignation as Lala Thornapple chattered on and on about her horses. I thought she was probably glad to have some visitors who were interested enough to listen, because the nurse didn't look the horsey type at all.

The stable yard was beautifully kept. There was not a weed or a wisp of straw to be seen. "You must have a jolly good groom," Henrietta commented, "to keep everything looking so neat and clean."

"Oh, I have," Miss Thornapple said happily, "I have."

We reached the first loose box. There was no welcoming head over the door. I felt sorry for Miss Thornapple, having horses so decrepit that they didn't fly to the door at the sound of footsteps. Nigella went to draw the bolt, but Lala Thornapple pushed her hand gently away and drew it herself, not without some difficulty, and opened the lower door. "Now this is the famous Genesis," she said proudly, walking into the stable and stretching out a

74

hand to fondle his neck. "Hello, you lovely boy, and how are you today?"

I tried not to gasp, but I couldn't help it. There was straw in the stable, beautifully bedded and laid with banked up sides, there was a water bucket filled to the brim with clean water, and there was a full hay net hung in one corner. But there was no Genesis. There was no horse at all. I looked, and I looked and I blinked, and I looked at the nurse, we all looked at the nurse, and the nurse shook her head firmly and put her finger to her lips.

"Of course," Lala Thornapple said, "he's quite an old boy now, aren't you my lovely? But you should have seen him in his youth, you should have ridden him. He was a flyer, you know, it took me all my time to hold him once he got going. It's the dressage you see, it develops all the muscles, it makes them very powerful, and Genesis was very good at dressage." She patted his invisible neck and turned to us. "Well," she said briskly, "let me show you the others."

We met several more invisible horses, even managing to make admiring comments, and we listened to a recital of their success in the early days of eventing. In the immaculate tack room there was a girl, carefully soaping an already spotless bridle.

"Ah Carol, my dear," Lala Thornapple exclaimed, "and how have my darlings been today?"

The girl was obviously prepared for this. She said in a perfectly serious voice, "Well, Dragoon's leg is very much better, the swelling has almost gone now, and Genesis has eaten up today, and they were all quite well-behaved when I rode them out this morning. Of course," she added, giving us a totally bland look, "the wind's dropped today, and that makes all the difference."

"It does, my dear, it does," Lala Thornapple agreed. She beamed at us in delight. "You see," she said, "I told you I had a very good groom."

I wondered what it would be like to be a groom to a yard full of invisible horses. How would you know which leg to bandage? How would you be able to tell if a horse had eaten up? And how on earth could you saddle up for exercise? I thought it was time to leave. Nigella obviously thought so too. She was already thanking Lala Thornapple for her kindness in showing us round as a preliminary to our departure. Henrietta was still staring at the girl groom. She looked as if she was about to say something to her, then changed her mind and turned away.

"But the saddle!" Lala Thornapple cried, throwing up her knotted hands in horror. "You haven't seen the saddle!" She gestured anxiously at her girl groom. "Get it down, Carol, dear, it's on the top rack, in the middle on the left-hand side."

Carol lifted the saddle down from the rack and placed it on the saddle horse on top of a snowy white unused stable rubber. It was beautiful; soft and supple and dark brown, deep-seated with thigh rolls and a suede seat and extended girth straps. Lala Thornapple looked at it for a long time, and I fancied that her eyes glistened with tears.

"Oh, no," I said instinctively, "we couldn't afford it. It's perfectly lovely, it's a wonderful saddle, but it's way out of our reach."

Lala Thornapple looked at me sharply. "How do you know you can't afford it?" she snapped. "I haven't told you how much it is yet."

76

"Oh," I said startled, "I'm sorry, I only . . ."

"Don't cross her," the nurse whispered warningly from behind my shoulder. "Humour her if you can." But Lala Thornapple was already beaming again.

"When I first bought this saddle," she said, remembering, "it was especially made for Genesis. I designed it myself and it was way ahead of its time. It isn't old fashioned you know, even now."

"No," Henrietta agreed warily, "it isn't."

"But of course it's no longer new," Lala Thornapple said with regret, "and although it cost all of fifty pounds to be made . . ."

"Fifty pounds!" Nigella couldn't restrain herself from exclaiming, it seemed such a paltry amount.

"It does seem a lot doesn't it?" Lala Thornapple agreed. "But it *was* made of the finest leather and suede, and the man who made it was a master saddler. Of course, I wasn't going to ask you *anything* like that for it; what do you say to thirty pounds?" She looked at us expectantly.

"Oh," Nigella said, aghast, "*we couldn't*!"

"Then what about twenty-five?" Lala Thornapple said kindly.

"But that's far too cheap!" I cried. "It's worth much, much more than that! We couldn't possibly take it!"

"You, young lady," Lala Thornapple turned on me with her eyes shooting sparks, "are far too stupid ever to become an event rider!" She turned her attention back to Nigella.

"Take it," the nurse muttered behind my shoulder. "Go on, tell her you'll take it. She'll be ever so upset if you don't, and I'll have to cope with her afterwards. Money means nothing to her, and she's had a lovely time showing you the horses. She'll relive all this for months."

So we took the saddle, Genesis' saddle, handmade from the finest leather and suede by a master craftsman, for the princely sum of thirty pounds. We were not proud of our bargain. We walked away from the immaculate yard peopled by ghosts and memories, leaving Lala Thornapple standing beside her nurse, waving her ruined hands; hands that had once guided a horse through an Olympic dressage test, and calling out to us that she might even come to watch the two-day event just for old time's sake.

Nobody said much on the way home. Only Nigella spoke, staring fixedly ahead into the twin pools of the headlights on the road. "When we're rich," she said, "and we can afford another dressage saddle, we'll take this one back and we'll leave it, just as it was, on the top rack, in the middle, on the left-hand side."

8

All in the Mind

"There seem to be an awful lot of horses and riders here," Nigella commented as we bumped on to the ground where the combined training competition was to be held. "They can't *all* be scholarship candidates."

"I expect some of them have just been invited to make up the numbers," Henrietta said, "to make it more of a competition."

I took no part in this conversation because I wasn't feeling well and it was taking me all my time to steer the horse-box. I had hardly slept a wink last night, I had just tossed and turned and worried ceaselessly about the dressage. I just knew that the test was going to be a disaster.

"They all look very professional, don't they?" Nigella said admiringly, as we turned into a parking space at the end of a line of smart horse-boxes. "You can tell it isn't just a horse show, all the horses are really expensive top quality animals."

"But then," Henrietta pointed out, "so is Legend." She glanced at me as if to suggest it was the rider who might prove less than satisfactory.

"I think I'm going to be sick," I said.

"Rubbish," Henrietta countered in an unsympathetic voice. "It's all in your mind. Don't be so feeble."

As I parked the horse-box, the people next door

gave us covert sideways glances. It wasn't, for once, because we looked so awful. Rather the reverse was true. The horse-box had been custom-built for our livery clients with gleaming black coachwork and a red trim. There was a Rolls Royce insignia on its bonnet. The sordid truth of the matter was that a hired box would have cost us fifty pounds and we couldn't have afforded it. As it was, after we had paid twelve pounds to have our unsuspecting pop group's petrol tank filled up, all we had left of the Training Fund in Nigella's bead-encrusted dorothy bag were eight single pound coins.

The Fane's jumped down from the cab and looked round with appreciation. The combined training ground was a magnificent sweep of sheep-nibbled turf. In the May sunshine the white boards of the dressage arena were brilliant against the emerald turf, and the show-jumps in their roped-off ring were a dazzle of red and blue and white. There was a small secretary's tent and some trestle tables set under a tree where ladies were already laying out cakes, sandwiches and paper cups for coffee and soft drinks. It was a lovely rural English scene, with even a Jacobean mansion away in the distance, but the sight of it all made me feel sicker than ever.

"I'll go and fetch the numbers," Nigella offered, "and the dressage timings. I expect they will be ready by now." She skipped off across the grass in her zippered ski-pants, newly laundered for the occasion. She had never been to a combined training competition before but already she knew the form; *Training the Event Horse* had taught her all she knew.

Doreen was at school, the combined training being

on a weekday, so we were without her dubious services as messenger and groom. Henrietta and I got Legend unboxed and took of his rugs and bandages. He was sweating slightly and I realized that I had over-rugged him, unaccustomed as I was to such luxurious draught-proof transport. I tottered around him with a rubber, drying off his wet patches and feeling absolutely dreadful. I didn't know where I was going to find the strength to mount, let alone ride a dressage test. I had never had such an appalling attack of nerves in my life and I was at a loss to understand it. Henrietta, observing that I was totally useless, tacked up. The dressage saddle had fitted Legend perfectly. The sight of it should have given me confidence, but it didn't.

I sat on the ramp and tried to read through the test. I was sure that I was going to lose my way.

> A Enter at working trot (sitting)
> X Halt. Salute
> Proceed at working trot (sitting)
> C Track Left
> E Circle Left 20m diameter . . .

Far from being familiar, it was as if I had never seen it before in my life, and when I got to the complicated bit with the circle off the centre line and the leg-yielding, the print started to move in front of my eyes.

Nigella came back. She handed me a number and a typed list of dressage timings. The tests were timed at seven minute intervals throughout the morning, leaving the afternoon free for the show-jumping. Mine was the eleventh test on the list, timed for

11.10 A.M., and there were thirty-one tests altogether.

"They're all scholarship candidates," Nigella informed me, "and they short-list twelve – I asked."

"You really must mount, Elaine," Henrietta said anxiously. "You have to do your schooling, then come back to smarten up, there isn't much time."

"And according to the rules," Nigella added, "you need to be riding in close to the arena twenty minutes before your starting time."

I tried to pull myself together. The first horse was already performing his test inside the white boards; in just over an hour I would be performing mine. I put on my hat.

"You'll be perfectly all right once you start schooling," Nigella said reassuringly, "honestly you will."

I hoped she was right. I checked Legend's girth and mounted, tucking the dressage test sheet into the pocket of the jeans I was wearing to protect my good breeches. Legend felt very alert and bouncy as I rode away from the horse-box to find a quiet place to school. The dressage saddle gave me a far greater area of contact and a vastly improved "feel", it was easy to imagine that I was actually part of Legend, not merely a passenger giving directions from on top.

I began to work Legend in around a majestic oak tree. He felt much fitter and livelier than usual and I made a mental note to tell Nigella to cut down his corn. It took longer than usual to get him to concentrate and to relax, but finally we got into our stride and I began to feel slightly better. My head was muzzy and my throat was dry, but the test had come back to me and I felt there was a sporting chance I might get through it without losing my way. In no time at all three-quarters of an hour had gone by and it was time to go and get ready.

Nigella had fetched coffee for us and I drank mine down gratefully to lubricate my throat. I put on my navy jacket and brushed up my hat, but when I leaned over to buff up my boots, my head felt as if it was going to fall off. I stood up and leaned against the side of the horse-box, agonized.

"Do come on, Elaine!" Henrietta called impatiently. She had sponged Legend's bit and oiled his hooves and pulled off his tail bandage. Nigella was giving him a last minute polish with a rubber. I tied on my number; it was thirteen. I felt awful again. If I was going to feel like this every time I had to ride a dressage test, I didn't think I would be able to stand it; my nerves would never last out. I would be a mental wreck. Perhaps Lala Thornapple was right after all and I was far too stupid ever to become an event rider.

"What happens if I ride a terrible test? What happens if we don't get short-listed for the scholarship?" I asked the Fanes. "What happens then?"

"We'll cross that bridge when we come to it," Nigella said firmly. She steadied the off-side stirrup whilst I struggled into the saddle. Legend rolled his eyes and pranced a bit. "He's having too much corn," I said, "he's too lively."

"Rubbish," Henrietta said crossly, "it's just because he hasn't had enough prep. Honestly, Elaine, I don't know what's got into you, you're being *hopeless*. Anybody would think you didn't want the scholarship!"

"I do," I muttered, "I've got stage-fright, that's all."

We made our way across to the dressage arena and watched one of the horses perform its test from the ropes which kept everyone twenty yards from the boards so that other horses should not affect the concentration of the one being judged. "Look," Henrietta said in delight, "he's having terrible trouble with his leg-yielding, he can't do it at all. He won't get any marks for that!"

Slightly heartened to see someone else making heavy weather of the dressage, I took Legend off to ride him in within sight of the steward who was in charge of the starting order. The judge was sitting with her writer in a Range Rover opposite the centre line at the C end of the arena and they gave the signal to start by a blast on the hooter.

If anything, this was more unnerving than the spoon and saucepan lid, and I worked Legend as close as I could get to the vehicle, hoping that by the time our turn came he would be used to it. The tests were running ten minutes late and I was glad of the extra time.

When my number was finally called Legend had settled and resigned himself to the idea of work. I knew that once he had reached this stage he would be very consistent, not easily shaken out of his stride, and very obedient; he might not be experienced nor very skilled at dressage, but he would try for me, and that was all I wanted.

We were allowed two minutes inside the boards to accustom ourselves to working in the arena before starting the test. This was a blessing because Legend didn't like the sparkling boards and leaned away from them, rolling his eyes. If this had happened during the test it would have lost us valuable marks. As it was, he soon got over it and we trotted out of the arena and waited at the top, just behind A. My hands felt clammy on the reins, my eyes felt hot, but I had nerved myself to the test and I was fully in control. The Range Rover sounded its hooter, this was it.

> A Enter at working trot (sitting)
> X Halt. Salute . . .

My nerves, my muzzy head, my dry throat, everything was forgotten in the solid concentration of trying to perform a good test. My world was reduced to the plaited neck and the pricked ears in front of me and the level thud of hooves below; contained within the white boards with their black letters; and directed by the printed sheet of the dressage test. Nothing else mattered. Nothing else existed.

Circle Left 20m diameter. I noticed that Legend bent his neck, rather than his whole body. My fault that, not enough leg, must do better next time. *K-M working canter*, on the right leg, thank goodness, but don't look down to see. *Sitting trot, A Halt, immobile 4 seconds*, moved off a fraction too smartly there due to Legend's over-anticipation. *K-M Change the rein at working trot*, turn up centre line, *circle 20 metres*, a better bend this time. *Leg-yielding*, started off all right degenerated into crab-wise trot, still, that's one over. Working trot, canter, turn down centre line, last of the leg-yielding; this time it's half-pass by accident, but at least we're trying. *D*

*working trot (sitting) G Halt, Salute. Leave arena at
A at free walk on a long rein.*

It was over. I rode across to the Fanes feeling
weak and light-headed. I could hardly believe that I
had got through it. It may not have been a well-
executed test, but we had done our best; we had
tried.

Henrietta slapped Legend on his neck as I rolled
out of the saddle. "It was a jolly good effort," she
said, pleased, "considering everything."

"We'll go and put Legend away, then we'll come
back and wait for the results to be posted," Nigella
said. She was flushed and excited, sure that we had
done well.

We stood by the score boards, waiting for my
marks to be posted up. Nobody seemed to have
done very well. Most of the marks were up in the
hundreds. Somebody remarked in a disgruntled
voice that it had been a ridiculously difficult test for
novice horses to perform; scholarship trial or no
scholarship trial.

The method of scoring was very complicated.
There were 140 marks which could be awarded for
the whole test, the test being divided into movements for which the judge awarded marks out of
ten, the total of marks were added, the penalty
points deducted, and the resulting figure deducted
from 140. Thus the lower the score, the better the
test.

When my score came up it was 81. It wasn't a
good score as dressage scores go, but it was good
enough to put me in the lead. Henrietta and Nigella
almost stood on their heads with delight. I went cold
and then hot, thought I was going to faint; then
bolted for the ladies' and heaved my heart up.

9

Too Awful to Contemplate

"The jumping's going to be nothing after the dressage," Henrietta said in a confident tone. "Absolutely nothing."

"The fences are easy," Nigella said, "look at them. The highest is only three feet six inches, and they're jolly well spread out, it isn't like a proper show-jumping course at all."

"It's just the combination fence you will have to watch," Henrietta warned. "Be sure you don't let Legend run out; you know he'll try if he thinks he has a sporting chance of getting away with it."

Legend and I were standing in the collecting ring waiting our turn to jump. My stomach was churning and I could see spots dancing in front of my eyes. At the end of the dressage tests I had lost my lead and dropped to third place. It was still better than any of us had expected. Now I had to get through the show-jumping. We had walked the course and the Fanes were right when they said it was not a difficult course; the only fences that presented any problems at all were the triple combination and the water jump. We were jumping in reverse result order and I was third from the last to jump. There had been a lot of clear rounds, the scholarship candidates seemed to be a lot better at show-jumping than they were at dressage. It was all very nerve-racking, and right at the last moment I had to shoot off to the ladies' again, clambering back into the saddle just as the horse in fourth place completed the fourteenth clear round. I rode into the ring feeling very shaky, knowing that I had to get a clear round. Anything less would be a disaster.

I cantered Legend in a circle, listening for the bell. Either he was feeling a bit strong, or I was losing my grip completely; but it took me all my time to hold him going into the first fence. He flew over it far too fast, and I heard his hind legs brush through the birch. I managed to steady him in time for the next fence, a Road Closed, and the fence after that, which was parallel poles. He was going on too strongly for the upright gate, but by putting in a big jump, he managed to clear it. I felt myself loosen in the saddle, but I pushed him on towards the water at a fair gallop, wanting to be sure he would make the spread and not wanting to give him much time to think about it. It was the first time we had ever jumped water. To do him credit, Legend didn't even hesitate; he took a flying leap and landed with yards to spare. By this time my arms felt like lead and I had to summon every last ounce of strength I had in my body to bring him back to a manageable canter. His neck felt like a piece of tensile steel, then, at the approach to the stone wall, he took me completely by surprise and put in one of his hateful, monumental bucks.

When the Fanes had first bought Legend, he had bucked me off lots of times; he had even bucked me off the first time I had ever ridden him. Gradually though, as I had learned to sit on and give him a wallop, instead of flying over his head, he had begun to desist, and now he rarely bucked. Today, he had clearly had enough of my feeble behaviour and he wanted to get rid of me. It was a miracle that I didn't fall off there and then, but I didn't. I managed to cling on and push him into the next fence and I was still hanging there by the skin of my teeth as we went, hopelessly fast, into the triple combination. I lost one stirrup over the first part, the other over the second, and when he ran out of the third part I fell over his dropped shoulder and landed in a little group of conifers.

For the rest of my life I shall never forget how it felt to pick myself up out of the broken flower-pots and flattened greenery as Legend flew round and round the ring at an enthusiastic gallop, looking mightily pleased about the whole affair. I had incurred three penalty points for a disobedience, eight for a fall, and every second spent stumbling after Legend was costing me another two penalty points for exceeding the time allowed.

By the time the ring steward had captured Legend and I had remounted, I was numb with despair. Anger was not far behind. It was anger that gave me the strength I needed to leg Legend into the combination again, get him over it without running out, and to finish the course. It was only when I reached the collecting ring that I noticed my left wrist had blown up like a balloon and that my hand was virtually useless. To cap all the other misfortunes, I had sprained my wrist.

"You can't possibly drive home with only one arm," Nigella said. "I shall have to drive the horse-box."

I knew she hadn't a driving licence, but I was almost beyond caring. Henrietta and I had had a blazing row and we were hardly speaking to one another. She seemed to think that I had thrown away all our chances on purpose. "You knew you had to watch him at the triple," she had raged. "You just let him run out! You didn't lift a finger to stop him!"

"I couldn't," I had said. "Once he got going he was too strong. He bucked, he's too fresh, I told you, he's having too much corn."

"That's right," Henrietta had shrieked. "Now it's our fault. Go on, blame us, we don't care!"

Nigella had been forced to intervene with calming words and now she was having to drive the horse-box home without a licence. If we had a crash, I knew whose fault it would be. I sat slumped against the door of the cab, feeling like hell. I had just about managed to live through what would quite possibly turn out to be the worst day of my life, and stretching ahead was a lifetime of penny-pinching and fund-raising too awful to contemplate. I just wanted to die.

But worse was to come. As we waited at the gateway of the combined training ground for permission to pull out on to the road, the officer in charge of directing the traffic walked across to us. His face looked grim.

"Oh no," Henrietta groaned, "he's all we need!"

The officer walked up to Nigella's open window.

"All right, young lady," he said in a threatening voice. "Where's your tax disc?"

Nigella stared at him, appalled. "I don't know," she said, "maybe it's fallen off the windscreen."

Henrietta got down on her hands and knees in the cab, pretending to have a look.

"You do have a tax disc?" he demanded, in a tone which implied that he knew perfectly well we hadn't.

"Yes . . . well, as far as I know we do . . ." Nigella faltered, unsure of her ground. "You see I don't . . . I mean, it isn't . . ."

"It isn't what, miss?" the officer said, staring at her with studied patience.

"What I mean to say," said Nigella, "is that it isn't really our vehicle."

The officer immediately took out his notebook and wrote down the registration number of the horse-box. "It wouldn't be a stolen vehicle, would it, miss?" he said in an expressionless voice.

At this, Henrietta sprang up from the floor of the cab. "It certainly is *not* stolen," she said in an annoyed tone. "It's borrowed from some very good friends of ours! How dare you even suggest it!"

"Now then, miss," the officer said sternly, "there's no need to lose your temper." He turned back to Nigella. "I shall have to see your driving licence, if you wouldn't mind."

"She hasn't got it with her," Henrietta said smartly. "It's at home."

"I didn't expect to be driving," Nigella confessed truthfully. "Our driver got bumped in the show-jumping," she waved an arm vaguely in my direction, "Elaine usually drives."

"And is the vehicle insured for you to drive, miss?" the officer enquired. "It *is* insured, I trust?"

"Of course it's insured," Henrietta snapped. She knew perfectly well that it wasn't; that Thunder and Lightning Limited only ever insured it for the hunting season.

I really couldn't stand any more of this. I lay back

91

in my seat and closed my eyes, overcome by giddiness, and wondering if there was room for me to pass out. I could see us all in court for driving a vehicle without a licence while it was not taxed and insured, and furthermore, I could see us losing our best livery clients, who's regular weekly cheques carried us through the winter. If we lost them we would be entirely ruined. Legend would have to be sold and I would be out of a job. I should have to go home to my father and begin again, searching through the Situations Vacant in *Horse and Hound*. It was altogether more than flesh and blood could stand. I let out a loud groan at the thought of it. The officer put his face to the windscreen and stared at me through the glass.

"She's broken her arm," Henrietta lied, "and quite possibly sustained internal injuries as well. We're taking her to hospital."

The officer's expression changed from one of alarm to one of fury. "Then why the bloody hell didn't you say so in the first place?" he demanded angrily. He stepped back into the traffic and waved us on furiously, anxious not to delay us a moment longer in case he was left with a corpse on his hands.

I must have looked almost as bad as I felt.

10

Where are the Horses?

"We weren't quite fair," Henrietta said, "we didn't realize you were really ill; we thought it was just nerves." She sat down on the faded tapestry bedcover.

"And we agree with you about the corn," Nigella said, "Legend *is* over the top. We've had to cut his ration by half, he's bucked us both off; Henrietta twice." She looked at me, shamefaced.

I wasn't going to say I told you so. I sighed and gave them a weak smile instead. I had been in bed for a week battling with a particularly virulent dose of 'flu. I was in no real hurry to get better; there didn't seem much to get better for.

"We've bought you a present," Nigella said. She laid a brown paper package on the bedclothes, where I could reach it. "We hope you like it."

"In fact," Henrietta said, recovering some of her spirit and looking smug, "we know you will."

In spite of myself, I was touched by this unexpected show of concern and generosity. "You shouldn't have," I told them, "you can't afford it."

"Oh, it didn't cost a lot," Nigella said, "at least, not compared with what it's actually worth."

I pulled myself up on to one elbow in order to investigate the bargain. I peeled off the paper. Underneath was a navy blue guernsey sweater. Mine.

"But it's my own sweater," I said, "my guernsey!"

"We thought you would be rather pleased to have it back," Nigella said, "so we spent the last of the Training Fund to redeem it. We thought you deserved it."

At the mention of the Training Fund, any pleasure I had felt in seeing my good guernsey again immediately evaporated.

"We won't be needing the Training Fund any more," Henrietta went on, "not since we've had this." She handed me an envelope. It was addressed to me, but the Fanes had opened it nevertheless. I was too weary to make a fuss. I pulled out the piece of paper it contained and opened it out. It was headed *The Hissey Training Scholarship for Potential Event Riders*, and the message was brief and to the point.

> The examiners are pleased to inform you
> that you have been short-listed for the
> above, and are hereby invited to further
> participate in a two-day event on June 20th,
> the details of which are enclosed separately.

I simply couldn't believe it. I read it over and over again. "We've done it!" I shrieked, "we're on the short-list!" I jumped up in bed, and reeled back against the pillows as my head started to thump and the Fanes blurred in front of my eyes.

"Yes," Nigella said in a pleased voice. "You are. But then," she added, "I always knew you would be."

"But I can't understand why," I said, "when there were so many others who did better!"

94

"The dressage was obviously more important than we thought," Henrietta said. "And, after all, it was potential they were judging, not necessarily performance, they obviously believe you both could do very much better, with the professional training and everything."

"So if you would care to recover," Nigella said, "we can start training for the two-day event."

With only a fortnight before the two-day event, there was no time to waste. Two day later I was out in the yard, and the day after that I got back on Legend and took him out to do some road work. My wrist wasn't up to anything more ambitious yet, but the swelling had gone down, and strapped up by Nigella in a crepe tail bandage, it felt comfortable and I was able to use my hand within reason.

Legend and I trotted along the quiet lanes between wide acres of ripening corn. The banks and verges were thick with primroses and the countryside looked fresh and green. Now and then we passed an isolated pink-washed timber-framed cottage with a couple of terriers yapping at the garden gate, or a fat cat asleep on the window-ledge. It was all very lovely and peaceful; even the inevitable wind was tamed today, reduced to a fresh breeze which made pleasant what might otherwise have been a day too hot for riding.

I rode along feeling pleased with everything. We had been very lucky so far. We had been lucky at the Point-to-Point, lucky at the horse show, and as it had turned out, even lucky at the combined training competition. I saw no reason why the same luck should not carry us through the two-day event.

If it did, Legend and I would have at least a foot in the door of the eventing world. It would be marvellous. Lost in satisfactory thoughts such as this, Legend and I turned off the lane into the bridleway that meandered round the back of the kennels. We didn't see Forster until we almost fell over him.

"Hello, Elaine," he grinned up at me, "imagine seeing you!"

"Yes," I said coolly, "Imagine." I wouldn't have stopped for anything, but before I could ride on by, he had caught Legend by the rein.

I stared at him angrily, my idyllic ride rudely interrupted. I had almost forgotten Forster in the last few weeks and I didn't want to be reminded now. "Let go of my rein," I said. "I'm busy."

"You don't look very busy," he replied, "you look as if you're having a nice, relaxing ride. I like your hair loose like that, it looks very pretty." He smiled at me, all white teeth and black hair and blue eyes and suntan. He was wearing jeans and an open-necked shirt with a heavy silver chain around his neck. I could happily have throttled him with it.

"What are you doing here anyway," I demanded indignantly, "lurking in the bushes and jumping out on people. Anyone would think you were a Peeping Tom."

"I'm not lurking in the bushes or jumping out on people at all," he said. "I've just been re-hanging a gate. It's called summer maintenance, it's part of my job."

I looked at the gate behind him and saw that this was clearly true.

"So, you're on the short-list," he commented. He

let go of Legend's rein, but he didn't move any further away.

"Yes," I said, surprised. "How did you know?"

"You forget," Forster said, "I know Felix Hissey quite well. I'll probably be with him at the two-day event. Perhaps I'll be allowed to buy you a drink?"

"You and me and Janie Richardson?" I said. "Wouldn't three be rather a crowd?"

He grinned.

"Well," I said crossly, "wouldn't it?"

"I do believe you're jealous," he said.

I denied it.

"You can come out with me tonight, if you like," he said. "I could pick you up at eight." He made it sound as if he would be doing me a favour.

"No thanks," I said. "Ask Janie Richardson."

"I already have," he said. "I'm picking her up at seven-thirty.'

"*Oh*!" I said, infuriated, "you *pig*!" I swung my foot at him angrily, Forster grabbed my ankle and pulled me out of the saddle. Legend walked off up the bridleway. I went to run after him but Forster pulled me back, pinned me against the gate, and clamped his mouth over mine. Then, before I had time to recover my senses, he was strolling off across the fields towards the white-washed buildings of the kennels with his hands in his pockets.

All this left me speechless. I picked up the nearest chunk of baked clay and hurled it after him. I'm not usually a good shot, but it hit him squarely on the back of his head. I didn't wait to see what would happen next. I ran down the bridleway to capture Legend, feeling that at least I'd made my point.

* * *

Later in the day, I was sitting on the tack room table staring at a photograph in *Training the Event Horse*. The photograph showed Genesis, in his handmade saddle, performing a half-pass at the Olympic Games. I looked at the grey horse carefully, pondering the angles of his head, the set of his neck, and the shape of his powerful, dappled hindquarters. Lala Thornapple must have been about forty-five when the photograph had been taken. She still looked young and slim and completely in unison with the horse; her legs firmly against his sides, and the reins running through her skilled, strong fingers.

Doreen came whistling into the yard on her bicycle to begin her evening stint, setting fair the stables for the horses who were still brought in at night. I hadn't realized it was so late. I put down the book and went to help. There were only three horses to bring in.

Legend was one, and The Comet, and Nelson. The last two were utilized as company for Legend when he was doing roadwork, and as transport and grandstand seats for the Fanes when we were schooling over the jumps and cross-country fences in the park.

I had collected the headcollars and was on my way out of the yard, when Henrietta appeared in a striped apron to tell me I was wanted on the telephone. "He wouldn't say who he was," she said in a disapproving tone, "but if you ask me, it's Nick Forster."

I walked back across the yard and called to Doreen to bring the horses in from the park.

"Don't let Doreen bring them up," Henrietta objected, "you know what a fool she is, she'll never be able to catch them."

98

"Ow," Doreen squawked, indignantly, "I will then!"

"All the same," Henrietta said despondently, as Doreen went off hung with headcollars and armed with a corn scoop, "I bet she won't."

I followed Henrietta into the kitchen. It was full of steam. Lady Jennifer was leaning over a bubbling jam kettle on the Aga, staring at the contents in anguish. Nigella was topping and tailing gooseberries in the sink. Lady Jennifer's latest project was a produce stall in the local market square in aid of the Red Cross. The Red Cross jam didn't appear to be doing very well; little saucers with drips of brown liquid on them were dotted all over the kitchen.

"I'm having the most *ghastly* time with this batch, Elaine," Lady Jennifer sighed. "it's an *appallingly* bad set, and it's been boiling for hours; it's *frightfully* concentrated, and the most *revolting* colour." It also smelled burned, but I hadn't the heart to say so. I went into the office and picked up the telephone receiver.

"Elaine," Forster's voice said, "I've got a lump on the back of my head the size of a grapefruit, and I'm thinking I might sue."

"Do," I said, "and I'll sue as well, possibly for assault."

Henrietta who had followed me into the office, looked up, startled.

"I'm not really all that interested in Janie Richardson," Forster said, "she's doing all the chasing, not me."

"But you are taking her out tonight," I said. "It wasn't a joke, was it?"

He didn't deny it.

"Look," I said impatiently, "what do you want? It isn't very convenient to talk at the moment; I'm just about to fetch the horses in." I rather wished Henrietta would go away, but neither of the Fane sisters had any qualms about opening other people's letters or listening in to their private conversations.

"Since you ask so nicely," Forster said, "I want to ask if you'll come out for a drink on Friday night."

A germ of an idea began to take shape inside my head. I still had to get even with Forster. I didn't want to sound too keen. "I might," I said, in a non-committal sort of way, "I'll think about it."

"Think about it now," he said, "I want to know."

"All right," I said, "I will."

"I'll call for you at eight," Forster said.

"Will there be two of us?" I enquired, "or three?" The line went dead.

"Do taste this, Elaine," Lady Jennifer said. She looked hot and bothered with her hair escaping from a scarf and blobs of jam all over her blouse, which meant it had to be washed again; it had already been laundered so many times that it was impossible to tell what its original colour had been. Henrietta and Nigella were now arranging jam jars in lines on the kitchen table.

"Would you like to go out on Friday night?" I asked them. "I've been asked out by Nick Forster, and I thought it might be rather jolly if we all went."

"What a simply *marvellous* idea," Lady Jennifer trilled. "It will be *infinitely* more fun, and so *very* sensible to go out in a crowd instead of a twosome; how *terribly* nice of you to suggest it, Elaine." She held out the jam spoon in an encouraging manner.

"Hrmm," Henrietta said suspiciously. She licked

her fingers and grimaced at the taste. "Does Forster know? Would he mind?" As she had been listening to our telephone conversation she knew pefectly well that he didn't know, and that he would mind very much indeed.

"Why should he mind?" I said innocently.

Henrietta gave me a conspiratorial grin.

"We'd love to come," Nigella said, "if you're quite sure we won't be in the way; we've had enough of gooseberries, one way or another."

I tasted the jam.

"I think you've forgotten to put the sugar in it," I said.

Outside in the yard I expected to see three heads hanging over the stable doors in anticipation of the evening feed. There were none. I sighed as I realized that Henrietta had been proved right and Doreen hadn't been able to catch the horses. I had provided myself with a spare headcollar and half a bucket of corn, when I heard galloping hooves on the drive. Almost at once, Nelson appeared under the clock arch, scrabbling his boxy feet on the cobbles in a desperate effort to keep himself upright, and there was Doreen clinging to his mane with her eyes panic-stricken and her face like chalk.

"The horses," she screeched, "we've got to save the horses!" She yanked at the headcollar rope in the nick of time to prevent herself from being decapitated as Nelson made for the safety of his stable.

"What on earth do you mean?" I shouted at her. "Where are the horses?"

"They all pushed out of the gate when I was

getting on Nelson!" she shrieked. "It wasn't my fault, Elaine. *Honest*!" She struggled wildly with the one-eyed bay, pulling his nose round to her boot, flailing at his ribs, and setting him in motion like a demented spinning top. "They've all galloped away down the road! All of them have gone, your Legend and The Comet, and the chestnut and the bay mare, and they'll all be run over by cars and break all their legs, and *oh*! Henrietta Fane's going to *kill* me!" At this her voice rose to such a bawl of hysteria that it brought the Fanes tumbling out of the kitchen door, still clutching their sugar packets.

I ran for the shooting brake.

11

Luck of a Kind

The park gate leaning open and the headcollars strewn across the drive bore witness to the flight of the horses.

"Stop! We must look in the park!" Nigella cried, "They may have come back!"

"Never!" Henrietta shouted. "They wouldn't come back! Go on, Elaine! Go *on*!"

I dithered helplessly at the end of the drive, not knowing which way to go.

"Left!" Henrietta commanded.

"No," Nigella shrieked, "right, look! There are hoof-marks on the verge!"

We bucketed along the lane, looking fruitlessly in gateways and across the fields of corn, our eyes raking the landscape for any sight of the horses, our ears alert for any sound that might give a clue to their whereabouts. Doreen took no part in this, she just leaned her head in the bucket of corn and wept and whimpered on about cars and broken legs, and was no use to anyone; yet she had refused to stay behind, and Lady Jennifer had been left to cope with Nelson, whilst the Red Cross jam boiled away unattended on the Aga.

With my nose practically resting on the windscreen I followed the hoof marks on the verge and the half-moon bruise marks on the tarmac. I didn't dare to think too much about what we were going to find along the way. I knew that apart from a seasonal policy to cover our hunter liveries and the people who rode our hirelings, we had no insurance whatsoever, and that the consequences of any accident, both in loss or damage to the horses, or in compensation claims from any other parties involved, could be catastrophic.

Henrietta and Nigella bounced up and down on the back seat in a fever of anxiety and impatience which grew even more frenzied as we neared the main road.

"If they've strayed on to the A12," Nigella moaned, clasping her hands over the back of my seat in an attitude of prayer, "God help us all!"

Doreen's wails increased in crescendo. Henrietta reached out and cuffed her into a silence broken only by an occasional strangled sob into the bucket. The hoof-prints led us to the junction where the lane met the main road. As I indicated to turn out on to the dual-carriageway, first to the left then to the right, in a welter of indecision, two things happened. The first was that the horses passed by. Led by The Comet they galloped across our vision with their necks stretched and their tails streaming and their hooves ringing out on the road. They looked neither to the left nor to the right, driven on like wild horses in a stampede by a line of nose-to-tail traffic following remorselessly on their heels.

The second thing that happened was that I stalled the shooting brake. The hand-brake didn't work due to Lady Jennifer's habit of driving round with it on, and as we slipped backwards down the incline, gathering speed, the Fanes screamed, Doreen upset the corn, and all was pandemonium. After a succession of bucks and leaps I managed to set the shooting brake lurching forward again. This time we shot straight across to the central reservation and narrowly avoided being cut in half by a Jaguar.

"Oh goodness, Elaine," Nigella gasped, "are you going to kill us all?" The tone of her voice suggested it might be the best way out of a nasty situation.

The pile-up of traffic behind the horses would not let us overtake. We scuttled hysterically in its wake, being hooted at by cars and sworn at by lorry drivers, and all the time we sounded our horn and flashed our lights, waving our headcollars out of the windows and crying uselessly that we were trying to catch the horses. Then the traffic suddenly started to speed up.

"The horses must have turned off!" Nigella cried, but by this time we were stuck fast in the middle lane, carried helpless as a stick in a stream, past the turning where the wide grassy verges bore the unmistakable dent of horses' hooves.

"Turn back! Turn back!" Henrietta screamed, but she could see it was hopeless. It was several miles before we reached a roundabout and sped back the way we had come, fretting and lamenting on the central reservation whilst we waited for the oncoming traffic to allow us to cross.

There was no traffic at all on the side road. We hurtled along with our eyes on the verges and it was only by sheer chance that Henrietta looked up and saw that the stampede was now coming in our direction.

"The brakes!" she shouted. "Elaine! Put on the brakes!"

With The Comet still in the lead, the horses crashed towards us up the lane. I jammed my foot on the brake and we flew forward, only the bucket saved Doreen from being pitched on to the windscreen. The shooting brake skidded across the road. Nigella, who had opened the door and jumped out before it had stopped, vanished from sight with a horrified shriek. She reappeared, still shrieking, holding out her arms in the face of the stampede.

The Comet, observing that his route was blocked, hesitated in his stride. His gallop became a canter and his canter became a trot. Then, in his own infuriatingly cool manner, he stopped on the verge and studied the distant pinewoods with profound interest, as if the skidding hooves behind were nothing to do with him at all.

We had actually got the headcollar on The Comet and the black horse, and everything might then have been all right, but for the car which came flying round the bend. To be fair to the driver, he hardly expected the lane to be full of horses, and there was no way, brake as he might, he could have avoided hitting one of them, slamming into its side and bowling it over on the tarmac. It seemed mightily unfortunate though, that the horse he hit was Legend.

The next hour was a horrific blur. I remember Legend struggling to get back on his feet with his flank torn open and his blood spreading in an ever-widening pool. I remember Doreen's screams and the terror in the face of the driver who shook and shook until his teeth chattered. I remember Henrietta racing along the lane like a maniac to find the nearest house with a telephone so she could summon the vet, and I knew that eventually the driver had driven off with Nigella to get the horse-box.

I know that the other horses were frightened and bewildered, and that other people arrived and an elderly woman fainted from shock and had to be laid out on the verge, so that by the time Nigella drove up in the horse-box, it was just like a battle scene with the blood and the smell of sweat and the body on the grass, and the weeping and the wailing, and the anxious shouts of complete strangers who, never having been close to a horse in their lives before, struggle manfully as people will in times of crisis, to hold on to the hirelings.

There was no time for tears or recriminations as we organized the transportation of the horses back to the stables, first Legend with his sides and his legs caked with blood, then the others by degrees, and ourselves and the shooting brake. It seemed to take forever to achieve all this, but at last it was done and I was standing in the stable holding the sweating, distressed bay gelding, whilst the vet swabbed and stitched and the Fanes stood with pails of bloody water, and Doreen wept quietly in a corner until Lady Jennifer came silently into the stable and took her away, gathering her up like an armful of crumpled laundry.

"You're lucky," the vet said finally, as he stood back to survey his handiwork. "There's nothing broken and it looked a lot worse than it really was. He's lost a fair amount of blood, but it was a clean injury and not too deep; it shouldn't leave much of a scar. He'll be as good as new in a few months."

We tried very hard to feel lucky. Afterwards we told ourselves over and over again how lucky we were to have a horse at all, when he could so easily have been irreparably injured or killed, and that the driver of the car could have been injured himself and have decided to sue. It had been luck of a kind, we supposed.

But standing in the lantern-lit stable on the blood-soaked straw, with our hair matted and our checks splashed with red, with the vet called from his fireside, and Henrietta in her sticky, striped apron, we didn't feel lucky.

We looked at our bruised and battered horse, and we knew that this was the end of the two-day event, the end of the training scholarship, and for all we knew, the end of an eventing career.

12

A Substitute Eventer

"Elaine," Nigella said, "Forster's here."

Friday night. I had forgotten.

"Tell him to go away," I said.

"I have," she said, "he won't."

"That's right," Forster agreed, "I won't."

He came into Lady Jennifer's little sitting-room behind Nigella, took her by the waist and placed her outside the door, closing it in her face.

"That wasn't very polite," I said.

"I'm not a very polite person. What are you doing?"

"I'm writing a letter." This wasn't exactly true. I was sitting at the bureau with a blank piece of notepaper in front of me and a pen in my hand, but I hadn't started to write, not yet.

Henrietta came in. She was wearing scuffed, pink, stiletto-heeled shoes, lurex tights, her black leg-warmers and a mini-skirt.

"Goodbye, Miss Fane," Forster said pointedly.

"Oh," Henrietta said, surprised, "do you want me to go? I thought I was invited. Before this happened, we were all going out together."

"All?" Forster looked at me suspiciously. "*All*?"

"Yes," I said wearily. "All. It was to be a sort of revenge."

"I see," Forster sat down on a small Edwardian

chair and rocked back on it, staring at me with narrowed eyes.

"Don't do that," Henrietta told him, "you'll break its legs."

"And if you don't leave the room," Forster said, in a conversational tone, "I'll probably break yours."

"I'd better leave," Henrietta said apologetically, "in case he does." She went out, resigned to more jam making for the Red Cross.

Forster got up and wandered over to the mantlepiece. He picked up a sepia photograph in a cracked rosewood frame. "Is this old Lord Fane?"

"It was," I said. "He died about ten years ago. He wasn't very good with money; I believe he drank."

Forster set the photograph down again. "I should think his family drove him to it."

"I do wish," I said, "that you wouldn't be quite so scathing about the Fanes."

Forster came over to the bureau. He wasn't dressed for going out. He was wearing cords and a jersey and a Husky waistcoat. "Who are you writing to?"

"I'm writing to the BHS to resign from the training scholarship," I said. "I thought if I wrote straight away, they would have time to invite someone else to the two-day event in my place. I haven't actually started it yet," I admitted, "it isn't going to be a very pleasant letter to write."

"Then don't write it," he said, "it isn't a good idea."

I stared at him curiously. "What do you mean it isn't a good idea? What did you come for, anyway? You must have heard about the accident. You must have known."

"Of course I knew," he said, "the whole village knew. The whole country probably knows by now."

"And you knew how I'd be feeling; you knew I wouldn't want to go out?"

"I knew that as well."

"Yet, you still came?" I said wonderingly.

"I still came." Forster leaned one elbow on the top of the bureau and rested his chin on his hand. I looked up at him, and he looked levelly back at me.

"You could have gone out with Janie Richardson instead," I said.

"I could."

"But you didn't."

"No, I didn't."

Henrietta poked her head round the door. "Would you care for some coffee?" she enquired.

"Go away," Forster said. He didn't shift his gaze from mine.

The head withdrew. "If she keeps popping in," Forster said, "I might easily break her neck as well as her legs."

"Why *did* you come?" I said.

"I came," he said, "just in time to stop you writing a letter you might regret." He pulled away the notepaper and crumpled it into a ball in his fist.

"But if I don't write it now," I said, "it will still need to be written; if not today, then tomorrow, or the next day, or the next."

"No," he said fiercely, "it needn't!" He hurled the crumpled piece of paper into the fireplace. "You can't give up as easily as that!"

I looked at him in astonishment, not knowing whether to feel hurt or angry. "I'm not giving up *easily*," I told him, "or because I *want* to, only because I *have* to!"

Forster turned away. He pushed his hands into the pockets of his waistcoat and glowered at the threadbare carpet. "Elaine," he said eventually, "this scholarship means a hell of a lot to you, doesn't it?"

"You mean it did," I said carefully. "It would have meant that Legend and I had a really good start, with all the professional help we needed. It would have given us a foot in the door of the eventing world; and of course, it would have been nice to have earned it ourselves, not to have been dependent on the Fanes to finance it. Yes," I admitted sadly, "the scholarship meant an awful lot, and I'm very, very sorry to have lost it."

"But you might not have completely lost it," he said.

"I could try again next year," I admitted, "but the way things are going I might not have a horse next year; if the Fanes get really hard-pressed, Legend could be the first to go."

"I don't mean next year," he replied, "I mean this year. I mean now."

I looked at him, surprised, to find that he still didn't completely understand. "But I *have*," I said, "I've completely lost Legend for this year, he won't be fit enough to do anything at all for at least three months. The two-day event's next week!"

"You've lost Legend, yes, but you could go on another horse, you could take a substitute! They allowed somebody to take a substitute last year; horses are always going lame at the last minute, they accept that!"

112

"Another horse?" The idea had not crossed my mind. It hadn't occurred to me that I could compete in the two-day event on any horse other than Legend. "But another horse . . ." I didn't really want to ride another horse; I wouldn't be able to do justice to a strange animal in the short time there was left to train before the competition, and anyway, I couldn't think of a suitable animal to be had.

"I honestly don't think so," I said, "if I can't go on Legend . . . there isn't a horse I can think of who could take his place; horses like Legend don't exactly grow on trees, you know, they're very hard to find."

"I realize that." Forster stared at the carpet. "It just seems such a wicked waste of an opportunity," he said, "to get so far, and then have to give in."

"I know," I said.

"So if there was something, *anything*, that was nearly good enough," he said, "at least you wouldn't be out of the running altogether. You'd still have a chance."

"Yes," I said doubtfully, "I suppose I would."

"After all," he went on, "they *are* assessing potential, they must have seen potential in your own performance, and they would certainly have seen it in Legend."

"I suppose so," I said.

"And in three months he'll be working again, so the chances are that he'll be completely fit by the time the course begins." I nodded in agreement. "So you owe it to everyone to try, to yourself, to Legend, even to the Fanes."

I frowned. "Well, if you put it like that . . ."

"Elaine," Forster said, "is there no other horse

113

even *remotely* suitable, that you could take to the two-day event?"

I stared at him silently, thinking of a grey horse who never lost his courage, a horse who could gallop, a horse who never, ever, flattened over his fences. It was a risk, I knew, but: "I do believe," I said, "that there is."

I went into the kitchen. The heat and steam and the sickly smell were overpowering. Lady Jennifer was ladling the Red Cross jam into jars. Henrietta was sitting at the table writing labels with her tongue between her teeth and her hair clinging damply to her forehead in little tendrils. Nigella was weighing sugar.

"Where's Forster?" they wanted to know.

"He's gone," I said. "I've just shown him out. And I would like you to know that I'm still going to the two-day event."

"As a spectator?" Nigella said. "Won't that be rather depressing?"

"Not as a spectator," I said, "as a competitor."

Henrietta looked up from the labels with her mouth open. "But you haven't got a horse," she objected. "How can you possibly . . ."

"I'm going on The Comet," I said.

"Not The Comet!" Nigella cried. "You're not thinking of taking The Comet to the two-day event!"

Henrietta pushed the damp hair off her face and looked at me speculatively. "What about the cross-country?" she wondered. "Will he run away?"

I shrugged. "The only question is, will he run in the right direction?"

"But the schooling," Nigella cried in agitation, "and the dressage! Will we have time to prepare?"

114

"We'll make time," I said.

I dipped my finger into one of the pots of jam and sucked it reflectively.

Everyone was silent, deliberating this new turn of events. Henrietta had stopped writing labels. Nigella's sugar lay forgotten on the scales. Only Lady Jennifer continued to fill up the jam jars.

"I should think The Comet might be *frightfully* good at eventing," she said.

13

An Evening with the Pony Club

"Are you sure you don't want any help with your dressage, Elaine?" Nigella said. She was walking by my stirrup as we left the little grass rick-yard which made an ideal, enclosed arena for our show-jumps. The Comet had jumped everything we had constructed, steadily and with the minimum of fuss. We had decided not to tempt fate by taking him over the cross-country course in the park; we had had enough anxiety and accidents, and the grey horse's performance over fences at speed had never been in doubt.

"No," I told Nigella. "Quite honestly, I would rather work by myself. It's a completely different test, so I'll ride a few movements at a time and learn it as I go along."

Nigella went off to help Henrietta to hose Legend's legs. He had been on three corn feeds a day at the time of the accident, and the enforced idleness had caused his legs to become puffy and heated. He was now on a non-heating diet of bran, sugar beet pulp and sliced roots and we were hosing each leg with cold water for fifteen minutes twice a day.

I rode The Comet out into the park and began to ride the test through. The hirelings ambled over and stood in an aimless little group outside the markers, watching our circles and our halts, our transitions and our serpentines. The Comet was stiff at first, and uncertain, but as time went on he became better

116

and better and it was clear to me that at some time he had been schooled to a very high standard indeed. I rode him back to the stables, pleased with the way he had performed, but at the same time, slightly troubled.

Before he had left on Friday evening, Nick Forster had asked me out again, and this time I had promised faithfully not to bring the Fanes. I hadn't been looking forward to telling them that I was going out without them, but in the event I was saved by Thunder and Lightning Limited who sent four complimentary tickets for a local DiscoNite at which they were making a live appearance. When I refused mine because I was already going out with Nick, the Fanes decided to give the extra tickets to Doreen and Brenda, so everyone was happy.

When it came to getting ready though, I hadn't a clue what to wear. I looked at the clothes in my worm-eaten wardrobe and I didn't seem to have anything suitable at all.

"Where are you going with Forster," Henrietta wanted to know, "that you have to make such a fuss?" Henrietta never made a fuss about clothes. She had thrown together an alarming outfit for the DiscoNite consisting of the lurex tights, the black leg-warmers, an elongate purple jersey that barely covered her thighs, and her scuffed pink satin stiletto shoes.

"I don't know," I admitted, wondering why on earth I hadn't thought to ask. "It could be a meal, I suppose, or on the other hand, it could be just a drink at a pub."

"Or it might be the cinema," Nigella suggested.

She was wearing tight black trousers, her red pill-box, her tap-dancing shoes and a black T-shirt with a moth-hole in the shoulder. "Why don't you wear this?" She pulled out the only classic garment I possessed, a cream linen suit.

The cream suit was more suitable for a wedding than a drink at a pub, but I struggled into it anyway.

Henrietta considered me with her head on one side. She had back-combed her hair until it stood out beyond her shoulders. Two long, thin plaits hung down in front of each ear. The effect was astonishing.

"You look far too colourless," she decided, "with your pale hair and your skin and everything. Can't you find something really bright to cheer yourself up?" She began to rummage through my things in the carved coffin-chest at the foot of my bed. Eventually she came up with a lime-green, nylon jersey. "Here, try this."

I tried it. It looked terrible.

"I can't wear this," I said, "it looks awful."

"You're right," Henrietta agreed. "It does look awful."

In the meantime Nigella had vanished in the direction of her own bedroom and returned with a crepe blouse in hot pink with a pie-frill collar and a sash. I put it on and looked in the mirror. The colour was very fierce.

"You still look boring," Henrietta said. She removed the sash from the waist and tied it round my head as if I was a Red Indian. "Now that looks much better," she said pprovingly.

"Oh," I said doubtfully, "I really don't know if . . ."

"Aren't you going to wear any makeup?" Nigella interrupted. The Fanes had painted kohl around their eyes and vivid blusher on their cheeks. Henrietta had small, metallic stars stuck cross her forehead. Standing together they looked rather like a cabaret turn. I was relieved to think I hadn't got to go with them to the DiscoNite.

I used some mascara and some lip gloss. Henrietta brushed aside my objections and applied some of her blusher to my cheeks.

I stared at myself in the spotted mirror. My reflection stared back at me. The sash around my head looked freakish. My cheeks appeared to be burning with a fever. The hot pink blouse didn't help. I ran downstairs. It was too late to do anything about it.

Nick drove down the Fane's pot-holey drive trying not to lose the exhaust pipe of his white, low-slung, sports car. He looked at me curiously. "Are you all right, Elaine?" he enquired. "You look a bit hot and bothered.

"Yes," I said brightly, "I'm fine." I got out a tissue and rubbed off some of the blusher when he wasn't looking.

We drove out beyond Westbury and turned into the forecourt of a rambling, timbered hotel called the Wild Duck Inn. The car park was overflowing and there were even a couple of coaches.

"It's busier than usual," Nick commented, "it's generally pretty quiet." He opened my door. "Do you have to wear that thing aroud your head?" he said with a trace of anxiety in his voice. "It looks a bit odd."

I had forgotten the sash. I snatched it off. "It was Henrietta's idea," I apologized.

Nick put his arm around me as we walked towards the main entrance of the hotel. "I'm glad you didn't decide to invite the Fanes along this time," he said. "I'm looking forward to a night on our own."

I waited in the beamed hall whilst Nick took our jackets to the cloakroom lobby. I felt a bit nervous. I wondered if Nick brought all his girlfriends to the Wild Duck Inn. There was a notice board with posters on it by the reception desk. I wandered over to it and read a few of the announcements just for something to do. Pride of place on the notice board went to a bright orange handbill. It said:

! TONIGHT ! TONIGHT !
The Midvale and Westbury Pony Club
DiscoNite
at the Wild Duck Inn, Fressington,
featuring
THUNDER AND LIGHᵵNING LIMITED
Live!

This was altogether too terrible to believe. I looked round for Nick, appalled. It would ruin our evening if we were to meet up with the Fanes. I had to tell him that we must leave at once. "Nick," I said urgently, "Nick, we . . ." but the district commissioner clapped a welcoming hand on each of our shoulders. "Jolly noble of you to support our little effort what? what?" he shouted. "Should make a tidy sum tonight if we all live through it, eh? eh?" He laughed energetically at his own joke and steered us firmly into a nearby bar where the Pony Club committee appeared to be bent upon consuming the maximum amount of beer in the shortest possible

120

time. Nick gave me a despairing look as we were separated by a raucous group of Pony Club associates. Pints flew back and forth. A martini was thrust into my hand and the district commissioner began a shouted conversation about the necessity of giving the members what they wanted, even if it perforated their eardrums in the process; all modern groups, he bellowed, were either damned louts or fairies, and Thunder and Lightning Limited were no bloody different. Whether they hunted or not, a spell in the blasted army would do them a power of good.

I listened to all this and I wondered how we could possibly make our escape. The district commissioner regarded the hunt servants as his own personal property. Not only that, but his brother-in-law was master of the Hunt and I knew that Nick couldn't afford to offend him. After a while, the district commissioner clapped his hands which seemed to be the signal for a general exodus to the DiscoNite. Nick managed to make his way to my side.

"We'll go in with them," he whispered, "then we'll leave; it's sure to be dark, they'll never notice." He squeezed my hand reassuringly.

In the ballroom where the DiscoNite was being held, it was pitch black except for a myriad of coloured lights pulsating to the beat of the terrifyingly loud music produced by the band. Thunder and Lightning Limited had been bald when we had first known them, now they had their hair dragged up to form a central spike dyed in alternate colours of orange, green, red and blue. They pranced and strutted across the stage wearing leather knee-breeches and bolero tops with flashes of lightning appliqued on to them. Their chests and their arms and legs looked hatefully white and puny and it was all simply hideous.

I could tell that Nick loathed it. We stumbled in the wake of the district commissioner who led us to some tables situated as far away from the band as he could get. Someone slapped drinks on to the table in front of us. The district commissioner sat down at the next table. "Rather like being in hell what? what?" he bellowed. He took some cotton wool out of his pocket and stuffed it into his ears, prepared to sit it out until the bitter end. Conversation was virtually impossible.

Nick and I began to plot our departure in sign language. We would get up and pretend to dance, working our way towards the exit, then we would make a bolt for it. We started to rise, but: "Well, if it isn't Busy Bee!" a fog horn voice proclaimed, and Brenda, vast in what appeared to be a pair of lilac pyjamas, plonked herself down at our table, making it rock, and spilling our drinks. Nick, who had hitherto kept his temper under trying circumstances, set his lips in a tight line. Brenda's face was plastered with her usual brand of orange panstick and her bleached, white hair was slicked flat on her scalp like a bathing cap.

"What's going on here, Busy Bee?" she bellowed. "Sitting in the dark with Lover Boy, are we?"

"Look, Brenda," Nick said threateningly, "take yourself off somewhere else. Elaine and I were having a private conversation."

"Private seduction, more like!" Brenda hooted. "You want to watch this lady killer, Busy Bee; if half what I've heard about him's true, he'll . . ."

Any further revelations were cut short by the arrival of Henrietta in the elongated purple jersey.

"Oh God," Forster said, aghast, "not *you*."

"Why shouldn't it be me?" Henrietta demanded indignantly, "I hardly expected to see you here, and Elaine knew *we* were coming."

Forster stared across the table at me in disbelief. His face in the disco lights went from red to orange to green. I looked at him helplessly, unable to deny it. Nigella appeared wearing the red pill-box with the veil, and with her came Doreen in tartan knickerbockers.

"Come and join the party," Brenda boomed, "the drinks are on Lover Boy!"

"Oh, thank you," Nigella said, gratefully sinking into a chair. "I'll have a campari and soda."

Henrietta and Doreen seated themselves expectantly at the table. Nick shot Brenda a venomous look and went to fetch the drinks. No sooner had he regained his seat than William arrived, very red about the neck, and two steps behind him came Janie Richardson. Far from being delighted, Nick sprang to his feet looking enraged. "What the bloody hell's going on?" he shouted at William. "What's *she* doing here?"

It was all very awkward. Janie Richardson sat down opposite me and stared round the table in an unfriendly manner. She was wearing a tight, silver dress and her hair was like a black bush. I thought it had looked a lot better under the silk hat.

Behind my back William was trying to explain himself to Nick. "She rang up after you'd left," he hissed. "I told her you were fixed up, but you know what she's like. She guessed you'd be here, and she asked me to bring her; I didn't want to come, but I couldn't very well refuse, *could* I?"

"I'm sorry about all this," Janie Richardson said, not looking it, "but the thing is that Nick was supposed to have been with me tonight."

"Is that so?" Henrietta exclaimed, pulling up her chair in an interested manner. "I thought he was rather keen on Elaine, he's been chasing her for ages."

"Of course, he could quite easily be attracted to two people," Nigella pointed out in a reasonable tone. "After all, he doesn't actually have to choose; it isn't like getting engaged or anything."

"That's not very fair though, that isn't," Doreen put in, "asking one girl out then taking another. I'd chuck him, Elaine, if I was you."

I wondered how much more of this I could stand. Things were getting pretty heated behind me, and William might well have ended up with a thump on his nose but for the district commissioner who suddenly spotted him and rose from his seat, overjoyed at having both whippers-in attending his DiscoNite. He clapped William affectionately on his back.

"Hunt jolly well represented tonight, what? what?" he whooped. "Got to support the young entry, eh? eh?"

This distraction gave Brenda the opportunity she had been waiting for. "Now look here, Cassanova," she said to Nick in a belligerent voice. "What the devil are you up to, asking Busy Bee out, when you're supposed to be with her?" She pointed to Janie, who jumped up from her seat and threw herself at Nick, unexpectedly bursting into loud sobs. Everyone at the table who had previously been

124

riveted by the turn of events, now looked embarrassed.

"Mind your own bloody business, Brenda," Nick said furiously, and taking Janie Richardson by the elbow, he steered her away, through the dancers and out of the exit, without even a backward glance.

"Well," Brenda said in disgust, "I bet that's the last we'll see of *him* tonight."

William did his best to apologize. "I'm very sorry, Elaine," he said, looking scarlet and very ill-at-ease. "It was my fault for bringing her, but she made me, she's ever so persistent."

I could believe it, but now I felt horribly unwanted, abandoned and miserable. How could I, in my plain, cream skirt and the unflattering, hot pink blouse, hope to compete with the exotic Janie Richardson with her coal black locks and her silver dress? I knew I couldn't, and the thought of it made me feel ill. "I want to go home," I said.

"You can come home with us," Nigella said comfortingly. "Brenda's driving; but we can't go yet, Henrietta's going to sing."

As she spoke, the deafening music suddenly died away and Solly Chell, the drummer with Thunder and Lighɔning Limited came to the edge of the stage and squinted into the interrupted dancers. "You there, 'Enry?" he bawled. "You ready?"

Henrietta jumped up, startled, and scampered off towards the stage. Everyone got up to follow, determined to have a better view. I followed them, not really wanting to, but not wanting to be left like a wall-flower with the district commissioner either.

Johnny Jones, the lead singer, handed the microphone to Henrietta. If I had been feeling less wretched, I might have been excited and even nervous for her. Henrietta sang all the time around the stables, composing little songs of her own to suit the occasion. We were so used to it that we no longer noticed, but we had never before heard her sing with the band – only informally, in the cab of the horsebox, driving home after hunting.

The band crashed into an introduction. The lights pulsed. The accompaniment was ear-piercing and strident, but Henrietta's clear voice soared above it. Even the youngest members of the pony club stopped yelling and listened. Everybody was entranced by the girl who stood in front of the band and sang like a lark. In her eccentric clothes, and totally unafraid, she could have been a pop star, yet somehow she managed to be nothing like one.

Intent on Henrietta's performance in spite of myself, I felt an arm steal round my waist. "I'm sorry it took so long," Nick whispered into my ear, "but I had to tell her once and for all that it was no good. She was a bit upset. I had to get her a taxi."

I felt weak with relief. I should have known he would come back. Now that he was standing beside me, I wondered how I could possibly have doubted it. We smiled into each other's eyes and joined in the appreciative hullaballoo for the girl in the elongated purple jersey as she jumped down from the stage.

14

Welcome to the Two-Day Event

"Welcome, welcome, everyone!" The portly figure of Felix Hissey stood on a small, raised platform which had been erected between the scoreboards. The familiar, ruddy-cheeked face which beamed from millions of pickle jars and sauce bottles on kitchen tables and supermarket shelves, now beamed down at us in person. "Welcome, welcome!" cried Felix Hissey again.

"Oh, do get on with it," Henrietta muttered impatiently. She had only half-plaited The Comet's mane, and was dying to get back to finish it.

"Welcome," Felix Hissey said, clasping his chubby hands together in delight, "to this very special two-day event, and a most special welcome to the Hissey Training Scholarship Candidates!"

We were back on the combined training competition ground, this time for the two-day event. In the box, The Comet waited; his fading dapples had been shampooed, his tail dipped in blue-bag, his hooves had been scrubbed, even the whiskers had been trimmed from his nose. He had submitted himself to all these attentions with his customary disregard and now, with his mane half-plaited, he waited for whatever might come next.

"And welcome," the King of Pickle continued throwing out his arms towards us in a gesture of universal joy and friendship, "to all the other competitors today, who have so sportingly agreed to make up the numbers; welcome! Welcome to you all!" He beamed round expansively once more, and clambered down from the platform to a scattering of applause.

"Is that it?" Nigella wondered. "Can we go?" But the chief of the selection committee was now on the platform.

The chief wore cavalry twill trousers with knife-edge creases, a Tattersalls check shirt and a BHS tie. He stared at us crossly, as if we had no right to be there at all, which was something of a shock, coming after Felix Hissey.

"The dressage will begin in exactly half an hour," he rapped, throwing up his chin in a defensive manner as if to stall any attempt at argument. "We expect every person to be riding in within sight of the starting steward at least fifteen minutes prior to their allotted time!"

"He makes it sound like a court-martial," Henrietta muttered.

"There will be an interval for lunch at one o'clock and the show-jumping will begin at two o'clock sharp!" The chief narrowed his eyes at us, as if we might regard this as unreasonable and begin to throw things. "Competitors will jump in reverse result order!" he barked.

"He might not be as bad as he seems," Nigella whispered. "He's probably very fond of dogs and small children, most of these BHS types are."

I couldn't imagine it.

"Accommodation for the horses belonging to the scholarship candidates has been arranged at the manor stables," continued the chief. "There is also dormitory accommodation for the candidates themselves if required!" He threw up his chin again and glared around as if challenging anyone to dare to apply for it. "There will be a veterinary inspection at nine o'clock tomorrow morning, the cross-country phase will begin at ten o'clock prompt, and there will be a short presentation ceremony at four-thirty!" Having delivered the last of the information at lightning speed, he walked sideways off the platform as if he suspected that there might be snipers in the audience.

"Are you nervous?" Nigella asked, as we made our way back to the horse-box. "You don't apper to be." She looked at me curiously, "you don't appear to be worried at all."

In some strange way I wasn't. It was as if all the happenings of the past few weeks had exhausted my capacity for worrying. The part of me that should have been worrying about the dressage, the show-jumping, the cross-country course, and the possible consequences of what I was doing, had run dry. There wasn't any worry left. "I'm not worried," I said, "not any more."

As it was half term, Doreen was with us and she led The Comet down the ramp of the horse-box. Henrietta opened her plaiting box and began to sew up the rest of his mane. We had plenty of time, The Comet didn't need very much preparatory schooling. I put on my navy jacket and my hat, Doreen pulled off the tail bandage and brushed out The Comet's tail. Nigella tacked up.

"It's remarkable that the saddle we bought for Legend fits so well," she commented, as she ducked under The Comet's belly to catch the girth. "It might have been made for him."

The Comet stood like a rock at the top end of the dressage arena; he stared into the distance, beyond the judges and their writers in the Range Rover, beyond the Jacobean manor house with its twisted chimneys and its topiary, even beyond the horizon. It seemed to me, waiting at A, that he might possibly never move again, but he was ready the second I closed my legs against his sides to begin the test.

Riding the test seemed to be more of a dream than reality. It slipped along quickly and effortlessly. I was conscious only of the flexing of the powerful neck contained by the unfamiliar double bridle, the grey ears set firmly forward, the scrubbed hooves flying in extension, thudding gently in canter, planted four-square on the turf at the halt. It all seemed so incredibly easy on the wise, grey horse, but then, I told myself, as we left the arena at a swinging walk on a long rein, he had probably done it all so very many times before.

For some reason known only to the chief, the dressage scores were not posted until all the tests had been ridden. Even before the last horse had left the arena, little knots of anxious people had gathered silently around the scoreboards.

The chief finally emerged from the secretary's tent with the result sheet in one hand and a stick of chalk in the other. He gave us a few sharp looks, climbed on to a chair, whipped round in order to ascertain that none of us had found this amusing, threw up his chin, and began to write.

The scholarship candidates' numbers were underlined in red to distinguish them from the non-participating competitors. The first candidate's score was 111, the next 94, then 101, then 89. "That's the best scholarship score so far," Nigella commented in a nervous voice; then as a 77 was posted, "that's better still."

Henrietta was quite unable to speak. She gazed intently at the board and picked furiously at the sleeve of her jersey. As we watched, the chief posted a score of 92 against another candidate's number; then he posted mine, 57.

The chief wrote it, looked at it, consulted the result sheet to check that he hadn't made a mistake, then threw up his chin and carried on scoring. When he had entered all the marks, he dismounted from the chair, looked quickly round for signs of rebellion, and observing none, vanished smartly into the secretary's tent.

The Fanes simply couldn't believe it. They stared at the scoreboard with their mouths open.

"Fifty-seven," Henrietta said incredulously, "*fifty-seven*?"

"It isn't possible," Nigella said in bewilderment. "They couldn't have given The Comet fifty-seven; there must have been a mix-up on the score sheets, someone must have made a mistake."

I knew there had been no mistake; fifty-seven was a fair mark for the kind of test The Comet had performed. He was older, he was not as supple, not as schooled, not as brilliant as he once had been, but it had been an admirable test, worthy of fifty-seven. "He deserved it," I told them, "it was a good test."

"It's not just a *good* test, it's incredible!" cried

Henrietta. "You've got the most fantastic lead! The nearest mark is seventy-seven; you're twenty points ahead! The others will *never* catch you up!"

"I don't suppose they will," I said, but then, remembering the set of the iron neck, the plank-like jaw, and the awful relentlessness of the grey horse's gallop, I added; "Unless we break our necks on the cross-country course."

We made our way towards the trestle tables set out around one of the ancient oak trees, where Felix Hissey was welcoming everyone to participate in his free luncheon. Doreen had almost finished hers. There was a powerful smell of pickled onions.

15

If You're in a Pickle

"Whatever you do," Henrietta said anxiously, "don't give him the *slightest* chance to get away from you, keep him *really* collected. Once he gets his neck out, you'll have no chance of stopping him at all."

"I wonder if I should tighten the curb-chain another link?" Nigella fretted at The Comet's immobile head, slipping her fingers behind the curb-chain to satisfy herself that it was tight enough, and pulling up the cheeks of the curb to test its efficiency. The Comet tried not to notice, concentrating his attention on the far distance, where tiny specks of traffic were visible, moving across the horizon.

"I think you should both stop fussing," I said. "He isn't going to run away."

Because of the reverse result order, I was last to go in the show-jumping. There had been ten clear rounds so far, six of them by short-listed candidates. The liver chestnut gelding inside the ropes took off too close to a white-painted gate and brought it thudding down. He had looked set for another clear, and a sympathetic groan went up from the small crowd of spectators seated on canvas chairs under an awning fronted by a banner which proclaimed *If You're in a Pickle – Make sure it's Hissey's!*

I could see the rotund figure of Felix Hissey himself seated under the awning. He was talking to Nick. As I gazed at them in an abstracted manner, my attention was suddenly caught by two people seated by them; two people whose faces were alarmingly familiar.

"Nigella," I said in dismay, "isn't that . . .?" But the liver chestnut gelding was cantering out of the ring and now there was no time. The ring steward called out my number. The Comet and I trotted into the ring. I pushed him into a canter and we circled around, waiting for the bell. The Comet was perfectly calm, perfectly manageable. As I had known he would, he cantered purposefully through the start, taking all the jumps in his stride, soaring over them accurately and obediently to finish with a clear round, well within the time allowed.

As we cantered through the finish I glanced into the crowd under the awning. Nick looked pleased, Felix Hissey was clapping his hands in delight. The two seats which had been occupied by the familiar-looking people were now empty. I closed my eyes and whispered a little prayer for myself and The Comet; praying that I had imagined it; that Lala Thornapple and the nurse had never been there at all.

The Fanes and I hadn't liked the sound of the dormitory accommodation; we had brought sleeping-bags and we were going to spend the night in the horse-box. Felix Hissey was providing a fork supper for everyone under the awning and Henrietta, Nigella and Doreen had gone off to investigate this, leaving me to take The Comet over to his stable at the manor.

On the way I stopped in the shadow of a small spinney to allow The Comet to graze. But The

Comet preferred to stand and stare into the spinney, so we both stood and stared into the spinney, made ghostly by its silver birch trees, and I leaned on the fence, listening to the small sounds of life around us, and The Comet's breathing.

"Elaine?"

Someone called my name softly. It was Nick, creeping up behind us like a thief in the night. He came and rested his arms on the fence beside me. We stood for quite a while, looking into the spinney with The Comet standing silently beside us. "Have you walked the course for tomorrow?" Nick wanted to know.

I told him that the Fanes and I had walked it earlier, all four miles and twenty-eight fences of it, through woodland, over grass and along tracks. I wanted to say more, I wished with all my heart that I could confide in Nick, that I could tell him what I had begun to suspect and ask him what I should do, but all of this was made impossible by his friendship with Felix Hissey. So everything I might have said remained unspoken, and I stared into the spinney, thinking, but unable to speak.

"If you're worried about the cross-country," he said, "I'll be there. I'll be driving Felix round in the Range Rover; if anything happens, if the old horse takes off, I won't be far behind."

"Thanks," I said, "I appreciate it." My voice sounded distant, even to my own ears.

"Elaine," Nick said gently, "what's the matter?"

"Why should anything be the matter?" I said. I blinked furiously, glad of the shadows, quite unable to cope with sympathy.

"You've won the dressage by a huge margin, you

got a clear round in the show-jumping," he said, "aren't you even pleased?"

"Of course I'm pleased," I answered. "Why wouldn't I be?"

"Because something tells me that you're not," he said, "something tells me that you're not pleased at all." He removed his elbows from the fence and turned his back on me, staring across the shadowy park towards the distant crowd of people gathered around the awning. "Something tells me that you're sorry you came, sorry I even suggested it."

There was nothing I could say to this. I just stared down at the long, lush grass growing beside the spinney, grass that The Comet didn't want. "I don't want you to think I'm not grateful," I said, "because I am."

"I don't want you to be grateful," Nick said, his voice low and angry. "I just want to know what's gone wrong between us in the space of a few days. I thought we understood each other after the other night; I thought there was something definite between us. Now I'm not so sure."

"It isn't anything to do with you and me," I told him. "It's nothing to do with the way I feel. After all this is over, I might be able to tell you and then you'll understand."

"And perhaps I won't," he said wearily. "I can't understand you, Elaine. I'm not even sure that I want to try."

I didn't call after him as he walked away. After a while I continued on my way towards the stables behind the Jacobean house with its twisted chimneys black against the sky. The Comet walked beside me;

he wasn't exactly invisible, but he was as insubstantial as a ghost or a memory in the twilight.

"If all this fails," Henrietta said, as she knelt at The Comet's feet and sewed up his bandages, "and something terrible happens today, we can always go back to fund-raising, and show-jump The Comet. I can't imagine why we haven't thought of it before."

"We haven't thought of it before," Nigella pointed out in a harassed voice, "because he's a bolter." She was very het-up about the cross-country. She pulled up the surcingle and slipped The Comet's rubber-covered reins under the stirrups and leathers. "Are you *positively* sure you don't want the double bridle, Elaine?" she asked me for the umpteenth time. "I'm sure you won't be able to hold him in the snaffle."

"The snaffle's fine," I assured her. "I can't possibly risk taking him in a double, I wouldn't be able to cope with all those reins, especially when they get slippery with sweat, and anyway, I wouldn't want to risk hurting his mouth. I'm sure to get left behind over a couple of fences."

"Hurt The Comet's mouth?" Henrietta exclaimed incredulously. "What a joke!"

I pulled on my navy guernsey and slipped my number-cloth over it. Doreen stood by holding my safety helmet and the cross-country starting times. The horses were being sent off at five minute intervals and I was the last one to go. I had less than half an hour to prepare.

Nigella was working herself up into a state of total panic. "Do we need over-reach boots?" She began to fling various articles of tack out of the locker in a frantic effort to locate them.

137

"If she's looking for over-reach boots," Henrietta called, "tell her they're here, on the ramp."

"What about vaseline?" Nigella wanted to know. "Do we need to vaseline his legs?" She ran to the back of the horse-box in order to consult *Training the Event Horse*. It had lost its dust jacket and there was hoof oil on the cover. I couldn't imagine what the library were going to say when, or if, she ever returned it.

"Please don't panic," I said. "There' no need. It's going to be all right, honestly." I could remember Nigella saying similar reassuring things to me at the Point-to-Point. It seemed ironic that I should be repeating them now. "I'm not going to get bolted with, we're not going to fall, nothing is going to happen to us."

Nigella stared at me. Two bright spots of colour burned on her cheeks. "How can you possibly know what is or isn't going to happen?" she demanded. "Why are you suddenly so confident?"

I put on my safety helmet and fastened the chin strip. I couldn't tell her why. "It isn't a difficult course," I said, "it isn't exactly Badminton." I strapped my watch to my wrist and wrote my starting and finishing times on my shirt cuff with a ballpoint pen.

As I went to mount, I saw that Nigella had left *Training the Event Horse* open on the ramp. Genesis was there for all to see, being hung with laurel wreathes after his victory in the Olympics. I tipped the book closed with my boot. It toppled off the side of the ramp and landed in the water bucket. Nigella fished it out, appalled.

"They'll make you pay for it now," Doreen

138

informed her. "They won't take it back, they're ever so fussy, libraries are."

I took The Comet's rubber-covered reins from under the leathers and pulled down the irons. "I wouldn't worry," I said. "I doubt if we'll need it after today."

Horses trickled home as The Comet and I waited for the signal to start. Horses returned dripping with sweat, with pumping sides and gusting breath, horses returned lame, others flew through the finish with their heads in the air, looking as if they would do it all again. Their riders looked red-faced, hot and triumphant, or pale and strained; one returned sodden from a ducking, slipping and squelching like wash-leather in the saddle, another came on foot and in tears, leading a horse with a twisted front shoe, comforted by parents.

The Fanes stood to one side looking fraught and anxious and five minutes seemed like fifty, but at last the flag was dropped, the stopwatch started, and The Comet and I were cantering away down the hill towards the first fence.

Over the first and the second fences The Comet flew, his bandaged legs setling into a regular, strong gallop, his steady head, pricked ears and his firm, plaited neck reassuringly familiar. Down towards the first drop fence he went, steadying with his powerful shoulders, jumping down and down and putting in a stride between the fences and down and down again, then up a short incline and over the tallest but least awkward of the Helsinki steps, just as I had planned it; then a stiff gallop and a huge leap over a hog's back constructed from telegraph poles, and on again, settling into the steady rhythmic gallop, following the orange direction flags down to the water.

It was here that The Comet and I met our first problem. The bed of the swift-running river was sandy, and as The Comet landed he pecked badly as his front feet sank and stuck in the sand.

I flew out of the saddle and up his neck, only saved from a soaking as he threw up his head in a valiant effort to pull out his front feet, and knocked me backwards into the saddle again, plunging forward and cantering gamely across the shallows. I had lost my reins and one stirrup, I was splashed and almost blinded by the water, but pushed onwards by my flailing legs, The Comet leapt up the sleeper-faced bank on to dry land. I barely had time to recover my lost iron and my reins before were over a stone wall, racing over four timber fences set for galloping, and into the woodland.

In the woodland it was dry and dense. The track was twisting and narrow and it was impossible to gallop. It was very silent and I was conscious of The Comet's laboured breathing, of my own breathless gasps, and the crackle and crunch of dead twigs and leaves under the steadily cantering hooves. It was quite a surprise to be suddenly confronted with a post and railed ditch with a jump judge sitting solemnly beside it on a shooting stick. The Comet put on a spurt and lengthened into it, managing to retain enough impulsion to carry us over the wide, low hedge which followed on immediately afterwards, bringing us into a lane with an unexpected clatter of hooves.

Made cautious by recent experience, we

approched the second river crossing with care, trotting up to it slowly and dropping off the bank, fully expecting the bed to be soft; it was hard. We splashed across to the opposite bank making watery clopping sounds on the river bed, and jumped out over a low rail. After a gate, a wicket fence, a small bank, and a tight double constructed out of two fallen trees, we were approaching the zig-zag rails and only eight fences from home.

The zig-zag rails had been the fence I had not liked the look of when we had walked the course the previous day. They were a Z shape of silver birch poles and we had to jump all three poles. Cantering up to it, it looked an impossible mass of angles and I tried desperately to remember exactly where I had planned to jump each one. I needn't have worried; The Comet made nothing of it. Jumping exactly where I asked him, slipping in an extra stride here, and lengthening a stride there, he sailed over like the veteran he was, never faltering, as we went on to clear the elephant trap with its sloping gate and yawning pit, up and launching into space over the ski-jump, then down, down, a seemingly endless succession of drop fences with the Fanes and Doreen standing at the bottom. I was feeling tired now, and even The Comet's powerful stride was beginning to flag, but as we breasted the hill and the bandaged legs flew stoutly onwards toward the quarry steps I saw the Range Rover crusing along about a hundred yards away, and looking up the hill, I could see little knots of people under the oak trees. We were approaching the run in.

We pinged through the bullfinch and cleared the chicken coops, there was nothing in front of us now but a level sweep of turf and the finishing posts. There was no danger, though, of The Comet starting to accelerate; he had no reserve left. He couldn't have bolted to save his life. We cantered in wearily to the finish, level with the Range Rover, out of which the Fanes and Doreen and Felix Hissey and Nick tumbled, flinging themselves at The Comet, slapping his wet, hot sticky neck, shouting their congratulations.

Everyone crowded round, wanting to touch the exhausted grey horse with his sides heaving like a bellows, as if he was a good luck charm. Even the chief was there, barking "Well done!" and "Jolly good effort!" Felix Hissey clasped his hands and cried "Wonderful! Wonderful!" The Fanes were jumping up and down with excitement and Doreen was trying to get through the crowd with rugs for The Comet, sniffing and wiping away tears with the back of her hands, overcome by the emotion of the moment.

It would have been marvellous but for the small, determined figure who came running and pushing through the throng, hotly pursued by another figure in a dark blue dress with black shoes and stockings. Lala Thornapple hurled herself at The Comet's lowered and dripping head, clutching wildly at him with her crippled, twisted hands. "Genesis!" she cried, "I knew it was you the minute I saw you! I knew it!"

The chief looked at the grey horse, and at me, and at Lala Thornapple, and his chin flew up and down, and the nurse stared at me, appalled. "Tell her it isn't true," she pleaded, "tell her it's impossible."

I slipped down from the saddle, ran up the stirrups, unbuckled the surcingle and the girth. I lifted off the saddle and placed it into Nigella's frozen, stupefied arms. I took the rug from Doreen, standing like a village idiot, with her mouth agape, and threw it over The Comet.

"I think she might be right," I told them, "I think The Comet is Genesis."

16

What Do We Do Now?

I stood in front of the selection committee in the secretary's tent and they all stared at me, their faces registering disbelief, irritation, and disappointment. Outside, a small crowd of competitors and their supporters waited, impatient, watchful and muttering.

"And you actually admit," a tall, thin woman with greying hair said in a perplexed voice, "that you substituted the grey horse for your own, knowing perfectly well that he was an ex-Olympic eventer?"

"My own horse was injured," I said, "he was knocked down by a car. He won't be fit to start work again for three months, and The Comet was the only other horse available. If I hadn't decided to come on him, I would have had to resign from the scholarship, but I didn't want to do that; I really needed to win a place," I added despondently. "I really wanted to. We all did." I thought of Legend with his leg inflated like a balloon, of the Fanes waiting dejectedly outside, and even of Nick, who had done his best, but who would quite possibly never want to speak to me again.

"But you did *know*," another BHS type said, his eyes incredulous, "that the horse you entered as The Comet was, in fact, not The Comet at all, but Genesis?"

"I didn't know for sure," I said, "I only suspected.

144

I'd seen the photographs in the book, and in Lala Thornapple's house, but I didn't know *absolutely*, not for certain, not until after the dressage. I'd guessed by then; I'm not very experienced you see, I haven't been properly trained in advanced riding, and I knew he couldn't have performed a test like that unless he was a very brilliant, exceptional horse."

"And the owners?" the tall, thin woman said. "Did the previous owners know? Did they tell you?"

"The previous owners hadn't a clue," I said. "To them he was just an old grey horse who jumped like a stag, but had a reputation for being a bolter; he didn't look like an Olympic champion, there was nothing about him to suggest it. He was always very reserved, a secretive sort of horse . . ."

"And you didn't think to mention it to them?"

"No," I said. "I wasn't sure anyway, until yesterday, and they would only have laughed. They wouldn't have believed it, nobody would."

Felix Hissey leaned cross the trestle table. For once he wasn't beaming and his round eyes were worried. "What about young Forster, Miss Would-Be-Event-Rider?" he asked. "Did you tell him?"

I had expected this. I couldn't bear the thought of Nick being implicated in any way. "You must believe me when I tell you that I didn't say a word to him about it," I said. "Nick Forster knew nothing."

Felix Hissey leaned back in his chair, satisfied. "I believe you," he said. "I know you, Miss Would-Be-Event-Rider, and I know you wouldn't lie."

I looked at him gratefully. Nothing about Felix Hissey was a pretence. He was a genuinely nice man.

"You do know," the chief barked, throwing up his

chin and glaring at me as if there was a chance I might deny it, "that the scholarship was intended for *potential* event horses and riders, *potential*, not proven?"

"I did know," I agreed, "it was in the conditions of entry."

"So you knew you were breaking the rules?"

"It wasn't quite as straightforward as that," I objected. "I suspected that I might be, but I couldn't be sure, and all the time I hoped that I was mistaken."

"But you weren't mistaken, Miss Would-Be-Event-Rider, were you?" Felix Hissey said, scratching his round head in an abstracted manner. "You weren't mistaken at all."

"The question is," the tall, thin woman said, "what do we do now?"

The selection committee looked baffled.

"She'll have to be eliminated from the competition," the BHS man said eventually, "and she'll have to be disqualified from the training scholarship. It's really most unfortunate for all concerned, but there's no way round it that I can see."

I was hardly surprised. It was no more than I expected, and probably less than I deserved.

"I think you had better go outside," the tall, thin woman said, not unkindly, "whilst we talk it over."

I turned to leave, hating the thought of emerging from the tent in front of all those curious and accusing eyes. But the chief sprang to his feet, ready to direct a strategic manoeuvre. He unlaced a flap in the rear of the tent, stuck out his head to ascertain that the coast was clear, then propelled me through it. "Make a run for it, girl!" he rapped. "Can't have

146

you running the gauntlet; we'll detail someone to tell your friends."

I bolted for the horse-box, reflecting that the BHS knew what they were doing when they appointed men like the chief.

"I just don't know what to say to you, Elaine," Lala Thornapple said, and her eyes, despite the pink-flushed cheeks, were contrite. "I've been in to see the selection committee and I've told them that you couldn't have known for sure that the horse was Genesis. How could you? You had never seen him in your life before, except in a photograph!" She ran her crooked hands through the grey horse's mane still crimped with its plaits. "Why, who would have thought that he would have still been going strong after all this time? But then," she added fondly, "he always was the most amazing horse."

"Why did you part with him?" Nigella wanted to know. "How could you have sold him, loving him as much as you did?"

"I didn't," Lala Thornapple said. "I went into hospital for an operation on my hands. It was unsuccessful, and the surgeon told my husband that I would never regain the use of them. He didn't want me to ride again after that, knowing that I would never be fully in control, especially on a horse like Genesis. He sold them all before I came home; I expect he thought he was acting for the best."

We fell silent, imagining Lala Thornapple coming home to an empty stable yard; finding all her beloved horses gone. No wonder she hadn't been able to accept it; no wonder she had been forced to pretend.

"I tried to trace them afterwards," she said, "but

147

it was hopeless. Most of them went abroad, as they often do, top class horses like mine; the English can't afford them. The money was well invested; it keeps me in comfort now, I suppose. My husband died soon afterwards."

"And The Comet just got sold on," I said, "getting more and more of a reputation as he went."

"He always was a very strong horse," Lala Thornapple said, "but I can imagine that if anyone took him hunting or anything like that, there would be no holding him; and once it got to be a habit, well, you know what horses are . . ."

"And we bought him," Henrietta said in wonder. "But we never guessed; we never knew."

"And Elaine got him in lieu of wages," Nigella said. "It's almost unbelievably ironical that she should end up with an ex-international eventer, without even realizing it."

"And for him to end up wearing his own saddle," I said, "that's the most unbelievable thing of all!"

"I want to ask you, Elaine, my dear," Lala Thornapple said, "if you would consider selling Genesis back to me. It would make me so happy; he could have his old stable back, and no horse in the world would be better cared for."

I knew this was true. I had known that Lala Thornapple was going to ask, so I was prepared for it. The nurse and I had discussed it previously and she had assured me that it would be the best thing possible for Lala Thornapple to have the real Genesis in the stables. I had thought carefully about The Comet and his future. I knew we couldn't use him as a hireling any more, he had caused too many accidents in the past and anyway, he deserved better than that. Today had also shown me that he was too old now for hard work, his heart and his gallant spirit were willing, but his legs were hot and puffy under his support bandages. Yet now the time had come to part with him, I loved him too much to let him go, and the fact that I knew he would walk away without a backward glance only made it harder to bear.

"I'll lend him to you," I said, "I don't want to sell him to you because . . ." I tailed off, not liking to finish, not wanting to say because you won't live for ever, and what will become of the old grey horse then, left alone in the empty stable yard.

"I know what you're thinking," Lala Thornapple said, "you think I'll die and he'll be sold again. Well," she sighed, and made a small gesture of resignation with her gnarled hands, "I'll die, I suppose, but if you agree to part with him, I'll make a will leaving him to you, together with enough money to keep him in comfort until the end of his days." She looked at me, and her eyes were round and anxious. "How would that be?"

I looked at the nurse in gratitude, knowing that this had been her doing. "I think that would be very satisfactory," I said.

"Welcome, Welcome!" cried Felix Hissey. "Welcome to this final prize-giving ceremony!! Welcome to you all!"

We stood at the foot of the raised platform waiting to hear the results. Nobody had either confirmed or denied that I had been disqualified from both the competition and the scholarship, but I knew that I must have been. Knowingly or unknowingly, I had broken the rules, and that seemed all there was to it.

"The results of the two-day event are as follows," Felix Hissey beamed down at me in what appeared to be an encouraging manner. My heart lifted slightly, then plummeted. "In first place with seventy-seven penalty points, Mrs Zara Gibbons' Flame Thrower, ridden by Selena Gibbons!"

A delighted cheer went up from the crowd. One or two people nearby turned to stare at me curiously; they knew that something had gone wrong, but they didn't know what.

"In second place," Felix Hissey announced, "Harvest Moon, ridden and owned by Timothy Whate!" Another cheer went up. I wondered if I could creep away without attracting too much attention, but decided that I couldn't. The Fanes and Doreen stood stoutly by my side; if they could stand it, then so could I.

"In third place," Felix Hissey continued, "Edwin Drood, owned and ridden by Mary Ann Maddox! In fourth place, Mrs Greta Shannon's Brown Paper Parcel, ridden by Davina Shannon! And fifth, Master Facey Romford, owned and ridden by Phillip Hastings! Finally," he cried, slapping his hands in a joyous manner, "in sixth place, Fox Me, owned and ridden by Amanda Willis!"

I joined in the general applause, feeling desolate. I hadn't expected to have been allowed to win; my own sense of fair play told me that it wouldn't have been proper. But I still felt bitterly disappointed and ashamed, not only for myself but for the Fanes, and perhaps most of all for The Comet, for the last event he would ever compete in, for a glorious career ended in dishonour, and all of it my fault. It was for The Comet that I could have wept.

"And now!" cried Felix Hissey, puffing out his chest grandly, "I have the most *enormous* pleasure in being able to announce to you, the names of the successful candidates in the Hissey Training Scholarship for potential event riders!"

There was a flutter of anticipation amongst the crowd. Felix Hissey beamed. The chief appeared with a list of names which Felix Hissey took from him with a courtly little bow.

"Scholarships have been awarded to the following," Felix Hissey announced. "Selena Gibbons and Flame Thrower, Mary Ann Maddox and Edwin Drood, Phillip Hastings and Master Facey Romford, Amanda Willis and Fox Me, Vivian Tintoft and Balthazar, and Alice Merryman and The Talisman."

Roars of approval greeted this announcement. The Fanes and I turned to leave. None of us could take any more. But Felix Hissey was holding up his hands for silence and the cheering died away.

"There is one more successful candidate," he informed us, "and although the Hissey Training Scholarship provides for only six successful candidates and six have therefore been awarded; by a unanimous vote, and through some entirely exceptional circumstances, we have decided to award an extra scholarship this year." Felix Hissey paused and drew a deep breath. "That scholarship, for displaying outstanding potential and admirable determination in the face of difficult and quite extraordinary circumstances, goes to Elaine Elliot and Another Legend, owned by the Honorable Nigella and Henrietta Fane."

The applause was simply deafening.

Sometime during the haze that followed, Lala Thornapple's nurse slipped an envelope into my anorak pocket. It contained a cheque for two and a half thousand pounds. With it was a short note.

> *Please don't refuse it* (it said).
> *Quentin Thornapple got a King's
> Ransome for Genesis when he sold
> him, and it's still only a fraction
> of his worth. Put it towards your
> training; finding Genesis again has
> made an old lady very happy.*

I handed the cheque to Henrietta. A year ago she had raised the money to buy Legend by selling the only valuable thing she possessed. Now I could repay her.

"Why are you giving it to me?" she wanted to know. "I thought we had agreed that The Comet was your horse; it's your money, not mine." She tried to give it back.

"No, no," I said, "it's for you. It's the money for Legend, repaid with interest."

Henrietta stared down at the cheque in silence. She didn't look at all pleased.

"But we've enjoyed owning an eventer," Nigella said. "We don't want to be paid back. We would rather put the money into the Training Fund."

"There's to be no more Training Fund," I said, "and no more fund raising. Now that I've paid you back for Legend and got a scholarship, I ought to be able to make it alone." I was trying not to be emotional.

I knew there was no future in being sponsored by the Fanes any more, but it hurt, more than I would have believed possible, to have to say it.

There was a silence in the horse-box apart from The Comet, eating his hay.

"Are you leaving us, Elaine," Nigella wondered, "is that what you are trying to say?"

Now that she had asked, I couldn't deny it. "I'd like to stay while Legend is recovering, and you will need help for the hunting season," I said "The scholarship training doesn't begin until the spring. I would like to stay until then, if you'll have me." It sounded awful, as if I was only staying because I hadn't anywhere better to go.

"Stay as long as you like," Henrietta said, "and leave when you like. I don't suppose we'll care, one way or another." Despite the matter-of-fact tone of her voice, I knew she was hurt. She would have died though, rather than have shown it. She turned away and stuffed the cheque into her pocket. In the year and a half that I had known her she had been irritating and difficult, she had been suspicious of me and sometimes bad-tempered, but she had never blamed me for Legend's accident. Although he represented all of her wordly wealth, and she knew, as I knew, that it had been my fault, she had never said a word.

"Well, *I* rather think," Nigella sadly, "that we'll all care very much indeed." Doreen came leaping into the horse-box, eating one of Felix Hissey's free currant buns. "Nick Forster's waiting for you, Elaine," she informed me. "I told him I didn't know how long you'd be, but he said he'd wait all the same."

153

I led The Comet down the ramp. He was to spend another night in the manor stables. It would have placed too much additional strain on his weary limbs to have expected him to travel home the same day.

Nick and I made our way slowly cross the sheep-nibbled turf. The stiff, grey horse walked between us. From the ramp of the horse-box the Fanes watched his progress. None of us quite knew what was going to happen next.

Ticket to Ride

Caroline Akrill

For Christine and Peter, and for Kenneth,
to remind them of our
Riding School Days

1

Last Straws

It was certainly Nigella's fault. By her reasoning, if every horse lasted a further week before being shod, and the blacksmith came every nine weeks instead of every eight, the resulting five visits a year instead of six would mean an annual saving of one hundred and sixty pounds.

This, then, was the result of it. Standing on the edge of a greasy bank, exposed to the vilest of East Anglian weather, lashed by rain, buffeted by winds; hands, thighs and face aching with cold; feet totally numb, the frostbitten toes probably snapping off one by one even as I stood.

"How far is the horsebox?" I asked.

Henrietta looked at me. Her cheeks burned red. Her hair, escaped from its coil, plastered the shoulders of her sodden habit. Her eyes, raised from the front hoof of the black horse, from the thin, twisted shoe which, despite manful efforts, she had failed to remove, were overflowing with vexation.

"How far is the box?" she repeated in a distracted voice. She dropped the hoof abruptly and took the black horse by the rein. He, after a few uneasy seconds spent pawing the air in order to ascertain that his leg was still attached to him, hopped anxiously at her side, his eyes rolling and the steam rising from his shoulders, as Hernrietta set off along the ridge of the bank stretching endlessly into the miserable, mud-filled horizon.

I took hold of Nelson, who had stood like a rock throughout the emergency, his one good eye straining after hounds, the water dribbling off his chin, and his saddle black like old washleather and squelched after them. At least, I told myself, this is the last time, the *very* last time. I am leaving tomorrow.

We walked, it seemed, for ever, but finally we reached a lane, and at the end of the lane, a pub. Henrietta handed me the black horse and vanished inside. After a goodly interval she reappeared bearing two small glasses. The contents of one of them almost blew my head off. The landlord of the pub, in a green apron, watched from the doorway with some anxiety.

"I haven't paid him," Henrietta gasped. "I don't seem to have any cash."

I searched my pockets without much hope and to my relief came across a pound note, folded small, and tucked away in more affluent times for such an occasion as this. I handed it to Henrietta who, without a word of acknowledgement, handed it to the landlord. This is the last pound, I told myself, that I will ever hand to Henrietta; but it might have been that anyway, since it was the last pound I had.

A hammer was produced, and a pair of pliers, and with the help of these we managed to remove what remained of the black horse's impoverished shoe. Barcloths were offered, saddles were rubbed, and we remounted and rode on in discomfort, clopping along the flooded lanes, through villages where the thatches poured and the guttering overflowed and every passing vehicle sent up a further douche of icy water.

There will be no more of this, I told myself, I am done with hunting. I felt myself done with many things, the Fanes included. But even now, as I looked through the slanting rain at Henrietta riding ahead, at the long and beautiful hair matted to the good blue habit, cut a little tighter in the waist and fuller in the skirt than was quite proper today, I wondered if my resolution would hold when the time came and if I would be able to leave quite easily. Yet, I *must* leave, I said to myself, there is no future for me with the Fanes.

Every joint in my body had set into a frozen ache by the time I realized, by the welter of orchestration as what shoes our horses retained rattled, clinked, and scraped on the concrete, that we had reached the sugar beet collection point where we had left the horsebox.

I struggled out of the saddle, my knees buckling under me as I hit the ground, and fumbled, agonized and blue-fingered, with straps and keepers and bandages.

We drove home with the heater on full and the windscreen pouring with condensation, to be received by a totally unrepentant Nigella who blamed the wet, the clay, and the sticky plough for our misfortune, and actually intimated that we had done her a personal disservice by managing to lose a shoe.

"I don't suppose you thought to bring it back with you?" she enquired, as if it might have been possible to wrench out the nails, hammer it flat, and reattach it to the black horse's foot.

By calling upon reserves of self-control I didn't know I had, I managed to endure all this without comment. It doesn't matter, I consoled myself, even though I had told Nigella it was a needless indulgence to take the horses out when there were no clients to escort; even though I had gone reluctantly, for Henrietta's sake. It really doesn't matter at all, because this is the last time I will have to put up with Nigella's misguided economies and her capricious penny-pinching. From tomorrow, it will be goodbye to all that.

Henrietta and I squelched through the kitchen. There was no need to remove our boots because the Fane residence boasted no carpets to speak of. In the icy vastness of the hall, the ornate plaster ceiling was mottled and patched with damp and the cavernous stone fireplaces were heaped with the same dead ash that had lain there eighteen months ago when I had first arrived as a hopeful young stable employee.

Now I trailed after Henrietta up the dusty, bare staircase and opened the door of my cheerless bedroom. My suitcase, already half packed, lay on the faded tapestry bedcover. Outside the tall, ill-fitting windows, the rain continued to pour down and the countryside was relentlessly grey. The room, with its monstrous carved wardrobe and coffin chest, was freezing, and its single decoration, a yellowing canvas of an angry Elizabethan lady clutching an orb to her flattened chest, her bald-lidded eyes following my every movement with venomous distrust, made it even less welcoming.

In the antiquated bathroom I fought the geyser and was rewarded with three inches of tepid water in which to soak my aching bones. I sat disconsolately in the stained bathtub trying to work up a lather with a hopeless sliver of soap and I thought about my future.

Tomorrow I would be leaving the Fanes to take

up my place on an all-expenses-paid eventing scholarship and in comparison with the discomforts I had endured at Havers Hall, I would be living in the lap of luxury. I imagined myself housed in a centrally-heated chalet, wallowing in a bath whose shining taps gave forth an endless supply of hot water, taking my place in a dining hall to be served with regular, properly presented meals. The thought of it momentarily banished any qualms I had about leaving the Fanes to cope with their financially precarious livery business, and as I rubbed myself dry on a balding towel, I told myself that all I had to do before I left was to wring six months' unpaid wages out of them at supper. In the light of past experience, I knew this would not be easy.

"Wages?" Nigella said innocently when I mentioned it. "Did we agree to pay you wages? I rather thought your board and lodging and the keep of your horse covered that."

She handed me a plate of frighteningly greasy stew concocted out of the leg of a casualty ewe deemed too good for hounds by the Midvale and Westbury Hunt and distributed as largesse to prospective puppy walkers "for the freezer". The Fanes didn't have a freezer.

"When I agreed to stay for the hunting season," I reminded her, "you agreed to keep Legend and to pay me twenty pounds a month. 'Pocket money wages' you called it. I'm not asking you for a fortune, it's only five pounds a week."

"It may not be a fortune to you," Henrietta said in a grumpy voice, "but it adds up to quite a lot. We're already overdrawn at the bank and there are

11

stacks of bills to be paid." She removed a well-chewed piece of mutton from her mouth and placed it on the side of her plate with a grimace of disgust. "This ewe," she said, "must have been run over the very second before it was due to die of old age."

"Now look here," I said crossly, determined not to let her change the subject, "you'll have to pay up because I'm absolutely broke. I gave you my last pound this morning, and I can't possibly go away on a month's course without a penny in my pocket."

Nigella carefully studied the piece of meat impaled on the end of her fork. "I rather suspect the mutton may have been too fresh," she decided. "I think we should have hung it for a few days before we cooked it."

"And *I* think we should discuss my wages," I said firmly.

"We are discussing them," Henrietta countered, "it's just that it's not awfully convenient at the moment. We're a little financially embarrassed."

I stared at her in exasperation. "It's *never* convenient," I said, "and you're *always* financially embarrassed. I've put off asking for as long as I possibly could, but it never gets any better, does it? People don't work for nothing," I told her, "they can't afford to, and besides, what's going to happen when you replace me? Whoever you get will expect to be paid a *wage*."

There was an awkward little silence.

"So you have definitely decided, Elaine," Nigella said, "not to come back after the course?"

"Nigella," I said, "you know I won't be coming back; we discussed it. I told you weeks ago."

"Well, yes," she agreed, "but I rather hoped you

12

might change your mind." She stared down into her stew and looked despondent. She was wearing a fearsome mohair jersey, its matted bulk filled with hayseeds, horse hairs, flakes of bran, and other, less easily indentifiable things.

"I haven't changed my mind," I said. How could I? Even if I wanted to, how could I go on any longer like this, without any wages, without any prospects? Surely even Nigella could see that it was impossible. "I'm going to advertise for a job in *Horse and Hound*. If you like, I'll write an advertisement for the vacancy as well and send it off at the same time." It seemed the least I could do.

"Er . . . no," Nigella said, "not yet, we'd rather not." She became suddenly very interested in her stew.

"We might not even bother to get anyone else," Henrietta remarked in a casual tone. "We may find we can manage on our own. After all, it isn't *that* difficult."

Remembering the state the yard had been in when I had arrived, I was astounded by this piece of ill-founded optimism. I turned to Henrietta, determined to make her retract it. "You seemed to find it difficult enough before I came," I snapped, "you didn't seem to find it particularly easy to manage then."

"What Henrietta actually means," Nigella said in a conciliatory tone, "is that we probably won't be looking for a replacement right away. We'll keep the job open for you in case you want to come back."

"That's very nice of you," I said, "but unnecessary."

"After all," she continued, "you don't know what

13

the course is going to be like. You might hate it. You might be homesick."

I wondered how she could possibly imagine that anyone could be homesick for a place like Havers Hall. I couldn't think of a single person who would want to live in it. Only the Fanes appeared not to notice its appalling discomforts; the Fanes and the rats, who scuttled nightly in the rafters above my head. Nevertheless, I was touched to think that they wanted to keep my job open in case I was unhappy on the course, even though they would be greatly inconvenienced by it. I opened my mouth to insist that they find a replacement at once, but was interrupted by Lady Jennifer, who darted into the kitchen clad in ancient tweed and a crumpled Burberry, trailing a faded Hermes scarf with a darn in it, and looking anguished.

"Elaine," she shrilled, "I'm so *frightfully* sorry not to be present on your last evening, but I was *hopelessly* delayed with the Meals-on-Wheels, and I'm already *desperately* late for the Village Amenities Committee. I shall have to fly this *very* second."

"It doesn't matter," I said, "honestly, I didn't expect it." I had grown very attached to Lady Jennifer and I knew I was going to miss her a lot. Now she fled across the kitchen towards her latest good cause, pausing only to grip my shoulder affectionately with her bony fingers.

"You've been the most *marvellous* help to us, Elaine," she trilled, "a tower of strength. I can't imagine how we shall *possibly* manage to survive without you. I feel sure the new girl won't fit in *nearly* as well." She knotted the headscarf under her pointed chin and made for the back door with her

14

mackintosh flying out behind her. The door banged shut.

I turned back to the Fanes in disbelief. Nigella gave her fullest attention to her plate, but Henrietta met my eyes warily.

"New girl?" I said.

Henrietta shrugged. "Oh," she said vaguely, "Mummy means whichever new girl we end up with, I suppose."

It was a lie and I knew it. "You've got a replacement for me already," I said accusingly, "you couldn't even wait until I was off the premises!"

Nigella sighed. She put down her fork. By this time everyone's stew was cold and beastly. "Elaine," she said, "we had to do *something*."

"But only a minute ago you said you would keep my job open for me in case I wanted to come back," I said incredulously. "You knew all the time that you had a replacement waiting!"

"We didn't want to mention it," Nigella said, "in case you were offended."

"Well, I am offended," I said, "I'm very offended. I've never been so offended in my life, and I think you've been incredibly underhand about it!"

"What did you expect us to do!" Henrietta demanded angrily. "Wait for you to make up your mind and then be left without anyone? Because we *would* have been left without anyone, wouldn't we? Since you have had your scholarship course to look forward to, you haven't cared what happens to us!"

I stared at her, shocked. "I *do* care," I said, "I don't know how you can suggest such a thing."

"If you cared," Henrietta blazed, "you would be coming back after the course, Elaine, but you decided not to. And now you're jealous because we've found someone to take your place – that's how much *you* care!"

I stared down at the lumps of mutton rising out of the glistening white globules of congealed fat on my plate. It was true. I *was* jealous. I hated the thought of someone replacing me, somone else doing all the things that I had done, getting to know and love the horses that I had known.

"Elaine," Nigella said cautiously, "it isn't that we wanted to replace you. We *had* to. It was your choice, after all, to stay or to leave."

I could hardly deny it. "But you could have told me," I said, "we could have discussed it together. You didn't have to be so secretive about it."

"She seems a good sort, anyway," Henrietta said in a hearty voice. "She's got some good ideas – she's going to take summer grass liveries and give riding lessons to the locals."

"But I told you to do that," I objected, "I thought of it ages ago. I made all sorts of suggestions."

"Oh yes," Henrietta said in a peevish tone, "you made *suggestions* . . ."

"We had lots of replies to our advertisement," Nigella said quickly, "fifteen altogether."

No wonder she hadn't wanted me to write one out. "If you wouldn't mind," I said, "I would rather not hear about it."

"We interviewed them last week," Henrietta said smugly, "the day you were out with Nick Forster."

"And I suppose you promised them a regular wage," I said, "even though you haven't paid me for the last six months."

"You needn't worry about your wages, Elaine," Nigella assured me, "honestly. We'll bring them to the training centre when we come to see you. It isn't

16

as if you won't see us again; we'll still be keeping in touch."

This was the first I had heard of it. "Will we?" I asked, surprised.

"You don't think we would just abandon you?" She dipped a crust of bread gingerly into the fatty gravy on her plate. "Not after all we have been through together?"

"And anyway," Henrietta said sharply, "there's Legend to consider. We still have an interest in him."

I didn't like the sound of this. "An interest?" I said.

"Well, yes," Nigella said, chewing at the soggy crust, "of course."

"When you say interest," I said carefully, "do you mean an interest as in personal interest? What exactly," I asked them, "do you mean by interest?"

"Why, personal interest," Nigella said, "naturally."

"And financial interest," Henrietta said. "After all, we found the horse in the first place, and I paid for him out of my own pocket."

"Now WAIT a minute!" I shouted. The legs of my chair squawked a protest as I started away from the table, confounded by this new piece of treachery. "You may have bought the horse to start with, but I paid you back in full – the horse is now *my* property!"

There was silence. Then: "It wasn't quite as simple as that, Elaine," Nigella said in an uncomfortable voice, "it was a very complicated arrangement."

"It wasn't complicated at all," I said heatedly. "You bought Legend for sixteen hundred pounds, you also gave me what you considered to be a totally

17

useless and dangerous horse in lieu of the wages you promised to pay me and never did. I sold the horse for two thousand pounds, and I paid you back the whole amount, including four hundred pounds in interest. Legend is mine. There's nothing complicated about it at all, it's perfectly simple."

"Ah," Henrietta said on a little note of triumph, "but you are forgetting an important little consideration known as potential."

"Whose potential?" I demanded.

"We bought an unschooled, untried, green horse, who bucked off everyone who tried him," Henrietta said. "He was just about worth what we paid for him. But, after we had disciplined him, got him fit, and schooled him up to competition standard, he was worth far more; double the price at least, possibly even treble." She helped herself to some more gravy from the stewpot, extracted a long hair from the second spoonful, and laid it pointedly beside Nigella's plate.

"After *you* schooled him!" I exploded. "Henrietta, *I* schooled him, *I* disciplined him, *I* got him fit and up to competition standard. *You* hardly ever placed your foot in his stirrup, apart from one occasion when I had a sprained wrist. Even then," I added with angry satisfaction, "he bucked you off."

"But you must admit that we helped," Nigella said. "You couldn't have done it on you own. We helped to raise the funds for his training, we helped to buy the saddlery, we organized the transport, we even helped to get you the scholarship. Do admit, Elaine, that you couldn't have done any of it without us."

I didn't want to admit it. I stared down at my horrible, untouched dish of casualty mutton stew, and I burned with fury. I had never imagined that the Fanes would claim a financial interest in my horse; an interest they knew I would never be able to repay; an interest which would bind and obligate me to them forever. If it was true, if they *were* still entitled to a share in Legend, I would never be free to pursue my eventing career, I would never be able to make any decision without consulting them first. I closed my eyes with despair and wondered how I would find the strength to endure it.

"I don't know why you're making such a fuss," Henrietta commented, leaning across the table and spearing a wizened roast potato on her fork. "It isn't as if we're actually asking you for the money." She flipped back a tress of hair that had trailed through her gravy. "It isn't as if we're being unreasonable."

"We've looked in *Horse & Hound,*" Nigella said, "and you can't get anything anywhere near Legend's standard for under ten thousand pounds. It's true, Elaine, honestly."

I knew it was true. "But what about me?" I asked bitterly. "I've done my part. I've kept my side of the bargain. I've organized your yard, I've increased your business, I've looked after your horses, I've found you new livery clients. I haven't been paid for any of it."

"Well, *that* isn't true," Henrietta exclaimed in an outraged voice. "We gave you a horse, we bought you Legend, we've helped with his training and saddlery, we've kept him for nothing, you've had free board and lodging yourself, *and* it seems that now you're to be paid five pounds a week backdated to last autumn. If you ask me, you've done jolly well out of us!"

"But five pounds a week isn't anywhere near a

proper wage for a trained and qualified groom," I said despairingly. "Even with board and lodging and keep of a horse thrown in, it's pathetic!"

"In case you haven't noticed," Henrietta flared, "we're not exactly well off ourselves."

"And anyway," Nigella said in a wounded tone, "you've been treated just like one of the family."

There was nothing I could say to this. I slumped back in my chair, defeated. It was pointless to argue any further. I stared up at the cobwebby iron chandelier above my head. Only two of its lights burned now out of twelve. When I had first arrived there had been six, then five, then four, then three; and now there were only two. After I have gone, I thought, there will be one, and finally none at all. Then perhaps someone will buy new bulbs, and then again, perhaps they won't. Somehow, and in spite of everything that had gone before, this gave my heart a little twist and I was forced to turn my attention back to the table. I put a piece of cold mutton into my mouth and chewed, and chewed, and chewed. It was not at all pleasant, but it gave me something else to think about.

2

No Fond Farewell

There was all of a sudden a crashing of hooves and, with a lot of flying manes and flapping New Zealand rugs, the Fanes dashed under the clock arch carried along by the horses who had spent the morning turned out in the park.

With Legend bandaged and boxed and my suitcase already on the front seat of the horsebox, I had steeled myself for this final confrontation. "Henrietta," I said, "what about my wages?"

Henrietta, poised to make the descent from the black horse's wither, set like a knife upon the end of his snaking neck, frowned. She wore an out-at-the-elbow sweat shirt and some ghastly striped purple, black and orange skin-tight trousers, the ensemble finished off with leg-warmers made furry with horse-hairs, baseball boots and a filthy scarlet hunt waist-coat. It was not an outfit to inspire confidence within the breast of a prospective livery client, but then, who knew when or if there would ever be more.

"You must give me something," I said, "even a few pounds would do."

Henrietta might have made a reply to this, had there not been a diversion as the bad-tempered chestnut, noticing that an opportunity had presented itself due to Henrietta's momentary inattention, nipped the black horse sharply on its flank.

The black horse shot forward as if propelled from a cannon, and Henrietta, true to a lifetime's instinct

21

never to loose the reins whatever the contingency, was towed backwards over his rump on the halter ropes of Nelson and the chestnut which were clasped in either hand. She landed on the cobblestones with a thud and a gasp, finally loosing the ropes at the moment of impact with the unexpected shock of it all.

Any further demands for my wages were cut off at this point and I could do nothing but stand speechless, as Nelson, the halter pulled completely from his threadbare little head, trotted unerringly into his own stable, and the black horse set off at a trot round the yard, snorting like a maddened bull, and lifting up his knees like a hackney. Even so, I still had hopes that the discussion might be resumed after Henrietta had struggled to her feet, looking fit to burst into flames, and I had come to and captured the black horse by his bobbing halter rope. It might have been, were it not for the fact that the bad-tempered chestnut suddenly spotted the grey cob livery.

The bad-tempered chestnut loathed and detested all of his fellow equines, but for some reason the grey cob was the horse he hated most of all. He bared his long, yellow teeth, flattened his ears, and flew at him with his tail whipping round like a windmill. The grey cob, fearing for his life, reared up against the onslaught and struck out with a front leg, emitting at the same time a shrill squeal of fright. The bay mare next to him, on whom Nigella had been sitting with a thunderstruck expression on her face, ran backwards in anguish, causing the rope of the chestnut pony on the other side to be snatched out of Nigella's hand. The pony, displaying true native instinct for self-preservation, immediately

22

bolted off back through the clock arch, splattering the walls with gravel as her flying hooves hit the drive. It was at this point that Nick Forster, who was waiting to drive me to the training centre, set up a constant and impatient toot-tooting upon the horn.

It seemed futile to ask again for my wages as Henrietta sped off after the chestnut pony with her auburn hair streaming out behind her, and Nigella fought to keep apart the bad-tempered chestnut and grey cob. Resignedly, I bolted the black horse into his stable and did the same with the bay mare before running for the horsebox.

"There isn't much petrol in the tank," Nigella shouted after me. "I don't know if I mentioned it!" Bearing in mind that I had failed to collect my wages and had not so much as a ten pence piece in my pocket, this was something of a *coup de grâce* on her part.

"You know, the Fanes have a point," Nick said, as we negotiated the narrow, banked lanes with the petrol gauge arrow pointing ominously to red. "They probably even have a valid case in law. Legend is twice the horse now that he was when they bought him, and you did enter into a sort of unofficial partnership to train him and provide his equipment. If you ask me, Elaine, I think you are possibly being a bit hard on the Fanes."

"I didn't ask you," I snapped. I was still feeling unnerved by the traumatic results of my last ditch effort to extract some money from Henrietta, and I was also nettled by the way Nick was apparently siding with the Fanes over Legend, when I had confidently expected him to be as outraged as I was. "And I don't agree with you. After all I've done for them, I think it's crass cheek to claim a share in a horse they have already been paid for with interest, especially as, true to form, they managed to dodge the issue of my wages to the bitter end. Honestly, Nick, I'm hopping mad and the way I feel at the moment I hope I never see the Fanes again as long as I live."

"If you don't, you certainly won't get your wages." He glanced across at my angry face and grinned. An unexpected curve in the lane escaped his attention and we swerved slightly. There was a muffled clunk from the rear of the box.

"Oh, do take care," I said crossly. "I don't want to arrive with a lame horse."

"If you speak to me like that," Nick pointed out sharply, "you'll be lucky to arrive at all."

We drove along in silence for a while. I didn't want to fall out with Nick, especially as he had taken an afternoon off from his job as first whipper-in to the Hunt in order to drive me to the training centre. I stared out of the window at the familiar Suffolk landscape. Drilling had already begun in the wide brown acres stretching out to meet the sombre darkness of the pine forests, and beyond, where the soil grew lighter and conifer gave out on to gorse and bracken, seagulls wheeled and mewled over the choppy wastes of the North Sea, and anonymous ships inched their way across the skyline. I had learned to love this county; becoming accustomed to the vastness of its skies, learned to tolerate the persistence of its winds. Now I was leaving and might possibly never see it again. I swallowed hard and turned my eyes to the road ahead.

"I'm sorry," I managed to say eventually, "I didn't mean to snap, but I've had such guilt feelings during the past few weeks about leaving the Fanes, and I suppose, if I allow myself to admit it, I've grown very attached to them in a way. Then, when I found out they had already found a replacement for me, and they were so difficult about Legend and I couldn't even get them to pay my wages, it was the last straw."

"Well, you needn't worry about paying for the petrol," Nick said. "I'll pay, and if you feel you must, you can pay me back when the Fanes pay you."

"Thanks," I said gratefully, "I appreciate it." He might just as well have said "when the cows come home" or "when your boat comes in" for all the promise it held in store.

We stopped at a garage for petrol and crossed the borders of Norfolk, Cambridgeshire, and Hertfordshire. By this time my thoughts had turned from the Fanes and the county I had left behind, to what might lie ahead. I began to feel nervous and even faintly sick.

Nick looked at his watch. "What time are you supposed to be there? Before six? We should just about make it." He glanced at my face. "Are you OK? You look a bit pale."

"I'm nervous," I told him. "I've lived for this moment for months; I've thought of nothing else and it's kept me going all through the winter, but now," I confessed, putting into words something I had not previously admitted to myself, "now that I'm actually on my way, I'm really not looking forward to it at all. I wish I wasn't going. I'm terrified."

Nick grinned.

"It's no laughing matter," I said indignantly. "I've actually reached the stage where I'm beginning to

25

doubt my own ability now. Remember, Nick, that I rode an ex-Olympic event horse in the two-day event when the final selection was made for this scholarship course, and all the other candidates were riding relatively inexperienced, home-schooled, novice horses. *Anyone* could have won on Genesis, even a fool could have won on him; so what if I've been deluding myself all this time? What if I turn out to be absolutely hopeless? What then?"

He tried to look serious. "It wasn't *just* the two-day event though, was it?" he said. "There were preliminary rounds before that, and then you were riding Legend. You *earned* your place on this course, Elaine, you didn't get it by foul means or by accident. You were chosen; so for you to say you might be hopeless is rubbish, and you know it."

I hoped he was right. "But it isn't only that," I said. "Suppose all the other scholarship candidates are well-heeled, public-school types and suppose I just don't fit in and they despise me? And whatever would they think," I added, struck anew with the ignominy of my situation, "if they found out I hadn't even got enough money to pay for the petrol to get to the training centre!"

Nick drove on in silence for a while. "When I first went to work for the Hunt," he said finally, "one of the first things I learned was that, because of my job, I would be loathed by some people and automatically accepted by others. I could never alter that, even if I turned myself inside out trying, so after a while, I learned not to try. This course is your big change, Elaine. It's your ticket to ride, and it's too good an opportunity to waste even a minute of it worrying about things you can't alter, things which aren't really all that important in the first place – and by the way," he added, pulling a wry face as the horsebox began to veer across the road, "I think we've got a puncture."

He steered the box towards the grass verge and I was out of the cab before he had hauled up the handbrake. Sure enough, the left rear wheelrims were resting on the tarmac and the tyre was as flat as a pricked balloon. Nick pulled open the personnel door. "There's a spare under the bunk; don't panic, I'll have it changed in a tick." A jack and some spanners landed on the lane with a clatter. I looked at my watch, it was a quarter to six. This *would* happen now, I thought in exasperation.

A second later Nick appeared beside me, looking thunderous.

"What's the matter?" I said anxiously. "Where's the tyre? Don't say it isn't *there*! I stared at him, appalled.

"I don't suppose it occurred to you to check the spare tyre?" he said angrily. "Because there's a slit in it I can put my fist through!"

I thought I might die of shock. The box belonged to livery clients and I remembered the day they had arrived late at a meet because of a blown tyre. "But Nigella was told about that!" I said. "She was supposed to have asked the garage to collect it *months* ago!"

"Well she didn't, did she?" he said furiously. "Or even if she did, the Fanes probably haven't paid their petrol bill so why should the garage care?"

I thought this was very likely true. "But there must be *something* we can do," I said. "Can't we mend it ourselves? Can't we blow it up somehow? I felt desperate enough to try anything, but I knew, even as I said it, that we couldn't.

27

Nick shot me a vengeful glance. "You'd better resign yourself to being late," he said. "We shall have to find a garage."

I looked round hopelessly. We were on a minor road, surrounded by woodland, and miles from any sign of habitation. There was not a telephone box, or even a cottage within sight. "But *Nick*," I cried, "*how*?"

He shrugged. "I suggest we either start walking or settle down for a nice long wait until another vehicle happens to come along."

"But we might walk for *miles* and not find anywhere, and there might not be another vehicle for *hours*!" I looked at my watch again in a panic. "It's already ten minutes to six!"

Nick ran a hand through his hair and looked at me with exasperation. "Well, what else can we do?"

I had to do something.

"Where are we?" I demanded.

"Berkshire," he said.

"I know we're in Berkshire," I said impatiently, "but *where* in Berkshire?"

I ran for the cab, found the livery clients' map, and opened it out on the bonnet. "We're not far from the training centre, Nick! Look, we're here." I grabbed his jersey and pulled him closer, stabbing at the patch of woodland with my finger. "It's about six miles. I have to get there, I'll have to ride it."

"Don't be silly, Elaine," he said. "You can't possibly ride it," he slipped an arm around my shoulders. "Stay here with me and wait. They won't worry if you're an hour or so late, and anyway, I won't see you again for ages . . ."

I was in no mood for anything like this. I pushed him away. "I'll call at a garage and send somone out

28

to you. I can manage my case and Legend can wear his rug, you can drop the rest of his things off later. I *can't* be late, Nick, they may lock me out, it is Sunday, after all. They may even refuse to take me if I don't arrive on time, the chief's a stickler for discipline!"

I ran round the back of the box and pulled frantically at the ramp handles. The thought of having to go back to Havers Hall and beg the Fanes to take me back was simply terrifying. I unloaded Legend, folded his rug over his shoulders and slapped the saddle on top of it. I did up the buckles of his bridle with trembling fingers, put his headcollar over it and knotted the rope around his neck.

Nick legged me into the saddle with obvious reluctance and handed me my suitcase. "I suppose you will remember to send someone out to find me?" he said crossly. "You won't just leave me here to rot?" He held on to Legend's bridle as I struggled to position the suitcase on the pommel and still remain in control. Legend arched his neck and pranced over the tarmac. He hadn't a clue what it was all about, but he was ready just the same.

"I will," I promised, "I'll stop at the first telephone box I see, and thanks Nick, for everything." I blew him a hasty kiss. In the circumstances it was the best I could do.

I left him standing in the lane; handsome, dark-eyed, and surly. "Damn and blast the Fanes," he called after me, "when or if I ever get back, I'll shoot the pair of them."

I had to laugh. It was such a relief to be in the saddle and on my way, and to hear him curse the Fanes and know he was on my side again.

"Make sure you get my wages first!" I shouted back above the urgent rattle of Legend's hooves.

3

Miracles Cannot be Wrought

The main stable yard appeared to be deserted. I led
Legend in the direction of a sign which said *Office
and Reception*. He had been perfectly equal to the
six mile trot, but the woollen rug and the travelling
bandages had caused him to become overheated.
Now his forelock was plastered to his face and a
gentle steam rose from every part. Polished equine
heads, busily chewing hay, popped over stable doors
at the sound of his hooves. I was feeling hot and
flustered myself and I was relieved that there was no
one to witness our unconventional arrival. On the
other hand, I was rather anxious in case I should
find no one to receive us at all.

Reception was empty and locked. I knocked on
the door of the office.

"Come in!" a voice barked.

I opened the door cautiously. The chief sat behind
a desk heaped with papers, memo pads, carbon
paper, two telephones, and a kilner jar half-full of
aspirin.

"I said, come in," he said impatiently.

"I can't," I told him, "I've got a horse with me." I
showed him the end of Legend's rein to prove it.

He frowned. "You are late, Miss Elliot," he said
in a terse voice. "You were advised to be here by
six. You were all notified; everyone received a
memorandum."

This was not a promising start. "The horsebox

broke down," I explained. "There was a puncture and I had to ride the last bit. I'm very sorry."

He waved me away in an irritated manner. "Get someone to show you where to put the horse and then report back to me."

"There isn't anybody," I said forlornly. "I've looked."

The chief sighed and came out from behind the papers. He wore old-fashioned breeches with crisply-pressed wings and the most beautiful brown leather boots, so close fitting and so neat that I couldn't imagine how he had ever managed to get them past his ankles.

I backed Legend away from the door to allow him safe passage and fell in behind as he strode away down one of the endless lines of immaculate loose boxes. Legend, who was probably missing his supper, dragged behind unwillingly, scraping his toes along the concrete. The chief finally halted and threw back the bolts of a half door.

"In there," he commanded.

I dragged Legend inside. With the sweat drying in crinkles on his shoulders, his plastered forelock, and his ears set firmly back, he had never looked more unimpressive and, disloyally, I wished he would buck up a bit and prance around in front of the chief. Instead he knocked over my suitcase as he made for the haynet.

I could see at a glance that the training centre was very hot on stable management; the loose box was spacious and spotless, the windows behind the bars sparkled, the bed was laid with banked-up sides, the manger had been freshly scrubbed and the water bucket filled to the brim. Only one thing struck a discordant note and that was the sound of music –

31

very loud, strident music – emanating from some-where further down the block. Obviously it struck a discordant note with the chief as well, because he looked furious.

"One moment, Miss Elliot," he said grimly, and hurried away towards the source of the discord. After a moment's hesitation, and not wanting to miss anything, I followed hot on his heels, leaving Legend struggling to chew a mouthful of hay with his bridle on.

As the music increased to a crescendo, the chief suddenly put on a spurt and flung open a stable door in a surprise attack. Inside the stable a slight girl in a red track suit was grooming a chestnut. When she saw the chief she reached out and snapped off a cassette player which was sitting on the window-ledge.

The chief looked as though he might blow a fuse himself. "Musical entertainment is not permitted in the stables, Miss Tintoft," he rapped. "This is a school of equitation, not a discothèque."

Miss Tintoft opened her mascara-edged eyes very wide and tucked her spiky orange hair behind her ears. "Well, I didn't know that," she said indignantly. "Still, I've only been here a couple of hours, I can't be expected to know everything, can I?"

"And neither," the chief added in an enraged tone, "are students allowed to wear coloured nail polish on these premises!"

Miss Tintoft put her purple talons behind her back and shrugged her narrow shoulders. "I've lost my remover," she said innocently. "I can't find it *anywhere*."

Even from behind I could sense that the chief didn't believe it. "You will hear more of this tomorrow, Miss Tintoft," he barked. "In the meantime, I suggest you familiarize yourself with the training regulations. I feel sure you were issued with a copy." He turned on his heel and saw me. "Kindly attend to your horse and report to the office immediately, Miss Elliot," he commanded.

I ran.

With Legend properly rugged and fed, and my suitcase at my feet, I sat on the edge of a wooden chair in the office. The chief looked at me sternly over the papers. In my lap I now had quite a few papers of my own. Memoranda guidelines, registration forms, rules and regulations.

"This scholarship should not be regarded as a holiday jaunt, Miss Elliot," said the chief, "it is *work*." He frowned at me severely, as if he doubted I knew the meaning of the word.

"I know," I said. "I'm prepared to work."

"There is no guarantee of anything at the end of the course," he warned. "Miracles cannot be wrought within one calendar month. True, there will be a team of four members and one reserve chosen from among you to attend the junior trial, but there will be other teams, better teams, more experienced teams, riding against you."

"Oh, yes," I said, "I realize that."

"Every member of every team will be hoping to catch the eye of the selectors, praying that they will be short-listed to represent their country at the Junior Olympics; but there is nothing, Miss Elliot, *nothing*," he emphasized fiercely, "to intimate that you have the remotest chance of being short-listed at all."

"No," I said, in a suitably humbled tone, "of course not."

"However," the chief continued, "if you work hard, if you prove that you have the talent, the aptitude and the dedication; if you prove yourself entirely reliable and capable, you just might."

"Well, yes," I said surprised, "I suppose I might."

"This establishment," said the chief, indicating with a vague gesture somewhere beyond the pile of papers, "is the finest training centre in the country; it has the highest standards, the highest percentage of examination passes, the most highly qualified staff; it enjoys an *international* reputation."

I nodded to let him know he was preaching to the converted.

"In order to maintain our standards, Miss Elliot," the chief continued, fixing me with a steely eye, "we like to choose our students with care. We do not take *anybody,* we accept only the talented, only the dedicated, we take only the cream of the cream."

I wondered if Miss Tintoft was an example of the cream of the cream, but the chief soon left me in no doubt that she was not.

"This is the first time we have played host to the Hissey Training Scholarship for Potential Event Riders," he said. "It is the first time we have taken in students who have not been hand picked for suitability, therefore it is in the nature of an experiment. If there are to be further training scholarships here, then this must prove successful. I trust that you and your fellow students will do your *utmost* to make it so." His tone indicated that from what he had observed so far this was not at all likely. "Miss Tintoft will conduct you to your quarters," he added. He shuffled some papers impatiently, and I got up, concluding that having been suitably chastened, I had now been dismissed.

I was outside the door when I was suddenly struck by something I had forgotten. I knocked on the door again.

"Come in!" bellowed the chief.

"I wonder if I could possibly use one of your telephones?" I asked him. "My friend's still waiting six miles away with two punctured tyres."

For the education of horse and rider the facilities at the training centre were impressive; even my first brief impressions confirmed that the chief had made no idle boast when he had proclaimed it the finest in the country. I followed Miss Tintoft, who said I should call her Viv, across yards where not a wisp of straw lay unswept, where the paintwork sparkled, where the gravel was raked into swirls, where pitchforks, brushes, and springboks were lined up with military precision.

"Amazing, isn't it?" Viv commented in a disparaging manner. "Wouldn't you think they'd have better things to do than make patterns in the gravel. Typical of the chief, that is." She walked across the next patch to show she wasn't going to be intimidated by any of it, leaving a line of footprints through the stones.

I kept my own feet on the concrete walkway. After my traumatic experiences with the Fanes and their tumbledown yard, I found the professional, meticulous efficiency of the centre very encouraging. I was sure that a month of top class instruction in such an establishment would greatly benefit my eventing career, and I was elated to think that I wouldn't have to pay for any of it. I could hardly believe my luck.

I couldn't wait to see the student accommodation, but disillusionment was literally just around the corner. Behind the immaculate yards where the horses stood knee-deep in straw, the training centre suffered an abrupt change of character. It presented a vista of ugly prefabricated buildings left over from the second world war, set amidst a landscape of mountainous, steaming muckheaps. There was a pungent smell of manure.

"Great, isn't it?" Viv said cheerfully. "Myself, I'd prefer to sleep with the horses."

She led me across to one of the buildings. It was grey and squat and depressing, and its name, emblazoned across the lintel, was NEWCASTLE. I thought it strange that a student hostel should be named after a northern city until Viv explained: "Duke of, not *city* of." She pushed open the door. "They're all named after famous riding instructors; there's a Berenger, a Fillis and a Solleysell and the newest one's called Podhajsky; it's not a memorial *I'd* care for."

I could see what she meant because the inside of Newcastle was worse than the outside. It didn't help that we walked headlong into an argument. A small, stocky girl with blonde hair and a hostile expression was berating the other occupants in no uncertain manner. She brandished an iron saucepan and her cheeks were flushed with anger.

"I haven't come all the way from Germany to be a cook!" she shouted. "I came here to train for eventing and nobody said anything to *me* about cooking!"

As I just happened to be the nearest, she handed

36

me the saucepan. "Now," she said with angry satisfaction, "*you* can be the cook."

I stood on the worn linoleum with my suitcase in one hand and the saucepan in the other. "I think there must be some mistake," I said. "I'm not the cook, I'm a scholarship student." The other people in the shabby little room seemed unconcerned.

"She hasn't come all the way from Germany at all," a girl, whose lank hair flopped all over her face, said in a confiding tone. "I know for a fact she lives in Halesowen."

The blonde girl overheard, "That is not the point," she snapped. "When I was at the Reitschule we weren't expected to cook as well as ride."

"Not to mention washing and cleaning," someone else said morosely.

"I wonder why she didn't stay at the Reitschule," the floppy girl said in a low voice, "if it was so much better there."

The blonde girl didn't rise to this. She threw herself into a vacant armchair. The springs had gone and she hit the bottom with a muffled thud. "Ha!" she exclaimed savagely, "even the chairs are broken!"

I turned to Viv in dismay. "Do we have to do eventing and *cookery*?" I asked her. I was bewildered and felt sure that it couldn't be so. There had been no mention of cookery in any of the chief's paperwork.

"We haven't got to *learn* cookery," Viv said in an exasperated voice, "we've just got to do our own. It's quite normal, all the working pupils have to cook their own meals as well, it isn't as if it's only us."

I should have known this from my own days as a

working pupil, but somehow I had expected scholarship students to receive slightly better treatment. Furthermore, I hadn't expected to be housed in a nasty little prefab with damp-furred walls and a one-bar electric fire. If anything, it was almost as bad as Havers Hall. "This is an *awful* place," I said, "surely they must be able to offer us better accommodation than *this*."

Viv shrugged. She clearly considered that we were all making a fuss over nothing. "Where did you expect to be accommodated?" she enquired. "The Ritz?"

"The thing that makes me wild," a tall girl with spots and a greasy fringe said in annoyed tone, "is that the chief dishes out all these memos, but he doesn't bother to tell us we have to do our own cooking and washing. Nobody does, they just leave us to find out for ourselves. If you ask me, it's a diabolical liberty and we ought to complain."

The blonde girl gave a scornful snort. "Who's going to care if you do complain?" she wanted to know. "Because you won't get any sympathy from the chief, I can tell you that. I can just imagine what *he'd* say. 'This is an equestrian training centre, Miss Merryman, not a five-star hotel.' – That's all the sympathy you'll get from *him*."

In spite of the stressful circumstances I had to smile; I could so easily imagine the chief saying it.

"Now at the Reitschule," the blonde girl went on, "they treat their students like human beings. We had really decent accommodation with central heating, tiled shower rooms, even a self-service cafeteria, and the whole place was *spotless*."

Already I could see that the Reitschule might become rather tedious.

"But as we're not at the Reitschule," Viv said in a cold voice, "I supose we'd better sort out a work rota, otherwise some people," she looked pointedly at the blonde girl, "won't do a tap." She searched through the pockets of her tracksuit and came up with a ballpoint pen. "Has anyone got any paper?"

Everyone looked blank except the tall girl who got up and unpinned a browning points of the horse chart from the wall. She laid it face down on the stained formica table. "Here," she said amiably, "write it out on this."

Viv yanked out two tubular-framed chairs from beneath the table, pushed one in my direction, sat down on the other herself and began to rule swift freehand lines across the back of the chart.

Whilst everyone awaited the outcome of the rota, I looked around cautiously at my fellow students. I had only seen them once before and then briefly, at the two-day event where the chief had been officiating, and where the successful scholarship candidates had been finally chosen. Then, they had just been anonymous competitors and rivals, uniformly black-coated for the dressage and show-jumping, or helmeted for the cross-country. It had not actually occurred to me that they might not be well-heeled, eventing types at all, but just ordinary, run-of-the-mill people like myself, and I didn't know whether to be relieved or disappointed. But then, I reflected ruefully, well-heeled, eventing types could afford to pay for their own training, they didn't have to try for scholarships given for publicity purposes by commercial enterprises.

"I don't know how I'll manage when it's my turn to cook," the girl with the floppy hair, whose name turned out to be Mandy, said in an anxious voice.

She leaned over Viv's shoulder and twisted a lump of hair nervously round a finger with the nail bitten to the quick. "I can't even boil water, and I'll never manage the cleaning either; I've never touched a washing machine, and I had an auntie who was electrocuted by a vacuum cleaner."

The tall girl gave a loud honk of laughter.

"You won't get electrocuted here," Viv told her, "unless you're thinking of plugging in the dustpan and brush." She got up from the table and pinned the rota on to the wall. We all gathered round to look at it.

There were seven scholarship students altogether, although only five of us had arrived so far. There seemed to be some doubt about one of the missing students as Alice, the tall girl with spots, had heard she had broken a leg out hunting, but as this couldn't be confirmed she had been added to the rota anyway in the hope that the information had been false. Over the twenty-eight days we were each allocated four days of cooking, plus one stint of washing, which meant that if we agreed to make our own beds and to make a conscious effort to keep the Duke of Newcastle tidy, we each cooked one day a week and did one shared stint of washing. Put like this it didn't sound so bad, and even Annemarie, from the Reitschule and Halesowen, had to agree that it was fair.

This being settled, and I having resigned myself to the fact that it was the instruction, not the accommodation, that was more important, I set out to explore the Duke of Newcastle.

My Ideal Home for the next four weeks was pretty squalid and a far cry from the luxurious centrally-heated chalet I had imagined. Leading off from the nasty sitting room, which doubled as a dining room, was a cramped hallway which managed to contain a further six doors. Four of these led into four identical little cells each containing two narrow divan beds separated by the sort of hateful little bedside cupboards which used to house a chamber pot. These didn't, because struck by the alarming possibility that the Duke of Newcastle might not even be blessed with indoor sanitation, I checked.

On top of the cupboards were bedside lamps made from Chianti bottles topped by fly-blown pleated paper lampshades, and the only other furnishing was a metal dress rail which presumably served as a wardrobe. All this made my bedroom at Havers Hall, with its half-tester bed, its carved wardrobe and coffin chest, positively palatial.

On the door of each cell was a notice. It said:

> *No smoking, alcohol, boots, food,*
> *electric kettles or male persons*
> *permitted in the bedrooms.*

It was signed by the chief. As I continued my tour of inspection I found many more similar notices also signed by the chief. In the bathroom, with its chipped porcelain and rotting lino, there was one pasted to the hot water cupboards.

> *This immersion heater must NOT be*
> *left on all night.*
> *ELECTRICITY COSTS MONEY.*

And in the dismal cubby hole that proclaimed itself the kitchen, yet another was sellotaped to the door of the refrigerator.

*This refrigerator MUST be defrosted
every THREE days. Biological specimens
and worm counts are NOT to be kept in
this refrigerator, it is for foodstuffs
ONLY.*

One wall of the kitchen was lined with open shelves stacked with saucepans with defective handles and odd lids. There were some piles of miscellaneous plates and mugs, and a drawer revealed a selection of assorted cutlery. In a cabinet, fronted with sliding doors of yellowing frosted glass, I found a half-empty packet of cereal, a jar of solidified Horlicks, and a vast selection of Hissey's pickles. Since Hissey's Pickle Company were sponsoring the scholarship course, this was a neat touch, but there was no sign of anything we could actually eat.

It was only when I opened the back door that I found a large carton bearing the grand inscription PROVISIONS FOR THE DUKE OF NEWCASTLE. I lifted the lid cautiously and saw a cold chicken, salad vegetables, milk, butter, bread, instant coffee and other welcome things. At least, I told myself as I carried the carton into the sitting room to show to the others, it's an improvement on the Fanes' mutton stew.

4

To Horse!

We were just breakfasting off the remains of the Duke of Newcastle's chicken, and wondering what had happened to the other scholarship students, when there was a knock at the door.

"Come in," Alice shouted, "we're all decent!"

"The door opened to reveal a tall girl in an immaculate cream woollen suit and a fur jacket. She had glossy brown hair coiled into a neat bun, her nose was rather too long, and her eyes were set close together which had the unfortunate effect of making her look like a snooty sheep. She smiled at us brightly.

"Good morning," she said in a superior, school-mistressy sort of voice, "I'm Selina Gibbons." She craned her well-groomed neck round the door in order to survey the room and the smile vanished. "What a *frightful* place," she said in distaste. She came inside, lifting her expensively shod feet up rather high, as if she expected to step into something unpleasant.

"Would you believe it," Alice said in surprise, "Selina Gibbons. I heard you'd broken a leg."

"I can hardly have broken a leg, can I?" Selina said sweetly. "Otherwise I wouldn't be here, would I? Otherwise my leg would be in plaster, wouldn't it?" She looked at Alice and frowned slightly. "Ought I to know you?" she wondered, then, before Alice could open her mouth to reply: "No," she decided, "I rather think not." She peeled off the thinnest of leather gloves. "Do you think that one of you could help me with my bags?" she said, adding, as none of us moved to do so, "*If* you would be so kind."

Mandy jumped up and began to haul in a set of matching suitcases from the doorway. Selina was already in the hall looking for her bedroom. The rest of us exchanged stunned glances across the breakfast table. It didn't take Selina long to inspect the Duke of Newcastle but although she was clearly somewhat discomforted by what she had seen, she seemed determined to put a brave face on it. She looked disapprovingly at the litter of crusts and milk bottles on the table. "I have breakfasted," she informed us, recoiling slightly as she noticed the chicken carcass, "so please don't trouble on my behalf."

"How very fortunate," Alice commented in a dry tone, "because there's nothing left anyway."

Selina favoured Alice with a tight little smile and stepped around us in order to inspect the rota. I wondered what her reaction would be when she discovered that she was expected to take her turn with the cooking and the washing but she made no comment. She seemed more interested in everyone's names.

"Vivienne Tintoft," she exclaimed, "not one of *the* Tintofts, surely? Not the Tintoft family who own the departmental stores?"

Viv, who had been spooning up the sugar left at the bottom of her coffee, dropped the spoon into the mug. "Come to think of it," she said, "my old man is in the retail trade."

"Really?" Selina looked round, interested.

Viv nodded. "He's got a market stall down the Mile End Road."

Selina wrinkled up her long nose as if she had just come into contact with a a bad smell. "A market *stall*?" she said, appalled.

"That's right," said Viv cheerfully, "handbags, belts, Indian sandals; you know the sort of thing."

Selina looked pained. "I'm not exactly sure that I do," she said.

Annemarie, who had been listening to all this with a bored expression on her face, now looked at her watch and announced that it was ten minutes to ten. There was a sudden flurry as everyone made for their cells because we were due for a briefing from the chief in the lecture hall at ten o'clock. Somehow I had found myself sharing a cell with Annemarie, and as we jostled one another for the benefit of the tiny spotted mirror on the wall, Viv appeared looking distracted.

"I *can't* share a room with Selina Gibbons," she groaned, "she'll drive me barmy. She's in there now lining the drawers with tissue paper and looking for fleas in the mattress. She's even brought her own sheets and pillowcases."

"I'll change with you, if you like," I offered. The truth of the matter was that I didn't feel I could face four weeks of Annemarie as a bedfellow. She had snored hideously and unceasingly all through the previous night until I, sleepless and distraught, had longed to be back under the faded tapestry bedcover at Havers Hall. Yet when I had mentioned it in the morning, she had denied it so vehemently that I half-believed I had dreamed it. I knew I would never dare to bring up the subject again.

Before she could object to sharing a room with

Viv, I left Annemarie sole use of the mirror and went to inform Selina that I was her new cellmate.

"Whoever shares a room with me," she remarked, as soon as I put my nose inside the door, "*must* be tidy. I do insist upon an orderly room." One of her smaller cases had turned itself into a typewriter. This seemed to be a surprising item of equipment to bring on a scholarship course, and Selina, following the direction of my eyes, snapped the lid shut.

"I do have rather a lot of personal correspondence to attend to," she said by way of explanation, "*private* correspondence," she added, as if she suspecgted I might be the kind of person who had a penchant for reading other people's letters. I withdrew.

We all arrived at the lecture hall together and sat down, taking up half of the first row of chairs. We were only five seconds ahead of the chief, who marched down the centre aisle in his gleaming boots and gave us a curt nod. He took up a position behind an ecclesiastical lecture stand and shuffled an array of papers.

"I shall not delay you long," he said, looking at us sharply, as if we were already late for three appointments and had really no right to be sitting there at all.

"So kind," Selina murmured. "It does take one a little time to settle in."

The chief stared at her as if he found her comment totally incomprehensible. "Hand out these sheets to the rest of the students," he rapped, "Miss er . . ." he paused to look down his list of names.

"Gibbons," Selina supplied. She took the proffered sheets and graciously handed one to each of us.

46

"Without a broken leg," Alice commented in a low voice, "*if* you would be so kind."

Selina gave her an icy look and sat down, folding her legs neatly under her chair like a professional model.

"Have you *see* this?" Annemarie hissed in my ear. "We have to be out in the yard by six o'clock, and we have to go out running for half an hour every day – *running*," she repeated in a scandalized voice.

"Silence, if you *please*!" the chief barked. "This is a briefing, not a ladies' coffee morning!"

Annemarie snapped upright in her chair.

"This morning," said the chief, "we shall begin with an assessment period in the indoor school, a break for lunch, followed by a further assessment of a restricted nature on the cross-country course. I shall be assessing capabilities, potential, and fitness, not only of yourselves, but of your horses – " he drew a deep breath as if to signify that there might be precious little to assess, "after which I shall draw up individual tables of exercise, work, and feeding for your horses, and set each of you appropriately timed periods of running, lunging without reins and stirrups, and riding, to produce maximum fitness and performance with a view to competing in the junior trial at the end of the month." He looked at each of us carefully to see how we would take this. We stared back at him in silence.

"Until I have worked out your individual programmes," he continued, "you will kindly follow the daily schedule."

"Which daily schedule is that?" Selina enquired sweetly.

"The daily schedule sitting on your lap," the chief snapped.

47

"Oh, I see," Selina said, undismayed. "I do beg your pardon."

Alice sniggered.

"You may now return to your quarters in order to change for the assessment lesson." The chief stared at Alice and narrowed his eyes. Alice stared back. The chief averted his gaze hastily. "I shall expect you to report to the indoor school in fifteen minutes precisely," he commanded.

"I may be a little longer than that," Selina informed him, "I have yet to unpack."

The chief's face took on a slightly darker hue. "Miss Gibbons," he said, "I repeat, I expect to see you in the indoor school in *fifteen minutes*."

Selina gave him a brave smile. "Very well," she promised, "I shall do my best." She got up to leave.

"Kindly remain seated until I give you permission to rise!" the chief bellowed.

Selina sat down again with a bump. Now it was her turn to look at the chief as if he might be insane. It occurred to me that he didn't appear to have had much practice in dealing with the cream of the cream.

"Rather natty, don't you think?"

Selina pulled a pair of breeches over her long, thin, elegant legs. They were cream, with velcro fastenings and soft, pale suede strapping from seat to calf, absolutely identical to the pair lying swathed in tissue in the bottom of my drawer, awaiting my first three-day event.

Resignedly, I took out my second best. Selina was already sporting a tweed coat by Weatherill, and had unpacked a pair of long riding boots which, even without looking, I knew would be handmade by

48

Maxwell. One could never compete; it would be ridiculous to try.

"As a matter of interest," I asked her, attempting to cram my hair into a net without the benefit of the mirror because Selina was already firmly installed in front of it, fiddling with a silky cravat, "why did you try for a scholarship? Why didn't you just pay for your training, and do the whole thing in comfort?"

Selina stabbed at the cravat with a gold stock pin. "Because one does rather like to feel that one has been accepted on merit," she said in a reproving tone, "not simply because one can foot the bill."

We made our way past the muckheaps, their familiar sweet, sickly smell shot through with powerful whiffs of ammonia, on our way to the high-powered frenetic efficiency of the yards where staff and working pupils alike were engaged in an unceasing round of activity. People hurried up and down the walkways, carrying saddles, draped with bridles and headcollars, half-buried under mounds of coloured rugs and striped stable blankets. Horses clopped in and out, springboks flew above the gravel, wooden water pails waited in rows beside the taps, hay nets were being stuffed and weighed in the barns, leather was being soaped in the tackrooms. In the large open-fronted boxes at the end of each row, electric groomers or clippers whirred busily, and from somewhere came the distinctive acrid smell of burned horn which told of a blacksmith at work.

We had all been out early to feed and muck out our own horses, and I had strapped Legend and washed his mane and tail. He seemed to have settled in perfectly and I found him looking over the top half of his door, interested in everything that was going on, but even so, he caught my step as I approached along the walkway and turned his bay head with its white star shining, and whickered a soft welcome.

On the front of the lower door was a perspex slot into which a card had been dropped. THE HISSEY TRAINING SCHOLARSHIP it read, and underneath our names, ANOTHER LEGEND, Owner/rider ELAINE ELLIOT. There was a space under this for further information, and although mine was left blank, most of the other cards around the yard had theirs filled in. RUG TEARER one said, and then BOLTS FOOD – LARGE STONES TO BE LEFT IN MANGER, and more unwelcoming, STRIKES OUT WITH FRONT FEET. I was rather glad I couldn't think of anything to write about Legend.

The scholarship students had all been allocated boxes in the same yard. Annemarie's horse, a well-made and compact part-bred Hanoverian, bought in Germany where Annemarie's father was a British serving officer, was stabled next to Legend. "He's small for an eventer, but he's got a lion's heart," she told me fiercely, as we led our horses across the gravel towards the indoor school. "He's good enough for the Junior Olympics, and I mean to get there. We haven't spent two months at the Reit-schule for nothing."

As we entered by the sliding doors, the chief was standing in the middle of the school eyeing his watch. "One moment!" he rapped, effectively halting us in our tracks as we began to prepare to mount. "Kindly make a line in front of me, *dis*mounted."

We shuffled ourselves and our horses into a line, surprised.

The chief marched up to Alice who had positioned

50

herself at one end of the line and peered closely at her face. "Better see the nurse," he said curtly.

Alice was astonished. "What for?" she demanded, as soon as she could find her voice.

"Spots," said the chief, "can't have a girl with spots. Unhealthy. Might be catching."

"Rubbish," Alice said scornfully, "it's my age."

The chief pointed his stick at her chest. "Button missing," he observed, flipping open her jacket. His eyes travelled downwards, "boot straps upside down." He moved on to Mandy, leaving Alice with her mouth agape.

Mandy stared at the chief like a mesmerized rabbit. She wore her hat with the peak pointing upwards and her awful floppy hair hung out all round.

"Hairnet?" the chief snapped.

Mandy jumped and grabbed nervously at her hair. "I haven't got one," she said.

"Obviously," the chief said in a dry voice. "Kindly see that you are equipped with one in future," He reached out and pulled the peak of her hat straight. Mandy flinched. I think she actually imagined he was going to box her ears.

The chief looked Selina up and down almost approvingly. "Very good, Miss Gibbons," he said. Selina smiled at him in an ingratiating manner.

Annemarie was next. She stood like a ramrod with every item of her kit clean and correct and her boots shining like mirrors, but even so, the chief found something to complain about. "Be good enough to remove your earrings, Miss Maddox," he said sharply. "This is a centre of equitation, not a West End nightclub."

Beside me, Viv let out a strangled squeak of mirth.

51

Annemarie began to fumble with her ear lobes. "Yes sir," she said.

It was my turn. The chief frowned and stared at my neck. I waited for him to say it was dirty, because I hadn't been able to have a proper wash all day. Every time I had tried to get into the bathroom it had been occupied by someone else. I had ended up washing just my hands and my face in the kitchen sink, over a pile of dirty dishes that nobody would accept responsibility for – the rota not being very specific about things like washing up. However, it wasn't my neck he was looking at.

"I would prefer a collar and tie to a roll-necked jersey, Miss Elliot," he rapped. "This is a formal lesson, not a hack in the park."

"I'll change it," I promised, "before the next lesson."

"You will indeed," he agreed, and he passed on to Viv.

Viv's lips were pressed together and her cheeks were pink with the effort of keeping herself under control, but the chief was more prepared for her than any of us could imagine.

"Hands to the front," he barked. "Get them out."

Viv held out her hands obediently, palms uppermost.

"Turn them over, Miss Tintoft," the chief said impatiently, slapping his boot with his stick to indicate he was in no mood to be trifled with. "You know perfectly well what I want to see."

Viv turned over her hands. I saw with relief that the talons were no longer purple.

"Ah," said the chief with satisfaction, "I see that the varnish has been removed; all that remains now is for the nails to be trimmed." To everyone's astonishment he put a hand into the pocket of his impeccably-cut tweed jacket and produced a pair of scissors. "Will you do it or shall I?" he enquired.

Viv stared at him, aghast. She couldn't have looked any more horrified if he had suggested amputation of the fingers. "I'm not having them *cut*!" she yelped. "It took me *years* to grow these!"

"Nevertheless, Miss Tintoft," the chief said in a deadly voice, "either you cut them or I shall. Alternatively, you may prefer to leave the training centre; but I assure you that you will not mount a horse in this establishment with fingernails resembling those of a Chinese mandarin."

There was a tense silence as they faced each other, but at the end of it Viv sighed deeply and took the scissors. One by one the talons fell and vanished into the tan. The chief pocketed the scissors with a thin smile of satisfaction.

"Ride! TO HORSE!" he bellowed.

5

A Little Miracle

"Check your girths!"

"Take your reins!"

"Down irons!"

"Prepare to mount!"

"Ride – MOUNT!"

With the chief's instructions ringing in our ears like machine gun fire, we progressed into our saddles in a succession of jerks, like badly manipulated puppets. It was two years since I had received any formal instruction and I had been rather dreading this; afraid I would have forgotten all that I had learned.

"Leading file, prepare to lead off on the right rein!" bellowed the chief.

We all looked round anxiously and I saw with relief that I wasn't the only one to hesitate. Typically, Annemarie was the first to move forward, electing herself to the position of leading file.

"Ride – pre-pare to walk!"

"Ride – WALK!"

Somehow we managed to achieve an orderly procession and the chief began to work us gently at the walk and trot through turns, circles and transitions, making no comment, but taking in every ill-timed movement of our hands and legs, every falter in our horses' strides with his gimlet eye.

In between concentrating on my own performance and trying to keep Legend on the track – he would

54

have much preferred to give the kicking boards, with their painted letters, a wider berth, and I realized that he had probably never been ridden indoors in his life before – I studied the other scholarship students to see what sort of competition I was up against for a place in the team for the junior trial.

Annemarie, as one would expect from someone who had studied at the Reitschule, was a highly disciplined and faultlessly correct rider who clearly expected and extracted the same exact discipline from her little bay horse. If there was a criticism to be made it was that she seemed rather too stiff, a little too unyielding, and I noticed that for much of the time the bay gelding was slightly overbent with his chin tucked into his neck. I knew, even without seeing them perform, that they would be formidable competition for the dressage and the show-jumping, both of which demanded precision and total accuracy, but I was not so sure how they would fare across country when scope, speed, and initiative all had a part to play.

Alice had gained her early riding experience in a dealer's yard, and you could tell by the way she rode her huge, handsome, iron grey, The Talisman, that she was fearless. She had told us appalling stories of how she used to display the prowess of the equine merchandise by jumping them over some spiked iron railings into a municipal park. This had rarely failed to impress potential buyers and if any horse injured itself, it was shunted round the back of the premises and sold off cheaply to the trade as damaged stock. Obviously this sort of training had developed a natural tact, an ability to get the best performance out of any horse, and I reckoned that Alice and The Talisman would be hot stuff across country, but I looked at Alice's long, loose, style of riding, and I wondered about the dressage.

Selina's plain, three-quarter bred gelding was totally redeemed by the beauty of his colour, a hot, bright, deep chestnut, with not a white hair to be seen. His name was Flame Thrower and he looked a wise, sensible, bold horse, who reminded me very much of a horse that Hans Gelderhol had been eventing at the time I was in his yard training for my Horsemaster's Certificate. The resemblance was so striking that I made a mental note to ask Selina how he was bred, to find out if they were related. Selina was a good rider, who had obviously been very well taught; on top of everything else she seemed to have going for her, I found this rather irksome.

Viv rode just in front of me on her own chestnut, a long-striding, powerful horse called Balthazar, who walked with a swinging stride and carried his tail gaily. Viv rode him in a relaxed and stylish manner and they were so well matched that they were a pleasure to watch. In fact all of the scholarship students rode well and were a pleasure to watch, apart from Mandy, but then Mandy and her pretty bay hose, Fox Me, were something else.

How Mandy had ever managed to qualify for the scholarship course, or even achieve sixth place at the two-day event, seemed a mystery, because to watch her floundering aimlessly round the school, cutting the corners, staring wild-eyed at the chief whenever he barked out a command, falling further and further behind the ride until she suddenly realized and legged Fox Me on so urgently that he arrived abruptly with his nose bumping into Legend's tail, it was clear that she was a total stanger to formal riding instruction.

All this became eventually too much for the chief to endure and he was obliged to halt the ride and enquire waspishly if this was a special performance, or if she always rode like an Irish tinker. Mandy stared at him in terror, not knowing whether it was meant to be a compliment or not. The chief then proceeded to give her a lecture on co-ordination of hand, leg and seat in order to produce a balanced, working pace which would enable her to keep up with the ride.

I was sure that most of this was lost on Mandy and I mentally crossed her off the list of possibles for the junior trial, feeling sure that her sixth place at the two-day event could have been nothing but a fluke. It was heartening to count up and realize that as there were five of us left, I could count on being reserve at least provided the final student did not turn up. I was in need of this sort of comfort because Legend, irritated by the sudden jostling of Fox Me, and not enjoying his taste of indoor life in the least, was not on top form.

The enclosed arena had put a constraint on him and I could feel that his paces were not as fluent and free as they usually were. It was also difficult to keep his attention as the slightest noise, a stirrup iron scraping along the kicking boards, or a bird fluttering in the rafters above, made him tense. When some-one ran up the steps and along the gallery, which extended for the entire length of the building, he bunched up and bounced like a rubber ball into the centre of the school, momentarily displacing the chief from his central position.

"Control, Miss Elliot, control," he said in an irritated voice, "this is an assessment period, not *El Rodeo*."

I coaxed Legend back on to the track, feeling humiliated. I knew that I must be making a very poor impression, second only in awfulness to Mandy. It even struck me that were the Fanes present to compare our performance with that of the others, they would probably decide on the spot that I was not a fit person to ride the horse in which they so tenaciously claimed an interest.

Troubled with such thoughts, I fell into line with the others as the chief set up two jumps, one at either end of the school, in order to assess our show-jumping prowess. It was at this particular moment that one of the sliding doors opened, causing Legend yet more anxiety, and a tall, lean, young man entered the school, leading a startling roan horse with white stockings extending to above every knee, a broad blaze between its wall eyes, and its tail carried as high as a banner.

We all stared. If the chief had considered Mandy's riding like that of an Irish tinker, then surely he was now faced with one in the flesh. The new arrival wore a faded brown riding hat with the ventilator button missing, a checked shirt with the sleeves rolled above slim, brown elbows, a red neckerchief, and skin-tight jodhpurs worn with short, beige, elastic-sided suede boots.

The chief straightened up with the cup and pin he had been attaching to the jump stand still in his hands. He threw up his chin. "Entry to the indoor school is expressly forbidden whilst there is a lesson in progress," he snapped. "There is a notice posted on the door – I suggest you consult it."

"But I'm supposed to be taking part in this lesson," the young man protested in an impeccable voice which signified an expensively privileged education. "I'm on the scholarship course; my name's Phillip Hastings."

The chief looked fit to explode. "Then, Mr Hastings," he said, "you will also be aware that you were supposed to arrive prior to six o'clock yesterday evening!"

"I got the wrong day, I'm afraid." Phillip Hastings had the grace to look somewhat shamefaced. "I thought it was today the course started. I actually thought I was early."

The chief closed his eyes for a moment and then heaved a deep sigh of resignation. "Mr Hastings," he said, "be good enough to remove that object from around your throat and this afternoon, ten minutes prior to the cross-country assessment, kindly present yourself for my inspection at the office correctly attired for formal instruction, wearing a collar and tie, a jacket, and *long* riding boots."

The rest of us watched with interest whilst the chief made a rapid assessment of Phillip and the amazing roan horse as he drilled them round the partly constructed show-jumps. It was galling to see at once that there was another scholarship candidate who was sickeningly good, and that the roan horse, despite its eccentric and somewhat off-putting appearance, was fluent, obedient, and expertly schooled.

"He's one for the team, anyway," Viv whispered, "I'd lay a bet on it." Forcing myself to agree with her in a matter-of-fact voice, I felt my heart sink like a lead weight in my chest.

Lunch, with Alice in charge of the catering, was not a success. Alice's idea of cookery was a fried egg slapped on to a piece of hard, blackened toast, and even this was not achieved without a lot of bad-tempered banging about and a haze of smoke, which hung above our heads as we waited uneasily at the table.

Selina, who had somehow managed to finish the assessment period looking as cool as a cucumber with not even the slightest of marks on her beautiful breeches, looked aggrieved as Alice thumped down the plates in front of us.

"Are *all* of the eggs broken?" she enquired.

They were, because Alice had not been able to find a spatula and had lifted them out of the pan with a dessert spoon. She had even managed to drop one of them on to the kitchen floor, but I only discovered this later when I happened to slip on the patch of grease it left behind.

Phillip, who didn't seem to object to the squalid interior and hideous surroundings of the Duke of Newcastle in the least, ate his egg without complaint. He told us that his father, who was insisting that Phillip went to university to study Law, had refused to finance his eventing on the grounds that it would interfere with his studies, but had been foiled by Phillip gaining a place on the scholarship course. If he could get a place in the team for the junior trial and be short-listed for the Junior Olympics, he hoped to use it as a lever to persuade his father that he was good enough to make a career out of event-ing. "But if I don't do it this time," he told us, "I'm sunk, because I'm due to take up my place at Magdalene in September."

I couldn't help wondering what the Fellows of Magdalene would think of Phillip, because when he had removed his shabby riding hat, we discovered that he had dyed his forelock platinum blonde.

Viv, who had described to us how she had pasted her own hair with powdered bleach and hydrogen peroxide, and had sat for hours with her head wrapped in aluminium foil like a Christmas turkey before applying a henna rinse to achieve the present flaming orange colour, was quite jealous.

"What did you use?" she wanted to know. "How long did it take?"

"Heavens, I didn't do it *myself*," Phillip said, shocked by the thought. "I had it done professionally at André Bernard."

Annemarie succumbed to a choking fit at this piece of information and had to retire to the kitchen for a draught of cold water.

To finish the meal, Alice presented us with mugs of strong, thick coffee.

"What's this," Selina wanted to know, "gravy?"

"If you don't like it," Alice said truculently, "make your own."

"I shall do that," Selina said and, rising from her chair, she disappeared in the direction of the kitchen and returned shortly afterwards bearing recognizable coffee in a china cup and saucer. "I took the precaution of bringing my own," she explained. We couldn't help but be impressed. You had to hand it to Selina, she had thought of everything.

We rode out to the cross-country course after lunch, tweaking up our girths and checking that each other's bridle straps were tucked into their keepers. Phillip was now formally attired after being inspected and approved by the chief; I was wearing a shirt and tie; Selina had encased Mandy's floppy hair in one of her own nets; Annemarie was without her gold studs; and even Alice had cobbled a button on to her jacket and altered her boot straps, although whether or not she would see the nurse about her spots was open to conjecture.

We worked our horses in on the long sweep of grass that led into the first fence of the cross-country course. It was heaven to be riding outdoors again, and Legend obviously thought so as well because he seemed to be quite his usual eager self, flipping out his toes at the trot and bouncing off into canter, shaking his glossy bay neck and making his mane fly. Slowly, my confidence began to return.

The chief, who was concerned not to overtax our horses, most of whom had hardly settled in after their long journey the previous afternoon, gave us five fairly straightforward fences to jump for our assessment, comprising the first two and the final three obstacles of the full cross-country course. They consisted of a plain post and rail; a tiger trap – a triangle of dry pine poles which made a hollow noise when you tapped it; a sheep pen of wattle fencing; a bank of tractor tyres – wide ones on the bottom, narrowing to smaller car-sized tyres on the top, and ridged with a telegraph pole; and finally, a modest square-trimmed hedge. None of the fences was over three feet in height, although the tiger trap and the tyre fence had bases which stretched to five feet as we discovered when we were allowed, two at a time, with the others minding our horses, to walk the course.

Annemarie went first, achieving a clear and correct, if rather tight-fisted round, and Phillip followed, his roan displaying, as we had known it would, an effortless ability to clear the fences in a relaxed manner, which I saw by my stopwatch was also deceptively fast. I felt sure that Magdalene College had lost a law student, as Phillip seemed a certainty for the junior trial and even the Olympic short-list.

Selina went next on Flame Thrower and theirs was a cool, professional performance, lacking only the drive and urgency of the real thing. Viv and Balthazar started off at a powerful canter which increased in speed as they went, too fast, into the sheep pen and Balthazar took the second wattle fence with his back legs, detaching it from its roped moorings. This meant a delay for Alice and The Talisman, who had been circling round the starting point. Viv cantered back to us with a rueful grin and a nonchalant lift of her shoulders.

"She'll never make the team with that attitude," Annemarie commented, "she didn't even bother to judge her strides. She just left it to the horse; she couldn't care less. She wouldn't have lasted five minutes at the Reitschule."

"Oh, *wouldn't* I?" Viv interspersed from behind somewhat unexpectedly, as Alice and the Talisman thundered past us on their way to the first fence. "Well, we shall see, won't we, when the team is announced, whether the Reitschule has done *you* any good or not!"

As it was my turn next, I removed myself hastily from what promised to develop into a lively argument, and took Legend away to warm up. As we circled round, I saw The Talisman flatten the second half of the sheep pen and caught a glimpse of the chief's agonized expression as he went forward to strap it yet again. I could see that combination fences were going to be troublesome for the Talisman and

Balthazar, both bold, strong, free-striding horses with a common disregard for anything less substantial than a telegraph pole.

When the chief raised his arm as a signal for me to start, I cantered Legend strongly towards the post and rails, he jumped it easily and leapt onwards, his eyes already fixed on the tiger trap. He extended into it and flew over and we turned towards the sheep pen. I steadied him, sitting down hard in the saddle, determined not to go into it too fast, because Legend, although not as big as either Balthazar or The Talisman, could produce a huge raking stride where necessary, and I had already paced out the pen and decided that two shorter strides would be preferable to negotiate the second half with absolute accuracy. So I held him back, releasing him for the first half, but not so much that I couldn't get the two canter strides inside to meet the wattle fence perfectly. We sailed out and on over the tractor tyres and the clipped hedge in triumph, and as we cantered back to the others, I slapped Legend's neck gratefully, feeling him vindicated from the morning's disastrous performance.

"Come back, Miss Elliot," shouted the chief, "and give me one stride at the sheep pen!"

I turned Legend back and my feeling of exhilaration died as we approached the pen again, knowing that of all the students who had gone so far, none had been asked to take the fence again. I pushed Legend on hard and he responded magnificently, thrusting forward with his powerful hocks, his front legs flying. He soared up and over the first wattle, took one flying stride in between and rose over the second like a bird. Well, I thought, as we trotted round the tractor tyres without a backward glance, if the chief had wanted one stride, we had certainly given him one. He didn't call us back a second time.

Mandy was last. We all stood with our hearts in our mouths as she cantered Fox Me towards the first fence, expecting her to fall off or let the horse refuse. He sailed over. He did the same at the tiger trap, and they turned towards the wattle sheep pen and jumped it neatly and effortlessly as if it had been no more than a couple of cavelletti. We were stunned.

The chief was clearly stunned as well because, when the pair finished, he called them back to do it again. Fox Me faced the post and rails for a second time without the least hesitation, he sailed into the tiger trap with total confidence and no thought of refusal, while Mandy, with absolute faith in his ability, and hindering him not one whit by superfluous aid or instruction, sat aboard him, radiant.

The chief was visibly perplexed by the problem this presented to him as an instructor in the fine art of equitation. One could see that whilst on the one hand his impeccable standards of excellence were appalled by Mandy's passive untutored method of riding, his instinct made him reluctant to interfere with the fragile balance of their totally successful partnership, lest he destroy with discipline and conventional technique something which was god-given and somehow sobering to watch.

Much as the chief must have itched to tear Mandy's riding apart, and make her begin again from the basics, he resisted it totally. For the whole of the course he made only minor adjustments to her riding position, for the sake of her chances of gaining a place in the team, and out of respect for a partnership based on a perfect understanding.

Seeing all this take place served to increase my respect for the chief albeit, after the incident at the double, somewhat reluctantly. It was inspiring to realize that even he could recognize a little miracle when he saw one. But watching Mandy and Fox Me negotiate the sheep pen smoothly for the second time, and pondering upon the slightly unwelcome possibility that they were now back on my list of possibles for selection, I felt in need of a little miracle myself.

6

Once More, With Feeling . . .

By the end of the first week, we had settled into our daily routine. We stumbled out of bed to the shrilling of many alarms at a quarter to six, gulped a cup of coffee, and clad in the stable workers' uniform of jeans, long rubber boots, and lovat anoraks or quilted waistcoats, set off for the yards alongside the working pupils and the early duty staff. Our first job was to muck out our horses and scrub out and refill the water buckets. Then we removed the horses' night rugs, gave them a brief grooming, which included washing off any dirty patches, picking out their feet, brushing straw out of their tails, and laying their manes, and we put on their day rugs. Whilst all this was going on, a numbered and weighed hay net was delivered, and a muck cart, pulled by a mini-tractor, collected the dirty bedding stacked neatly on a spread sack outside each stable.

Feeding followed; the feeds mixed in accordance with the charts devised by the chief detailing individual menus for each horse. While the horses ate their breakfast we helped to rake and sweep the yards, until not an alien speck or wisp remained for the chief to see when he carried out his daily inspection.

At eight thirty we scholarship students were scheduled for our half-hour run around the perimeter of the cross-country course. This was supervised by a member of staff to make sure we didn't cheat. For the first few days this was simply murder; we staggered along with aching calves, gasping breath and stitches, limping back to the Duke of Newcastle in agony. Naturally, only Selina had managed to come properly equipped with running shoes. The rest of us had to make do with rubber boots, jodhpur boots, or shoes that managed to be even less suitable. Nevertheless by the end of the week most of us were beginning to find it less of a strain and more enjoyable – all except for Mandy, who flopped along behind looking absolutely exhausted.

After the run we had breakfast – the box marked PROVISIONS FOR THE DUKE OF NEWCASTLE never failed to appear on the doorstep whilst early morning stables was in progress. By nine thirty we were back on the yards. A thorough strapping for the horses was the first task, from whence we were called away individually to endure ten minutes lunging on a round, piebald, pony who appeared to do little else but trot and canter round in circles every day of his life. We swung our arms and legs and did various exercises designed to supple us, improve our balance, and strengthen and deepen our seats. All it did for us at first was to increase our aches and stiffness. The lunging period, according to the chief's daily schedule, was to be extended by ten minutes every week until in the last week we were being lunged for forty minutes each day. The thought of it, as we reeled away after just ten minutes, was frightening.

At eleven o'clock we had to be tacked up for our first lesson of the day which was usually dressage, followed by a circuit of the show-jumping arena, and at twelve thirty we rugged up our horses again, skipped out their boxes, fed them, and went for lunch.

We were out on the yards again at two to prepare for the afternoon's cross-country instruction, during which the chief cruised between fences in a Range Rover. It was a two-hour period, but as a lot of it comprised standing about and discussing technique, it was not too taxing, and at four thirty we returned to the yards, and were allowed half an hour's break for tea. At five we skipped out the stables again, shook out the horses' beds for the night, topped up their water buckets, changed day rugs for jute rugs, the evening feeds were mixed and another hay net delivered, and the yards were raked and swept again for the chief's evening inspection at six.

After supper we reported to the tack room to clean our saddlery in order that the whole procedure should be repeated again the following day, and although there was still lots of activity going on in the yard – horseboxes and trailers constantly coming and going as outsiders brought along their own horses for evening instruction, and we were allowed to watch the lessons from the gallery, or from a vantage point on the cross-country course if we wished – all we ever wanted to do in the first week was to plod wearily back to the Duke of Newcastle and fall into bed.

On Saturday morning I had a letter from Nick. It read:

Dear Elaine,

Thanks for sending the garage – I really enjoyed my three-hour wait. Lots of cars came along between the time you abandoned me and the arrival of the truck, but

I didn't flag them down because I knew you'd remember me eventually – if I waited long enough (story of my life).

Typically, the Fanes were unsympathetic when I got back, implying that the puncture must have been our fault – well, you know the Fanes . . . but you'll be pleased to hear I didn't lose my temper. I did tackle them about your wages, but only time will tell if it did any good.

I'll call in and have another go at them because I understand the new girl has moved in, and I want to see if she's the wonder woman she's made out to be (might also be pretty), and I'll tell you the news when I see you, which will be on Monday – I'll call for you at 2.30 P.M.,and don't say you can't because I know you've got an afternoon off, I checked.

Trusting you're top of the class,
    Love etc.,
      Nick.

I had very mixed feelings about this. Nick had dropped off the remainder of my things late on Sunday evening after the garage had fixed the horse-box. At the time, he had still obviously felt very piqued about the incident because he had simply left the box of equipment in the yard, from where I had retrieved it the following morning. I had been feeling guilty about not remembering to call the garage earlier and had been meaning to ring and apologize. Somehow, there had not been the time and I was pleased that he had written now and relieved that he had apparently forgiven me.

His reference to the Fanes, though, stirred up unwelcome emotions. I had been too busy to give them much thought in the past week. While I certainly did not want to hear about the new wonder woman, because I felt that the wages the Fanes were paying her were rightfully mine, I was dismayed to discover that I felt jealous at the thought of someone else grooming and exercising the horses that I had loved – and I *had* loved them, even though I was only now beginning to realize just how much.

After lunch on Saturday, we discussed the technique of jumping fences involving water, and now we stood in a group and watched Selina and Flame Thrower approaching a telegraph pole situated in the middle of a small lake which necessitated jumping into and out of two feet of water. For once, Selina was in trouble. She had entered the lake too slowly and too cautiously, and Flame Thrower, having allowed himself to be ridden into the lake, noticed the telegraph pole too late to be reconciled to it. He refused.

The chief, standing on the bank with his beautiful boots inches from the water and with a tweed cap on his head, hailed her irritably: "Back, Miss Gibbons, come back! Try again from the rise; this time with more impulsion!"

Selina turned the bright chestnut horse away from the pole and they splashed towards the bank. Flame Thrower's tail hung in a sodden lump, and Selina's beautiful breeches were becoming wetter by the minute. They set off again from the rise, cantering into the water and throwing up clouds of spray, but the chief was having none of it.

"Impulsion, Miss Gibbons," he bellowed, "does *not* mean you merely increase the speed!"

Selina halted the horse's progress towards the obstacle and they foundered through the water towards the chief. By this time they were both dripping wet.

"I am perfectly aware of that," Selina said in an

incensed voice, "perfectly. But it is extremely difficult to work up either enthusiasm *or* impulsion,
when one is drenched with filthy water, and the
horse does not like the look of the obstacle one is
approaching one little bit."

Surprisingly, the chief didn't lose his temper; in
fact, he seemed to find Selina's obvious discomfort
rather amusing. "Quite," he said, "but if you expect
to be accepted as a serious candidate for the junior
trial, you must imagine that you are riding for your
country; you must ride as if your life depended upon
it; you must ride at that obstacle with body and soul
united in determination to get over – even if you are
killed in the attempt."

Selina stared at him with pursed lips. "I came on
this course for the good of my career," she said. "I
didn't realize I would be expected to die for my
country." Nevertheless, she turned Flame Thrower
away and set off again from the rise. This time she
gave it everything she had and they sailed over. The
chief sent her back to the yard to change her clothes.

The next fence presented a different problem,
being an uphill double. The chief began with a
lecture on gradients, explaining how the horse's
stride naturally lengthened going downhill and shortened going up. He made us dismount and pace the
distance between the rails on foot. Each rider, he
said, should be familiar with the natural length of
their horse's stride, and, by taking into consideration
the gradient and the speed, should calculate whether
it would be sensible to achieve four long, six short,
or whatever other combination of strides were
necessary in order to present the horse correctly at
the second part of the double.

Viv went first on Balthazar. They approached it at

a powerful gallop which shook the ground, flew over the first part, took three huge, raking strides, and finding themselves still inconveniently far away from the second part, chanced it anyway with a vast leap which, though mighty and courageous in its attempt, could not be high enough to clear the top rail. Balthazar hit the timber with an impact that would have knocked the hind legs off a lesser animal, and cantered back to us with not so much as a mark on his cannon bones.

The chief was furious, and told us that if the fence had come towards the end of the course, and taking into consideration horse and rider fatigue and the gradient involved, to attempt to take a solidly fixed double at such a punishing pace would be a recipe for disaster; the result of which would probably be two broken legs for the horse and a broken neck for the rider. After a short interval spent trotting in circles to ascertain that Balthazar was indeed still sound, he dispatched them to try again, and this time they approached it at a more sober pace, achieving four comfortable strides between the fences and two clean jumps.

Alice went next on The Talisman, who was very enthusiastic about his jumping and not easily controlled. He got away from Alice on the approach, threw up his head and raced at the double, landing a long way in. This upset Alice's stride calculations, and as she struggled to check him, he hesitated, put in an extra one, and took off too close to the second part, slamming the rails with both pairs of fetlocks and almost pitching Alice over his head as he landed. He trotted back to us on three legs with blood welling from his off-hind coronet.

Alice flung herself out of the saddle and knelt to

examine the damage. "I knew damned well he wasn't going to make it as soon as we took off," she said in an angry voice. The chief sighed and ordered her back to the yard to seek medication.

Phillip and the amazing roan went through the double in perfect copy-book style and they were followed by Annemarie and her little bay horse. It was clear that he would have attempted to jump over the moon if she had asked him, but the fact that he was small and close-coupled, meant she had to jump him with deadly accuracy and place him every inch of the way. This suited her disciplined way of riding but it meant that they were slow, and I had noticed that the little horse had been at full stretch when we were working over spreads. Brave as a lion he might be, but even his courage and Annemarie's ambitious determination couldn't give him the scope he lacked to turn him into the potential top class event horse she so desperately wanted him to be. He would do his best, but it was clear, as we watched him, that as the fences got higher and wider, and as the pace got faster, his best wouldn't be good enough. The only person who didn't see this, or who wouldn't allow herself to see it, was Annemarie.

Mandy followed Annemarie, and although she appeared to close her eyes and leave it all to Fox Me, he leapt the first part, and with four swinging, perfectly judged strides, met the second part exactly right and soared over. There was nothing the chief could say to this so he said nothing.

It was my turn last of all. I had worked out that Legend, who had a naturally long, floating stride, would shorten due to the gradient, taking four normal uphill strides inside the double, bringing himself exactly right for the second half without any adjustment from me. Being an economist by nature, I could see no justification in asking for shortened and lengthened strides if the same result could be accomplished more effortlessly without. It seemed that my calculations were right, because Legend did it beautifully and as he swept through the double it felt deceptively easy. It probably looked too easy as well because the chief sent us to do it again, this time with instructions to get three long strides between the fences.

I felt this was a bit unreasonable, especially as he had been furious with Viv for attempting it, but I knew Legend could do it and I took him at it from a good distance away, feeling the power from his hocks and the thrust of his shoulders as he flew forward. He rose over the first part, and with my legs clasped urgently to his sides, he flew onwards with three enormous strides that ate up the ground, soared over the second part and landed perfectly. It was simply marvellous.

"Now do it again," the chief commanded, "and give me five short bounces."

I couldn't believe it. I trotted Legend up to him feeling indignant. "But I've already been over it *twice*," I said, "and he's done it beautifully both times."

"Allow me to be the judge of that, Miss Elliot," the chief snapped. "This time I want to see you take it slowly, with lots of impulsion, and absolute control."

I could hardly refuse. I rode back to the approach line, gritting my teeth, bursting to retort that I had been in absolute control both the previous times.

I sent Legend forward towards the double yet

again, but this time, because he would have liked to race at it as before, I sat down hard and held him back, feeling the stretched muscles and tendons pulling in my calves and my heels, and the energy being contained by the reins until it was as if I held a coiled spring in my hands. Legend's dark hooves pounded on the turf, his neck arched and his ears strained forward. I placed him at the first part, releasing him only enough to allow him to jump, collected him, held him for one, two, three, four, five, short, bouncing strides, released him dangerously near to the second part, and up he went, up almost like a lift, and over, tucking up his hind legs to clear the rail. We had done it. I looked at the chief in triumph, but he was already waving me on towards the next fence. "Ride on! Ride on!" he shouted. "Continue over the next jump." He didn't even say well done.

I rode on feeling angry. I didn't know why the chief should be trying to humiliate me, but I felt he had sent us again and again at the double in the hope that eventually we would make a mistake. Well, we hadn't. I was fiercely proud of Legend and I leaned forward in the saddle and rubbed his neck with my knuckles as we cantered on up the rise. "We'll show the chief," I told him, "we'll get fitter than the others, we'll work harder than the others, and we'll make the team, he'll *have* to choose us. Then we'll show *everybody* what we can do."

We thudded towards the brush fence situated on top of the rise, and suddenly Legend began to falter in his stride. This was very out of character as he wasn't the sort of horse to spook at a perfectly straightforward fence, but he would certainly have stopped had I not legged him on energetically. He took off with reluctance and might even have turned back in mid-air had it been at all possible, due to the surprising nature of what lay behind.

Two people were standing beside the wings. They were Nigella and Henrietta Fane.

Where Own Horse Welcomed

I managed to pull Legend up after a few strides and I stared at them, speechless.

"I don't know why you're looking at us like that," Henrietta said in an annoyed tone, "you knew we were coming; we said we would bring your wages."

"They said in the office it would be perfectly all right to come up here," Nigella said, "as long as we kept out of sight, and didn't get in the way." She wore a vast, shapeless jersey above some grubby lilac culottes, and below them, her hunting boots.

As I still hadn't said anything, Henrietta said, "I suppose you do still *want* your wages? Nick seemed to think you were pretty desperate."

"Why," I asked her, "have you brought them?" I looked at her suspiciously because I didn't actually believe it.

"Of course we've brought them," Nigella said, "why else would we be here?"

"Other than to see Legend, of course," Henrietta put in swiftly, in case for one moment I might imagine they had softened in their attitude.

"Well, if you *have* brought my wages," I said, "I would rather like to have them, please."

Henrietta pulled a crumpled brown envelope with a window in it out of her appallingly ancient anorak. She held it out to me wordlessly and I took it from her.

"We haven't managed to pay you everything that

we owe you," Nigella was forced to admit now that she was faced with the presence of the envelope, "but we did manage to pay you half – well," she added, as I took out and counted the five ten pound notes it contained, "almost half."

Inside the envelope there was also a folded piece of paper. I opened it out, expecting it to be an IOU, but it was no such thing, it was a garage bill.

To recovery of Horse Box registration number SPD 347W	£24.50
To repairs to two punctured tyres	4.20
V.A.T. At 15%	4.30
	£33.00

"I think this belongs to you," I said. I held it out to Henrietta.

She made no move to take it.

"Now look here," I said angrily, "you don't actually expect me to pay the garage bill out of my own wages? *I'm* not responsible for the upkeep of the horsebox. It wasn't *my* fault the spare tyre hadn't been repaired!"

There was at this point an approaching thunder of hooves, which necessitated a timely removal of ourselves to a safe distance in order to avoid being trampled by Phillip Hastings and his amazing roan horse.

We watched him rise up over the brush and canter strongly onwards before we resumed our conversation.

"But Elaine," Nigella protested, "if you hadn't used the box to come to the training centre, the second puncture might never have happened and the clients would have had the spare repaired. *We* wouldn't have been expected to pay."

"But you expect *me* to pay," I blazed back at them furiously. "Even though you claim to have a financial interest in my horse, you don't seem at all keen to share responsibility when it actually comes to parting with hard cash!"

"We weren't supposed to have been using the horsebox at all," Henrietta countered angrily. "We only allowed you to use it out of kindness. If you had hired a box it would have cost twice that much!"

"And as you hadn't paid me any wages for six months," I said bitterly, "you knew I couldn't do that."

There was a dreadful silence after this broken by the sound of more hooves as Viv and Balthazar breasted the fence and pounded onwards.

"What have you come for, anyway?" I asked them in a dispirited voice.

"We came to bring your wages," Nigella said, "we came to see how you were, to see Legend, and to tell you our new girl has started and that things are looking up for us."

"She's shutting off half of the park so that we can make our own hay for the winter," Henrietta said in a satisfied tone. "She's giving riding lessons on the hirelings, *and* we're to take horses for breaking and schooling. That's not to mention the grass liveries; we've already got two of those."

"In other words," I said, annoyed, "you've come to gloat."

"Not gloat, Elaine," Nigella protested, "we just

80

thought you'd like to know how things are, so you won't feel so guilty about leaving us in the lurch."

"Nigella," I said crossly, "I don't *feel* guilty about leaving you in the lurch."

"Oh yes you do," Henrietta said, "Nick told us."

I stared at her angrily, wounded to think that Nick had seen fit to repeat what I had regarded as our private conversation.

Annemarie came over the brush, glaring at us as she cantered past. The little bay's neck was ridged with wrinkles due to being held so furiously in check. Legend began to sidle and shake his head, anxious to be away.

"As you will shortly be very prosperous due to all this increased business," I said, " perhaps you'll feel able to drop your ridiculous claim to a share in my horse, especially as you've replaced me so advantageously that you'll never need my services again."

Henrietta frowned. "Why should we," she demanded, "when we're entitled to it?"

"It isn't just the money, Elaine," Nigella pointed out, "we don't want to jeopardize your career in the least. We *like* having an interest in an event horse, it's opened up a whole new world for us. We've never had more fun than we've had in the last eighteen months."

Henrietta made no move to agree. She stared down at her sawn-off wellingtons, the toes mended by means of a patch from a cycle puncture repair kit. If this was true, she wasn't going to allow me the satisfaction of hearing her say it.

"And we're all so looking forward to coming to the junior trial," Nigella continued, adding anxiously, "you will want us to come, won't you . . . it will be all right, won't it?" As I made no reply but continued to stare angrily at Henrietta, she blurted out, "Mummy told me to say she misses you *terribly*."

I didn't want to hear this. I didn't want to hear any of it; not how much Lady Jennifer was missing me, not how the new girl was going to achieve miracles – miracles that if I had stayed and been less determined to pursue my own eventing career, I might have achieved myself. "I have to go now," I said, "I'm supposed to be under instruction and already the chief will be wondering where I am." I made to turn Legend away.

Henrietta looked up. She eyed me in a speculative manner. "I suppose you've already got a new job organized for when you finish the course?" she said. "We haven't actually seen your advertisement in *Horse & Hound*, but we could have missed it, of course."

"I suppose you *have* advertised, Elaine?" Nigella said in a worried voice. "Because with only three weeks to go, there isn't a lot of time left."

I didn't need Nigella to tell me this and I didn't want the Fanes to know I hadn't placed an advertisement yet. Nor did I want to admit, even to myself, that the reason I had hesitated was that I had hoped that their new groom would be useless, and that they would beg me to go back. Despite the awfulness of Havers Hall, despite the way they had behaved over Legend and my wages, I realized that I was missing *them* terribly – Lady Jennifer, the horses – *my* horses – and even the Fanes themselves. But nothing, nothing in the world, would have allowed me to confess it, and so I lied. "Yes," I said, "I advertised under a box number. I've found a place."

There was a silence. Then: "I expect they offered

you better wages than ours," Henrietta said in a quizing tone.

"Since I wasn't shown your advertisement, I wouldn't know what wages you offered," I snapped, "but I'm sure it wouldn't be difficult to offer better wages than you paid *me*."

"Well, if you're going to be like that about it," Henrietta retorted, "if you don't want us to know what you *do* consider to be a decent wage, I'm sure we don't want to know anyway. I'm sure we're not all that interested."

"As a matter of fact," I told her, "I'm getting fifty pounds a week."

"Fifty pounds a week!" Nigella gasped. "Really?"

"And free board and lodging and keep for Legend," I added.

"Goodness," Nigella exclaimed, "we can't really compete with anything like that."

"And time off for eventing?" Henrietta enquired.

"And time off for eventing," I said.

"And use of a horsebox?"

"And use of a horsebox."

"With a room of your own, not having to share with others?"

"Yes."

"Heavens," said Henrietta. I could see she was having difficulty in swallowing all this, which was hardly surprising since it sounded unlikely, even to my own ears.

"Where is it?" she said.

"Where is what?" I said, holding up Legend who was by now digging a hole in the turf with an impatiently flailing foreleg.

"The job, where *is* the job? Which county?"

"Oh," I said vaguely, "I've got a choice of two or

three similar places and I haven't decided which to take yet."

Nigella suddenly turned away. "When you go," she said in a strained voice, "you will leave us a forwarding address, won't you? We don't want to lose touch."

"Because of Legend," Henrietta added quickly, before I could think it was me they wanted to keep in touch with. "We shall need to know where he is."

For some appallingly sentimental reason my eyes suddenly filled with tears and I jerked Legend away almost roughly. I said, "I really do have to go now. I'll see you at the trial, I expect."

Mandy and Fox Me now appeared over the brush and I loosed Legend to canter after them.

"Elaine . . ." Nigella began in a choked voice as we bounded past, "we . . ." but I couldn't turn back and, blinking hard, I rode on in a wide arc, past the brush fence to be confronted with the Range Rover bumping along gently, followed by the rest of the class.

"Fall in, Miss Elliot," the chief barked from the driver's window. "I want to see you take the brush again, and this time I want to see a more decisive approach; I want to see *positive, controlled* horsemanship."

I trotted Legend back down the rise and set his head towards the brush once more. This time he didn't hesitate, and when we landed, the Fanes were nowhere to be seen.

Later the same day, when I returned to the Duke of Newcastle after the evening stint of tack cleaning, I found a piece of the Fanes' ancient notepaper with a crest on it in the bottom of my suitcase, borrowed

84

Viv's ballpoint pen, and I was just about to help myself to an envelope from the stack of papers beneath Selina's bed, where she also kept her typewriter and a professional-looking camera, when the bedroom door opened.

"Elaine!" Selina exclaimed in a shocked voice. "How *could* you snoop into my private belongings, when I have *expressly* asked you not to!"

I got up, feeling guilty. "I'm not snooping," I said defensively, "I'm only desperate for an envelope. I've got a very important letter to write and when I tried to ask for one, you were on the pay phone in the lecture hall and you waved me away."

Observing that I hadn't disturbed her stack of type-written papers, Selina softened. "Well, you may have an envelope, of course," she said sweetly, "but please remember never to touch my belongings again. I do set a very high value on personal privacy."

From the way she locked me out of our bedroom when she was busily engaged on her typewriter I knew this to be true, so I took the proffered envelope with suitably humble thanks and left her to it.

I went into the sitting room and sat at the formica-topped table. Alice sat at the other end reading a romantic novel with a lurid cover, absently picking at her spots. Mandy sat in front of the electric fire, its one bar glowing bravely, with her Sony Walkman clamped over her floppy hair. Annemarie was slumped in an armchair, deep into *Die Klassiche Reitkunst*. Phillip and Viv were in the kitchen making toast and coffee.

Painstakingly I began to word my advertisement:

Experienced girl groom, Horsemaster's Cert., prepared to consider any situation where own horse welcomed. Write Box . . .

8

Washday

"Do you have to get a job to go to after the course?" Viv wanted to know as, after morning stables on Monday, we prepared for our stint at the washing rota. "What about your old man? Couldn't you go back to him for a bit?" She raised her head from the collection of empty Vim cannisters, rusting Brillo-pads and dried up tins of boot polish which cluttered the clammy little cupboard under the kitchen sink. She handed me a packet of detergent.

I thought of my father and his little terraced town house with its minute paved backyard, "my patio," he called it, his rented garage three streets away which housed his beloved Morris Minor, twenty years old and still, as he proudly boasted, "in show-room condition," and his modest building society savings account. We lived in different worlds my father and I, and I knew I could never go back.

"There's nowhere to keep Legend," I said, "my father doesn't really like horses, and I know he'll think I'm crazy when I tell him I'm not going back to the Fanes. He thinks they're wonderful, especially Lady Jennifer." The detergent was set into a solid brick. I tore off its cardboard wrapping, laid it on the draining board and began to break it up with a fork. "No, I'll have to get a job, it's the only answer."

Viv slammed the cupboard doors shut and straightened up. She trundled the old-fashioned twin-tub washing machine out of its corner, causing alarm amongst a family of spiders. "Perhaps we should swop fathers for a while, you and me," she suggested. "My old man may have the money, but yours sounds as if he's got the sense to leave you to live your own life." She connected the hose to the tap and turned on the water.

I looked at her, interested. "You mean if you hadn't got the scholarship, you could still have had the training anyway?" I hadn't realized that there was so much money to be made out of selling Indian sandals and belts, and I thought it fortunate that Alice didn't know of it because she was always making snide remarks in front of Selina about people who could afford to pay taking up places on scholarships designed for those who couldn't.

"I could, but it's got to the stage where I won't take his money, so I probably wouldn't have."

"But you do *want* to event?"

She shrugged her narrow shoulders in a typical gesture as we watched the water splash into the machine. "How does anyone know *what* they want," she said, "especially with an old man like mine, always interfering, making arrangements, paying for things; finishing school, a hairdressing course, a secretarial course. I've hopped out of them all, but he never gives up, and now I've got Balthazar. It started off with just a few riding lessons, then a better instructor, then suddenly I'd got this horse, the best horse money could buy, and it seemed a waste really, not to event, because everyone said he could do it, and here I am . . ." she looked at me in genuine despair. "If only he'd just leave me alone and give me a chance to decide what *I* want to do."

I sprinkled some lumpy detergent into the water

and it whirled round on the top, partly submerged, like a cluster of icebergs. "But surely," I said, "you wouldn't put up with all this," I waved an arm around the Duke of Newcastle's incredibly squalid little kitchen, "and the work, and the running, and the lunging, and everything, if you didn't *want* to do it? No one would."

As the water began to steam, she looked up and gave me an elfin grin. "Ah, well, that's my competitive spirit asserting itself, isn't it? I'm going to get into the team now, just to spite Annemarie and the bloody Reitschule. Just for the satisfaction of seeing her face when the chief reads out my name and not hers; because that little Hanoverian of hers isn't going to make it, he hasn't got the scope."

We began to load the first wash into the machine, and I reflected that already intense rivalries had sprung up between the scholarship students, between Alice and Selina, and between Viv and Annemarie who had only shared a cell for one night before war had been declared. Now Annemarie shared with Mandy, and Viv with Alice.

"Anyway," Viv declared, "I'm glad you haven't got too much money, Elaine, because money spoils. It changes your values, and, if you haven't actually earned it yourself, it stunts your growth and makes you lose your direction until, in the end, you doubt your own ability and lose your self respect." She grabbed a pair of jeans out of my hands before they hit the water. "Don't put *those* in – they'll dye everything blue!"

I could see that this might well be true, but it didn't stop me wishing I had some money; just enough to pay off the Fanes and to secure a roof over our heads for me and for Legend. "What about your mother?" I wondered. "Do you get on all right with her?" My own mother had left home, for a man fifteen years her junior, when I was ten.

Water suddenly began to fly about and splash over the sides of the machine although the lumps of detergent still bobbed on the top in an unpromising manner. I slapped on the lid, hopping to contain it.

"My mother's dead," Viv said gloomily. "If she'd been alive things would be different – we got on famously, my mum and I. She didn't expect me to be anything other than what I was, what I wanted to be, but my old man married again and I've got a stepmother now – oh, you should see her Elaine, she really thinks she's somebody and I *hate* her. She hates me as well but she pretends she doesn't, so I won't live at home any more. I live with my gran. The old man hates it and he's forever trying to get her to send me back, but she won't, and I won't go back, not while *she's* there, I couldn't stand it." She grinned at me, her humour suddenly restored. "So there you have it, but don't tell anyone, Elaine," she warned, "I'll skin you if you do!"

"I wouldn't," I protested, "I promise I won't say a word."

The washing machine now began to vibrate in an alarming way and to creep across the kitchen until it reached the limit of its cable where it rattled and fretted with impotent fury. We halted its progress by propping a corner with *Die Klassiche Reitkunst*.

After a noisy interval the machine turned itself off with a small bang. I lifted the lid cautiously. The clothes were bound together in a distressingly tangled lump, speckled with undissolved detergent.

"We can't have got it hot enough," Viv concluded. She turned the dial on the side of the machine to

BOIL. I watched with some trepidation as the water began to bubble and steam billowed, but at last the speckles turned to suds. "That's done it," Viv said in a satisfied voice. "It'll be done in no time."

Soapsuds worked their way between the lid and the top of the machine, inching slowly down the sides and threatening the safety of *Die Klassiche Reitkunst,* then, with a mighty whooshing of the rinse and more furious vibratings, they were banished and the cycle came to an abrupt end. We pulled out the jumble of clothes and put them into the spinner. They seemed terribly hot.

"They certainly look clean, anyhow," Viv observed as she transferred them to the laundry basket, then abruptly her tone changed. "Cor strike a light, Elaine," she groaned, "just take a look at these."

I looked over her shoulder and saw that she was holding up Selina's beautiful breeches. They were hardly recognizable. All the lovely soft creamy suede strappings had shrunk to a quarter of their original size; not only that, but they were transformed into something utterly repulsive, dark and slippery and slimy to the touch, like raw pig's liver.

"It must be because we boiled them," I said, appalled, "they're ruined!" It was small consolation to look at the rest of the breeches and see that they had survived because they had self-strappings.

"We'll have to do something," Viv said, "Selina will go mad. She'll go absolutely barmy."

We couldn't think of anything. We stood in the steamed up kitchen and we stared at the breeches, aghast.

"We'll try drying them," Viv declared. "First we'll get them dry, then we'll iron them out flat, but we'll

90

stretch them as much as we can now, whilst they're still wet."

We pulled at the breeches until we heard the stitching begin to pop, then we fetched the electric fire and held the strappings as close to it as we dared. With the steam from the machine and the hot clothes and the strappings, the Duke of Newcatle's kitchen turned into a turkish bath, the windows poured. My hair hung lank to my shoulders and Viv's orange spikes stood on end so that she resembled a frightened cockatoo. In spite of all this the strappings were no better when they were dry. In fact they were worse. They toasted to a crisp and when we tried to iron out the crinkles, they broke up like biscuits. It was simply terrible.

There was only one thing to do. I ran for my cell, rummaged through my drawer and found my own identical breeches lying in their tissue, lovingly wrapped against their day of glory, and I substituted them for Selina's ruined ones. Viv crept out of the Duke of Newcastle's back door and buried the remains of the old ones in the muckheaps with the fish slice.

"There's a *devastatingly* handsome young man asking for you in the yard, Elaine," Selina beamed round the door of our cell as I brushed my hair and fixed it with a slide. "Have you known him long?" She came in and settled herself on her bed in anticipation of some interesting gossip. For someone who could be incredibly tart with anyone she suspected of showing an interest in her affairs, she showed an extraordinary curiosity about every last detail of other people's lives, and never tired of asking questions.

91

"About eighteen months," I said. "He works for the Midvale and Westbury Hunt."

"Does he really," she said, impressed, "and does he wear scarlet? I should think he would look simply divine in scarlet."

"Yes, he wears scarlet," I said, "he's first whipper-in."

"Oh, how marvellous!" Selina clasped her hands together and looked beatific. "And is it unbearably romantic?"

I remembered the mud, and the lost shoes, and the rain, and Nelson's saddle, black, like old wash-leather. "No," I said, "not very, it's a plough country."

"Not the hunting," Selina said crossly, "I mean the relationship."

"Oh," I said in a shocked voice, "I couldn't *possibly* tell you that. I set rather a high value on personal privacy." I snatched up my good navy guernsey and smiled at her vexed expression as I made for the door.

I walked through the yards, looking for Nick. Everywhere was unusually quiet as Monday was a rest day at the training centre; no horses were exercised, no lessons were given, and only a skeleton staff were retained in order to feed, water, and attend to basic necessary duties. I looked in to see Legend on my way past his box, but he was busy with a hay net and couldn't be bothered with any acknowledgement other than the cock of an ear in my direction.

Nick was waiting in the car park, leaning with his elbows on the roof of his white sports car, and smoking a cigarette. He was wearing his best Italian suede trousers, an open-necked shirt with a cravat, and a hacking jacket. I could see why Selina had considered him devastating.

"I thought we'd go for a picnic," he said.

"A picnic?" I looked doubtfully at the sky which was cloudy and a little threatening. "Is that a good idea?"

He stuck the cigarette in the corner of his mouth and opened the passenger door for me, squinting his dark fringed eyes against the smoke. "As I've actually been shopping for the food, it had better be."

I studied him cautiously as he got into the driving seat and slammed the door. He didn't seem to be in an awfully good mood and I wondered what had annoyed him. We had had many a bitter battle in the past because of his uncertain temper, but I didn't feel like an argument today – after my first week at the training centre, I was too tired for one thing.

"What's the matter?" I asked him. "Is everything all right?"

"Everything's fine," he said shortly. "I just don't feel like seeking company, that's all, and anyway, we've got to talk."

This sounded unpromising, especially as he immediately pushed a Streisand cassette into the tape deck which made talking out of the question. He drove on, and I sat silently, as the cassette played and the throttle roared, and the main road became a side road, the side road became a lane, the lane became a cart-track, and the cart-track petered out on to a grassy bank beside a meandering stream sheltered by a copse of hazel trees, golden with catkins.

"Oh," I said, delighted. "It's lovely – how did you know it was here?"

Nick opened up the boot and pulled out picnic things which included two mohair day rugs with the initials MWH on the sides. "I once had a girlfriend who lived in Crookham," he said.

I flopped down on one of the rugs, feeling rather squashed. Nick had had a lot of girlfriends in the past, and if rumour was to be believed, not all of them had been single either. I watched him open a bottle of white wine with a practised hand, and accepted some in a plastic tumbler. He sat down on the rug and looked at me in an expectant manner.

"Well?" he said.

I looked at him in surprise. "Well what?" I asked.

"Perhaps it would help if I gave you a clue," he said. "On my way over, I popped in to see the Fanes."

"Oh, yes," I said, "and *was* she pretty?"

He looked at me for a moment as if he didn't know what I was talking about.

"The new girl," I told him, "you know, wonder woman."

He frowned. "No," he said, and after some consideration, he added, "she's tough, strong, efficient, and capable, but she isn't pretty."

"I see," I said. "So she *is* as good as they said she was." I stared down into my plastic tumbler and felt my heart drop several inches because I had believed the Fanes capable of exaggeration, and now I knew they had told the truth. "What does the yard look like?" I asked him.

"The yard looks tidy, the cobbles are weeded, the boxes are properly mucked out, the horses are well strapped." Nick regarded me steadily over the rim of his tumbler. "She's worth every penny of fifty pounds a week."

I didn't believe it. "The Fanes aren't paying her that much," I said incredulously, "they couldn't afford it!"

"But it's the going rate for an experienced groom, isn't it?" Nick asked in an even tone. "After all, it's what you'll be getting."

I took a sip of wine. "I'd like to think so," I said, "but I'll bet you anything that the Fanes aren't paying her more than fifteen pounds a week, less probably."

"Plus use of the horsebox, a room of her own, time off to compete, and keep of her own horse?"

"Has she got her own horse?" I said, nettled by the idea. "They didn't say."

"They said quite a lot to me," Nick said, splashing more wine into his tumbler – the bottle was already half empty.

"Don't you think we should have something to eat?" I suggested. "You're not supposed to drink and drive."

"We'll eat when you've told me what you told the Fanes," he said coldly, "unless what Henrietta said was true and you didn't intend to tell anyone about where you are going after the course."

With my mind still gnawing away miserably over the success of the new girl, I hardly heard what he said. I rolled over and looked into the stream. "Tell me about the riding lessons and the grass liveries," I said. After all, I thought, it's me she's replacing, I'm entitled to know.

The next minute I was hauled up into a sitting position by the neck of my good navy guernsey and Nick's furious face was next to my own. "Tell me about *your* new job, Elaine," he said in a dangerously quiet voice.

I stared at him, quite unable to speak.

"Or don't you want me to know?" he continued. "Perhaps Henrietta was telling the truth for once, was she, when she said it was to be a secret?" He let go of my guernsey and turned away. "You could have told me," he said in disgust, "you might have spared me having to hear it second-hand from the Fanes."

I let out a sigh and put down my tumbler. Now I could see why he had been in such a bad mood, what all the dropped hints about wages and time off to compete had been leading up to. Trust the Fanes, I thought resentfully, to cast a blight even when they couldn't be present to do it in person.

"It isn't true," I said. "Honestly, Nick, I haven't got a job, not yet, I've only just sent off my advertisement."

He turned back to me, scowling, not knowing whether to believe me or not.

"I haven't," I assured him, "I just couldn't bear the Fanes to think I hadn't got anything at all, when they were so cock-a-hoop over wonder woman, so I made it up. Anyway," I added, "you need money to advertise, and until they brought my wages, I hadn't any."

This reminded me that I still owed him the petrol money and I searched through my pockets and presented him with it. He took it, but reluctantly. Now I had explained how things were, I knew that he believed me, but it was a little while before his humour was restored.

We lay on the hunt day rugs and stared into the stream.

"Now you've finally got away from the Fanes," Nick told me, "you have to steel yourself to forget them. They've found someone else to feel responsible for their equine cripples and to run their business, so you can put them behind you and set your sights on better things."

"It would be a lot easier if the better things were already in sight," I said, "and if the Fanes didn't insist on having a stake in Legend." Also, I thought rather miserably, it won't be easy to forget them. The Fanes, the unbearable, irritating, eccentric, irreplaceable Fanes, were going to leave a big gap in my life. We fell silent, thinking about the Fanes.

"Once," said Nick, "a horse and a chance to event were all you wanted."

"And now," I said, feeling desolate, "it's all I've got."

The first spot of rain fell upon the back of my neck. Nick immediately jumped to his feet and began to throw things into the boot of the car.

"I don't think we'll bother with the picnic, after all," he said in a cheerful voice, "I'll take you for tea in Crookham instead. I know the perfect place."

I didn't doubt it.

9

Such An Excellent Store

The following week we were to ride the cross-country course as a whole for the first time. It was a testing course, consisting of twenty-nine fences up and down-hill, through water and woodland, and even though the chief had drilled us over the most awkward fences individually, we were all anxious about it by the time the day came. When Phillip, whose turn it was to cook, suggested a fried breakfast, we all groaned.

Phillip was visibly disappointed as, far from objecting to being included on the rota, he had actually been looking forward to showing off his talents as a chef. He contented himself with laying our beastly formica table with elaborate care, lining up the cereal packets and the bowls, putting out side plates, searching out saucers for our motley collection of mugs, scraping the marmalade into a basin, and decanting the milk into a jug; he even cut up the butter into neat little squares.

"Gorden Bennett," Alice commented when she saw it, "who's coming for breakfast, the Queen?"

Alice was not riding because The Talisman still had a puffy leg as a result of hitting the double. He was not actually lame, but the chief had decided he should do light work only until the leg was back to normal, and he had appointed Alice timekeeper and starter for the cross-country. She was not looking her best this morning, having finally been persuaded to see the nurse, who ran a mini-surgery in the yard two mornings a week to deal with bites, kicks, sprains, crushed toes, lice, ringworm, bumps on the head, and all the other minor ailments and accidents that working pupils and students were wont to suffer from. Nurse had issued Alice with some green acne ointment which made the spots look even more unsightly, and Alice, who didn't care what she looked like, made a point of plastering her face with it before every lesson to annoy the chief who, suspecting that she was being insubordinate, but unable to do very much about it, gave her some searching looks.

Selina appeared for breakfast, still in her track suit and running shoes, having managed to finish the morning run looking as immaculate as when she had started out. "Well, this *is* an improvement, I must say," she said. She settled herself at the table and looked round approvingly.

Mandy, flushed and wheezing, flopped into her chair with her Sony Walkman still in place, and Phillip, setting an evenly browned rack of toast in front of us, plucked the earphones off the top of her head in protest. If it had been anyone else, Mandy would have snatched them back, but as she was in love with Phillip, she switched it off and gave him a cow-eyed look of adoration.

Annemarie, whose table manners left a lot to be desired, threw herself into the vacant chair, grabbed a piece of Phillip's beautiful toast, piled three squares of butter on to it, flattened it with her knife, stirred her coffee with the blade and plunged it, still dripping, into the marmalade. Despite this appalling display, she still complained unceasingly about the

99

quality of our accommodation, comparing it unfavourably with that of the Reitschule.

"I wasn't able to find a jamspoon," Phillip apologized, "sorry."

Annemarie paused with loaded toast inches from her mouth. "There aren't any jam spoons to be found in this hole of a place," she said with her customary disgust.

"And even if there were," Selina pointed out, "*some* people might not know what they were for."

One by one we got up from the table and went to get changed for the cross-country. I managed to be ready first and was sitting on Mandy's bed, having just negotiated the loan of a hairnet from Annemarie, when the door burst open and Selina appeared, looking furious.

"These breeches have *shrunk*!" she raged, her face white with temper. "Lilywhites promised me *faithfully* they were pre-shrunk and machine washable!"

I had forgotten about the breeches, but now I saw with dismay that the velcro fastenings only reached to her knees, and the waistband didn't meet at all. In retrospect, this was hardly surprising because my breeches were two sizes smaller than the ones they had replaced, but it had been a fact I had failed to consider in the anxiety of the moment.

There seemed nothing for it but to tell Selina what had happened. I opened my mouth to confess everything and offer to buy her a new pair of breeches, but she was not to be interrupted.

"I think it's utterly disgraceful," she stormed. "I shall create the most *almighty* scene, and what is more, I shall close my account!" She raced out of the cell, still wearing the breeches, to ring the store from the pay phone in the lecture hall.

Annemarie, who knew the story of the breeches, looked after her with vengeful satisfaction. "Now there's going to be trouble," she said, "just you wait."

I didn't have to wait long, Selina returned a few minutes later, looking serene.

"What did they say?" I breathed, trying hard not to sound over-anxious.

Selina smiled at the memory. "Well, of course, they were *most* apologetic," she said. "I must admit to being positively warmed by their concern. They intend to take the matter up with the manufacturer, and naturally, they are sending an immediate replacement."

"Well . . . naturally," I said, "I mean . . . why not?"

"I must say they are such an *excellent store*," Selina went on in a self-congratulatory tone, "but I am, after all, one of their most valued customers." She sat down on the bed and peeled off the offending breeches and, after a moment of thoughtful hesitation, held them out to me. "They should be just about your size now, Elaine," she said in her sweetest voice, "do please take them, and no . . ." she held up a restraining hand as my jaw fell open, "please don't try to thank me, they are no earthly use to me, after all." She rose from the bed, patted my shoulder in a queenly gesture, and went off in her lace-trimmed knickers to hunt out her second best.

I continued to sit on the bed with the breeches on my lap, feeling stunned, but Annemarie folded up and fell across her bed in a paroxysm of helpless,

101

hysterical laughter. I suppose that even at the Reit-schule, it would have been considered a pretty good joke.

The chief stood by the Range Rover watching us work in our horses, beating an impatient tattoo on his boot as Alice sweated over a heap of papers on the tailboard, sorting out the draw for our starting order, and working out the times.

We were wearing our jerseys, our cross-country hats and safety harness, we had been given number cloths, and our stopwatches were strapped to our wrists. Our horses had studs screwed into their shoes to give them extra grip, their bandages were sewn on, their legs smeared with vaseline to assist them to slip instead of scrape over the fixed fences in the event of a mistake. All this made it as nerve-wracking as the real thing.

The chief supervised us individually as we gave our horses a sharp gallop to clear their wind, and sent us to Alice to collect our times, set to start at ten minute intervals. I had never given Legend his pipe-opener so close to starting before, and now I could see that it had been a mistake because he got excited and began to plunge about in an agony of impatience, knowing exactly what lay ahead and desperate to get on with it. I knew that event horses often became so wound up before the start of the cross-country phase that they jibbed out of sheer nerves at the last minute, napping, rearing and running backwards, losing valuable seconds after their starting time and often needing three people, one either side and one behind, to get them to approach the start at all. I didn't want Legend to get the habit, so I took him well away from Alice and her stopwatch, and with one eye on my times, written on my wrist with Viv's ballpoint, worked him steadily into a calmer frame of mind.

Viv and Balthazar went first, thundering away in a purposeful manner towards the first fence. Phillip set off ten minutes later, the roan horse's tail flying, and its white stockings flashing in the sunshine. Annemarie followed, looking tense and determined, and I was next.

As my starting time approached, I worked Legend nearer and nearer to Alice, slowing to a working trot and finally to a walk, so that as Alice began our count-down we were walking towards her, drew level, and cantered away on the exact second.

"Neat work, Elaine!" Alice bellowed, and Legend, realizing that we were off, gave a leap of joy.

It was a glorious morning, sunny and fresh, with a deep blue sky and a keen little breeze. The trees were coming into leaf, and the parkland over which the cross-country course was set was awash with a froth of white and yellow daffodils. The afternoon spent with Nick had helped me to resolve to put the Fanes and their affairs behind me, and to concentrate my energies exclusively towards Legend and my eventing career. The early morning running and the extra hours spent in the saddle were already having a beneficial effect on my health and fitness, and I felt confident and happy as we thudded across the turf. I was ready for anything.

Legend cleared the first fence easily, galloped over the tiger trap almost without noticing it, and had gained so much superfluous speed out of sheer *joie de vivre,* that I was forced to sit down hard in the saddle and fight to steady him as we flew downhill towards the telegraph pole in the middle of the shimmering lake. Showers of sparkling droplets flew into the air as we hit the water and cantered strongly towards the pole with more than enough impulsion to satisfy the chief, who was currently nowhere to be seen. Legend jumped the pole, landed with a tremendous splash, crossed the shallows in a succession of high-spirited leaps and bounds, gained the bank and pounded onwards towards the uphill double where The Talisman had cut his fetlock. As before, he cleared it easily, taking four effortless strides in between the fences and sailing cleanly out over the second part.

Things began to go awry after that because, perhaps made over-confident by past success, we took off too close to the brush where the Fanes had sheltered and scraped over the top in a hail of twigs, and followed this by making an appalling mess of the zig-zag rails.

There were four separate parts to the zig-zag, all set at different angles and varying distances and I somehow managed to misjudge Legend's stride and speed, placing him either too close or too far away from every rail, whilst he, calling upon every last ounce of athletic ability in his body, got over somehow, but not without a hammer blow to his front or hind shins each time, and a devastating peck on his final landing.

I didn't deserve to be still in the saddle by the end of it, but I was, just, and I struggled back over the pommel from halfway down his shoulder as he recovered his balance and trotted on, but with a peculiar, halting gait. I pulled him up and looked down, feeling sick with fright, to see what damage he had done to himself and saw the cause of it –

yards of trailing bandage unwinding itself from his near fore; my stitching had come undone.

I jumped down to the ground, feeling shaken, and not helped by the fact that Legend was still eager to continue and was in no mood to stand still whilst I retrieved the lost bandage, repositioned the gamgee tissue, and wound up the crepe again, blessing the fact the I hadn't cut off the tapes and still had some method of securing it. Legend pranced and fidgeted as I fumbled with the tapes, knotting them several times for security, and the precious seconds ticked away. To make matters worse, a distant flash of reflected light told me that the chief was standing by the Range Rover with his binoculars trained upon us.

I cursed him as I clambered back into the saddle, knowing that I would be in deep trouble later and would probably have to spend hours sewing up bandages to prove I was capable of doing it properly. We cantered on. Legend, to my relief, appeared to be perfectly sound.

The next two fences, approached cautiously, with due regard to stride, speed, height and distance, we jumped clear, and now we entered a natural hollow, where a succession of narrow drop fences had been cut like giant steps out of the hillside. Perched on the very edge of each step was a timber jump made of railway sleepers, increasing in height as one descended and the steps themselves also widened on the descent, so that it needed a clever, scopey horse to negotiate it.

Legend, his bay head lowered to evaluate each step as it appeared below us, plummeted down the first, landed, rose again immediately over the first sleeper, plummeted again, took a stride, soared upwards, dropped down to land on the step below, took two strides, leapt, and as I struggled to remain in balance, dropped and landed safely at the bottom.

I clapped his neck as we cantered on, hoping that the chief had been watching our copybook descent. He hadn't, because when I looked up, I saw that he and Annemarie were engaged in energetic pursuit of the little part-bred Hanoverian who was playing a spirited game of catch-as-catch-can between the next two jumps. He had clearly deposited Annemarie, who had a grass stain on the seat of her breeches, at the steps which, because of his lack of scope, had become his personal bogey.

With a feeling of resignation, I reined in Legend and stopped my watch as Annemarie and the chief, both clearly infuriated, made alternate swoops at the little bay, and Selina appeared at the top of the steps to begin her descent. Mandy, I felt sure, would not be far behind and I knew that by this time Alice's timekeeping would be in a hopeless muddle and the chief would end the morning practically deranged with fury.

Selina appeared beside me, looking, I thought, rather pale after Flame Thrower's descent of the steps. She stopped her watch and observed the chase which was still going on ahead of us.

"Do you think we should assist?" she enquired.

"No," I said, "I don't think so."

Selina watched the chief stalking the little bay, who with a guile born of many similar occasions, waited until he was within a hair's breadth of his rein before throwing up his head and trotting out of reach.

"No," she said with a little smile, "I don't think so, either."

* * *

106

The door of the Duke of Newcastle opened and Phillip came in with the morning's post; an airmail letter from Germany for Annemarie, two typewritten envelopes for Selina, and a parcel for me, untidily wrapped, tied with orange baler twine, and addressed in Nigella's wandering hand.

Inside the parcel I found a vast, shapeless, blue jersey with red sleeves. Nigella had worn it when she had won a point-to-point in the days when we were shamelessly pot-hunting in aid of Legend's training fund. *It was lucky for me,* she had written, *so perhaps it will be lucky for you, Elaine.* I laid it on my bed and remembered when we had bought it from *Help the Aged* on Lady Jennifer's duty day. We had had to buy two jerseys, one blue and one red, and had cobbled the sleeves of one on to the other to achieve something like racing colours. It was hideous and so enormous that I could never wear it, but I was made to feel a little emotional by the thought which had prompted her to send it, especially as she had pinned to it the rest of the ten pound notes to make up the balance of my wages.

We wondered, Elaine, Nigella's letter continued, *if we could possibly come and see you on your next free afternoon. We really need to talk to you and hope you will agree . . .*

I could have refused. After all, I had decided to forget the Fanes completely and concentrate on my career. But, what difference will it make, I asked myself, to see them one last time? And suppose they've changed their minds and decided to relinquish their claim to a share in Legend? How much more satisfactory it would be to leave them on affectionate terms.

I went to find Selina and asked if I could borrow two of her envelopes.

She frowned. "I will *give* you two envelopes, Elaine," she said, "because I hardly expect them to be returned, but if you are likely to require any more, you can buy perfectly good Basildon Bond at the village store."

I took the envelopes, scribbled a note to Nigella telling them to come the following Monday afternoon, hunted out the garage bill, put it in the other envelope, and tucked three ten pound notes and three single pound notes in with it. Then I sealed them both. At least my side of the slate was clean. Now it was up to the Fanes.

10

Their Own Familiar Fields

Monday turned out to be rather dramatic, one way and another. Because the weather had been so perfect, we had all been for a long, blissfully leisured hack on Sunday evening, and so we spent part of the morning cleaning our tack. I went to collect the headcollars, which were kept in the yard store for convenience, and slipped over to the office to see if there was any post because I had been rather expecting a letter from Nick. Instead I got a short note from my father hoping I was enjoying the course, informing me that he would be coming to the junior trial with Lady Jennifer, and enclosing five pounds. He, at least, was confident that I would make the team.

I wandered through the car park, hung with headcollars, marvelling at the amount of correspondence Selina received every day, and stopped in my tracks to admire a beautiful pale green Rolls Royce, which crunched silently across the gravel and came to a halt just in front of me. A small, portly man in a dark suit and a silk tie emerged from the driver's seat.

"Hello," he said in a cheerful voice, "are you a student?"

I replied that I was and I wasn't, and I explained about the scholarship course.

"In that case," he said, "perhaps you would be

kind enough to hunt out my daughter for me. I believe she's on the scholarship course as well."

He smiled at me in an encouraging manner. He seemed very pleasant, very well-spoken; but possibly, I thought, a man of steel, a person not to be trifled with. I went.

I hadn't even asked who his daughter was, but I put together the authoritative manner and the Rolls Royce, and I concluded that the only scholarship student who could possibly be his daughter was Selina.

I found her soaping the underside of her saddle, wearing a pink nylon overall to protect her navy blue track suit. She looked surprised when I said her father was waiting to see her.

"I thought he was in Montreal this week," she said in a perplexed tone, as she removed her overall, patted her already immaculate hair, and followed me out into the yard. She looked even more surprised when they came face to face. Her visitor looked rather taken aback as well.

Selina opened her eyes wide with astonishment. "Why," she exclaimed, "it's Mr Tintoft, isn't it?" She turned to me looking rather distressed. "This isn't my father, Elaine, it's Mr Tintoft, head of the departmental stores."

There didn't seem anything I could say to this. I just stared at them both and wondered what was happening.

Mr Tintoft was staring at Selina with an outraged expression on his face. "And you, young lady, are Jane Lejeune, unless I am very much mistaken," he said in a furious voice. "You and I already have one score to settle, and now look set for another, if you are here for the purpose I suspect."

110

Selina summoned up her most imperious manner and held up a restraining hand, "Mr Tintoft, I think you are mistaking me for someone else," she said firmly. "I don't actually know you at all, we have never been introduced, and I only recognized your face from the newspapers.'

"And I recognize *your* face from the newspapers," Mr Tintoft retorted in a heated voice, "and if you've come here, sailing under false colours, the way you sailed into my stores . . ."

"I can assure you, Mr Tintoft," Selina cut in sharply, "that you are totally mistaken, *totally*," she emphasized, "and if you imagine that my being here has anything at all to do with your daughter, I can assure you again, that it is *positively* untrue." She turned to me for confirmation. "Elaine," she commanded, "tell Mr Tintoft who I am."

"Selina," I told him, "Selina Gibbons."

"And why am I here?"

"Training for eventing," I said, "trying for a place at the junior trial."

Mr Tintoft stifled a bark of incredulous laughter. "And just how old is a junior these days?" he enquired.

"Under twenty-one," Selina said, and the corners of her mouth quivered.

Mr Tintoft stared at her for a moment and then his shoulders began to shake with supressed mirth. He turned to me, still standing beside them, taking it all in and not understanding a word. "I think, if you wouldn't mind, you had better fetch me Vivienne," he said.

I left them giggling together like a couple of first-formers and went to find Viv. She was soaping a bridle in the tackroom. Her dungarees were splashed with water and there was a smear of glycerine saddle soap across her cheek.

"Viv', I said, "your father's here."

She stared at me and her face went very pale. "What for?" she whispered. "What does he want?"

"I don't know," I said helplessly, "I expect he'll tell you that."

She dropped the whole bridle into the scum-covered water and it hit the bottom with a dismal clunk. "Hell, Elaine," she said, "oh *hell*." She sounded as if she might burst into tears.

There was nothing I could do or say, but:"Oh, *Viv*," I said, remembering, "you said he sold sandals along the Mile End Road."

She looked up at me, tight-lipped. "So it's Knightsbridge," she said, "what's the difference?"

"There's a lot of difference," I said.

She looked down at the scummy water and then unexpectedly spat into it. "Well, you can stuff the difference," she snapped viciously and, racing off out of the tack room, she slammed the door so hard that a tin of louse powder jumped off the shelf.

Viv didn't appear for lunch, she stayed in her cell with her transistor turned on full blast. Selina's expression didn't encourage questions and I didn't ask any. Mandy was the only other person present, but as she had her life support machine clamped over her ears, she was not much company. I felt rather glad that the Fanes were coming because at least I would have someone to talk to.

Henrietta and Nigella arrived at three, looking fearsome. Nigella wore a calf-length cotton skirt whose hem dipped everywhere and a yellowing shawl with a long fringe which might have been cashmere and once very fine, but now was just dubious. Henrietta wore Nigella's mohair jersey, her own purple mini-skirt which showed a lot of thigh clad in mustard yellow tights, and her terrible leg warmers. Their wild and beautiful hair looked as though it hadn't been combed for a week, although Nigella had made some attempt to tidy hers by securing it at the back of her neck with a bucked D-piece from the bit rings of a pelham bridle.

We paid a courtesy call on Legend, and then walked through the park, admiring the daffodils, with the sun warming our backs. The Fanes seemed subdued and I guessed that something was troubling them. I knew that they would only tell me about it in their own time and so we talked about the course and the other students, and how Legend was performing, and what I thought our chances were of getting into the team for the junior trial.

"And what about you," I said eventually, "how's the new girl?"

There was a pause, during which we stopped walking and Henrietta removed one of her scuffed, pink stiletto-heeled shoes in order to examine the heel, which had worn down far below its tip.

"The thing is," Nigella said in an uncomfortable voice, "that we're in rather deep trouble at the moment."

"It's true, Elaine, honestly," Henrietta added as if, for some reason, I might disbelieve it. She replaced her shoe, and as in all moments of stress, fell to picking at the cuff of the mohair jersey.

"What sort of trouble?" I asked.

"Oh," Nigella said, a note of inevitability in her voice, "it's *financial*."

113

"Yes," I agreed, "I suppose it would be." After all, every one of their problems stemmed from lack of finance, one way or another.

"The rats have eaten the electricity cables," Henrietta said.

"What did you say?" I looked at her in astonishment. Whatever I had expected, it certainly wasn't this.

"They've eaten the electricity cables, gnawed off the plastic coating. Rats do, apparently," Nigella said.

"So we've no electricity," Henrietta said, her pride forcing her to add, "but we've got candles, and the Aga, naturally."

"Oh," I said, "naturally." I imagined them sitting at the kitchen table in the candlelight, walking up the cold, dusty staircase by the light of a single, flickering, flame.

"We've had the electricity people in, and we've got to have the whole place rewired," Nigella said, "it's going to cost two thousand pounds."

"Goodness," I said, it sounded an enormous amount. "Have you got it?"

"No," Nigella said.

"What about the bank," I suggested, "Won't they help?"

"Mummy went to see them, of course," Henrietta said, "but they consider they've helped us enough. We already owe them quite a lot, they're threatening to foreclose."

I wondered how much they owed the bank, hundreds? thousands? As if by mutual consent, we all sat down on the grass.

"They want us to sell," Nigella said, "in fact, it's rather worse – they're going to force us to sell."

114

This was terrible news. "But what about your business?" I asked them. "What about your new girl? Your improved prospects?"

"We haven't got a new girl anymore." Nigella kept her eyes on her shoes, the red tap-dancing shoes with the scraped sides that she regarded as her best. "She's left."

"*Left*?"

"She turned out not to be suitable after all," Nigella said. "There were . . . difficulties."

"Difficulties?"

"She wanted more than we could afford to pay," Henrietta burst out, "and she complained all the time, about the room, about the food, about there not being any hot water, and then . . ." she tailed off.

"And then?"

"And then the lights went out," Nigella said.

I could have laughed, it sounded so ridiculous, and so very typical of the Fanes, but I could see that it was also tragic. "If you sell," I asked them, "what will happen to your business?"

"The business will have to close," Nigella said, "after all, it's the land which will bring in the money to repay the bank – the house isn't worth anything, its practically a ruin."

It was the first time I had heard her admit it. "But the horses," I said, "what about the horses?"

"We'll sell them wherever possible," she said "and those we can't sell we'll have put down. That way, at least the kennels will benefit." She looked up at me, knowing that I would take this badly. "There isn't really any future for some of them," she said, "and at least they won't be shipped on the hoof or anything awful like that. They're put down kindly in their own familiar fields. They don't know, after all, what's going on."

I had known the answer even before I had asked, but now I thought of Nelson with his stitched up eye socket and his threadbare coat, of the bad-tempered chestnut whom nobody loved, of the black horse who never stood still, and of the beautiful bay mare who was never sound for more than a few months at a time. My heart gave a frightening lurch as I realized how it would end for them, and I knew that I should never be able to bear it. "We can't let it happen," I said, "there must be some way, there must be *something* we can do."

"Well, yes," Nigella said, "there is *something*" She began to twist the end of her ghastly shawl and she looked embarrassed. "The thing is, Elaine," she began, "we know how awkward it would be for you to come back now, and by now, I mean after the trial, especially with your new job prospects and everything . . ."

"And we couldn't pay you fifty pounds a week," Henrietta put in almost sharply, "so there would be no point in promising it."

"But if you would consider coming back to us," Nigella said, "we think things might possibly be all right."

I looked at them in despair. I was incredibly touched by their naïve belief that my expertise would have such a beneficial effect on their business that they would be able to surmount even these new and totally impossible difficulties. But for the life of me I couldn't see how I could earn two thousand pounds immediately. I could continue with the grass liveries and the riding lessons, we could break and school horses, and perhaps we could still make our own hay for the winter, but none of this would bring in money quickly, or in sufficient quantity, to satisfy the bank.

"Nigella," I said, "how will my coming back make any difference?"

Nigella seemed reluctant to answer this, and so it was Henrietta who replied.

"If you come back," she said, instantly more cheerful, "we can sell Legend. You can buy another cheap, unschooled youngster to replace him, we can pay our bills, and then we can start all over again."

Even knowing Henrietta as well as I did, I couldn't believe she had said it. "Sell *Legend*?" I said, appalled.

"Well, why not?" she wanted to know. "He'll be worth a bomb after all this intensive training, especially if he gets picked for the Junior Olympics. We'll get twenty thousand for him at least, it's a *fortune*." It seemed to her to be the perfect solution and she looked at me expectantly. "What do you think?"

I lay flat out on the grass, feeling absolutley stunned. The Fanes had offered me the chance to go back; they actually *wanted* me to go back, but they made sure I could never accept by expecting me to sacrifice Legend. Yet, if I didn't go back, the hire-lings would be sold – or slaughtered. Whichever way I looked at it, the situation was equally horrendous.

"I think I've been hit by a sledgehammer," I said.

11

Hard Going

Halt at X, rein back four steps, proceed at working trot, (sitting) . . . I squeezed Legend into a trot, and fixed my eyes beyond the end marker in order to keep him absolutely straight.

"Stop!" the chief shouted. "Stop and begin again, Miss Elliot, and this time I want to see a more fluent rein back, counting, if you must, one-two-three-four, not one-two-three-and-a-half!"

I took Legend back to X, halted, counted four whole strides back, squeezed him again into a trot, and this time I got as far as E.

"Stop!" commanded the chief. "Circle at E, Miss Elliot, means circle at E, not just before E, and not just after E. Accuracy, obediance and control are the essence of dressage; do it again please!"

We did it again, and again, before the chief professed himself satisfied. We repeated our halts, our leg-yielding, our transitions, and our turns-on-the-forehand so many times that my head began to spin and I felt panic rising in my chest. Legend, sensing it, stiffened into resistance, and the chief, raising his eyes to the heavens in a supplicatory gesture, finally waved us out and called in the next student.

Three weeks into the course, the work somehow seemed harder instead of easier. I was sure that I was putting maximum effort into my work and still it didn't seem to be enough to please the chief, who constantly stopped and corrected me, making me ask Legend to repeat movements and jump fences time after time, even when I felt sure our performance had equalled that of the other students.

I rode away from the arena, took Legend into the shade and dismounted, running up the irons and loosening his girth. With the team due to be announced at the end of the week, I felt sure we hadn't a chance of being chosen, and if we weren't, I knew that the fault would be mine and not Legend's. I've been too long without formal instruction, I thought, and in the time I have been with the Fanes my riding must have deteriorated badly without my realizing it.

I watched Phillip perform a fluent rein back into sitting trot under the now approving eye of the chief, and turned away, not wanting to see. Legend nudged my pockets hopefully and I found him a peppermint. He found it difficult to eat, rolling it round in his mouth and getting it mixed up with the bits of double bridle, an expression of deep concentration on his face. If I sold you, I thought, if I found a good home for you, a family home, a comfortable well-off home, with someone to love you as much as I do, somebody who is a better rider than I am, would you really mind? Would you even notice?

I leaned my head on his silken neck, sick to my heart.

The next morning had been set aside for show-jumping practice. The fences in the paddock were not high, in fact hardly any of them exceeded three feet six inches, and they were also set at a good distance apart. Although there were spreads, uprights, combination fences, and the course included a water jump and a change of direction, it was still a far cry from the high, angled close-set fences of the professional show-jumping arena.

The chief had continually stressed the importance of the show-jumping phase, and warned us again and again against being over confident or ill-prepared, because easy as it may look, a fence down in the show-jumping could lose us a close-fought competition. At the junior trial, the show-jumping would be phase two, following on after the dressage tests and coming before the cross-country. This set us rather a different problem from the three-day event proper, where it came at the end of everything, after the dressage, the roads and tracks, the steeplechase, and the cross-country, when the show-jumping phase was designed, not as further punishment for a horse and rider already tested to the limit of their endurance, but as an exercise to prove that they were still fit and supple enough to jump an accurate, intelligent round. Then, it was full of pitfalls for the tired or complacent horse and rider, but at the junior trial our horses would be fit, fresh, and bursting for action. We had to gauge their pre-ring preparation exactly right. They needed to be sober and obedient enough to go in and jump a clear round, but not having had their sparkle blunted for the cross-country.

Due to the dry, sunny weather, the ground was already baked and hard, and all of our horses wore support bandages, tendon boots and over-reach boots as we rode into the jumping paddock, where the fences sparkled, white, green, red and blue in the sunshine. The chief, still wearing his long boots and his jacket, although as a concession to the unseasonably hot weather he had exchanged his tweed cap for a straw trilby, positioned himself inside the marked off arena with his stopwatch and a starting bell.

Annemarie went first. She achieved what was so very nearly a clear round due to a brilliant display of precision riding marred only by the bay tipping a pole off the triple spread.

"If she'd let him crack on a bit at that and really stretch out his neck, he might have managed it," Viv grumbled. "Still, I'm glad he didn't." She had never offered me any information on what had happened when her father had arrived, and I had never asked, knowing that if she had wanted to discuss it, she would have done so.

We watched Alice and the The Talisman go round the course, rattling every fence but, by a miracle, not knocking down a single pole. Although it looked awful, and sounded worse, this was quite a feat on Alice's part, as The Talisman had little or no respect for coloured poles, knowing perfectly well he could plough through them without the slightest injury to himself if he chose. Theirs was not a copybook round, but it was exciting and, as The Talisman cantered out of the arena with his hooves scarred with paint, we heaved sighs of relief.

Mandy and Fox Me went next, sailing round in their usual magical manner; their perfect understanding and the pretty bay horse's undoubted courage and exceptional ability stood them in good stead both across country and in the show-jumping arena.

Phillip and the roan horse also achieved a clear round and so did Selina and Flame Thrower, the latter combination jumping each fence in a neat, methodical manner, as if they had been doing it for years. Viv and Balthazar looked fit to make it four in a row until the powerful chestnut ran out at the last part of the triple combination, earning Viv a verbal lashing from the chief. She took Balthazar at it again, sullen faced, and this time they jumped it perfectly.

It was my turn. I had walked the course previously and worked out speed, stride and distance for every combination, noted the approach, groundline, height and spread of every fence. I was determined that we should jump clear and we did. Legend soared over the fences, clearing them with inches to spare, making nothing of them at all. Even the chief found nothing to complain about.

"Very good, Miss Elliot," he said as we cantered through the finish.

As we trotted across to the others, I leaned over and slapped Legend's neck, feeling a surge of relief and renewed confidence. Perhaps this was the turning point, perhaps there would be a place for us in the team after all. Surely, I told myself, I would be a fool to consider giving up Legend now, surely nothing, not even the Fanes, would be worthy of such a sacrifice?

Getting a grip on my emotions and my common sense for the first time since the Fanes had spilled out their devastating news, I suddenly found I could think positively again. I felt sure there was no need to have the hirelings shot. Why not offer them free to approved homes, so that they could live out their remaining years peacefully in semi-retirement? I knew that *Horse & Hound* was always full of advertisements from people of limited means who had the facilities but not the ready cash. *Companion wanted for youngstock* – That would do for the black horse; *Bombproof elderly hack, about 15hh wanted by gentlewoman with back complaint* – that would suit Nelson perfectly; nothing I had seen sprang readily to mind as suitable for the bad-tempered chestnut, but I was sure we would be able to place them all eventually. We might even advertise them ourselves, with a brief description of each. Why, I would even draft and pay for the advertisement myself. I didn't see how it could fail.

Fired by such thoughts, I turned my attention to the problem of the Fanes themselves. Wouldn't they be better suited in a smaller place anyway, somewhere more economic and easier to run than Havers Hall? In my imagination I saw them installed in a comfortable three-bedroom cottage with full central heating and a fashionably coloured suite in the bathroom. It all seemed so terribly simple and obvious that I was amazed it hadn't occurred to me before.

"Letter for you, Elaine."

Phillip dropped the familiar, crested envelope on to my plate. He looked exhausted and, looking round the table, I saw that everyone did. Viv looked pale and no longer bothered to apply her makeup. Alice, despite liberal applications of green acne ointment, had broken out in a fresh rash of spots across her chin and forehead. Mandy had dark shadows of fatigue under her eyes and a cold sore on her lip. Annemarie was tense and bad-tempered, and even in repose her square face was set like a piece of granite. Only Selina appeared unaffected by the general tension now that selection was just three days away; sailing graciously through it all, confident probably, that her rightful place in the team was totally secure.

The letter was from Lady Jennifer, written in a spidery hand below the Fane crest.

My Dear Elaine,

The girls have told me about their plans to resolve our little difficulty, and I am writing to say that I would not dream of asking you to part with Legend, in fact I positively forbid you even to consider it. It was frightfully thoughtless and unfair of them even to suggest such a thing – you must forget it entirely and concentrate your energies on getting into the team for the junior trial – we will all be there to support you!

You must promise me you will not waste even a second worrying about what I am sure is only a temporary setback; the bank have been terribly understanding in allowing us a fortnight's grace before any decision is made and one is always so incredibly optimistic that everything will turn out all right.

Good Luck!
   and lots of love
      Jennifer Fane

My heart warmed towards Lady Jennifer as I read the letter. It was so typical of her to make little of their problems in order that I should be able to concentrate on the course. Well, I wouldn't let her down. If it was within my capabilities to get into the team, I would do it. I would also take her advice and postpone any further action on the implementation of my plans for the rescue of the hirelings and for the future comfort of the Fanes themselves until after the junior trial.

A fortnight would give me all the time I needed.

* * *

Due to the hard going there was to be no cross-country practice that afternoon, but a lesson in the indoor school instead. We were all husbanding our horses' legs carefully, knowing that a sprain, or concussion on the iron ground could put us out of the team.

I took Legend into one of the tan surfaced lunging rings to give him some gentle work on both reins in lieu of the morning's work he was going to miss, and he trotted round, flexing his neck and reaching for the bit, swishing his silky black tail. Despite the injuries he had suffered in a horrendous road accident the previous year, I was pleased and relieved to see that he was as sound and level as ever.

After the lunging, I replaced Legend's bridle, roller, and side-reins with a headcollar and took him out to graze from the end of a rope. He had been used to long periods of freedom in the park at Havers Hall, and even in the winter I had turned him out in a New Zealand rug for a few hours two or three times a week to encourage him to relax and keep his temper sweet.

I had noticed some particularly long, succulent grass growing in the shade of a copse at the end of the show-jumping paddock, and I took him there. Legend tore great mouthfuls out by the roots, and I watched him idly, glad of a little relaxation myself, listening to the satisfying sound of his champing jaws. I started to think about the Fanes, remembered Lady Jennifer's instructions, and thought about Nick instead.

I didn't expect to see him again before the junior trial because they were in the middle of whelping at the kennels and he was taking a draft of experienced, older hounds, to a hunt in the north on Monday, and was expecting to be away for a few days. He had made me promise to ring him though, on Saturday, as soon as the names of the team had been announced. Good or bad, he had insisted, and good or bad I had promised.

Thinking about all this, I gradually became aware of approaching voices, angry voices, on the other side of the copse, and as they got nearer, I recognized them as belonging to Annemarie and Viv who had met up while hacking in the park.

"Your horse stopped at the combination," Annemarie was saying in a scornful voice, "at least my horse doesn't *refuse*. You don't get anywhere in eventing if your horse is a coward."

"Balthazar didn't stop," Viv said in a furious voice, "he ran out. He ran out because *I* let him run out, it was *my* fault. Your horse knocked the last rail off the triple because he couldn't make the spread, he may never *refuse*, but he still can't do it, he hasn't got the scope. Balthazar *can* do it, he's physically capable of it. Your horse isn't and that's what counts in eventing!"

In the silence which followed I held my breath.

"What did you say?" Annemarie asked in a hard little voice.

"I said," Viv repeated with a weary sigh, obviously already wishing she hadn't, "that your horse can't cope with spreads. He tries, he's bold enough, and brave enough, but he just hasn't got the reach. For heaven's sake, Annemarie, you ride him, you ought to *know*."

"No," Annemarie shouted, "I don't know! You're wrong! He can do it, he *can*, and I'll prove it! I'll show you!"

There was all of a sudden a scattering of gravel

from the drive which bordered the paddock, and Annemarie and her little bay hurtled through the gap and charged towards the marked out arena with its painted fences. Annemarie's hat, which she must have removed because of the heat, bounced away across the grass like a rugby ball.

"Come back, you fool!" Viv yelled in an agonized voice. "You know you're not allowed to jump without supervision, you haven't got your hat on either!"

But Annemarie was not listening. I watched, horrified, as she steered her horse towards the triple, minus support bandages, minus even a preliminary balancing canter, and pushed him hard at it with her legs. Any other horse would have refused, point blank, to tackle it, but the little bay part-bred Hanoverian, trained to a high standard of discipline by the Reitschule, summoned his lion-like courage, steadied, lengthened, gathered himself, took off, and powered by his own determination and Annemarie's willpower, flew upwards and cleared the poles. Then he landed with a sickeningly jarring impact on his front legs, buckled to his knees, and sent Annemarie hurtling over his ears, to land headfirst on the baked, iron-hard ground.

The little bay horse managed to struggle to his feet, but Annemarie didn't. She just lay where she had landed as Viv on Balthazar, and I, dropping Legend's headcollar rope, tore across the parched grass towards her.

12

Questions and Answers

I stayed, staring helplessly down at Annemarie, whilst Viv galloped to the yards to bring assistance. I tried desperately to remember the first aid I had learned for my Horsemaster's Certificate but all I could think of was that I should loosen any tight clothing, especially at the neck. I couldn't get to Annemarie's neck because she was lying face downwards and I dared not try to move her. I was sure she must be dead and I felt sick at the thought; sick and dizzy and very, very frightened.

The chief's Range Rover had arrived and he was pulling a stretcher out of the back, when sudenly, terrifyingly Annemarie rose from the ground into a sitting position and stared at me. "What happened?" she demanded.

"Lie down at once, Miss Maddox," the chief barked, "you must remain perfectly still."

Annemarie lay down again obediently with her boots together and her hands pressed to her sides like a toy soldier. "Where's my horse," she hissed to me, "is he all right?"

I didn't want to answer this, because I knew perfectly well that he wasn't all right. "He's with Legend," I said, "he hasn't gone far. I'll catch him in a minute."

Annemarie nodded, satisfied. The chief, helped by an ashen-faced Viv, rolled her gently on to the stretcher. While they were doing so, I ran to pick up

Annemarie's hat and laid it on her chest, like a crusader's shield, hoping that the chief would just think it had fallen off before she hit the ground. She would be in trouble, I knew, for jumping without supervision, and there would be punishment enough when she saw what had happened to her little bay horse, because I realized, as I walked towards the two horses in the shade of the copse, that something heartbreakingly awful had happened to him when he had landed.

Legend was still pulling grass greedily, but the little bay was just standing with his head lowered, patches of sweat forming on his neck, his nose pinched with pain, and his two front legs already beginning to fill. I had been afraid that he might have broken something, but as I picked up the end of the broken rein and took Legend by his halter rope, the brave little horse moved forward slowly and reluctantly. Together we made painful progress into the yard and I was able to shout to one of the working pupils to go and ask reception to call out the vet as an emergency.

While Annemarie was transported to hospital to have her head X-rayed for possible skull fracture, the vet was in the stable with her horse; feeling, probing, injecting with anti-inflammatory and pain-killing drugs, and giving instructions for the use of diuretics, cold pressure bandages on the injured legs and support bandages on the hind legs. Extra thick bedding was laid, an extra blanket was provided, and at the end of it the little bay stood with bulky dressings strapped to his front legs, trying to rest one after the other, too uncomfortable to attempt to lie down, his mash untouched, his hay net ignored. There was nothing broken, the vet said, nothing that

129

time wouldn't heal, and in six months, eight perhaps, or ten, he would be almost as good as new. Of course, tendons which had been so badly sprained might never be quite as strong again, but with careful treatment there was no reason why he shouldn't make a full recovery, provided that one faced the fact that he was unlikely to event again.

Viv had gone to the hospital with Annemarie and I stayed in the yard at lunchtime, unable to face the inquests and speculation I knew would be taking place inside the Duke of Newcastle. I strapped away gloomily at Legend as he pulled at his haynet and for the first time since I had first set my heart on an eventing career, I considered the moral aspect of testing a horse to the limits of its ability, when the consequences could be something like this – or even worse.

I knew that Annemarie had done a stupid thing out of anger, hurt pride and deep, burning ambition, and I was sure that in the same situation, I wouldn't have reacted in the same way, and yet, goaded almost beyond endurance, could I be *that* sure? I realized that we were still only on the bottom rung of the eventing ladder, and that further up, the wastage in horses was high; they broke their bones, their tendons were irreparably ruptured, their hearts gave out. It was all very well for a human athlete to test his own abilities almost to breaking point, but was it fair to form a partnership where one half of the combination had no voice and had no way of saying, "stop now, I've had enough."

Troubled by these and similar thoughts, I went to look again at the little bay horse with his hugely swollen, hot, painful legs, and his heart-wrenchingly miserable expression, and I felt a hopeless anger because there was nothing I could do. There was not a glimmer of hope, not a crumb of comfort that I could offer. And I knew that the pathetic creature I was looking at could have been any horse, it could have been my horse, and unless I was very, very fortunate, one day it would be.

After the initial shock of Annemarie's accident had worn off, the other scholarship students soon recovered their spirits, but I didn't, and Viv was still upset by what had happened as we set off round the perimeter of the cross-country course on our early morning run the following day.

"What will happen to Annemarie?" I wondered. "Will they send her home?" By a miracle, the X-rays had shown no injury to her skull at all, although the hospital had insisted on keeping her for a few days under observation. She was, as Viv said ruefully, and not without a touch of reluctant admiration, a tough nut in more ways than one.

"How can they send her home?" Viv said. "She'd have to go back to Germany, and what would happen to her horse then? He's not fit to travel anywhere. No, the chief will have to keep her here. He'll probably end up giving her a job on one of the yards."

"She won't think much of that," I said, "not after the Reitschule."

Viv allowed herself a little grin as we pounded around the lake and began to run up the rise. "I doubt if we'll hear very much about the Reitschule in future."

"But we'll never hear the last about her losing her place in the team," I panted. Annemarie had not yet been told how severely her horse was injured, and we all knew what a devastating shock it would be for her. None of us was looking forward to the day she came back from hospital.

"I wouldn't lose any sleep over it," Viv told me, "she might still get to ride in the team after all."

I looked at her in astonishment as we laboured up to the top of the rise. "How?" I gasped.

Viv made no reply to this. She just patted the side of her nose in an admonitory gesture and, gaining her second wind, sprinted off down the hill.

The following morning I received the first replies to my advertisement. I took them into the bathroom and locked the door in order to gain some privacy because Selina was in the bedroom, doing some surprisingly early typing.

Two of the letters I tore up at once and flushed down the lavatory; the first being from a small suburban riding school who offered keep for my own horse – *we presume he lives out,* they said, and caravan accommodation, plus a wage of eight pounds and fifty pence for a six-day week. The hours were 8 A.M. until 8 P.M. with an hour for lunch and two ten-minute coffee breaks.

The second was from an active, retired gentleman who required an attractive and lively female companion for horse-related activities – photograph essential. I dismissed this as being highly suspect.

The third letter I just couldn't believe. It was the perfect solution to all my problems. It offered a wage of fifty pounds a week, plus accommodation for my own horse, use of a cross-country course, indoor school and BSJA regulation jumps for training purposes, a horsebox was available if required, time off for competitions was negotiable, hostel accommodation would be provided for myself (with other staff), and I could start whenever suitably convenient. I didn't even have to attend for an interview.

I sat on the side of the bath feeling rather shaken. I had been worried that nothing would come of the advertisement, that at the end of the course, there would be no prospect in view. If this had happened, I would have had to turn Legend out for the summer, paying rent for grazing, whilst I found other work, as a shop-assistant perhaps, or a waitress; that, or sell Legend and go back to the Fanes, either of which would have made me exceedingly miserable.

But the more I looked at the letter, beautifully typewritten on headed notepaper with the logos of the BHS and the ABRS on either side, the more worried I became. In the end I had almost convinced myself that it wasn't genuine; that someone had played an unkind practical joke; that it was altogether too perfect a solution to be true.

There was only one thing to be done. I had to go and find out.

I unlocked the bathroom door, ran out of the back door of the Duke Of Newcastle, past the steaming muckheaps, across the yards, dodging horses, pupils, and staff, and arrived, panting, at the office. I opened the door.

The chief regarded me with irritation from behind his desk. "There is a notice outside requesting people to knock before entering," he snapped, "this is a private office, Miss Elliot, not a public right of way."

"And I want to be sure that this is a genuine letter," I said, "not just someone's idea of a joke." I placed the reply to my advertisement on top of his memorandum pad.

He looked at it. "Ah," he said. "That."

"So you do know about it," I asked him, "you have seen it before?"

"Of course I've seen it before," the chief looked at me as if I might easily be out of my mind. "I wrote it." He pointed to the signature. "I even signed it, but if you still doubt it, I can show you the copy."

"I don't want to see the copy," I said hastily, "I just want to know if you are serious. Do you really mean it?"

"Of course I mean it," he barked, "why else would I have written it?"

I sat down abruptly on the little wooden chair. "But how did you know it was me?" I asked him, "when I advertised under a box number?"

"Miss Elliot," the chief said patiently, "there is a system in existence which has evolved in order to prevent embarrassment to both parties when an advertisement carries a box number. Normally you place your reply in an outer envelope listing the people to whom your reply should not be forwarded. In your case I listed the only person to whom my reply *should* be forwarded."

I stared at him, impressed. "But how did you know I was going to advertise anyway?"

He sighed. "Haven't you realized yet, how quickly word travels? Your friend Nicholas Forster is a good friend of Mr Felix Hissey, who is sponsoring your scholarship course, and is in constant touch with me to keep abreast of your progress."

"*My* progress?"

"Not just *your* progress, Miss Elliot," the chief said impatiently, "everyone's progress."

"Well, yes," I said, "of course, but I still don't really understand why you should want me to work here, unless you're offering me a job out of the kindness of your heart, out of charity, because you know I'm in a difficult position."

"I don't offer people jobs out of the kindness of my heart," the chief snapped, "only if I consider I can put their talents to good use."

"But what talents have I got?" I wondered. "I'm not trained to teach, and I know you don't think much of my riding ability."

The chief threw up his chin in an enquiring manner. "What makes you think that, Miss Elliot?"

"Because you're always picking on me during instruction," I said, "making me repeat things, because I never seem to be able to please you."

The chief rested his chin in his hands and regarded me thoughtfully. "Has it never occurred to you that I might be spending more time on you because you are the most promising student on the course?" he said.

I couldn't believe it. "No," I said, "no, *never*."

"Good," he said in a satisfied voice. He handed me the reply to my advertisement. "You may be needing this. You may be requiring to reply to it."

"Yes," I said with conviction, "I shall certainly need to reply."

"If your reply is in the affirmative, Miss Elliot," said the chief, eyeing me sternly, "you will be required to train for Assistant Instructor's Certificate and progress upwards until you hold a full BHSI qualification. You could then specialize in preparing students for three-day eventing, if you so desired."

"I suppose I could," I said, "if I so desired."

135

"And do you so desire?" the chief wanted to know.

"I don't know," I said, "I've never even considered it."

"Then go away, Miss Elliot," he commanded. "Consider it."

I got up from the chair. There was one last question I wanted to ask. "Why did you go to the trouble of aswering my advertisement, when you could have just called me into the office and offered me the job face to face?"

The chief looked up at me and he very nearly smiled. "I like to have everything in writing, Miss Elliot," he said, "efficient, orderly documentation is the key to the smooth running of every establishment."

I was suddenly overwhelmed with gratitude and affection for this brusque, far-seeing, kind-hearted man. "Oh!" I exclaimed, "I'm so *terribly* grateful."

He picked up a few papers, as if they had suddenly demanded his instant attention.

"Be sure to close the door on your way out, Miss Elliot," he said.

13

Selection Day

We filed into the lecture hall on selection day, feeling tense. Annemarie was not with us. The chief had broken the news to her as gently as he was able and, as we had known she would, she had taken it very badly. She had stayed on her bed with her face to the wall, refusing to eat or to speak for a day and a night, after which she had got up and taken over the nursing of her little bay horse with justifiably contrite devotion. Everyone agreed that Annemarie had needed a lesson, but in paying the price of blind ambition, it had been tragic that her horse had suffered most.

The chief was already installed behind the lecture stand when we arrived, straightening his papers impatiently. "Hat off, Mr Hastings," he snapped, as Phillip took his seat wearing the sailcloth cap he habitually wore in front of the chief; "this is a team selection announcement, not *La Tour de France*."

Phillip removed his cap somewhat reluctantly to reveal his platinum forelock, now showing quarter of an inch of dark regrowth. The chief threw up his chin in a startled manner, leaned forward to ascertain that it wasn't a trick, or a wig, and decided to ignore it. He rustled his papers officiously. "Hrmmmm," he said.

I took my seat feeling reasonably confident. After my interview with the chief, I fully expected to be included in the team, together with Phillip and

137

Selina, whom I considered to be the other two certainties. As to who would make up the rest of the team, I honestly didn't know.

Mandy and Fox Me were incredibly consistent if one looked at them entirely from the performance point of view; but everything depended on whether the chief would go for results alone, because Mandy was by no means a top class event rider in the making. She would be hopeless if she was separated from the pretty bay horse.

Balthazar was a splendid horse; big, brave, scopey and capable of producing a good dressage test. And whilst Viv had been well taught and was a good rider, it was true to say that every mistake Balthazar made could be directly attributed to her inattention. Viv had everything going for her, she had the ideal horse, the ability, the opportunity, but somehow her heart wasn't in it. She didn't have the temperament or the dedication for a tough competitive sport like eventing. She resented the discipline, rules irked her, routine bored her, attention to detail made her impatient. Nevertheless, in spite of all this, Viv and Balthazar could not be discounted.

As for Alice, she was certainly dedicated, but in her own inimitable way. She was tough, and she was determined, and she had a horse of a like mind in The Talisman. One got the impression that, even if the chief decided not to choose them for the team, they would make their own way up the eventing ladder in the end. Perhaps this was a sign that he would chose them. I didn't know.

I looked along the row at their faces. Mandy looked absolutely petrified; Alice wore her see-if-I-care anyway expression and rather a lot of green acne ointment, and Viv's face was totally blank. Two of them will be disappointed I thought, but as it happened, I was wrong.

"In a few seconds' time, I shall read out the names of the team members for the junior trial," the chief barked. "There will be five names, comprising four team members and a reserve. The identity of the reserve will not be decided until just before the trial. The reason for this is that the choice of the final team may not be wholly dependent upon ability. Many things will have to be considered; emotional stability, fitness, accident." He looked at us severely over the lecture stand as if he suspected we might not agree that this was fair.

He picked up the top sheet of paper. "The team for the junior trial is as follows," he announced. "Elaine Elliot, Phillip Hastings, Alice Merryman, Vivienne Tintoft, Amanda Willis."

Everyone whose name had been included let out a long sigh of relief, and then, as it occurred to us whose name had been omitted, our necks swivelled towards the person sitting on the end of the row, and we all stared at Selina. Selina smiled back at us in a serene manner.

The chief marched out from behind his lecture stand. He handed a pile of memoranda to Selina. "Be kind enough to hand these out, Miss er. . ." he said, "and perhaps you should take this opportunity to explain yourself to your fellow students." He favoured us with a curt nod and strode off as if he had a train to catch. The door banged shut behind him.

Selina stood up and began to hand out the memoranda giving each of us the benefit of her bright, schoolmistressy smile.

"For a start," she informed us, "I'm not Selina

Gibbons at all. Selina was unfortunate enough to break a leg whilst out hunting with the Cottesmore and was unable to take her place. I was allowed to come instead, and my name is Jane Lejeune." She paused expectantly, awaiting some reaction to this piece of information, but we were all too taken aback to do or say anything.

Viv recovered first. "Wait a minute," she said, "you're not *that* Jane Lejeune, the one who does all sorts of different things and then writes about it in *The Sunday Times*? You're not the one who took a job as trainee sales-assistant at my old man's biggest store and wrote about all the fiddles!"

Selina inclined her head in a modest little gesture of acknowledgement. "I'm afraid so," she said.

Viv collapsed back in her seat. "Blimey," she exclaimed in an awed tone, "it's a wonder the old man didn't have the hide off you." She looked at Selina with a new respect.

I suppose I should have guessed, after all, I had been there when Selina had been unmasked by Mr Tintoft. I had heard it all, but then the name Jane Lejeune had meant nothing to me because I had never read *The Sunday Times*, the only newspaper the Fanes ever took was *Horse & Hound*.

"Do you mean you're not really a student?" I said, mystified. "Do you mean you don't want to event at all?"

"Certainly not," Selina said firmly, "I already have a very promising career in journalism."

Now that she had admitted it, I wondered why I hadn't suspected something like this before. There had been clues enough – the typewriter, the endless correspondence, the curiosity, the professional camera under her bed, the lengthy telephone calls.

"You're not going to write about us though, surely?" Phillip said in an incredulous voice. "Who would be interested if you did? Wouldn't it have been better to have infiltrated the eventing world at the top?"

"Not at all, Phillip," Selina said, with a gracious smile. "I could hardly have held my own at the top, and the famous faces are already very well documented. But who knows about the people struggling to get a foothold on the bottom rung of the ladder? Who knows the discomfort, the sweat, the heartache, the *agony* suffered by the hidden people of eventing?" She beamed at him winningly. "I think people are going to be *most* interested."

I coud see her point, but Mandy's mouth sagged. "You don't mean we're going to be in the papers – not the *Sundays*," she said aghast, "I don't know what my dad will say when he knows."

"Only with your permission, of course," Selina said hastily, "and naturally, if you would prefer, I can change your names and you would remain quite anonymous."

"And it is *The Sunday Times*," Phillip pointed out, "it isn't as if it's the *News of the World*." He seemed rather delighted with the idea.

"Well, I suppose if it isn't in the *News of the World*," Mandy said doubtfully, "it might be all right, because my dad might not even see it."

Alice, who had sat silently throughout all these revelations, and now had her grounds for disliking Selina removed in one fell swoop, came to life. "You certainly fooled me," she said grudgingly, "you could pass for a potential eventer any day."

This was praise indeed from someone like Alice, and Selina preened. "I did have a marvellous horse

141

though," she admitted, "and hours of expert coaching before I came; but I was rather good, wasn't I?"

"But now you're not in the team," Alice went on, "what about the horse? Because if he's going spare, you could lend him to Annemarie, then at least she'd have something to ride for the rest of the course."

It seemed a splendid idea. "But I'm afraid it can't be done," Selina said with regret, "the horse I rode isn't Flame Thrower at all, he's an intermediate event horse and he belongs to Hans Gelderhol. He's being collected tomorrow to go back into training for Burghley."

"So it *was* the horse I remembered," I exclaimed, "and I had assumed he might just be related!" Altogether, I seemed to have been rather dim-witted about the whole affair.

"I must admit to feeling a qualm when I discovered that you had trained with Hans Gelderhol," Selina admitted, "especially when you mentioned the similarity to the horse he had been eventing at the time."

"No wonder you were so good," Alice said, with a smart return to her previous acerbic form, "riding an intermediate event horse."

Selina chose to ignore this remark. "Well, now that there is absolutely no need for secrecy," she said in a satisfied tone, "I shall spend the rest of the weekend taking photographs." She beamed round at us, tore the chief's latest memorandum into tiny pieces, tossed them into the air in a gesture of smug finality, and left the lecture hall before the pieces had even reached the ground.

We, who were left, looked at one another, dumbfounded.

"Wouldn't you just believe it," Alice trumpeted, "*The Sunday Times!*"

Later that day I rang Nick at the kennels to give him the good news. "That's fantastic," he said, "not that I had any doubts anyway, I knew you'd do it."

"Would you do something for me?" I asked him. "Would you call in and see the Fanes before you take the hound draft and tell them for me?" I wanted them to know, but I wasn't at all anxious to speak to Henrietta and Nigella again, not until after the trial. I had enough to occupy my mind as it was.

"I was going to tell you about the Fanes," he said, "I don't know if you've heard from them recently, but I dropped by the other day and it seems that wonder woman's left."

"I know," I said, "they came to tell me."

"So you probably already know," he said, 'that they're selling up."

I didn't believe it. "They can't be," I said, "I knew they had problems, but the bank has given them a fortnight to put things right – I know it's true because Lady Jennifer told me herself." But even as I said it my elation started to ebb away and a familiar sinking feeling began in my chest.

"I don't know about that," Nick said, "but there's a *For Sale* notice at the bottom of the drive, and when I arrived the girls were loading pictures into the shooting brake."

I remembered the dusty, darkened oil paintings lining the staircase and the galleried landings. The best had long since been taken away, leaving bare, oblong patches on the walls. I knew the ones that were left were hardly worth selling; they were just rather poor portraits of Fane ancestors painted by unknown artists. Everything of value had already gone from Havers Hall; Henrietta had sold her Vile secretaire in order to pay for Legend, and I myself had carried a valuable Cantonese vase up the escalators to Harrods Fine Art department so that we could pay off the saddler, the corn merchant, the blacksmith . . .

"Nick," I said, "they *can't* have decided already, they *can't* have given up hope, not just like that."

"I think they must have decided," he said, "they've already told us to . . ." he tailed off, not wanting to continue.

There was a silence.

"Oh no," I whispered, "they haven't . . . they couldn't . . . Oh, Nick, not the *horses*."

"No," he admitted, "not yet, they're not – they're a bit . . ."

I knew what he was trying to say; that after a hard season's hunting they were all too thin. A few months out at grass at this time of year would make all the difference, especially now there was no need to shut off half the park for the winter.

"Elaine . . . are you still there?"

"Yes," I said, "I'm still here."

"They told me – Henrietta told me, that they asked you to give up Legend."

"They did, and I almost considered it, but Lady Jennifer wrote to me, she said that I shouldn't." In her letter, I thought, she had made light of their difficulties, she had said it was only a temporary setback, and they had a fortnight's grace and were optimistic that something would turn up. She had probably told me this knowing all the time that nothing would turn up, having already instructed the estate agents to call. Such an action was typical of

144

someone who devoted her life to the welfare of others, without giving a thought to her own perilous circumstances.

"I'm glad you *didn't* consider it," Nick said in a grim voice, "whatever their problems are, you must *never* consider giving up Legend, he's your future."

"But what about *their* future?" I asked him miserably. "The horses haven't any future at all, and I don't think I shall be able to bear it."

"Would you be able to bear it any better if they were sold at auction?" he wanted to know. "Would you have preferred the Fanes to do that? Because I'm surprised they *didn't*. They would have got meat money for them, after all; so that must be something to be thankful for."

I tried to feel thankful. I knew that being humanely destroyed in their own familiar fields was far preferable to being sold on the open market; to being loaded on to one of the hellships which transported meat cattle on the hoof to the continent, then being docked and herded into huge container lorries and driven for days without food or water, to be finally butchered in some foreign abattoir. I knew I would have sold Legend, I would have sold my soul, I would have died before I could let that happen. Yes, I knew it was better, but I couldn't feel thankful, it was too unbearably, heartbreakingly sad for that.

"I thought we might have been able to find homes for them," I said, "I thought there might be some way . . ."

"Look, Elaine," Nick said, "I'm beginning to think I shouldn't have told you."

"If you hadn't," I told him, "I would never have forgiven you."

145

"But as I have told you, you must make me a promise."

I knew what that would be. After all, I had already promised Lady Jennifer the same thing.

"You mustn't think about it, worry about it, until after the junior trial," he said, "the house won't sell, just like that. It'll take months, perhaps years to find a buyer. And the horses are safe for two months at least. Nothing's going to happen yet, *nothing*," he emphasized, "is going to change before the junior trial. Promise me Elaine, that you won't try to do *anything*, that you won't let it spoil your chances next week – *promise*."

"I promise," I said. After all, what else could I say.

"And after the trial," he said, "we'll worry about it then; we'll talk about it, and if there's a way, if there's anything at all we can do, we'll do it."

"All right," I agreed.

"But we won't part with Legend," he assured me, "whatever we may decide, it won't be that."

"Thank you," I said, and miserable though I was, I was grateful and gladdened that he cared enough about the Fanes even to want to discuss their problems, when not so very long ago, he had despised them.

"By the way," Nick said, "did you get any replies to your advertisement?"

"The chief replied," I told him, "he offered me a job. I can stay here and work on the yards as a member of the junior staff."

"And will you stay?" he asked.

"It looks as if there won't be any alternative," I said.

14

No Substitute

I woke because someone was shaking me. I sat up in bed feeling alarmed. I knew it couldn't be Selina because stertorous breathing was coming from the other bed. After an energetic afternoon with her camera, she was dead to the world.

"Elaine!" Viv's voice hissed urgently. "Hell, I thought you'd never wake up!"

"Viv," I whispered anxiously, "what's wrong? Are you ill or something?" In the moonlight filtering through the Duke of Newcastle's ineffective curtains, I could now make out the shape of her, kneeling beside my bed.

"I've come to say goodbye," she said in a low voice. "I've decided to take off. Now. Tonight."

"Take off?" I struggled up into a sitting position, hardly able to take it in because I was still half asleep. "What on earth do you mean? You *can't* be leaving, not *now*. Not in the middle of the *night*!"

"Sssssh," Viv hissed urgently, "don't go and wake *her*," she nodded towards the dark hump in the next bed, "she's all I need!"

"But why are you going?" I still couldn't believe it. "What about Balthazar – are you taking him?" For one minute I could see her, muffling his hoofs with the Duke of Newcastle threadbare towels, in order to lead him silently out of the yards.

"No, I'm leaving him," Viv said, "for Annemarie."

"For *Annemarie*?" I stared at her, stupified.

"Look Elaine," she said, "I would have gone before, I'm not really into all this eventing, you know I'm not. I just sort of slipped into it, and after what happened to Annemarie's horse – well, I know it isn't for me, but I wanted to hang on to be sure I'd got a place in the team, and now I know I have, I can leave. It's as simple as that."

"You'd leave Balthazar for *Annemarie*," I said, appalled, "after what she did to her own horse?"

"That was partly my fault anyway," Viv said, "and Balthazar's more the horse for someone as ambitious as Annemarie than ever that poor little bay was. She'll find a different problem when she rides Balthazar, and it won't be pushing him to the limits of his capabilities, it'll be letting him go as much as he wants to. I've no worries about him, he can look after himself."

I could see that this might be true; "*I* wouldn't do it," I told her, "I wouldn't let anyone else ride Legend."

"But then," Viv said, "not everyone's as selfish as you are."

There wasn't time to feel offended. "Where will you go?" I asked her. "Will you go back to your gran?"

"Well I shan't go back to the old man," she said bitterly. 'He really had plans for me, I can tell you. Six months with this top eventing coach, six months there, a string of event horses – I'd probably even have ended up at the Reitschule. No, I've had enough of eventing, thanks Elaine, you're welcome to it."

Although I knew in my heart that she was right to leave, I didn't want her to go now, not alone, in the middle of the night. It was dangerous. Anything could happen to an unaccompanied young girl. "You're not to go now," I said, grabbing her arm, "wait until the morning, wait until daylight. I'm not going to let you go. I'm going to wake the others."

"Elaine," said Viv in a voice of deadly earnestness, "if you even so much as open your mouth, I'll knock you out cold with the lamp."

"*Viv*!" I was aghast, more so because I knew she meant it.

"There's nothing you can do to stop me," she said, "I've made up my mind, and if I'd realized you were going to be so awkward about it, I wouldn't have bothered waking you."

"Oh, *Viv*," I said sadly, "what will you do now?"

"Well," she said, considering it, "to tell the truth I've always thought I might like to have a go at acting, you know. I might audition for RADA or LAMDA, or somewhere like that; it's hard to get in, but I might just make it, and that's something Mr Fixit really *can't* interfere with."

But he'll try, I thought, he'll really try. She got up and made her way silently to the door.

"Viv," I said, "he only interferes because he loves you."

She paused. "Yes," she said shortly, "maybe."

"And I'm sorry you're leaving," I said, "I'm really sorry."

"So am I," she whispered as she slipped out of the door. "If I'd known I wasn't staying, I wouldn't have cut my nails."

I lay back on my lumpy pillow and I heard the Duke of Newcastle's back door click shut behind her. I lay awake for a long time thinking of the slight girl with the orange hair driving along the dark,

149

empty roads, and the man with the silk tie and the pale green Rolls Royce who, although he knew many things, had never learned that money, ambition, or even love, were no subsitiute for freedom, understanding and respect.

"Step into the office for a moment, Miss Elliot," said the chief as he marched along the walkway in front of the stable where I was strapping Legend.

I replaced Legend's rug and roller and hurried after him, dropping my grooming kit box outside the stable door and kicking over the bottom latch.

The chief took up his position behind his desk and ledged his beautiful boots, out of habit toes up heels down, on the brass footrail. He took off his tweed cap and laid it on top of a pile of memoranda.

"Have you any money?" he asked.

I stared at him in astonishment. "Not very much," I admitted, "about forty pounds."

"Any savings? Any private income?"

"No," I said, "nothing at all."

"What about your father," he demanded, "is he rich?"

"No," I said, "I'm afraid not." I was beginning to feel rather alarmed.

"You do realize," said the chief, "that eventing is a very expensive sport?"

"Oh yes," I assured him, "I do."

"And that most people, if they don't happen to have well-heeled connections, need a sponsor in order to meet their expenses."

"Yes," I said. I couldn't see for the life of me what he was getting at.

"Then how are you, Miss Elliot, on your fifty pounds a week, less stoppages, going to afford it?"

"Well," I said carefully, "my horse won't cost me anything to keep . . ."

"You'll have to keep him shod," the chief pointed out, "you have to provide his equipment, clothing for yourself, registration fees, entry fees, petrol, veterinary fees. Even leg washes and worming powders," he said, "cost money."

I couldn't think of a reply to any of this.

"Have you ever heard of the Horse Trials Support Group?" he asked.

I said I thought I had, but then again, I couldn't be sure.

"It comes under the umbrella of the BHS," he said, "and every so often, when funds allow them to do so, they offer their support to potential top class event riders with promising horses in order that they may continue to event – usually riders with a good deal of winning form and experience behind them."

I wondered what he was going to suggest. I hadn't a good deal of winning form and experience behind me.

"I have already had a preliminary talk with the chairman," said the chief, "and I put forward a suggestion that they might consider giving you some assistance in the form of a modest grant."

"A grant? For me? To help with Legend?" It seemed hardly possible.

"Of course," he said, "it is by no means certain that they will agree . . ."

I still couldn't grasp it. "Do you mean they would give me *money*?"

"Miss Elliot," the chief said in a testy voice, "a grant usually consists of money, and in the case of a grant from the Horse Trials Support Group, it is usually a contribution, a percentage of travelling and competition expenses."

"But they'll never give money to *me*," I said, "they've never even heard of *me*."

"That may well be true," he agreed, "nevertheless, they are going to brief a member of the selection board for the Junior Olympics who will be officiating at the junior trial, and as a result of his report, they may decide that you are worthy of consideration, and you may be allowed to put your case before a special committee."

I stared at him in amazement, and already my mind was churning with possibilities; alarming, incredible possibilities.

"I *will*?"

"You might," the chief replied in a dry tone, "if you perform well at the junior trial."

I reeled out of the office, hardly daring to contemplate the viability of the plan already forming in my mind. If the grant from the Horse Trials Support Group was big enough, it might be utilized to bail the Fanes out of their present difficulty.

"Gordon Bennett," Alice commented morosely, as with an appalling succession of crashing blows, Annemarie and Balthazar demolished the triple combination, leaving the coloured poles scattered around the jumping arena as if they were no more than matchsticks. 'She'll have to be put in reserve. If we have to have her in the team, we'll be sunk."

Viv's abrupt removal from the scholarship course had caused something of a furore the following morning, when the letter she had pushed under the office door for the attention of the chief had been discovered. Mr Tintoft had been summoned, and he had arrived without delay, spending almost an hour with the chief, but at the end of it, Balthazar had been formally offered to Annemarie, and the chief had announced that Miss Tintoft had resigned from the course for "family reasons".

Now though, we were left with the problem of putting together Annemarie and Balthazar with less than a week to go before the junior trial.

Due to her high-powered instruction in Germany, Annemarie was an excellent, correct, disciplined rider, but compared to the average English rider, she appeared to be rather stiff, unyielding, and unsympathetic. She had schooled her own part-bred Hanoverian horse herself, and he was accustomed to her style of riding, but Balthazar, being a much longer-striding, free-moving horse, used to Viv's more relaxed approach, was not, and he resented it.

There had been difficulties aplenty over the cross-country course, but now, in the confines of the show-jumping arena, it seemed to be even worse. The chief had devoted most of his time to trying to overcome their problems; but as there was not enough time to re-school the horse to respond to Annemarie's expectations, it had to be the other way round; Annemarie had to adapt herself to Balthazar. She was trying very hard, but it was not easy for either of them.

We, who were the rest of the team for the junior trial, sat on our horses and watched from outside the arena, biting our glove ends as Balthazar fought against Annemarie on his approach to the fences, throwing up his head, hollowing his back, and dropping his hind legs on to the poles. Timber scattered, wings rocked, the powerful hooves flew, as Annemarie over-collected the chestnut horse, chopping his flowing stride, upsetting his natural balance and bungling his take-offs. The chief held his hands over his ears as the sound of falling timber went on all around him, and yelled at her to relax, to give more rein, to try somehow, anyhow, to achieve some rapport with the big, confused gelding. To give Annemarie her due, she improved a little at every session, and she never uttered one word of complaint, but in the short time left to us it became clear that Alice was right. If we had to call on Annemarie and Balthazar for the team, our chances of success would be virtually non-existent.

A few days before the junior trial, the chief staged a mock trial of his own. We rode the dressage test we were to ride on the day, we went round the show-jumps, and we finished by riding the whole of the cross-country course. The results were hardly encouraging.

Somehow we all managed to produce abysmal dressage tests; even Phillip, who was never less than consistent, got a poor mark. Legend blew up completely, shied at the markers he had seen every day for the past three weeks, refused to settle, and got the worst mark of all. Mandy lost her way three times, blundering along hopelessly, until the chief was forced to intervene with directions. The Talisman refused to walk and did all the walking movements at a jog trot, and the best score was achieved by Annemarie and Balthazar which, while it gave a much-needed boost to their morale, was pretty depressing for everyone else.

We scraped round the show-jumps, with two clears; Phillip and Mandy. Legend took a pole off the double, The Talisman managed to knock the brush fence over, which is practically impossible to do, and Annemarie and Balthazar knocked down every other fence.

Things were hardly any better when it came to the cross-country. Legend was still far too exuberant, despite the fact that I had doubled his riding-in time, and got into trouble almost immediately at the uphill double, pulling away from me at the approach and landing too far in, screwing himself up and over the second part by a miracle, but losing me over his shoulder in the process. I was unhurt, but over-cautious after that, and we finished with three penalties.

Phillip, who seemed to be jinxed, fell into the lake when the amazing roan lost its footing unexpectedly on the approach to the telegraph pole and vanished in a cloud of spray, reappearing on the other side of the obstacle trotting energetically towards the bank, with Phillip floundering after him. This made for a nightmare round as far as Phillip was concerned – sopping wet clothes, slippery reins, a saddle like a waterchute and, to cap it all, a severe attack of stomach cramp, which the chief supposed to be brought on by nerves.

Mandy and Fox Me flew round in their customary charmed manner, but due to lack of brainpower missed out two fences entirely which meant instant elimination from the cross-country phase. Finally, Alice suffered a crashing fall off The Talisman when he unexpectedly applied his brakes at the zig-zag rails. She galloped through the finish with her face awash with blood – it turned out to be only a nosebleed, but it was very nerve-racking all the same. The round accomplished by Annemarie and Balthazar was a battle from start to finish and appallingly slow, but at least they didn't hit a single fence which was an improvement on previous rounds.

After this disastrous showing, we rode back to the yard feeling stunned. The chief, surprisingly, didn't appear to be unduly concerned, and when we returned to the Duke of Newcastle, after attending to our horses, we found that Selina, who had had a field day with her camera during the mock trial, and whose suitcases were already packed against her removal the next morning, had cooked a farewell celebratory supper.

It was at the precise moment that she was walking into the room bearing aloft a cracked casserole dish, preceded by a delicious aroma of casseroled chicken with herbs, cream, and white wine, that Phillip, who have been spasmodically bowed over by his stomach cramp, suddenly slumped on to the table, and fell sideways, and in slow-motion, into a senseless heap on the linoleum.

Less than an hour later he was wheeled into the operating theatre to have his appendix removed.

15

Junior Trials

"Gordon Bennett," Alice remarked, staring down into a chasm the width and length of which would have accommodated a family saloon car, situated below some hefty timber rails. "I don't know why they didn't go the whole hog and line it with broken bottles." I knew how she felt. It was a tough cross-country course for the junior trial.

We had marched around it with the chief the previous evening, and now, in the early morning before we began to prepare for the dressage, we walked round it more slowly on our own. Two miles of varied terrain and eighteen difficult fences under a sky which, if gathering clouds were anything to go by, promised the added complication of rain. I had never doubted Legend's ability to tackle any course so far, but now I thought of the obstacles I had seen, the table, the blind drop, the Normandy Bank, the coffin, the birch rails set on the edge of a fast-running stream with a watery landing, and the gaping trakehner, and I trembled.

Annemarie stared at the fences with her lips pressed into a tight line. If she was frightened, she wasn't going to admit it. Mandy was pale, but then she was always pale, and as there was nothing left of her nails to bite, and her hair was enclosed in a hairnet at all times on the instructions of the chief, she gnawed her knuckles instead. Only Alice showed no outward sign of nervousness and, as a concession to appearances at the trial, she had purchased some spotcover makeup. Unfortunately it was a pasty pink, and the combination of the makeup, the angry eruption of the spots, her own sallow skin, and her mustard yellow team sweatshirt was pretty dire.

The team sweatshirts were a not altogether welcome surprise because they were casual dress uniform for the trial and turned us into walking advertisements for our sponsor. Across our chests we carried the slogan HISSEY'S PICKLES LEAD THE FIELD, and below it a pickled onion and a gherkin wore jolly smiles and silly little riding hats. The general effect was distressing, but as they had been presented to us with great ceremony by Felix Hissey himself, we could hardly refuse to wear them. Only Alice gloried in hers, mainly to annoy the chief who winced every time he saw us wearing them.

We walked on, pacing our distances, checking landings and take-offs for the going, working out the shortest route between the fences, deciding which line to take over fences which offered alternatives, wading into the stream to test the bed for stones, holes and firmness, calculating speeds, strides, and the effect of uphill and downhill gradients. None of us had very much to say. How different it would have been, I thought wistfully, if it had been Viv, Selina and Phillip in the team; then it would have been almost enjoyable – and more important, then we would have had a chance.

The dressage was scheduled to begin at nine, and my courage suffered another setback when I discovered that I had been drawn first. After all that had gone before, the horrendous mock trial, and Phillip's appendicitis, it seemed the final straw. "Oh well," I told Legend, as we set out at a quarter to eight under a sky of unrelenting grey cloud, "somebody had to be first, and at least it will soon be over and done with."

Under the chief's critical eye, we had all schooled our horses thoroughly and diligently the previous day, and as soon as I put Legend to work I could feel that it had paid off. He was no longer bursting out of his skin, he was alert, responsive and sensible.

At eight thirty I rode back to the temporary stabling to change. I stripped off the Hissey sweatshirt and the jeans I had worn to protect my breeches, tied my stock, buffed up my boots, put on my good navy coat and brushed my hat. The rest of the team, supervised by the chief, unfamiliar in a suit and a bowler hat, busied themselves with Legend, oiling his hooves, brushing out his tail, wiping the bits of the double bridle which had been purchased by means of the Fanes' training fund. Just before mounting I skimmed through the printed test for the last time to refresh my memory.

With less than fifteen minutes to go, more riders were now working their horses steadily in the exercising area. Knots of people could be seen gathering outside the little grandstand at one end of the dressage arena, and the judges were strolling across the grass towards their caravan. Amongst them, I knew, were the selectors for the Junior Olympics, and one of them had a special interest in me. We may not have a chance as a team, I thought, but I must do well, I *must*, for everyone's sake.

I worked Legend gently behind the arena, waiting for the starting steward to give me the signal which would allow us a few valuable minutes inside the boards before the test began. I could think of nothing but the importance of performing a good

159

test in front of the people inside the judges' caravan. Nothing else mattered. I knew that Legend had never been on such top form – the month of instruction and fitness training had made an enormous difference to us both, and if we couldn't do it today, we probably never would.

The signal came, we trotted forward into the arena, and as we did so the clouds suddenly parted and everywhere was bathed in sunshine. The white boards sparkled, the black letters danced, and shimmering auburn highlights appeared on Legend's silken neck.

We stood at the scoreboards, holding our breath as the scorer mounted the ladder. My score went up first. It was sixty-four. It seemed to be a good score, but everything now depended on the general standard. The next score went up. Seventy. Then the next, sixty-eight. And the next. One hundred and five. Yes, it was a good one and I felt myself sag at the knees with relief. Alice's was the next score and it was quite a way down the board. When she had seen her drawn number she had not been too dismayed because she was not at all superstitious, but, "Wouldn't you just believe it," she had commented in an acid voice, "*thirteen*." The score which appeared opposite her name was a respectable seventy-one.

Annemarie, who had produced a surprisingly fluent test, marred only by Balthazar's occasional shows of irritated head-shaking and tail-swishing, was given sixty-nine, and Mandy, whose test had been threatened by one black moment when she had hesitated, unsure of the next movement when circling back on to the track at sitting trot, and had been saved by Fox Me who slipped into a canter as they hit the letter, thus anticipating at a most fortuitous moment and reminding her of what came next, was given a seventy-nine. By the end of the score posting, I was fourth individual overall, and the Hissey Training Scholarship Team were lying third out of nine teams.

It was an unbelievably marvellous beginning, and it had an instant effect on our damaged morale. Alice let out a mighty whoop of joy, Mandy continued to stare up at the boards as if she had seen a heavenly vision, and Annemarie smiled for the first time in two weeks. As for me, I stopped thinking of myself as an individual, and remembered that we were supposed to be a team; we *were* a team – and it was high time that we began to think, act, and ride like a team. A chance to ride for the scholarship team in the junior trial had been the one thing that all of us had wanted. Well, we were here, we were lying third after the first phase, and now we would go out there and fight.

"We can do it," I told the others, "I'm *sure* we can do it."

"Not before I have taken my photograph, if you wouldn't mind!" Selina, sportingly clad in a quilted anorak and culottes, was already engaged in journalistic operations, removing anxious competitors and their supporters from her path in her most charmingly authoritative manner. "I'm really *so* sorry – Would you excuse me? Will you move a little to the right, Mandy? Could you look up at the scoreboards for me? Would it be possible for you to look a little more worried, Elaine? – Oh my goodness," she said in a pained voice, "where did you get those *terrible* jerseys?"

* * *

161

Mandy jumped first in phase two, the show-jumping. It was not a difficult course; we confidently expected Fox Me to go clear and we were not disappointed. They cantered round in a blithe manner, making nothing of the course, clearing the spreads, the combinations, and the uprights, and trotted out to a scattering of applause.

Alice was next and as the bell rang she pushed The Talisman into a canter and they went through the start towards the first jump. There was no doubt that Alice had benefitted enormously from her month with the chief. Her seat was much stronger and she was far more positive and co-ordinated in her riding. I watched with a thumping heart as she jumped a clear round knocking, but not dislodging, the gate and the wall. Now it was Annemarie, and this really would be the test.

Balthazar bounded through the start and Annemarie, in her anxiety not to over-collect him, let him go too fast in the first fence and his hind legs trailed through the brush. Luckily, this was unpenalized but it was not a promising start. They jumped the next two fences clear and approached the double. I held my breath as Balthazar sailed over the first part, took two flying strides, and leapt out without any trouble at all. Now there was a wall for which Annemarie sat down and shortened him, too much I thought, far too much, but no, they were over, and already lengthening towards the water, clearing it, and on into the triple combination, over the first part, two perfectly timed strides, over the second part, three strides, and over the last. It was an incredible performance for Annemarie and Balthazar and Annemarie obviously thought so as well because she seemed to lose her concentration with the relief of it. Balthazar picked up too much speed, and galloped, hopelessly fast, into an upright plank jump, Annemarie caught him back in the nick of time, Balthazar climbed over it, and by a miracle managed not to dislodge the top plank, but by then, their luck had run out and they took the last fence in a shower of poles, scattering a row of conifers, breaking two pot plants, and even knocking over one of the wings. Nevertheless, we were all delighted, because for Balthazar and Annemarie, a round with only four faults was a great achievement.

Having stayed at the ringside to watch Annemarie's round, I now ran for Legend, took him twice over the practice fence, and rode into the ring and through the start, feeling nervous, but optimistic. Legend jumped a perfect round, flowing over the fences, never putting a polished hoof out of place, and we cantered back to our swelling band of supporters, triumphant.

The Hissey Training Scholarship Team had now gathered quite a following; Viv had arrived; so had Alice's mother, who was an older, gruffer, taller version of Alice; Mandy's parents were there, filled with awe and excitement but rather clueless about what was going on; even some relations of Annemarie had come from Halesowen in lieu of her parents who were still in Germany. There was Selina with her camera; there was even Felix Hissey himself, rotund, beaming with delight at our unexpectedly good showing so far, and of course, there was the chief, who, when he received the news that after the show-jumping the team had moved up to second place, and I was lying third individual overall, gave a curtly satisfied nod, as if it was no more than he would have expected anyway.

But it was now the end of the first day, and nobody had arrived for me; not the Fanes, not my father, not even Nick. I couldn't imagine why this should be and I felt hurt and offended. I knew the Fanes had problems of their own to contend with, but they had all promised, even Lady Jennifer had promised in her letter, that they would attend.

"Never mind," I told Legend as we walked together across the sunlit turf towards the temporary stabling, "they'll come tomorrow. I know they'll come tomorrow." They had better come tomorrow, I thought angrily, after all I am planning to do for them.

The next morning I stood outside Legend's temporary stable wearing Nigella's lucky red and blue jumper, the side seams of which I had cobbled together to give it some semblance of shape. I'm wearing the Fanes' colours, I thought, and they will never know. I had no idea what had happened to them, to my father, and to Nick, but I had given up all hope of seeing them now, and I had no room in my mind for speculation. Every scrap of concentration was directed towards riding clear across country, for the team, for the selection committee, for the Horse Trials Support Group Grant, for the chief, for Felix Hissey, and for Legend. I slipped on my number cloth, put on my hat, fastened my safety harness and called good luck to Alice and The Talisman as they set out towards the start with the chief walking beside them.

Mandy had already ridden her cross-country, and Fox Me had gone brilliantly, cantering through the finish with one refusal at the blind drop, and no time penalties. He stood now, spent, as Mandy sluiced him with buckets of warmed water, his nose almost touching the ground, water cascading off his belly and his chin.

Annemarie, second of the Hissey Team to ride, limped in leading Balthazar. She had sustained a bruised thigh and a thorough soaking when the big chestnut had fallen on top of her at the running stream, and she had a gathering bruise on her cheekbone where she had fallen again at the angled triple. Despite this, she was triumphant, and Balthazar, though showing vermilion on the insides of his distended nostrils and pouring with sweat, looked magnificent, and hadn't a scratch. "He's a fantastic, wonderful horse," Annemarie declared, "another month and I shall have his measure." This was a new, humbled Annemarie to the one we had first known, and Viv, collecting buckets and scrapers for the washdown, caught my eye and winked.

The next horse returned to the stable block horribly lame and bleeding from a deep gash above his hock. I turned away and closed my heart to it. After Annemarie's accident, I had confessed my doubts about the moral aspect of testing a horse to its limits to the chief. He had answered my questions by replying that there was no clearcut answer, but that all event riders asked themselves the same question sooner or later and could only answer for themselves and with their own conscience. I had made a bargain with myself which was that if I ever felt that Legend had stopped enjoying it, if I ever had cause to suspect his soundness, fitness, or mental attitude, I would stop.

Putting these thoughts and my worries about the absence of the Fanes, my father and Nick firmly out of my mind, I led Legend out of his stable, tightened his girth and surcingle, checked his bandages, boots and bridle, smeared his legs with vaseline from the communal tub, secured the headpiece of his bridle to his forelock plait with tape to minimize the risk of losing the bridle in the event of a fall, and mounted up. I left the yard to a chorus of heartfelt good wishes. Both Alice and I had to go clear if the Hissey team were to hold their position in second place.

I rode towards the chief who was waiting for me in the exercising area where the riders who were to go before me were warming up. "The Talisman is over fence one and two," said the commentator. I trotted up to the chief feeling my throat tighten. Legend flexed his neck and threw out his toes as if he was in a show class, his black plaits sharp and firm against his bay neck.

"The Talisman is clear at number four . . ."

The chief made a wry face and held up crossed fingers.

I worked Legend steadily, gave him his pipe-opener, and resumed some slow, sober work at the trot and canter. I could feel his eager excitement and his impatience but he didn't lose his manners.

"The Talisman is clear at number eight and nine. . ."

I cantered Legend in some slow figures of eight, doing some deep breathing to calm my nerves.

"The Talisman is clear at fourteen and fifteen. . ."

"Good old Alice," I thought, "whatever else she might be, she's a trooper."

"The Talisman is clear at sixteen and seventeen. . ." and then a ghastly silence until, blessedly, "The Talisman is clear at the final fence. No time penalties."

Now it was up to me.

* * *

166

The chief walked me down to the start. Beyond the finish I could see the saddle being dragged off The Talisman as Alice went to weigh-in. Selina was taking photographs.

At the starter began the countdown, Legend stood like a rock. I could almost hear his heart beating.

"Eighteen, seventeen, sixteen . . ."

"*Elaine*!"

". . . fifteen, fourteen, thirteen . . ."

"ELAINE!"

I tried to ignore it, but I couldn't. I turned.

"I thought we'd be too late," Henrietta panted.

". . . twelve, eleven, ten . . ."

"Go away," I implored her, thinking that whatever frightful news she was bringing, I couldn't possibly hear it now. "I'm busy – this is *important*."

". . . nine, eight, seven . . ."

"But so is this important," Henrietta said in a desperate voice.

"Not *that* important, Miss Fane," said the chief firmly. He took Henrietta by the collar of her anorak and tried to pull her away backwards, out of range.

"Don't," Henrietta shouted, struggling red-faced, "I only want . . ."

". . . six, five, four . . ." The starter struggled to hang on to his concentration.

". . . to tell Elaine that we're RICH!" Henrietta squealed.

". . . three, two, one – GO!"

Legend shot like a bullet past the starter, covering the turf in mighty leaps. I knew I shouldn't be thinking of anything except the course, the team, and the selection committee, but I just had to know. I looked back.

"What do you mean?" I shouted, and I saw that

Henrietta had managed to wriggle out of her anorak and was now flying after Legend in her purple tights and legwarmers, and that after her came the starter, and after him the chief, still gripping the anorak.

"The picture in your bedroom – the Elizabethan lady," Henrietta shrieked, "It's worth a FORTUNE!" At this point, unable to sustain such a headlong flight in her stiletto-heeled shoes, she fell face-down on the grass and was captured by the starter, and I, feeling Legend already beginning to lengthen into the first fence, burst out laughing as he soared up and cleared it.

"It can't be true," I told him, "it *can't* be."

Legend, instead of answering, rose in a beautifully effortless arc over the gaping trakehner and landed without a falter in his stride.

"Oh *Elaine*," Lady Jennifer's voice said admiringly, "that was *terribly* good."

I glanced towards the direction of the voice and caught a glimpse of Lady Jennifer and my father, standing arm-in-arm. Has the whole world gone mad, I asked myself, or am I hallucinating?

Down we went towards the coffin, over the first pole, took one downhill stride, then the ditch was below us, and with one mighty uphill bound, we were over the other pole and climbing the rise towards the blind drop.

"Another Legend clear at fences two and three . . ."

The blind drop had caused a lot of trouble and it had been where Fox Me stopped, so I was ready for Legend when he faltered, not at all keen to jump into the darkness of a copse when he couldn't see anything beyond. I collected him firmly and pushed

168

him on. He cocked his ears at it, lengthened, rose up and plummeted, throwing out his forelegs and pecking slightly on the landing. I lost a stirrup but we were over and cantering on towards the log pile. Next came the birch rails with the watery landing, and the table which, although it had looked almost unjumpable from the ground, looked perfectly feasible from the back of a horse. Legend made nothing of it.

"Another Legend clear at fences six and seven . . ."

Now we were faced with the Telegraph "W", and as we approached it, it seemed to be a mass of jumbled angles. I knew Legend wouldn't make any sense of it until it was too late, and I had already decided to take him over the two points. I collected him, he jumped, took one short stride, and bounced over the second point. Scattered applause came from people standing at one side and the judge raised her flag.

"Another Legend clear at fence eight . . ."

Obstacle after obstacle vanished under Legend's soaring hooves and the nearer to the finish we got, the more our joint confidence increased and the easier each fence became. My heart grew lighter with every jump as I realized that we were probably going to win, that the team would retain their second place, that I wouldn't have to part with Legend, that the Fanes were going to be all right and their horses would be saved.

Finally, standing by the last fence, I saw Nick, holding in his arms the biggest bottle of champagne I had ever seen in my life.

"Another Legend clear at the last fence. No time penalties," announced the commentator.

I almost fell out of the saddle. Somebody undid the girth and put it into my hands. Someone else threw a rug over Legend. I weighed-in in a daze. The Fanes seemed to be everywhere.

"Sothebys say it might fetch half a million," Henrietta said in a satisfied voice as if our conversation at the countdown had not been interrupted. "So we don't have to sell after all and we can keep the horses."

"And we thought we'd do hunting breaks in the winter, and riding courses in the summer," Nigella said, "residential, of course."

"So you need your BHSI," Henrietta said, "but it shouldn't be too difficult. After all, you've got your Horsemaster's, and that's a start."

"We'll do up the house," Nigella said. "Every room will have hot and cold running water."

"And we won't want to sell Legend, if that's what you're worried about," Henrietta said. "In fact, now that we're rich, we'll give you our share, at least," she added, her natural caution getting the better of her, "we'll think about it."

"And as our home is going to be your home anyway," Nigella said, "you'll want to come, won't you? Now that Mummy and your father are going to be married."

"*Married*!"

"Oh Elaine," Lady Jennifer trilled, her face radiant. "Don't you think it's a *frightfully* splendid idea?"

"The gardens are very run down," said my father confidingly, "but I feel the terrace would make a splendid patio."

"Excuse my butting in on what I feel sure is a

private celebration," Selina said in her most charming voice, "but could I *possibly* trouble you for a photograph? Would you take off your hat, Elaine? And could you, Nick, just pretend to pour some champagne into it?"

The bang, as Nick opened the jeroboam, almost made Legend jump out of his skin.

"What a terribly amusing idea," Lady Jennifer shrilled as champagne foamed and flowed into my best cross-country hat for the benefit of *The Sunday Times*.

Felix Hissey appeared at my elbow, his jolly face alight with the glory of having his team finish second and one of their number first overall and now a certainty for the Junior Olympics. There was to be a party, he announced, for everyone, but first I was to be taken to be personally congratulated by the head of the Olympic Selection Committee.

"Now?" I said, alarmed by the thought of it. "But I can't, I have to look after Legend." Legend, who had cantered through the finish looking fit for another twenty miles, was wearing his sweat rug and a headcollar and showing enormous interest in a packet of polo mints being opened by Nigella.

Henrietta took his rein. "We'll look after him," she said, "I'll wash, and Nigella can scrape."

"And I'll cut off his bandages and plaster him with kaolin," said Nick. He passed the jeroboam to my father and took the saddle out of my arms. "Go on," he said, "and prepare yourself for a surprise."

I followed Felix Hissey to the judges' caravan overlooking the deserted dressage arena. He opened the door, indicated that I should precede him in a courtly manner, and shut the door smartly as soon as I mounted the steps. The head of the Selection

Committee sat the table in front of the wide window and he looked at me for a long time without speaking.

I didn't speak either. I couldn't. I had trained in his yard, I had taken his every word as gospel, I had admired him above all others; I had watched him endlessly, adoringly, as he schooled, trained, gave his attention to more talented, more` attractive people than I; and yes, I had been in love with him, as young girls often are with their mentors, and I had resented the fact that to him, I was just another working pupil, just another acolyte in his firmament, and because of this I had refused his help and I had sworn that I would make it on my own. And glory, I thought suddenly, by the skin of my teeth, and by the width of my fingernails, I have got this far without him, and now is the time to feel triumph, and yet, surprisingly, there is none.

"Well, Elaine," Hans Gelderhol said gently, "I did warn you it would be a bumpy ride."

"Yes," I admitted, "it has been."

"And I did say that there would be bruises, and damaged dreams, and frustrations along the way."

"Yes," I said, "and you were right, there were."

"But you have done more than I ever hoped for you," he said, "you went out alone and you found your job, and your sponsor, and your event horse, and now you have a place in the Junior Olympic Team."

"Yes," I agreed, "I've done all that." I could hardly believe it – yet it was true.

"And now you will go on and learn more, and in two years, or three, or perhaps four, it might be Elaine Elliott, instead of Hans Gelderhol, who is

European Champion. I am now forty years of age," he told me, "I can't go on for very much longer."

Forty! It couldn't be true, but looking more closely I saw the fine lines around the famous hazel eyes, and the grey hairs amongst the blonde, and I realized that he was not the golden boy of eventing any longer.

"It would be ironic, would it not," he said with a wry smile, "for you to be the one?"

"It would," I said, "but it might not happen." My eyes strayed to the window, and to where in the distance a little group of people walked beside a bay horse wearing a sweat rug, his head lowered, his tail swinging gently about his hocks.

"Might not happen?" exclaimed Hans Gelderhol. "Might not *happen*? What does this mean? Does it mean that you have lost your spark, does it mean that you are no longer the girl I remember, the blue-eyed girl with the blonde hair and slight build, not strong enough and not wealthy enough for eventing, but who burned with ambition and spurned my offer of a job, of help, because she wanted to prove she could do it on her own? What do you mean, *might not happen*?

"I'm not sure that I know myself," I said, "but I do know that situations change, and people change, and ambitions change with them. I *was* determined to succeed, I wanted to show you I could do it, I wanted your admiration. I wanted success, too, and fame perhaps, and love, I wanted that most of all, but I didn't know it, and it seems to me that until these things are within your grasp you can't evaluate them, you don't know their true worth until you get close enough and then you find out a lot of unexpected things, and oh, I'm not explaining this very well," I told him, "but I've found something that might be more important than all of it. Look," I leaned over the table and I pointed to the bay horse and even from so far away I caught a flash of purple tights and I saw that Henrietta had an arm around Legend's neck and that her head was beside his head. "Do you see my horse," I asked him, "and the people with him, just turning into the stabling?"

He nodded, squinting intently in the direction of my finger; he was a little short-sighted now, the golden boy of eventing.

"Well," I said proudly, "that's my family."